"It feels right.

"Sitting with you in my car, walking beside you, holding hands, being here. It all fits." Noel traced a line along Lyrissa's earlobe with a fingertip.

"Really?" Lyrissa rasped. *Don't lose it! He's pulling out the big guns!* Her body, especially her heart, wasn't listening. "Let's not get intense. I find you attractive, too." Lyrissa flashed a sassy smile. "We can enjoy each other. Nothing heavy."

"That's what you want? A casual affair?"

Lyrissa congratulated herself on the blinding inspiration. In one fell swoop she could further her real agenda and satisfy her craving for him. It was purely physical, she told herself. Those stories of forever romance she'd inhaled as a teen had messed with her head. All her shivering came from too many months of abstinence after her last breakup. Scratch the itch and it would go away.

Wouldn't it?

Other Contemporary Romances by
Lynn Emery

GOTTA GET NEXT TO YOU

LYNN EMERY

Tell Me Something Good

HarperTorch
An Imprint of HarperCollinsPublishers

HARPERTORCH
An Imprint of HarperCollins*Publishers*
10 East 53rd Street
New York, New York 10022-5299

Copyright © 2002 by Margaret Hubbard
ISBN: 0-380-81305-X

First HarperTorch paperback printing: May 2002

HarperCollins ®, HarperTorch™, and ◆™ are trademarks of Harper-Collins Publishers Inc.

Printed in the United States of America

Visit HarperTorch on the World Wide Web at www.harpercollins.com

10 9 8 7 6 5 4 3 2 1

1

Lyrissa Rideau stood beside her boss, barely able to believe he was about to introduce her to *the* Georgina St. Denis. She'd chosen her clothes for the occasion with great care. The soft dove gray silk suit was conservative without being too severe. A rose blouse beneath the jacket softened the look.

"It's a pleasure to finally meet you, Mrs. St. Denis." Shelton Taylor's voice dripped old New Orleans Creole charm. "Welcome to Taylor Gallery."

Georgina St. Denis held a carved mahogany walking cane, but didn't lean on it. Her iron gray hair was brushed back into a French twist at the nape of her neck. "Thank you, Mr. Taylor." She inclined her head ever so slightly and gazed at Lyrissa, a question in her eyes.

"This is my assistant, Lyrissa Rideau." Mr. Taylor turned to Lyrissa.

Lyrissa nodded to Mrs. St. Denis with deference. "Hello."

Mrs. St. Denis gave her a cool smile that was more a dismissal than a greeting, yet Lyrissa was hardly intimidated. In fact, she was practically giddy at her own good fortune. No, that wasn't accurate. Good fortune implied luck. But luck had had little to do with this meeting. Lyrissa had made this day a *reality*. A careful word in the right circles she'd carefully cultivated for the last three months had borne fruit. Today the plum had dropped right into her lap. Perfect.

"Come this way to my office." Mr. Taylor paused and turned to Lyrissa. "Would you please get us some coffee?"

"Of course," Lyrissa said.

"I'll have decaffeinated café au lait," Mrs. St. Denis said over her shoulder as she walked on ahead as though she owned the place. "Doctor's orders."

Anxiety flittered across Mr. Taylor's face. "Would you mind, Lyrissa?"

"No problem. I'll get it from CC's Coffee House," Lyrissa said quickly.

"Thank you," he whispered, handing her a twenty-dollar bill. "Here. Say a prayer for me. This woman is just as likely to eat me alive as hire me," he muttered before scurrying off after the imperious woman.

Lyrissa laughed. Georgina St. Denis had a reputation for being a rottweiler in pearls. She should feel guilty. After all, Lyrissa was the indirect cause of the poor man's panic attack. Yet she was too happy at the prospect of getting close to the St. Denis family art collection to feel anything but triumph.

She strode past Mr. Taylor's office and around a corner down another hallway. The storage room had a wide door that led to the alley and a loading dock. A muscular young man was unpacking a massive cast-iron sculpture.

"Kevin, I'm going out to get coffee for a potential client. Do you want something?

He stood straight and wiped his forehead with the back of his hand. "Nah, I'm okay. What's wrong with the coffee we got?"

"It's not decaf café au lait," Lyrissa intoned in a voice to imitate Georgina St. Denis.

" 'Scuse me!" Kevin grinned at her. "Guess we'd better start stockin' the good stuff."

Lyrissa waved a hand. "Not necessary. Her highness won't be back soon. We'll be visiting the royal palace from now on to see her art collection. Sure you don't want anything?"

"No way. I'm in training. Nothing but bottled water for me these days." The young man was on the Southern University wrestling team.

"What discipline," Lyrissa said with a grin and left.

She walked back down the hall toward the side entrance and paused outside Mr. Taylor's office door. The murmur of voices came through the smooth oak, but she couldn't make out the words.

"Maybe if you pressed your ear to it you could hear better," a deep voice said.

Lyrissa jumped and turned sharply. "I, I work here, and . . ."

Her voice died away when she looked into a pair of eyes the color of dark amber with a hint of green. Shapely, masculine eyebrows lifted above them. The man stood at least six feet three inches tall. His skin was the color of vanilla caramel candy. His face was framed by dark thick bronze curls cut into a short, neat style that suited him. The custom fit navy linen and silk jacket did not disguise broad shoulders. Lyrissa imagined an equally broad chest covered in downy curls. For a moment she forgot to be embarrassed as she pictured this man naked to the waist. Before she could undress him further he spoke again, breaking the spell.

"You get paid to eavesdrop?" His full mouth lifted at one corner as his dark eyebrows arched even higher.

"Yes. I mean, of course not!" Lyrissa blinked her way back to reality. His smart-ass tone pinched a nerve. "May I help you?" she said in her best chilly tone.

"Nice collection," he said, untouched by the frost in her voice. He waved a large hand back toward the main gallery. "Mr. Taylor deserves his reputation, Ms. . . . ?"

"Lyrissa Rideau. I assist Mr. Taylor in acquisitions and appraisals." She extended her hand. She felt a shock of warmth like a soft electrical charge at the sensation of his large hand closing around hers. His palm was dry and smooth. He smiled and revealed even white teeth. Her breath went shallow for a split second at the sight. This man went from being merely tall and good-looking to drop-dead gorgeous in the blink of an eye. He let go of her hand too soon.

"I'll just look around a bit more."

"Yes." Her answer was more a sigh than a word. She watched his broad back retreat.

Mr. Taylor opened his office door. "I'll just check on that, Mrs. St. Denis." The short wiry man literally bowed his way out into the hallway. He bumped into Lyrissa. "Where's the café au lait?"

"Um, just on my way," she said, craning her neck to keep the stunning vision in sight.

"Excuse me," Mr. Taylor said sharply. "This is Georgina St. Denis, okay? You don't keep this woman waiting for *anything*."

Lyrissa took in a deep breath, then let it out. "Right, right. It'll just take me a few minutes to get it."

She flashed an encouraging smile at her jittery boss, then scurried out the side entrance. Thankfully the coffee shop wasn't very crowded. Frank, one of the owners, helped her. He filled a small black insulated pot with decaffeinated coffee, then added hot, frothy milk that formed white foam on top. As she'd promised Mr. Taylor, Lyrissa was back at the gallery within five minutes. She went to the kitchen and put the pot, white china cups, and a matching sugarbowl on a red lacquered Chinese serving tray. With skills gained from working her way through high school and college as a waitress, she balanced the load expertly on one hand.

The handsome gentleman appeared from nowhere again. "Need help?" he asked in that sonorous voice that could melt the clothes off the coldest woman.

"I've got it, thanks." Of course, Lyrissa stumbled and the cups rattled ominously.

"Here, let me." He opened the door to Mr. Taylor's office.

Lyrissa rushed to block his view into the room. She imagined Mr. Taylor's eyes bulging with alarm. Mrs. St. Denis was known for her obsession with privacy.

"Thanks, but I'm fine. This is a private meeting and— damn!" she muttered when the carafe of coffee wobbled.

He steadied it with one quick motion. "There you go."

Mrs. St. Denis sat in one of six forest green leather chairs arranged around an oval table. "What in the world is going on? Well, it took you long enough to get here!"

"I'm sorry, Mrs. St. Denis. But—" Lyrissa began, then realized the royal disapproval was directed at the man beside her.

He smiled at Mrs. St. Denis. "It's not easy finding a parking space around here, Grandmother. Let me help you, Ms. Rideau." He took the tray from Lyrissa and set it on a long rosewood table against the wall.

Her mouth open in surprise, Lyrissa barely registered his action. She held her arm up as though the tray was still there. "Grandmother?" she repeated.

He flashed another dazzling smile at her. "Noel St. Denis at your service. I'll pour."

Mrs. St. Denis pursed her lips as she accepted a cup from him. "We don't have much time, Noel Phillip. We have a meeting at the office in another hour."

Noel St. Denis shook his head. "We've got plenty of time. Henderson cancelled. Ms. Rideau?" He handed Lyrissa a cup.

"Thank you," she managed to mumble as she sank into a chair across from Mrs. St. Denis. Noel sat in the chair next to his grandmother.

"Ah, here we are." Mr. Taylor came back in. He looked at the newcomer.

"My grandson, Noel. He's the CEO of Tremé Corporation," Mrs. St. Denis said with obvious pride.

"Pleased to meet you." Mr. Taylor shook hands with him. "Here is a sample of the kind of report we would complete for you if you hire the Taylor gallery to catalog your art collection."

Mrs. St. Denis put her cup down on the table and took the report. The others were silent as she read one page, then flipped to another. Lyrissa studiously avoided gazing at Noel St. Denis. She was sure her concentration would dissolve if she looked into those arresting eyes again. A St. Denis, she reminded herself. The phrase "forbidden fruit" popped into her head. Noel St. Denis was from a wealthy old New Orleans Creole family. Correction: make that *the* old New Orleans Creole family. The St. Denis clan was on the A+ list. These were the same people who Lyrissa had learned to love to hate. Mrs. St. Denis seemed to epitomize the breed. Her long, thin nose tilted up so that she continuously looked down at everything and everyone. Lyrissa revised her impression of Noel St. Denis. The fluid walk that had so captured her was more arrogance than grace, she concluded. That charming smile held a trace of condescension. *Nice reality check, girlfriend.* Lyrissa knew their kind only too well. Her family had been slighted and snubbed for at least two generations by these people.

Fortified, she glanced at Noel. He was staring at her intently. Lyrissa assumed an impassive expression. Despite her effort not to be affected, a tingle traveled up her arm as though he'd touched her again.

"What does provenance mean?" Mrs. St. Denis tapped a page with one polished fingernail.

"It means the origin or source of the item—how it was acquired," Mr. Taylor replied.

"We would list which auction company or dealer sold you the item," Lyrissa put in. "But of course, in your case, most of the items were inherited."

"Yes, such a fantastic family collection!" Mr. Taylor's eyes gleamed.

"Of course, we would describe how your ancestors acquired each piece," Lyrissa added and watched the older woman carefully.

"I see," Mrs. St. Denis said. She closed the folder. "Most of our collection is spread out. Over the years we've had a tendency to exchange and lend out paintings, sculptures and the like. Among only family, of course."

"Naturally," Mr. Taylor purred. "More café au lait?"

"Thank you." Mrs. St. Denis reached out the cup to Lyrissa without looking at her.

Lyrissa pushed down the urge to snap at the old bat. Instead, she smiled sweetly and rose as though serving a St. Denis was a pleasure. When she returned to her seat, Noel was studying her with a hint of amusement in his eyes.

"We would do our appraisals on-site. No problem," Mr. Taylor said, beaming at her.

Mrs. St. Denis frowned. "We? I don't want another gallery or museum brought in. If you can't handle a collection of this magnitude—"

"I meant myself and Lyrissa," Mr. Taylor broke in quickly. "No, no. Taylor Gallery would handle everything. Ms. Rideau has a master's degree in fine art and is working on her Ph.D. in art history. She has over twelve hours of course work from Lindenwood University in professional fine art evaluation."

Mrs. St. Denis looked at Lyrissa carefully for the first time. "Really?"

Lyrissa smiled. "Yes. My particular interest is Louisiana Creole art, especially the influence of immigrants who came to New Orleans from St. Dominique," Lyrissa said, meeting Mrs. St. Denis's gaze with confidence. Though upper crust Creoles could still make Lyrissa feel socially inferior, she had no doubts about her credentials.

"Very good." Mrs. St. Denis nodded to her slightly, then turned to Mr. Taylor again. "Noel's secretary will get you a list of the collection."

Mr. Taylor smiled with relief and joy. "Excellent! Then we—"

"Wait," Mrs. St. Denis raised a hand as though she were a queen shushing a subject. "It's not complete."

"I don't understand. You don't have a complete list?" Mr. Taylor's bushy brows came together.

Noel cleared his throat. "Not complete in the sense that some of the descriptions are vague. For example, pictures may be described without naming the artist. And in some instances we're not sure which relatives have what pieces."

"How many items are we talking about?" Lyrissa asked through clenched teeth. She'd thought locating her family's painting would be the easy part.

"We're not sure," he said with a lift of one shoulder.

"You own possibly the most important private collection of Creole and French art in the south, and you don't know where most of it is?" Lyrissa blurted out before she could stop herself.

"All the pieces are in the family," Mrs. St. Denis said crisply. Her light brown eyes flashed a warning signal.

Mr. Taylor rushed in to head off the rising storm. "I'm sure the entire collection has been well cared for. The St. Denis family has a reputation for refined tastes and a keen appreciation of fine artwork."

"Precisely." Mrs. St. Denis gave Lyrissa one last scouring gaze before turning to Mr. Taylor. "Apparently your employee isn't familiar with our family history."

Lyrissa realized she'd made a tactical error. Her grandmother had warned her hundreds of times about her smart mouth. She affected an apologetic expression. Noel seemed about to say something—to rescue her? she wondered—but she hurried to reply, "I certainly didn't mean to imply otherwise, Mrs. St. Denis. It's just such a surprise, given the value of your collection. I do know that your hard work and attention to detail made Tremé Corporation what it is today."

The older woman's severe expression relaxed in the face of a personal compliment. "Well, my husband and I built the business together." She sighed. "But the young woman has a point. There's no excuse for not having a complete list."

Lyrissa said a silent prayer of thanks. At least her quick tongue had gotten her out of this tight spot. "Actually it's not uncommon in large, wealthy families for art to be spread out." She smiled widely at the older woman.

"Yes, yes," Mr. Taylor said. "Now I'll go over our contract with you."

"I'll go out front to make sure Kevin doesn't need help in the gallery. I look forward to seeing you both again," Lyrissa said, smiling at Mrs. St. Denis and then eyeing Noel. She closed the door behind her and clasped her hands together. "Yes!"

She was still grinning when she walked to the main gallery. Kevin had arranged the placement of a cast iron sculpture of three dancers in flight on a granite pedestal. He stood back, both hands on his narrow hips, to examine his handiwork.

"How's that, Lyrissa?" he asked.

"Perfect. Any customers here?"

"A lady is in the red room looking at the paintings. I'll bet she's just killing time on her lunch hour."

"How can you tell?" Lyrissa played their usual game. Mr. Taylor had trained the young man to spot the serious customers with money to spend.

Kevin grinned. "For one thing, she acted too snooty to me. Real rich folks don't waste *any* time on us little people. They don't see you at all."

Lyrissa laughed. "You've learned well, my son. Take those two," she said gesturing toward Mr. Taylor's office. "They're the *real* thing. Old money and old family name."

"I gotcha. We better smile when they treat us like dirt." Kevin joined her in laughter. "I'll get back to the salt mines." He headed for the storage room again.

Noel St. Denis stepped from behind a wide decorative screen that came from Madagascar. "We're not as bad as you think."

"Oh I, uh . . ." Lyrissa looked into his shrewd eyes and decided flattery wouldn't work. She gave him her most winning smile. "You got me."

He smiled back. "It's okay. Grandmother is used to being in charge."

"Mrs. St. Denis is still with Mr. Taylor?" Lyrissa glanced over his shoulder.

"Yes." He walked around looking at the art on display. "The agreement seems fine. They're just chatting about mutual acquaintances."

Lyrissa followed him at a respectful distance, as she did with most wealthy customers. He stopped in front of a wooden sculpture by Frank Hayden. Noel circled the panel of smooth walnut fashioned in swirls. While he studied the art, Lyrissa studied him. Her first impression had not changed: he was one fine man. Yet she felt sure he had an inflated ego to match his good looks. His bearing said he was as used to getting his way and being in charge as his grandmother. Watching them together, it was obvious that he was the apple of his grandmother's eye— handsome, spoiled, and arrogant, Lyrissa mused. One tall package of everything she detested. Or should. He turned to face her, his striking face radiant with pleasure. Unexpectedly, desire flowed through her body like warm milk.

"The wood seems to pulsate with energy," he said in a reverent voice. "It tells a story, like a griot."

She moved closer to him as though drawn by a magnet. "The lines are sinuous, inviting you to touch it. You'd expect it to be warm like a living thing."

"Yes," he said, now looking at her instead of the sculpture. "So beautiful, it's hard not to touch it."

Lyrissa watched the movement of his lips. His words seemed directed at her, not at the sculpture. She tried hard to ignore the insistent prickle in her hips as she stepped away from him.

"Of course, that's the genius of a great artist, to breathe life into his creation. He makes us feel it as much as see it," she murmured, still staring at his mouth in fascination.

Noel gazed into her eyes steadily and took a step toward her. "I definitely feel it."

The room, indeed the whole world, tilted in his direction. The air between them crackled with electricity—at least, that's what Lyrissa would have sworn at that moment. Then Kevin walked in.

"I think they sent us the wrong catalogues," Kevin said, peeling stiff cellophane wrapping from a package.

"What?" Lyrissa felt a bit dazed.

"These are for some medical supply company." Kevin held up a stack of glossy brochures. The wrapping snapped and crackled as he wadded it up into a compact ball.

Kevin glanced from her to Noel, who was now studying the dancers' sculpture. "Oops, bad timing. Sorry."

"No, no. We're talking about the art," Lyrissa stammered.

The young man gave her a puzzled look. "Right, you're with a customer. You okay?"

"Fine. I'll, uh, look at those later, Kevin," she said.

Lyrissa gave him a thin smile. Kevin nodded, then left. Noel hovered near, the subtle scent of his cologne drifting out to tickle her nose. She fought the urge to close her eyes and follow it until their faces touched.

"You know, I'm not that educated on art. Maybe you could teach me more," Noel said, an inviting inflection in his tone.

"I . . ."

Lyrissa shivered with anticipation at spending hours alone with him. Before she could make a more coherent reply, the front door opened. A tall, elegantly dressed woman came in. She wore a short olive wrap skirt and an ivory cotton blouse.

"Noel, I can't believe my eyes!"

"Hello, Felice." Noel met the woman halfway and they embraced.

Felice took off her sunglasses. She glanced at the expensive watch on her slim brown wrist. "My God! It's ten in the morning and you're not hard at work conquering the business world," she teased.

"I manage to stumble out into the sunshine now and then," he said with a soft laugh.

Lyrissa felt another shiver at the sound. Then reality bit hard. The haze she'd been in dissipated and she saw clearly. Felice Gerard was from another old Creole family. As she and Noel exchanged pleasantries and referred to a party they'd both attended, Lyrissa felt the familiar feeling. It was as though she stood looking through the window of an exclusive club she could never join. Felice threw her head back and let out a silvery laugh.

"Oh, Noel! You're so *funny,*" she trilled, a delighted expression on her face.

"Actually the party wasn't so bad. At least no one got drunk and fell into the fountain this time," he said with a devilish glint in his eyes.

"I'll be in my office if either of you needs assistance," Lyrissa said and nodded to her small office. It was located right near the entrance. A glass wall allowed her to see the front door and into the main gallery.

Noel turned to her. "I'm sorry, Lyrissa. This is Felice Gerard. This is—"

"I come here all the time. Hello." Felice waved a hand at Lyrissa as though her name wasn't important.

"Good morning," Lyrissa said stiffly. She fought to maintain a smile.

"I'm going to rent art for our annual sorority charity function. You know, it dresses up the club ballroom," Felice went on.

"Then Ms. Rideau will be able to help you. She's an expert," Noel said and moved to stand beside Lyrissa.

Felice raised one delicately arched eyebrow as she looked at them. "Ye-es, I'll bet."

That was the last dash of cold water Lyrissa needed. The mystique of Noel St. Denis had been effectively doused. "Excuse me," Lyrissa said in a flat tone and headed to her office, leaving the door open. Once inside, she opened a folder without reading its contents. Instead she listened carefully to Noel's and Felice's conversation.

Mr. Taylor came out of his office with Mrs. St. Denis. He held the elderly woman's elbow lightly. "I'm certainly looking forward to seeing the famous St. Denis collection. To think I'll be the one that will unite it under one roof."

Mrs. St. Denis patted her gray hair. "We might even arrange an exhibit at a local museum."

Mr. Taylor's eyes widened with pure joy. "That's a fantastic idea! I could contact the New Orleans Museum of Art right now. I know the curator and she'll be downright ecstatic at the prospect."

"First things first, Mr. Taylor," Mrs. St. Denis said. "We need an appraisal. We're considering a limited sale at some point."

Lyrissa's head snapped up at that. A sale? She had to move fast, then. In today's market, a Jules Joubert painting would bring on serious high bidding from collectors. Yet the painting was not theirs to sell.

"Hello, Mrs. St. Denis," Felice called out gaily. "Did I hear you say something about an art auction? Why, that would be a wonderful fundraiser for the St. Mary's Academy booster committee. We could—"

"Hello, Felice," Mrs. St. Denis cut in with a dry tone.

"How is your grandmother? I hope Charlotte is feeling better after her fall."

"Grandmother is a resilient lady. She didn't even break a bone. Remarkable, for a woman her age. But then, we're a strong breed." Felice flashed a toothy smile.

"Charlotte was always a tough old bird," Mrs. St. Denis tossed back.

"Er, yes." Felice blinked at her rapidly.

"Goodbye, Mr. Taylor," Mrs. St. Denis said. "We'll be in touch soon." She glanced at Felice without affection. "Goodbye, Felice. Noel, I've kept you away from the office too long. I'm ready," she added before Felice could answer.

Noel shot a significant look at his grandmother, but she seemed not to notice. "Nice to see you, Felice."

"Give me a call," Felice purred. "Daddy is having one of his famous fishing events at our camp in a couple of weeks. You'd love it."

"I'll get back to you," Noel said.

"Be sure you do," she said, dropping her voice to a soft, intimate timbre. Felice walked away from him with hips swaying.

Lyrissa watched from her vantage point and rolled her eyes. *Oh, please,* she muttered to herself.

"I'll get the car in a minute, Grandmother. I want to say goodbye to Ms. Rideau," Noel said and headed to Lyrissa's office.

Mrs. St. Denis pursed her thin lips in an expression of displeasure, but said nothing. She nodded distractedly as Mr. Taylor prattled on excitedly about the collection. Noel strolled into Lyrissa's office as though he belonged there. Noting his serene confidence, Lyrissa was sure there had never been a time when he didn't feel he belonged.

She stiffened her spine, determined to resist his unsettling ability to get her blood pumping. Thinking about the wide social gulf between them helped, a little. A small shock of heat went down her back when he walked right up to her.

"Thanks for the personal attention," Noel said with a winning smile that could soften any heart of stone.

Lyrissa put on a reserved smile. "We work hard to give special treatment to *all* our clients."

Noel lifted one dark eyebrow at her. "I understand," he said without losing his good humor. A teasing glint lit his gorgeous eyes. "I look forward to seeing you again soon."

She cleared her throat. His cocky expression seemed to say, *It's not over, lady, I'll get to you yet.* Lyrissa added a bit more ice to her attitude. "Goodbye, Mr. St. Denis," she said in her most formal tone.

Noel merely nodded and left. Only when he was several yards away did she let out a long breath. She watched his graceful stride as he went through the glass doors and down the sidewalk until he was out of sight. She shook her head slowly. *If only he weren't a St. Denis,* she groaned inwardly. Warning signals clanged that she shouldn't even think about it. After a few seconds she realized the clanging sound was actually the phone on her desk ringing. Her eyes still on the door, she picked up the slim receiver.

"Hello. Yes, they're just leaving now," she said. "Don't worry. We'll have our painting back in the next few weeks."

2

Noel eased his pearl white Infiniti I30 into downtown traffic on Poydras Boulevard. His thoughts were still at Taylor Gallery. Lyrissa Rideau had left a strong sensory impression. He could still smell the subtle floral scent of her cologne. Each time she'd moved, the scent floated toward him, faint enough to tease and make him want more. Then there was the way she moved. Her shapely legs, revealed beneath her short gray skirt, could stop traffic. Like a camera, the image in his mind moved up her fine figure to her face. She had smiled at him and the hairs on his arms stood at attention. But she'd been reserved, almost disinterested. Noel wasn't used to that reaction from women, at least when he noticed. The plain fact was, he rarely did. Women came to him. Few of them were restrained about it. Maybe that was it. He simply hadn't recognized a more modest approach. His grandmother's voice broke into his attempts to solve the puzzle.

"I'm surprised you're not on your cell phone to the office or speeding to get back there." She gave him an appraising glance.

"Nothing urgent going on there today," he reminded her, stopping at a red light.

"There's always something urgent when you run a business, son. Staying one step ahead of your competition and customers is urgent," she said, quoting a small portion of her usual lecture on succeeding in business.

"Yes, Miss Georgina," Noel said, using the name most people called her. He shrugged. "Carlton is there."

"*That* doesn't reassure me," was her short reply.

The light changed and Noel turned onto Camp Street. Ahead was the twenty-story office building that housed Tremé Corporation.

"Look, that last little problem wasn't entirely his fault. I should have reviewed—"

"Of course it was his fault," she shot back. "If he worked for any other corporation he'd be sorting mail by now. Being my grandson is the only thing that saved his backside."

Noel sighed. He couldn't offer much in the way of excuses for his stubborn cousin. Carlton managed the real estate arm of the family business. He'd recently miscalculated the per-square-foot cost of a large warehouse. The result was that he'd signed a two-year lease with a packing firm that barely covered the cost of its maintenance. "He's working on a fix now."

Noel turned into the parking garage next to their building and inserted his magnetic parking card into the slot. The long orange and white bar across the entrance rose slowly.

His grandmother snorted undelicately. "Right. Knowing him, he'll alienate the client and we'll end up with another empty property. Do the words 'cash flow' mean anything to that boy?" she said with a sigh of frustration.

"Calling him a boy doesn't help things, Grandmother," Noel said with his own sigh.

"Humph! When he grows up, I'll stop," she said, her tone no softer.

For the last two years Noel had been dealing with his resentful cousin daily. The rivalry between their fathers had extended to the next generation. At least, as far as Carlton was concerned, it had. Uncle William, Willie to the family, still openly fumed that Noel had been made CEO instead of Carlton. Uncle William had been forced to retire because of health reasons. Noel's father, Richard, ran his own small but lucrative import business part-time. He preferred a flexible schedule that allowed for lots of time for golf. Tremé Corporation demanded long hours and sacrifice. Neither appealed to him.

Noel parked his car in his reserved parking space. He got out and went around to help his grandmother from the car. "Don't start with him today, all right? We have to pull together as much as possible."

Miss Georgina took his hand briefly as she stood, then let go. "Give your cousin that speech. Include his father while you're at it."

Noel closed the door and turned on the car alarm. "No need. I'm sure *you* will," he murmured.

"Darn right," she snapped and marched purposefully to the elevator.

They didn't speak again during the ride up to the fourteenth floor. Miss Georgina's grim expression worried

Noel. When the elevator whisked open, they walked through a set of glass double doors. Tremé Corporation took up the entire floor. Dark blue carpet stretched down the hallway that led to other hallways to offices. They turned to the main suite and went through another set of double doors, this time of dark oak panel.

Edwina, Noel's secretary, smiled when they approached her desk outside his office. "Hello, Miss Georgina. How are you?" Eddie's voice and smile faded when she saw the older woman's expression.

"Good morning," Miss Georgina said in a curt tone.

Noel opened the door and stepped aside to let her enter his office first. He paused before following her. "Eddie, please tell me we've got fresh coffee."

"Going to be one of those days?" Eddie wore a look of sympathy.

"Again," Noel retorted.

Eddie stood. "I'm pretty sure Josephine made a fresh pot ten minutes ago. I'll go check in the kitchen and fill up a pot for you. I think she brought some of her special muffins, too."

"Thanks." He rubbed his midsection as he went into his office and shut the door.

Miss Georgina eyed him. "You shouldn't skip breakfast and then drink a lot of strong coffee, Noel Phillip. You'll ruin your stomach."

"Dealing with difficult relatives is what will ruin my stomach," he replied with a sideways glance at his willful grandmother.

Miss Georgina sat down in a dark red leather chair. "I can deal with Carlton," she said with a wave of her hand.

Noel sat down at his desk. "Yeah right, Carlton."

"More important, what are you going to do to raise capital?" Miss Georgina fixed him with a steady gaze that sent lesser souls fleeing.

"Eddie is typing up a draft proposal right now. Naturally Carlton isn't pleased about possibly selling even one piece of art. And I'm sure Uncle Willie knows every detail by now." Noel rocked back in his captain-style chair. "But they're not the only ones who will howl about the collection."

"I own the St. Denis collection, and they darn well know it," Miss Georgina said imperiously.

"It's almost a family legacy, Grandmother. Especially the way Great-grandfather's will read."

Miss Georgina scowled as though ready to do battle. "He left it to your grandfather to administer as he saw fit. Our lawyer assures me that's as good as ownership."

Noel nodded slowly. He doubted even his thunderous Uncle Laurence would want to tangle with an angry Georgina St. Denis. "We'll need to raise at least two million in cash reserves to see us through the next three quarters—"

A knock at the door interrupted him.

Eddie came in with a tray. "Hot coffee and banana nut muffins. I warmed them up for you."

"You're an angel in disguise." Noel sprang out of his seat and took the tray from her. He set it down on a credenza that matched his desk.

"Thank you, dear." Miss Georgina gave her an endearing smile and Eddie nodded and left them alone. "Sit down, Noel." She shooed him back to his seat while she poured out a cup of coffee and put a muffin on a saucer.

"Thanks, Grandmère," he said, using the childhood endearment.

"Now tell me more about this proposal." Miss Georgina placed the cup and saucer in front of him on the desk.

"I'm going to sell three warehouses and renegotiate two leases that will be up soon." Noel took a sip of coffee. "Ahh, I needed that."

"Yes, dear. Now, what else?" Miss Georgina sat down with her own cup of coffee.

"There's a good chance we can get financing for construction of the office park through the Louisiana Public Facilities Authority." He paused to nibble on his muffin.

"Of course. It will have a positive economic impact on a blighted area of the city. Sound reasoning so far. I can't imagine the board not realizing it." Miss Georgina's brow furrowed as she sat drinking coffee deep in thought. "You know, I—"

"No, Grandmother," Noel broke in before she could finish. "You're retired and the doctor says you should rest. I don't want you getting into this dogfight."

"So you do expect trouble." She raised a dark eyebrow at him.

"I'm not worried. Matter of fact, don't say anything to Carlton. He'll just dig his heels in even more and say you're playing favorites."

"But I could help with Laurence and the others. I'm sure the board will support you if I—"

"You don't think I can handle it?" Noel squinted at her over the rim of his cup.

"Don't be ridiculous! You've taken hold of this company and put it back on the right track." Miss Georgina leaned against the soft leather. "Willie was so stuck in the past. I would have had to orchestrate his ouster if he hadn't retired."

Noel knew she would have done it, too. His grandmother never flinched from tough decisions. Especially when it came to saving the St. Denis family reputation and fortune. They both gazed over at the large oil portrait on the opposite wall. A younger Miss Georgina sat in a chair. Her hair then was black and waved in the style popular in the forties. Noel's grandfather stood behind her, one hand on her shoulder. He was a light-skinned man with gray eyes and thick black hair. His expression was staid, yet there was a soft light of kindness behind it.

"Ten years and I can still hear his voice," Noel said quietly.

"Yes." Miss Georgina stared at her late husband a moment longer then turned to Noel again. "Now, back to the present."

"The board meets again in one month. I'll be more than ready by then," Noel said in firm tone.

"In other words, butt out," Miss Georgina said dryly.

Noel grinned at her. "Something like that."

There was another knock at the door, then it opened. Carlton came in. He kissed Miss Georgina's forehead. "Hello, Grandmother. You're looking well. Noel." He gave Noel a curt nod.

"Good morning, Carlton," Noel said mildly. "By the way, thanks for getting that report to Eddie for me."

"I could have gotten the figures from all four quarters if I'd had more time," Carlton said with a tight smile. "I'm sure the meeting would have gone better."

Miss Georgina stopped in the act of reaching for a muffin. "What meeting?" she asked sharply and glanced at Noel.

Noel pushed down a spurt of irritation. "I met with Larry Hardison about the mortgage on the Crowder Boulevard strip mall."

Miss Georgina put down her coffee cup. "Why? What's wrong with Crowder Plaza Mall?"

"The place is dying a slow death since that Super Discount Mart opened in the new mall," Carlton spoke up. "I never thought we should have renovated that dinosaur."

"We're talking a lot of jobs, Carlton. Crowder Plaza is in a poor neighborhood. They need that grocery store and the Dollar General. Not to mention the beauty shop," Noel said, repeating the same arguments he'd used with his cousin before.

"If we lose money, then we'll have to make a decision to unload the least profitable assets. Crowder Plaza certainly fits that description," Carlton said.

"I agree with you. But I won't make that decision unless I have to," Noel said with an edge to his tone.

"Meanwhile, the red ink flows," Carlton tossed back.

"The city council is working on making that area a free enterprise zone. West Services, Inc. is close to opening a customer service call center nearby."

Carlton spoke directly to Miss Georgina as though they were alone. "Both could be months, maybe even a year or more away. *If* either happens, Grandmother."

Noel struggled not to lose his temper. He glanced at his watch. "Aren't you meeting with Julie and Andre in fifteen minutes about the Algiers properties?"

His cousin faced him with a cold expression. "Thanks

for reminding me. The new tenants I signed will make the warehouse and business park very profitable."

"Good. See you at three for our staff meeting." Noel stared at him steadily.

Carlton's frozen expression cracked into a rigid smile. "Right," he said, then turned to Miss Georgina. "I'll see you Sunday, Grandmother." He gave her another kiss goodbye, looked at Noel once more, then strolled out.

Noel slapped the arm of his chair. "Arrogant little—"

"He has a good point about the Plaza, son," Miss Georgina cut in.

"I know!" Noel admitted with a sour expression as though agreeing with Carlton hurt.

"We're a business, not a charity," she went on firmly.

"Businesses have a responsibility to the community, Grandmother."

"The St. Denis family has done more than its share for this parish." She went on about the charities they contributed to.

As she talked, Noel ground his back teeth in frustration. Since he'd taken over the company, he'd implemented his own style of management. An important part of it was to change the way they did business. He intended to do more than write checks and attend fancy fundraisers. Noel had spent hours convincing Miss Georgina and the board members, most of whom were family, that his ideas would be good for Tremé Corporation's bottom line.

"Grandmother, this is the twenty-first century. Businesses have to be community partners," Noel said quickly when she stopped to take a breath.

"I know what century it is," she snapped, her dark eyes flashing. "I'm seventy-seven, but I'm not senile."

"Yes, ma'am," Noel said. "I meant—"

"I know what you meant." Miss Georgina gazed at him for a few moments. "You're itching to tell me to shut up and let you run this company."

"I wouldn't dare say such a thing." Noel's mouth lifted at one corner. "Not as long as you're carrying that cane."

Miss Georgina laughed and relaxed in her chair again. "I don't know why I put up with your insolence."

"Because we're so much alike." He grinned at her.

"No, you're like Phillip. Thank God for that." Miss Georgina stood. "Call a car to take me home. I've pestered you enough for one day."

"I'll get Marlon to drive you." Noel called their courier in the mailroom to take Miss Georgina home in the company car.

She gazed at Noel steadily. "What did you think of Miss Rideau? She seems competent." Her gaze seemed to look straight into his thoughts.

Noel hadn't been raised in the St. Denis clan without learning how to think fast. "Her credentials are very impressive," he said evenly. Still his memory flashed on a pair of full lips that seemed to beg for kisses.

"For all his fawning over us, Taylor will probably get her to do most of the real work." Miss Georgina continued to study Noel closely as she spoke. "She's very pretty. Nice figure, too. Reminds me of what's-her-name, that woman you were dating last year."

Noel scowled. "There's no comparison. Shauna's biggest interest was shopping," he said without thinking. "I doubt she'd know a Picasso from one of those mass-produced paintings they sell at the mall."

"Ms. Rideau did impress you."

Before Noel could respond, Marlon stuck his head in the door. "Hey, Miz St. Denis. Ready to go?"

"Yes, she is," Noel said promptly. "Goodbye, sweet Grandmère." He pecked her cheek.

Miss Georgina tucked her purse under an arm. "I get the hint. Stay out of your personal life, too. We'll talk later, dear."

"I'm sure we will," Noel murmured in a long-suffering tone.

She turned a warm smile on Marlon. "Now, young man, let's see if you can drive me home without breaking the sound barrier this time."

Noel sat down again and tried to concentrate on the pile of work on his desk. An image of Lyrissa's large brown eyes and luscious lips kept floating into his head. Before he plunged into a stack of invoices, Noel took out his Palm Pilot. He tapped the key that opened the address book then found the phone number of Taylor Gallery.

I'm only following your advice, Grandmother, he thought as he dialed the number. Paying attention to business. The sooner we get started on the appraisal, the better. "Ms. Rideau, please."

Two days later Lyrissa walked into Copeland's on St. Charles Avenue and glanced around for Noel St. Denis. The popular restaurant was packed, as usual. She'd left her Honda Accord at work and taken a cab since there was little parking on the lovely streets of the Garden District. She paid the driver and walked into the restaurant wondering just what she was doing here. Noel St. Denis had made his invitation sound like business. Still her pulse had inched up when he suggested they meet over lunch. Mr. Taylor had been far from being annoyed he wasn't invited—he'd been *delighted*.

"Leave at eleven and beat the crowd," her boss had said with enthusiasm.

So here she was, about to have lunch with one of the most sought after bachelors in New Orleans. Lyrissa was determined not to make a fool of herself. She glanced at her wristwatch. Ten minutes early to prepare herself before he arrived. A harried but smiling waiter dressed in a crisp white shirt and black pants approached.

"How many?" he asked.

"Two, non-smoking," Lyrissa said, anticipating his next question.

"This way, please."

He led her into the dining area to a table near the window that faced St. Charles. In no time she had a glass of water with a slice of lemon and a basket of warm bread in front of her. Lyrissa quenched her thirst, absentmindedly sipping as she gazed down the tree-lined boulevard. Flowers bloomed everywhere. Late spring sunshine painted the scene a cheery yellow. Yet Lyrissa's thoughts were on the task ahead of her.

Noel St. Denis was a wild card, she mused. She'd been prepared to face Miss Georgina, as the woman was called. Lyrissa had spent the last six months learning about her. Her grandmother and great-aunt had given her the history, but Lyrissa had used her own contacts to find out recent information. Convinced she'd be dealing with Miss Georgina, Lyrissa had not spent much time investigating her grandchildren. Of course, she knew of Noel. He had a reputation as handsome, somewhat aloof, and completely devoted to the family business. She had been told that he was a discreet ladies' man. "Very selective" was the phrase she'd heard more than once when it came to his choice of female companions. Lyrissa concluded that meant his women had to meet the usual upper-class old Creole family criteria, the right pedigree, lots of money, and of course, the right skin color. She gave a soft hiss of disgust. She was prepared to deal with Mr. Personality.

At least, she thought so . . . until Noel suddenly towered over her.

"Sorry I'm late," he said, his deep voice rumbling. His full lips parted in a captivating smile. "Hope you haven't been waiting long." He put one hand on the back of her chair.

She blinked rapidly. His subtle, spicy cologne wrapped around her. "No, just a few minutes, really," she managed to get out, fighting to catch her breath. The man exuded a kind of magnetic force.

"Good. Iced tea, please," he said to the waiter like a man used to being served promptly. "I had a meeting that ran too long. And you know how traffic is downtown."

"Yes, of course," Lyrissa murmured.

Noel unbuttoned his jacket, smoothed his green and tan silk tie, and sat across from her. She gazed at him as he picked up his menu. The noise around them faded in and out as she watched every move he made. He wore a dark khaki suit of a light fabric. Despite his muscular build, he looked perfectly at ease in business attire. Lyrissa imagined him dressed casually in a knit short-sleeved shirt hugging his broad chest, golden brown arms glistening in the sunlight. What would he look like in body-hugging blue jeans that outlined solid thighs? Even better, how would he look in swim trunks? She tilted her head to one side. Her gaze slid down his chest to the chocolate brown leather belt around his slim waist.

"Is something wrong?" he asked.

She snapped out of her reverie. "Excuse me?"

"You seem preoccupied. Guess my social chatter needs work." He smiled that charming smile.

Lyrissa reluctantly gave up her vision of his hard body gradually shedding clothes. She drank deeply from her glass, thinking that she'd have done better to splash the cold water on her face. Still, the maneuver gave her time to recover. Two minutes into their conversation and she had the man practically naked in her mind. Sure she'd just broken the world speed record for Lusting After a Single Male, she cleared her throat and forced a smile.

"I should leave the office behind. It's just that I have so much work piled up."

"Then I won't waste your time with small talk." Noel gazed at her with an amused expression.

Lyrissa blushed. This lunch was definitely not going according to her plan. Noel was in the driver's seat and she didn't even remember giving it up. "That's not at all what I meant, Mr. St. Denis."

"Noel."

She ignored the warmth his invitation inspired. "I'm sorry. You were saying?"

"I'll call you Lyrissa, if you don't mind," he continued, staring at her intently. "You don't, do you?" His baritone voice rolled out the red carpet, enticing her to greater intimacy.

"N-no," she stammered then wanted to kick herself for

sounding so graceless. *You have definitely lost control. Correction: you never had it.*

Just then the waiter arrived. "I'm sorry, folks. We're just so busy. Are you ready to order?"

Lyrissa sagged with relief as Noel turned his attention from her. He ordered a shrimp remoulade salad and more iced tea. She clutched her menu as though it were a lifesaver. All too soon it was her turn. The waiter looked at her.

"And for you, ma'am?"

Lyrissa prayed her voice wouldn't come out as a squeak. She sipped more water. "I'll have the spicy grilled fish and a garden salad," she said, surprised at how normal she sounded.

Noel leaned toward her. "Lyrissa—"

"I've read about the St. Denis art collection," she cut in smoothly, careful to wear a placid expression. "The history of the art is a big part of the history of your family."

He hesitated as though debating whether to give in or continue his seduction. Lyrissa squared her shoulders and gazed at him steadily. They seemed to be sizing each other up. She hoped he hadn't detected the chink in her armor. Two many months of forced celibacy, she told herself. That had to be it. *Just hang on, girl.* Noel nodded as though conceding for now, at least. Lyrissa had no doubt he'd try again. But she'd be ready next time.

"The St. Denises have always been pack rats," he said with a grin and sipped some iced tea.

"Pack rats with very good taste," Lyrissa replied.

"You haven't seen all the strange things in attics and spare rooms." He leaned forward and lowered his voice.

"Don't tell anybody, but some of my relatives are a little peculiar."

"I think we can safely say that secret came out years ago," she tossed back, then gasped. Her rapid-fire mouth had gone off again.

Noel laughed. "Trust me, the rumors aren't half as wild as the truth."

Lyrissa felt her cheeks burn. When would she learn to think first, then speak?

"So you know all about the St. Denis family?" Noel sat back when the waiter appeared with their food.

"More tea and water?" the waiter asked.

"Yes, please," Lyrissa said, her throat already dry as dust. She waited until he'd filled both glasses, then darted off again. "I did search through articles about the collection. The most recent one I found was written about eight months ago."

"Right. That was when the Amistad Center displayed several old family documents." Noel used his fork to spear a succulent shrimp.

Lyrissa stared at the way his mouth closed around it. She looked down at her plate when he glanced at her. "Uh, yes. I noticed that Miss Georgina is listed as the owner. But you mentioned the collection is somewhat spread out through the family."

"Some pieces were gifts to my great-great-grandfather. He's the one who gathered all the art and made it into a collection. He was an art lover. He scavenged family attics."

"I see."

"We're famous for having maiden aunts and confirmed bachelors with no kids. So to keep valuable items from being lost, he made it his business to keep the family legacy intact." Noel chewed a bit of lettuce, then glanced up.

"Harland St. Denis was a man of foresight. Most African-American families haven't been able to preserve that much of their history." Despite her low opinion of the St. Denis clan, Lyrissa's compliment was genuine.

"You have done your homework, Lyrissa," Noel said with an appreciative expression.

She shivered at how his deep voice rolled out the syllables of her name. "It's part of my job, of course." Lyrissa concentrated on cutting a small square of fish.

"What else have you dug up on us? None of the nastier family skeletons, I hope."

Lyrissa glanced at him sharply. "Not at all. The St. Denis family has a fine reputation. I wouldn't dream of . . ."

Noel put down his fork. "Relax. I'm just kidding. Look, I'm not my grandmother. She takes the whole 'protect the family name' thing very seriously."

"And you don't?" Lyrissa eyed him with interest now.

"Don't get me wrong, I'm proud of my family. But I know not all my ancestors were saints." He lifted a shoulder and picked up his fork again.

What an understatement! She'd done her homework, all right. The St. Denis family had not only a generous helping of eccentrics, but their share of robber barons as well. Some of the best pieces in the famous family collection had been stolen. Lyrissa would right at least one particular wrong.

"If you say so," she replied with a tight smile.

Something in her tone must have caught his attention. He looked at her with an intensity that could have started a fire. Lyrissa swam against a strong tide that threatened to pull her into those smoky amber eyes. Noel wore the ghost of a smile as though very much aware of his effect on her.

"Tell me about you, Lyrissa."

She blocked the start of another shiver when he said her name. She was determined to make her body behave.

"I received my BA degree from Dillard University in fine arts. I completed my master's in art history at Tulane. Now I'm working on a Ph.D. with a concentration in art administration. I'd like to be a curator at a major museum one day." Lyrissa knew she was babbling, but couldn't help it. If only he'd stop looking at her like that.

"Smart and ambitious. I knew it from the moment we met. But I meant, tell me something about you *personally*." He pushed his half-eaten salad aside.

"Personally," she repeated, gazing back at him.

"It's only fair, since you know so much about me."

"Not that much, really," Lyrissa said. "All I know is that you have an MBA from Loyola. You became CEO of your family's corporation three years ago, after your uncle was forced to retire. Since then you've reorganized the company."

"Very good. Now what's my favorite color?" His mind-numbing smile flashed again.

She was ready this time. Lyrissa wore a serene expression as she met his gaze. "My interest is professional."

Noel didn't respond immediately. He seemed to be deciding on his next move. His expression didn't change, but his direction did. "Okay, let's talk business. What are collections like ours worth?"

"Difficult to say, until I get at least a general idea of what we're talking about. But obviously it's valuable."

"Yes, we know that. Has Taylor Gallery handled similar

appraisals?" Noel drummed the fingertips of his right hand on the white linen tablecloth.

Lyrissa took a small bite of fish and chewed slowly. Let him wait for a while, she thought. At last she dabbed her mouth with her napkin. "Similar, but not as large. I suppose Mrs. St. Denis is preparing her will and needs a dollar figure."

"That's part of it," he said vaguely. "Tell me this, how long will the appraisal take?"

"How long will it take for you to get me the list and track down where each piece is?" Lyrissa asked.

Noel drew a cream colored legal envelope from his inside jacket pocket. "Here's the list." He opened it and took out the folded sheets.

Lyrissa put down her fork and took them from him. She scanned five pages of the neatly printed list for several minutes. Each page contained two columns describing works of art.

"You don't have the artists' names or locations indicated on over half the items. Do you have another, more complete list?" She held up the sheets of paper as though they were useless.

He sighed deeply. "Now you see the problem."

"You don't have any idea where fifty percent of the most valuable privately held collection of Creole and African-American art is?" Lyrissa said sharply. There was no mistaking the criticism in her voice.

"We have a general idea," Noel said, an abashed expression on his face. "But as we told you, it's all in the family. At least, we're pretty sure."

"You're pretty sure," she repeated.

"It's really not that bad, Lyrissa."

"Noel, I—"

"We've made progress!" he cut in. "You called me by my first name."

Lyrissa pressed her lips together. "Let's talk about how we can begin, despite the difficulties."

"Yes, let's," he said brightly and bent his head close to hers.

They talked about how she would proceed with the appraisal for another thirty minutes. Lyrissa spent most of that time taming her reaction to being so close to him. She felt drained by the time they said goodbye. On the other hand, Noel had a decided spring in his step as he strode toward his car. She wanted to slap the arrogance from his stride.

For the rest of the day she was in a bad mood without quite knowing why. Fighting New Orleans rush hour traffic to get home didn't help her relax. She unlocked the front door to the two-story family home and tossed her leather briefcase on the foyer table. Her grandmother and Aunt Claire came from the living room.

"Tell us all about it, dear. Is he as handsome as they say?" Aunt Claire bubbled, her dark eyes bright. "We've been dying to find out all day."

"Claire, please!" Mama Grace snapped. She turned to Lyrissa. "Where is our painting? I hope those thieving pirates haven't sold it." She wore a deep scowl.

Lyrissa sighed heavily. The tight feeling in her neck traveled up to her temples. "Can I at least sit down?"

"Of course, cher," Aunt Claire clucked like a mother hen. "I have your favorite—iced mint tea." She started off down the hall toward the kitchen, then stopped and turned around. "Don't say anything until I get back."

Mama Grace took Lyrissa's hand and led her to the sofa. "Take your shoes off and put your feet up."

Lyrissa knew very well the attention, though sincere, was to get her back on the subject of the painting. Aunt Claire came back and fussed over her. Soon Lyrissa had a tall glass of tea in one hand, a napkin on her lap, and two sets of eager dark eyes gazing at her expectantly. Her grandmother and aunt sat on the long paisley print sofa facing her.

"I don't know where the painting is. But," Lyrissa hastened to add, when she saw their disappointment, "Mr. Taylor is busy with the Hayden exhibit and working with Dillard on its collection. Which means—"

"*You'll* handle the St. Denis appraisal. Bravo, Lyrissa!" Mama Grace clapped her hands.

"Clever girl! We'll have our ancestor's magnificent painting back where it belongs in no time," Aunt Claire added.

"And we'll knock Georgina St. Denis off her high horse once and for all." Mama Grace sat back with a look of satisfaction.

"Don't get happy just yet," Lyrissa cautioned. "Getting that painting away from Georgina St. Denis won't be easy."

"You can do it. Don't let her intimidate you," Mama Grace said sternly.

"Right," Lyrissa whispered, more to herself than to Mama Grace.

She sipped her tea as Mama Grace and Aunt Claire talked. Lyrissa could still feel Noel's sensual charisma flowing over her like a satin sheet. A small voice told her Mrs. St. Denis might be the least of her worries.

3

Lyrissa gazed at the grand St. Denis family mansion as she approached it. Somewhere in there was the key to retrieving her family legacy. Mama Grace had told her stories about their magnificent ancestors for as long as she could remember. Past family glory was all Mama Grace and Aunt Claire had to hold onto. They had lived a life of genteel near-poverty for years before Lyrissa was born, always teetering on the edge of a financial crisis. Yet Mama Grace did have an abundance of pride to pass on. Her grandmother and great-aunt always held their heads high in public. Still she knew how much it hurt them to be treated inferior by the "best" old families.

Pride helped Lyrissa deal with the subtle and blatant insults she suffered as a child. Feeling second-class, never good enough, had taken a toll on her sense of worth. With each accomplishment she'd had to overcome doubt in her

own ability. Now she would deliver the mother of all pay-
backs to those high and mighty New Orleans society Creoles. Lyrissa tingled at the prospect of throwing each
taunt back in their smug faces. She'd show them what the
Jouberts were made of!

She parked her car in the circular driveway, and headed
up the steps. For a moment she stared at the front door—
made of beveled glass with an oak frame—then she rang
the bell. A tall, dark woman wearing a white uniform
dress opened it after several minutes.

"Good morning, I'm here to see Mrs. St. Denis,"
Lyrissa said.

"You the lady from the art gallery?" The woman
blocked the door as though she were a security guard.

"Yes, Lyrissa Rideau." She took one of her business cards
from a side pocket of her briefcase and handed it to her.

"Hmm." The woman studied it as though considering
its authenticity. "Come on in. Can't be too careful these
days. I'm Rosalie. Been keeping house for Miss Georgina
fifteen years."

"Thank you," Lyrissa said with a respectful nod, then
entered the foyer.

The parquet floor gleamed. On either side of the wide
hall were long antique tables. Each held a tall vase filled
with fresh spring bouquets. Several feet ahead a staircase
curved gently to the west and up to the second floor.
There was also a small elevator of wrought iron. Lyrissa
recognized it as one commonly made around the turn of
the century for private homes of the wealthy. Rosalie
turned to give her another once-over.

"Rideau, huh? I went to school with a Clarence Rideau.
Know him?" Rosalie asked.

"The name doesn't ring a bell. But then, I've got a million relatives." Lyrissa smiled and shrugged. "I'll ask my grandmother."

Rosalie seemed to warm a bit. "Betcha he's one of your cousins. And don't get me started on having too many kinfolks. Most of the time one of 'em wants to borrow money or be fed." She waved a hand.

Lyrissa laughed. "And I'll bet you can't say no."

"Humph! Guess again," she retorted with spirit. "So you gonna count up their fancy doodads." Rosalie's tone seemed to be the seal of approval.

"Yes. I'm looking forward to it. There are some beautiful things here." Lyrissa walked over to an ornate mirror, early nineteenth century, that hung on the wall. Its wooden frame was painted an antique gold.

"Yeah, if you like old stuff. Me, I prefer modern furniture. These things give me the creeps, buncha antiques from dead folks."

"You make it sound like the house is haunted," Lyrissa teased.

"Sugar, I wouldn't be here if it was," Rosalie replied with a grin. "But some of them old people was real mean."

She nodded to a line of oil portraits that hung on the wall along the staircase. Lyrissa walked over to get a better look. Two grim men and two haughty women stared straight ahead. All were dressed in period clothes from bygone eras. Small brass plates bore their names.

"They don't look too cuddly, do they?" Lyrissa murmured.

"My granddaddy used to say that bad deeds get attached to things," Rosalie said somberly. "Guess that's why I don't like antiques."

Lyrissa shivered at the tone of her voice. "There are happy memories attached to antiques, too."

"Uh-huh." Rosalie gazed at the portraits a second longer, then looked at Lyrissa again. Her expression brightened. "Better show you to her highness before she starts fussin'."

"I'm ready," Lyrissa said and tugged on her skirt to straighten it. "Will Mr. St. Denis be here, too?" She tried to make the question sound casual.

"Which one of her sons you talkin' 'bout. Richard, or Willie?" Rosalie gestured for her to follow.

"I mean her grandson Noel." Lyrissa felt the heat once again just saying his name.

Rosalie looked at Lyrissa more closely and a sly smile spread across the housekeeper's face. "I wondered why he showed up."

"They both met with my boss about the St. Denis collection," Lyrissa said too quickly and blushed. Rosalie's knowing expression was like an X ray right into her mind.

"Uh-huh. Mr. All-work-no-play usually goes to the office by seven in the morning and don't leave until six in the evening. He must really be interested in the *collection*. Here we go."

Rosalie walked off before Lyrissa could lob a comeback. They went down the hall past a set of beautiful carved oak doors. Lyrissa wanted to stop and examine them, but didn't. They proceeded to another set of doors that slid apart.

The lovely sitting room, smaller than the formal living room for entertaining, was decorated in soft pink, gray, blue, and moss green. An antique rug of pink roses with green leaves covered the floor. A set of dark rose-colored chairs matched a Queen Anne sofa in soft green-and-pink-patterned upholstery. Blue drapes covered large windows that overlooked a patch of lawn. Groups of family photos in silver frames lined the top of a console table. One larger than the rest stood alone on a marble mantel. The frame was sterling silver studded with marcasite. A handsome man with a thick mustache stood ramrod straight in the black-and-white photograph.

"How wonderful!" Lyrissa forgot her reserve. She studied the pictures as though she were at a museum photo exhibit.

"That's my papa," Miss Georgina said with pride from her seat at an antique desk.

Lyrissa started. She'd been so absorbed in taking in the decor that she hadn't even noticed Mrs. St. Denis was sitting quietly in the room.

"Etienne Rohas. French and Spanish blood."

"And African," Lyrissa added without thinking.

"Qu'est-ce que c'est?"

"She said African. Most likely West Africa by way of Cuba." Noel's deep voice came from another corner of the room. He must have slipped in from a back entrance. There is no way she wouldn't have felt his presence upon entering the room.

He wore a wide smile. His even white teeth sparkled against the creamy brown skin of his face. A sky blue dress shirt stretched across his broad chest. Narrow hips tapered down to muscular thighs covered by navy pin-striped slacks.

"Hello again, Lyrissa," he said.

"Hi," Lyrissa managed.

Miss Georgina shot Noel a glance heavy with meaning. "Interesting," she murmured.

"Our African ancestor came from St. Domingue, now known as Cuba, in seventeen eighty-two," he said mildly despite his grandmother's tight expression. "We do have African blood, Grandmother."

"I know that," Miss Georgina snapped. She gave him a look that could have cut through steel.

Lyrissa cleared her throat. "Your home is lovely," she said to ease the tension.

"Thank you. Please sit down, Ms. Rideau."

"Here. Best seat in the house." He ushered Lyrissa over to a pair of leather chairs facing Miss Georgina's desk. He sat next to her.

"My grandson tells me you weren't pleased with our list." Mrs. St. Denis fixed her with a stony gaze.

"More information on the items would certainly make the process easier," Lyrissa replied carefully. She wondered just how much Noel had told her about their meeting.

"Your job is to catalogue and appraise our family art," Mrs. St. Denis said.

Lyrissa swallowed a tart reply itching to slip from her lips. She couldn't afford to get tossed out on her butt the first day of this assignment. She would have to face her furious boss. Worse still, Mama Grace would throw a fit that would make Mrs. St. Denis seem like a pussycat. Noel seemed to take great delight in watching the two strong women face off. Lyrissa ground her teeth with the effort, but succeeded in plastering on a subservient smile.

"Of course. I only meant you would have the report faster if the list were more complete," Lyrissa said.

After a few beats, Mrs. St. Denis gave a slight nod. She wore the expression of a queen granting reprieve to an offending subject. "Time is a consideration. But I don't think you'll have a difficult task."

Rosalie came in. "Miz Olivier is on the phone for ya. Somethin' 'bout a problem with the St. Augustine charity ball."

"Can't Beatrice do at least one thing without calling me?" Mrs. St. Denis muttered in irritation. "I'd better take this call."

Noel stood. "I'll show Lyrissa where to begin. My grandfather's study has a small display room next to it," he said to Lyrissa.

Mrs. St. Denis flashed him another silent message, but merely nodded. She watched them leave, then punched a blinking button on the phone before her. "Yes, yes, Beatrice. Now what?"

Lyrissa walked beside the tall, handsome man very much aware that Mrs. St. Denis was not pleased. "Rosalie can show me the way. I know how busy you must be."

"No problem," he said with a charming smile.

"Uh-huh," was Rosalie's arch comment as she headed off in the opposite direction.

As she followed him back to the antique doors she'd so admired, Lyrissa had the distinct feeling she was walking into trouble. Being alone with Noel would be a distraction. She wanted to get rid of him so she could snoop around. The fact that he had an uncanny knack for turning her on was an even better reason.

"Here we are. Grandfather's inner sanctum." Noel swept a hand around, indicating a large study. Two walls consisted of floor-to-ceiling bookcases.

"What a marvelous collection of old books!" Lyrissa crossed the thick carpet to read the spines. Many had titles in French.

"So you're a book lover, too." Noel joined her.

"I could spend hours in here," she said, brushing her fingertips along the embossed leather covers.

"What a great idea. We could spend them together." Noel wore a bland expression when Lyrissa glanced at him sharply. "—Working on completing the list, of course."

"Of course." Lyrissa stepped away from him. He was far too sure of himself for her taste. "You mentioned a display room?"

"Through here." Noel went to a door set in the opposite wall. He opened it and waited for her to follow.

To her dismay, the door was narrow and she brushed against him as she entered the room. Her pulse raced at the brief contact. Still she remembered her real purpose for being here. She looked around. There were four long glass display cases. Two contained old documents. The others held antique eyeglasses, writing pens, and other items no doubt owned by St. Denis ancestors. Framed antique maps of New Orleans, Louisiana and Haiti hung on the walls.

"This is a small museum," Lyrissa said and looked at Noel. "These should be catalogued as well."

"Taken care of, ma'am. The Amistad Center will get these on permanent loan from the family."

Lyrissa nodded. The Amistad Center had been established to preserve African-American history. "Very good."

"We're not completely irresponsible," Noel said dryly.

"Why didn't you have them catalogue the art as well?"

"We need a professional appraisal." Noel stood aside so she could lead the way back into the study.

"I see. I assume I can work here after a tour of the house's art. I'll sit at this small table." Lyrissa started forward, but he put a hand on her arm. Her skin tingled at his touch through the fabric of her jacket.

"You'll need more room. Sit at the desk."

"Your grandfather's desk? Mrs. St. Denis might not like that at all." Lyrissa moved away to break contact and clear her head of bothersome fantasies forming.

Mrs. St. Denis came in. "I don't mind one bit. You'll have more room and your work will go faster."

"Right." Lyrissa suppressed a smile. She understood well that Mrs. St. Denis wanted Lyrissa far away from her grandson.

"The charity ball back on track?" Noel asked his grandmother.

"Thank God for Rosalie. Beatrice had totally bungled handling the caterers, but everything is fine now." Mrs. St. Denis walked to the desk and ran her fingers on its surface. "My husband's grandfather had this sent from New York."

"It's beautiful," Lyrissa said. She still hesitated to sit in the large forest green leather chair.

"Go on." Mrs. St. Denis gestured to the desk and chair. "Don't let us keep you from working." She shot a pointed look at Noel.

"I'd better get to the office. I'll see you later, Lyrissa. Maybe I'll join you two for lunch," he smiled at her.

"I'll probably be gone by then," Lyrissa said. "I have a class this afternoon."

"Oh, I see."

Lyrissa's pulse jumped again. Was that disappointment in his attractive brown eyes? "Goodbye." She calmly turned her attention to taking papers out of her briefcase.

"Goodbye," he replied, still looking at her.

"You can have lunch with me for a change," Mrs. St. Denis put in.

Noel turned to his grandmother with a boyish grin. "What a delightful idea. See you around twelve-thirty. He kissed Miss Georgina's cheek and left.

"Now, where do we start?" Mrs. St. Denis stood over her.

"Show me the items here in the house," Lyrissa said.

For two hours Mrs. St. Denis led her through the spacious rooms, giving her a history lesson on the St. Denis family. Lyrissa mused that it was a distinctly sanitized version. Rosalie had been right in her assessment of some of the St. Denis forebears. Miss Georgina characterized them as astute businessmen who amassed a fortune through hard work. Mama Grace wasn't alone in the opinion that more than a few had been ruthless robber barons. Yet Lyrissa had to admire their taste. The rascals had stolen well when it came to art. Finally they returned to the study. Mrs. St. Denis sat down heavily in a leather chair. She seemed winded and her face was lined with fatigue. Lyrissa started to sit next to her in the matching chair when Mrs. St. Denis waved her away.

"No, no. Sit at the desk, Ms. Rideau."

"Thank you," Lyrissa said.

Lyrissa sat down in the captain's chair behind the desk and gazed around the room. Around her were fine art, antiques, and wall-to-wall rare books. Rosalie appeared with a tray bearing glasses of iced tea. *A girl could get used to this,* she mused.

Mrs. St. Denis patted her cheeks with a napkin and spoke after taking a delicate sip from her glass of tea.

"There's more in the attic, but I'm afraid I can't climb up that narrow staircase."

She stood. "You rest, Mrs. St. Denis. I'll take it from here." Lyrissa felt a surge of excitement at being able to search on her own so soon.

"Sit and have some tea before you go back to work." Her invitation was more a command.

"Thank you." Lyrissa bit back her frustration and smiled graciously.

Rosalie handed Lyrissa a glass. She winked at her, then turned to Mrs. St. Denis. "I've got chicken salad, fresh romaine and chives, and sliced home-grown tomatoes. That okay for lunch?"

"Yes, indeed. Rosalie's chicken salad is famous," Miss Georgina said to Lyrissa.

"I'll call y'all when it's ready. Around twelve-thirty, as usual." Rosalie left.

"What's next?" Mrs. St. Denis asked.

"I'm going to look at each item again. I'll fill in missing information on the list such as the names of artists, country of origin, that sort of thing."

Mrs. St. Denis lifted her chin. "I believe in being candid. I wasn't happy that Felton Taylor assigned you instead of doing the work himself. But you seem meticulous in your approach. I like that."

"Thank you, Mrs. St. Denis," Lyrissa replied with a slight smile.

"We should have done this long ago. We had other priorities." Mrs. St. Denis took a deep breath. She seemed to have recovered from the effort to keep up with Lyrissa.

"Yes, ma'am. Tremé Corporation," Lyrissa said.

She nodded slowly. "Noel has done a wonderful job. Reminds me of his grandfather in that way."

The older woman seemed lost in her thoughts for a time. Lyrissa studied the oil portrait of Phillip St. Denis more closely. Noel had the same determined set to his chiseled features, the same finely etched jaw line as his grandfather.

She remembered her grandmother's description of Phillip St. Denis as an enlightened despot who ruled his family and company with an iron hand. Mama Grace had sneered that he was cut from the same mold as his ancestors, and just as callous. Lyrissa wondered if Noel shared that quality as well. Certainly he exuded an aura of power. His tall, well-developed frame implied physical power as well. The image of his well-muscled thighs and arms flashed in her head. Noel had a hard body that could make a woman sweat bullets. Still, he was a St. Denis. He came from a long line of Creoles who'd looked down on the likes of her. Back to business, she mentally ordered herself, glad the handsome distraction was out of the house. With any luck she would not see much of him.

"I understand that the artwork will be considered a corporate asset," Lyrissa ventured.

Mrs. St. Denis's bemused expression cleared. "My grandson's idea. We'll see."

"Still, it's important to document such valuable items. For inheritance purposes, if nothing else," Lyrissa said in a discreet reference to Miss Georgina's mortality.

The older woman waved a hand. "That's not an issue."

"I see," Lyrissa answered, although she didn't.

"I'll let you get to work." Miss Georgina stood slowly.

"Call Rosalie if you need anything. I'll be in my office."

"Thank you." Lyrissa watched her walk away. "Alone at last," she whispered.

The next hour passed quickly as she went back through the house and looked at each item. She went into the attic, a large room that was neat despite being packed with items. There were pieces of glazed pottery and small ceramic figurines, and several small paintings stacked against one wall. With the excitement of a child on a treasure hunt, she delighted in each new find of a significant piece of art. The discoveries heightened her anticipation of finding the one masterpiece she most wanted to see. Lyrissa's heart pounded each time she spied a frame. With so much to look through, she was sure "The Stroll" was within her grasp. She imagined removing it from its frame, rolling it up into a tube, and simply walking through the door with it. The St. Denis family wouldn't even miss it. After all, they weren't even sure of what they owned.

Lyrissa stood staring at a large framed map of Louisiana when it was still a Spanish colony. She traced a finger along the crescent outline of the old city of New Orleans. The Joubert and St. Denis families were from the same world, yet worlds apart. The distance was a good reason why she shouldn't entertain lustful fantasies about Noel St. Denis.

"I see you've found our own version of a flea market."

She spun around to find that her fantasy had materialized. *Speak of the devil.* Lyrissa cleared her throat. Her mind should be on her goal, not him. Noel smiled and her pulse rate revved like a racecar engine. He dipped his head as he stepped across the threshold into the attic. Lyrissa looked up at him, trying to recall every nasty story about

his family that she'd heard. If only that silk suit didn't
drape across his muscular body so well. Noel looked less
like a workaholic businessman than like a sexy black glad-
iator fresh from conquering foreign lands. He walked toward her radiating animal power and beauty in each step.
In a flash like a camera bulb going off, she imagined being
scooped into his arms and her mouth crushed against his.
Lyrissa gasped when he pulled off his jacket.

"I'll help get some of this stuff out of your way. Tell me
what you want." He hung the jacket on an old mahogany
coat rack nearby, then stood with both hands on his narrow waist.

She stared at the way his custom dress shirt molded to
his chest. Suddenly the dimly lit attic became an intimate
hideaway just right for a romantic assignation.

"What I want?" Lyrissa repeated in a dazed voice. His
eyes warmed the longer they looked at each other. She
cleared her throat and turned away. "I'm about to wrap
up here."

"Too bad," he murmured.

Lyrissa glanced at him to see a faint, seductive smile
curve his full lips up at the corners. Great! Mr. Lover could
see right into her lust-filled, dirty mind. He seemed to
have a "Gotcha!" glint in his eyes. She'd seen his type before. Noel St. Denis slipped neatly into a familiar category:
dog. Lyrissa pulled back her shoulders and faced him. Her
expression tightened as one eyebrow went up, the expression she used to brush aside unwanted male attention.

"Actually, I've got a lot of other business to take care of.
So it's all good," she said with a frosty smile. "Excuse me."
She stepped forward and waited for him to move. He
didn't.

"I enjoyed our lunch the other day. I suggest we meet again. In fact, let's meet regularly so I can get progress reports." Noel continued to smile.

"Mr. Taylor has already agreed to keep Mrs. St. Denis informed." Lyrissa tucked her legal pad under one arm. She maintained her distant demeanor even though he was disturbingly close.

"I've already spoken to him about it." His smile widened. "My grandmother put me in charge."

A muscle in Lyrissa's right cheek quivered as she clenched her teeth. "Yes, well. I'll be in touch," she said after several seconds.

"I look forward to hearing from you," he said, his voice like quiet thunder close to her face.

"Goodbye," Lyrissa said, clipping the word off as she maneuvered around him. She went down the stairs quickly without looking back.

"Ms. Rideau," he called after her.

Lyrissa paused, took a breath, then turned to him as he came down each step. "Yes?"

He took a business card from his inside jacket pocket. "This is my direct phone number."

I can do this. She took the small ivory square with gold foil lettering on it. Their fingers touched briefly, testing her strength. Ignoring the tiny needle of electricity, she lifted her chin. "I'll finish here. Then I'll need a list of your relatives' addresses for the rest of the collection."

"No problem. Let me know when you're ready," he said with a sober expression. He pointedly gazed at her mouth.

She nodded and walked away very aware that he was right behind her. Lyrissa put her tablet, pens, and pencils in her briefcase.

"What time is your class?" he asked casually.

"Four o'clock," she said without thinking.

"Then you've got time to stay for lunch," Noel replied. He looked at her when she glanced up. "To give us a quick report."

How could she refuse? She could lie. "All right," came out before she knew it.

As Mrs. St. Denis, Noel and Lyrissa ate lunch in the formal dining room, Lyrissa glanced up several times to find Noel looking at her. By the time the lunch was over, Lyrissa felt drained from all her efforts not to notice him. His grandmother watched Noel watch her. Finally she was on her way out the door.

"I'll be back on Tuesday morning around nine, Mrs. St. Denis. If that's a good time for you, that is," Lyrissa said. She frowned when Noel took out his electronic date book and tapped the small keypad.

"Fine, fine. Just call and remind Rosalie. She'll put it on my planner," Mrs. St. Denis said. She also noticed Noel's action. Her dark brows came together.

"Goodbye, Lyrissa." He held out his hand.

After a moment of hesitation, Lyrissa took it, but let go after only a split second. "Goodbye."

Noel's amber eyes flickered with some hidden message just for her. Or was she imagining things? Lyrissa nodded to Miss Georgina and walked away.

She spent the next few hours trying to shake off the effect of his smoldering gaze.

"I see something strange here in the cards." Lyrissa's great-aunt Claire pursed her ruby red lips.

"Don't be such an idiot," Mama Grace said. "Taking up

Tarot reading at your age." She made a rude noise to punctuate her scorn.

Lyrissa rolled her eyes. She loved her grandmother and great-aunt dearly, but they were a bit much at times. Still, Mama Grace was conservative compared to her baby sister Claire. A host of sterling silver bracelets tinkled musically each time Aunt Claire moved her arms. She was sixty-three going on sixteen. At sixty-eight, Mama Grace exercised full rights to be the authority as the elder sister.

"The Tarot is reliable. Look at what happened to Earl Collins. The cards—"

"Had nothing to do with it. Earl tripped over his big feet like he's done since we were children," Mama Grace said. "Now voodoo is a different matter."

"Will you two stop? Retirement means taking up knitting or Tai Chi, not witchcraft." Lyrissa plopped down into an overstuffed chair.

"Voodoo isn't witchcraft, it's a religion." Mama Grace shook a finger at her. "Besides, we're only exploring in the wonderful tradition of Miss Zora."

"True," Aunt Claire said.

"You know, Claire, I just thought of something. Lyrissa is doing what Miss Zora did." Mama Grace smiled with pleasure. "Isn't that wonderful?"

"Exactly, Grace. You hit it just right, as usual." Aunt Claire nodded at her sister.

Lyrissa sighed. Mama Grace and Aunt Claire had long been ardent admirers of Zora Neale Hurston. They had in fact become experts in Hurston's writings and her life as an ethnographer. Miss Zora, as they called her, had been an educated and daring young woman. In order to learn about the folklore and culture of poor blacks, she'd taken on the persona of a working-class uneducated person. She'd even gone so far as to be initiated as a voodoo priestess.

"God created a plethora of mysteries and there are just as many ways to seek the answers," Aunt Claire said.

"In fortune telling and chicken bones? I don't think so. You're retired librarians, for goodness' sakes! Give me a break."

"Don't be a smart mouth," Mama Grace shot back.

"Okay, fine. But I'll stick to what really works." Lyrissa nibbled on the small squares of fresh apple Aunt Claire had served her. "Does anyone want to hear about my first day working for Georgina St. Denis?"

"Of course we do!" Aunt Claire dropped the card she was holding.

"So tell us. How bad off is the old hellcat?" Mama Grace leaned forward with a gleam in her eyes.

"She's doing great, considering," Lyrissa said.

"Humph! Georgina St. Denis will live to be one hundred on sheer meanness." Aunt Claire scowled.

"Did you see the painting?" Mama Grace said.

Mama Grace referred to the reason Lyrissa would suffer Miss Georgina's tantrums. "Sunday Stroll on the Faubourg Tremé" was a magnificent oil painting done by their ancestor, Jules Joubert in 1819. It had been acquired by the St. Denis family under questionable circumstances. "Stolen" was the word her grandmother used regularly.

"I couldn't exactly do an inventory, Mama Grace." Lyrissa looked at her. "I'm going to take my time, get familiar with the house and the personalities."

"What personalities?" Mama Grace said.

"There's the housekeeper. She comes in four days a week." Lyrissa shifted in her chair.

"No problem." Aunt Claire shrugged.

"And then there's *him*." Lyrissa thought of broad shoulders covered by expensive fabric.

Mama Grace blinked in confusion. "Georgina's husband has been dead for almost ten years now."

"Her son lives in that new fancy suburb, Gentilly Estates," Aunt Claire put in.

"I mean her grandson, Noel." Lyrissa kept her voice neutral, despite the way her body responded when she said his name.

"Of course. They made him CEO of the company. Our friend Bessie knows a lot about them. Did she mention him, Claire?" Mama Grace gazed at her sister.

"She didn't say much. Bessie mostly knows about the older family members. What's he like?" Aunt Claire turned to Lyrissa.

Lyrissa stared ahead without seeing the lovely Louisiana landscape painting on the wall. She thought of lightly tan muscled arms. Phillip Noel St. Denis was like a quiet storm. He'd snuck up on her with his eyes the color of almond. Too bad he was an arrogant piece of work. Still, he had a body that inspired fantasies. Lyrissa was a normal female. Unfortunately, she was a female who'd hit a long dry spell when it came to finding decent male company.

"Lyrissa?" Aunt Claire's eyebrows formed twin arches as she exchanged a glance with Mama Grace. "I think we've got a little problem brewing," she murmured.

"Lyrissa Michelle, focus," Mama Grace ordered with a solemn expression.

"He's handsome, I take it," Aunt Claire said.

"He's okay." Lyrissa avoided her gaze. She hoped Aunt Claire hadn't developed a skill at reading minds.

"Hmm," was all Aunt Claire said in response. She continued staring at her great-niece.

"I was just thinking about ways to look around the house with them there."

"Sure you were." Aunt Claire glanced at Mama Grace again.

"Cut that out," Lyrissa said. "I've got only one interest in that family, to get back our property."

"If you say so." Aunt Claire seemed unconvinced.

"Concentrate on your priority and ignore anything else." Mama Grace stared at her steadily as though to detect any sign she'd do otherwise.

"No problem," Lyrissa replied in a firm voice. A tiny voice in her head said, *Liar.*

4

Lyrissa's best friend, Ebony Armstrong, gazed at her in amazement. They had met for lunch in a small soul food deli on the corner of Louisiana Avenue. Ebony worked as an attorney in a law firm with offices downtown.

"Let me see if I've got this straight," Ebony said. She brushed back her shoulder length braids. "You're doing an appraisal for the mighty St. Denis family, the people you're trying to stick it to. Sweet deal."

"You haven't met Georgina St. Denis." Lyrissa made a face.

Ebony laughed. "Like you can't handle her. What about this guy, Noel? Is the brother as fine as they say?"

"If you like that type." Lyrissa waved a hand as though dismissing him.

"Well, what type is he? Give me his stats," Ebony

pressed. She leaned across the table, one hand propped under her chin.

"About six feet three, built, medium sized. Dark brown hair with some red highlights. His eyes are a light brown, like cinnamon, sorta. Big shoulders, too." Lyrissa gazed off without seeing anything in the busy restaurant.

"So you're telling me the man is more than fine."

"I guess. He's what you'd expect from a St. Denis."

"Gotcha. Looks good and knows it. They say he's got a supernatural way with women. Sure you won't be tempted?"

Lyrissa's eyes narrowed. "I don't care what he looks like. I'm not into color-struck, stuck up—"

"Calm down, girl. I was just asking the question. Geez!"

"Now you've got your answer," Lyrissa tossed back.

"Everybody in here got my answer!"

Lyrissa blushed and lowered her voice. "I grew up with those folks looking down on me. Remember in school?"

"Hey, I was there. Damn right I remember." Ebony frowned. "It was no fun."

"Even the teachers treated us like crap." Lyrissa shook her head. "Our families thought getting us into St. Mary's was the thing. We caught all kinds of hell."

"Gotta admit it's a good school. We got a first-class education. Which is what they wanted for us." Ebony sighed.

"Yeah, we got an education, all right. In more ways than one."

Lyrissa learned her hardest lessons about bigotry based on skin color at St. Mary's Catholic School. The two friends sat deep in thought for several moments, reflecting on the past. Lyrissa and Ebony had really clung to each other for support back then. Both were outsiders, too dark and with hair too coarse to be acceptable to the light-skinned Creole girls.

"Anyway, back to the present. You're in the St. Denis fortress," Ebony said.

"Yeah, I'm in."

"You plan ahead. Honey, I never would have thought of what you're doing." Ebony wore an expression of admiration.

Lyrissa sighed.

"You're not doing anything wrong, just gathering evidence so you can get back what's rightfully yours," Ebony stated.

"It feels like I'm running a scam." Lyrissa frowned.

"No, no, no." Ebony tapped the table three times with her fist. "*They* pulled the scam."

"Guess I'm too jumpy. With my big mouth and quick temper, I'll probably mess up," Lyrissa said.

"You're doing great so far."

Lyrissa wondered again if she'd gotten in over her head. "I just keep wanting to come out and tell them. Fight head on, you know?"

"Their lawyers would blast you in a blink-blink. I say, get the ammunition you need to fight first and use the element of surprise." Ebony outlined the plan like a general.

"Yeah, yeah, yeah."

"Hey, you can do it. Just be cool, and when you're sure, take care of business." Ebony snapped her fingers.

"Right. Except for one little detail." Lyrissa leaned across the table.

Ebony gazed at her for a moment, then grinned. "Hit him fast and hard. I'll start plotting our legal approach. Just give me the evidence."

"I've got to figure out a way to get it first. These people aren't stupid." Lyrissa looked at her.

"You'll work it out." Ebony clapped her on the shoulder.

"Oh, sure I will."

Lyrissa laughed out loud but not because she was amused. Ebony certainly overestimated her ingenuity. Not to mention the other problem that she'd not counted on. Noel St. Denis was more than a distraction. He was a sharp set of eyes that could watch her every move. It had all seemed so simple three months ago when she set the wheels in motion for Taylor Gallery to be hired by Georgina St. Denis.

"This whole thing is gettin' tricky, girl." Lyrissa muttered. A vivid memory of golden brown eyes popped into her head.

"What do you think?" Mrs. St. Denis tipped her head to one side like a schoolteacher testing a pupil.

"Well . . ." Lyrissa hesitated to answer immediately.

They were in the study. Lyrissa almost forgot to concentrate on her one goal. Like the rest of the huge house, the library held paintings and other items she could happily spend hours examining. All were of historical interest.

"Don't be tentative or timid. I don't like either." Mrs. St. Denis waited.

"My special area has been New Orleans art history." Lyrissa continued to examine the painting.

"Even better, but we'll get to that later. Well?"

"Hmm, late eighteenth century. Dutch, I'd say. It's a Van der Weele." Lyrissa nodded as she continued to study the painting.

"Very good."

"Thank you," Lyrissa said.

"My French ancestor brought it here when he came over from Paris in 1735, I believe." Mrs. St. Denis paused for a moment. "You still haven't told me much about yourself. Where did you go to grade school?" Mrs. St. Denis looked at her hard.

"St. Mary's."

"Maybe you know my godchild Jeanine Bienville and my great-niece Monique Lacour."

The muscles in Lyrissa's neck tightened. She definitely knew them. They were members of the elite clique that had made her life miserable in high school.

"I'm not sure. It's been a long time," Lyrissa lied. She couldn't trust herself to talk about that group calmly.

"Possibly not. What about your family?" Mrs. St. Denis asked.

Lyrissa blinked for a second, then regained her balance. "My parents died when I was young."

"That must have been hard on you," Mrs. St. Denis commented. There was no pity in her voice.

"Not too much," Lyrissa said quickly.

Too quickly, she knew by the way Mrs. St. Denis looked at her. Was the old lady testing her again? She could well have hired a private detective to check out her new employee. Lyrissa would not have put it past her.

"I find that hard to believe." The older woman lifted her head and continued to gaze at her.

"My mother ran off and left me with my dad." Lyrissa spoke quietly. "She died young from living too wild—drugs, I think, but my family still hides the truth from me. My dad drank too much and ran his car into a concrete piling on Interstate 10 on the way to Baton Rouge one night."

She decided it was best to stick to the truth so she wouldn't have to remember a lie. Still, a tight knot of sadness formed in her stomach.

"I'm sorry to hear that." Mrs. St. Denis sounded sincere in a prim, socially-acceptable-thing-to-say fashion.

"Actually, I think my parents did the best they could. They both had lots of problems." Lyrissa shrugged.

"You don't blame them, then?" Mrs. St. Denis seemed intensely interested in Lyrissa's answer.

"No, in a way I don't. Mama tried, but she had it rough growing up. She used to play games with me, I remember." Lyrissa cleared her throat to stave off tears. "And Daddy was funny. They both made sure I didn't go hungry and got to school. Mama would show up on the playground with some toy every now and then."

"You're an unusual young woman. Not many children would be so forgiving," Mrs. St. Denis said.

Lyrissa saw an opportunity. "Can I ask *you* something personal? My dissertation will include at least a chapter on Creole culture. So I'm not just being nosy."

"Fair enough." Mrs. St. Denis sat back in her chair and put her clasped hands into her lap. "Fire away."

"Do you think of yourself as African-American?" Lyrissa chided herself that she'd not chosen her words better. "I mean—"

"I know what you mean." Mrs. St. Denis waved a hand at her. "You must understand something, my dear. Creoles consider themselves a distinct group, for the most part. Not white or black, but better." She wore a half-smile.

"Some prefer to be considered white, though," Lyrissa said.

"True. And why not? Take the Fouché family, for example. Their female ancestor was a fair-skinned mulatto, and her 'husband' a wealthy French planter. Their children were raised in the French culture and educated in Paris. They consider themselves more French than anything else. Shouldn't they be able to say who they are? They had little in common with the slaves or even most free blacks of the eighteenth century. Edgar DuMasse spoke six languages, wrote poetry, and composed music."

"But they did have African ancestry traced back to a slave brought over by Spanish explorers in 1698. To deny him is a kind of racism," Lyrissa said.

"I've never heard them deny it," Mrs. St. Denis said promptly.

"They don't go around claiming him, either," Lyrissa shot back.

"You really want to ask me about our ancestry." Her eyes narrowed.

"Well . . . I have to admit to being a little interested."

Mrs. St. Denis rose slowly. "You have a lot of work to do. I'll let you get to it."

"Yes, ma'am." Lyrissa pressed her lips together.

"Ring for Rosalie if you need anything," Mrs. St. Denis said in a clipped tone.

Noel came in and pecked his grandmother on the cheek. "Good morning, sweetheart." He gazed at Lyrissa with smoldering eyes. "Good morning, Lyrissa."

"Hello." Lyrissa looked away from him in self-defense.

"Your father is already here." His grandmother started for the door, clearly expecting him to follow.

"I'll be there in a minute," Noel said.

Mrs. St. Denis turned and glanced from him to Lyrissa with a tight expression. "Don't keep us waiting. We have important business to discuss."

"I won't be long. Besides, this gives you time to talk about me behind my back," he said with a good-natured smile.

"Amusing," Mrs. St. Denis retorted and walked out.

Noel turned back to Lyrissa. "Have everything you need?"

"Yes, thanks. I've got a lot of ground to cover today." She made a great show of opening a large book.

"Well, I won't get in the way, then. But if you do need anything—"

"I'll call Rosalie," Lyrissa cut in.

"I meant you could call on me." Noel walked over to where she sat and stood close to her.

"I'm sure I won't have to bother you. Mrs. St. Denis has given me access to quite a few of your family's old documents." Lyrissa tried to put in her tone every ounce of dismissal she could.

"Excellent. I'll see you later." Noel never lost his cool, confident exterior.

"Goodbye." Lyrissa maintained her ice maiden expression.

Noel smiled at her once more and walked away. His graceful stride only added to the sexiness that seemed to ooze from every pore. The conservative steel gray suit didn't disguise the muscular body beneath it. She watched his broad back until he disappeared through the double sliding doors. Lyrissa let out a long, slow breath. She'd have to keep a tight rein on her libido with him around.

5

Noel sat between his grandmother and father at the table in the sunny breakfast room. Richard Phillip St. Denis was his usual self, careless grace under fire. Miss Georgina chewed on her scrambled eggs as though they were nails, arched brows drawn down. If his grandfather had been alive, he'd have said, "Georgie's jaws are tight. Somebody's in serious trouble." Richard seemed blithely unaware of any stormy undercurrents. He behaved as though this was their normal Wednesday morning breakfast.

His grandparents had breakfast with each one of their three children every week once they'd grown up and left home. Spouses and grandchildren were included, of course. Noel's mother bowed out whenever she could. Noel glanced at his grandmother and then his father. He wished he'd had the foresight of his mother.

"So tell me, son, how are things down at the old salt

mines?" Richard picked up a thin crispy slice of bacon and bit off the end.

"As if you care," Miss Georgina said in a quiet yet steely tone.

Noel cleared his throat. He would try to head off the pitched battle this time. "Actually, things are looking up, Dad. Carlton and I have had two productive meetings."

Richard sipped coffee from a china cup with a red rose pattern. "Hard to believe Carlton listens to anyone but himself. He's just like his daddy."

"Your brother works hard." Miss Georgina stared at him in a way that would make most men tremble. Her middle child merely shrugged.

"Oh yeah? Well that's nothing to brag on. Noel says the whole damn place is about to collapse," he retorted.

"I didn't say—" Noel cursed silently.

Miss Georgina set her coffee cup down on the linen tablecloth with a thump. "And who do we have to thank for that? You!"

"I don't follow your logic, Mother," Richard said, his voice still mild. "Willie was CEO. The buck stopped with him."

Noel groaned inwardly. Why hadn't he just said "Fine" and not mentioned his cousin's name? Uncle Willie had been forced to give up the high pressure position because of his health. Diabetes and heart problems kept him ill. The stress of running a huge business had only made things worse. The sibling rivalry between his dad and his uncle Willie seemed to have been passed down to their sons. Things got worse when Noel became CEO.

"You're a St. Denis!" Miss Georgina snapped. "You have

a responsibility to protect what your great-grandfathers built."

"Here we go. Speech number twenty-five," Richard mumbled under his breath. He aimed a mischievous wink at Noel.

Noel scowled at him in return. He put down his fork and took one of Miss Georgina's hands. "*Family is* taking care of Tremé Corporation. Calm down, Grandmère."

Miss Georgina huffed for a few seconds more before her expression relaxed a bit. The French endearment from his childhood could usually soften the formidable woman's hard edges. She patted his Noel's hand and cast a sharp look of disapproval at her son.

"Noel understands even if you don't, Richard."

"Oh, give me a break," Richard said. His handsome brow wrinkled with irritation for the first time.

Noel sighed. He took a drink of strong Louisiana coffee to fortify himself. His grandmother and father argued in their own subdued, upper-crust manner. Noel tried to tune out the barbs. He searched for an appropriate opening to duck out on them both. A flash of dark rose fabric drew his attention.

Lyrissa passed by carrying a notepad and a large leatherbound book. Her dark hair was pulled back but loose curls framed her face. She glanced at Noel for a moment, then retreated.

"Excuse me," he said. His grandmother and father did not seem to hear him.

He went down the hall toward the library just in time to see her start up the stairs. The knee length skirt clung to her hips. The silk shirt was prim and provocative at the same time the way it draped her shoulders and breasts. Soft round hips and thighs that moved with a hint of sensuality took the simple outfit to a whole new level. Lyrissa climbed the first four steps, one hand on the banister. Noel's throat went dry as he watched the sway of her bottom. His imagination took over. The seductive rhythm suggested silky skin hugged tight by satin panties. Every move seemed an exclusive invitation for him alone. Noel pictured them headed toward his bedroom. Suddenly his pants were too tight and the room too warm.

"Ahem!"

"What?" Noel mumbled, reluctant to tear his gaze away from the arresting vision before him.

Rosalie stood with arms folded in the library door. "You lost somethin' up them stairs?"

Noel felt like a schoolboy caught looking up a girl's skirt. Luckily he recovered just as Lyrissa glanced back at them. At least, he prayed he had.

"I was going to ask Miss Rideau a question before I left for the office, if that's okay with you. By the way, breakfast was delicious, as usual." Noel smiled at her.

"Uh-huh," Rosalie walked off but looked back at him over her shoulder. Her expression shouted, *You're busted*!

"Good morning," Lyrissa said. She came back down toward him. "What was that about? I didn't catch what she said."

"Nothing. Rosalie is just . . . Rosalie." Noel lifted a shoulder. "So how are you today?"

"Fine. I didn't mean to intrude on your breakfast."

"Trust me, an interruption would have been nice," Noel said with a grimace.

"Excuse me?"

"Nothing. How's it going so far?"

"I've only just begun, Mr. St. Denis." She wore a quizzical expression.

"Right." Noel smiled sheepishly. "Guess it's obvious I'm trying to make conversation."

"Is there something in particular you want to know?"

Her neutral expression unnerved him. Most women warmed to him quickly. Lyrissa Rideau seemed unaffected by his attempts to be friendly. His resolve to chip away at this iceberg grew.

"Not really." Noel smiled at her easily. "Digging through dusty old books in the library must be tedious."

"Not at all. I find it fascinating," Lyrissa said with enthusiasm. She went on to talk about her methods and the sources she would use.

He smiled at the first sign of a thaw. Her eyes were bright with anticipation for the search. Her honey brown skin seemed to glow and it was catching. Noel moved closer to her as she spoke.

"There are so many archives I can use. I may even find documents at the Cabildo," Lyrissa finished, referring to the French Quarter museum. "But your grandmother's house is filled with historical treasures. I'm delighted every time I turn a corner."

"I'm glad you enjoy being here," he said softly, then blinked hard in surprise.

"Th-thank you," she replied. She gazed back at him then glanced away quickly.

He cleared his throat. "So tell me the truth—how hard *is* it to deal with my grandmother? Has she shared any of the dark family secrets?"

"She was a bit hesitant." Lyrissa's full mouth lifted at the corners. "But I think she's okay with it now. Just how dark *are* those secrets?"

The mere suggestion of a smile made her even lovelier. Heat seared his skin with force. Just a gentle curve of her lips could arouse him. Women had done far more to get his attention and he'd barely noticed. Yet here he was on fire, aching to touch her satin skin with his fingertips. He stood mesmerized by the way her mouth moved when she talked.

"What?"

"I assured Mrs. St. Denis that I'll be very discreet. I'm only interested in the history related to the artwork." Lyrissa stared at him curiously. "Are you okay with it?"

Noel took a deep steadying breath. He was making a fool of himself. "Sure, sure. Just don't expose all the family skeletons to the world."

"And have to face your grandmother? Shelton Taylor doesn't pay me enough," she said with an amused expression.

"I have a feeling you could hold your own." Noel smiled.

"I'm not willing to test that particular theory. Besides, you've only known me a few days."

"I can already tell just from watching you," Noel replied.

"So you've got your eye on me, huh? Sounds like you're suspicious like your grandmother." Lyrissa tilted her head to one side. A tendril of hair brushed her cheek and she tucked it back in place.

Noel watched the movement, wishing he'd been the one to comb his fingers in her hair. He cleared his throat and looked away. "I just meant . . ."

"It's okay. I'm used to scrutiny. After all, we're dealing with valuable family heirlooms." She smiled at him. "You should be cautious. Anyway, I'm trying not to get Mrs. St. Denis too irritated with me."

"A good idea. No sense grabbing a tigress by the tail."

Lyrissa laughed and the musical sound rippled over him like a refreshing summer shower. He enjoyed the way her eyes lit up when she was amused. The intimacy of their shared joke was intoxicating. He moved closer again. Her delicate floral scent pulled at him.

"Cashmere Bouquet body powder." He inhaled deeply. "I haven't smelled that in years. I didn't know they still made it."

"Are you saying I'm out of date?" Lyrissa raised an eyebrow.

"No way. It reminds me of my first love. Shana Travis was the belle of St. Francis Nursery School." Noel laughed.

"So why didn't you marry that wonderful little diva?"

"She tossed me aside like a dirty diaper. A pint-sized player turned her head." Noel affected a pained expression and placed a hand over his heart.

"Silly girl, to let a St. Denis slip from her fingers." Lyrissa stared at him with an inscrutable expression. "Of course, Travis isn't a name in the Creole social register."

Noel's gut tightened. He'd learned early about who was and wasn't acceptable to his family. His battles about choosing his friends, male and female, had begun early. He remembered Rasheeka, a beautiful little girl the color of teakwood. Lyrissa had hit a tender spot. His smile stretched his face tight.

"At four it wasn't exactly a tragic love story." He pushed away the memory.

Richard walked up. "Well, good morning. Noel, introduce us."

"Lyrissa Rideau, this is my father, Richard St. Denis. Lyrissa is with Taylor Gallery." Noel took a step back as his father reached out and took Lyrissa's hand.

"It's wonderful to meet you." Richard made the simple statement sound like a grand compliment.

"Hello. Nice meeting you, too," Lyrissa said. She glanced between them but said no more.

"I know, we look more like brothers than father and son," Noel said blandly. He waited for Lyrissa to fall for the legendary Richard St. Denis charm.

"You're taller," she replied. Her eyes widened. "I didn't mean—what I'm saying is—"

Richard blinked as though he'd been thumped on the forehead, but quickly rallied. He cleared his throat. "No, no, dear. Think nothing of it. So Noel has made an impression."

"You could say that," Lyrissa tossed back with a sideways glance at Noel.

Noel gazed at her expecting to see a flirtatious sparkle in her brown eyes. Instead he sensed dislike, even contempt, underlying her reply. He was puzzled. It had never been difficult for him to get female attention. In fact, it was often a downright nuisance. Lyrissa seemed underwhelmed by his charm. Strange and intriguing, he thought. Normally he would have been relieved. Instead, desire to pursue her sent a prickle of heat down his back.

"If you'll excuse me, I should get back to work." Lyrissa wore a cool smile that was not aimed at either of them. She went upstairs and disappeared unceremoniously.

"Lucky you," Richard said with a wink.

Noel headed back to the breakfast room. "I don't know what you mean."

Richard followed close behind. "Most of those academic types are twice as old and ten times uglier. You've got one luscious female right under foot."

"She's a professional here to do a job, Dad." Noel tried to block the image of her hips swaying as she walked. He failed. That bothersome heat wave came back.

"Whatever, the point is, you hit the jackpot. Use it to your advantage. You've got art, she's into art."

"You've got a dirty mind, Dad," Noel said.

"Then you got it honest." Richard grabbed his arm and stopped him. "I watched you watch her, son. I know that look."

Noel did something he hadn't done since he was twelve when asked about a girl. He blushed and tugged at his shirt collar. "What look?"

"You're hot for Ms. Rideau, and I don't blame you one bit. Go for it, boy!" Richard slapped his shoulder.

"Cut it out," Noel grumbled. "I don't try to jump every beautiful woman in sight."

"You have an appreciation for the finer things in life. It's in your blood. Especially when it comes to women." Richard sighed with satisfaction.

Noel shrugged. "She's attractive, but—"

"You said beautiful." Richard grinned at him.

"The point is, I don't spend my days chasing women. Not when the company is in such a sad state."

"You inherited your mother's skill at criticizing me in a most concise way." Richard scowled and went back to the breakfast room. Noel reluctantly followed.

"I was wondering where you both went for so long." Miss Georgina wore reading glasses as she scanned a section of the *Times Picayune*.

"I met Ms. Rideau. Lovely young thing." Richard settled back in his chair at the table.

Miss Georgina looked at him sharply. "Stay away from her."

"Relax, Mother. She didn't warm up to me." Richard poured more coffee into his cup from a ceramic pot.

"I'm not worried about that," Miss Georgina shot at him. "She's not interested in an aging Casanova."

"Wait a minute!" Richard was the picture of wounded male pride.

"She'd cut you down to size, then quit. It would be fun to watch. But we'd lose time finding another appraiser." Miss Georgina went back to reading.

"You underestimate me, Mother. But it's a moot point." Richard grinned at Noel. "I wouldn't stand in the way of my own son."

Miss Georgina dropped the newspaper and stared at Noel. "What is he talking about, Noel?"

"Nothing," Noel put in quickly. "As usual, Dad has an overactive imagination." He could have added that Richard also had an overactive libido.

"If you say so." Richard let a lift of one dark eyebrow punctuate his statement.

"I hope you're not going to be such a fool, Noel Phillip." Miss Georgina frowned at him.

Irritation made the hair on Noel's neck stand up. "I can make my own choices."

"Don't be ridiculous!" Miss Georgina tossed her linen napkin on the table.

Noel let out a long sigh of exasperation. "Why the hell are we even discussing this?"

"Watch your language, young man," Miss Georgina warned.

"I'm sorry." Noel waved a hand in the air. "Look, there is nothing, I mean *nothing*, going on between Lyrissa and me." He gave his father a stony look that only brought a careless shrug.

"I should hope not." Miss Georgina appeared satisfied with his declaration.

Noel was now irritated for another reason. His grandmother and parents held onto the old prejudices about social station. They had always tried to control his choice of friends and romantic interests. He knew well what his grandmother's simple response meant. Still, he did not want to bring up an old battle. Older and wiser, he pushed back the urge to return fire.

"My full attention is on the company," Noel said in a tight voice.

He tried to convince himself more than his grandmother. Falling for Lyrissa—or anyone—wasn't in his five-year plan. Falling in love wasn't smart at all. Flirting, yes. A hot, short, and sweet love affair, definitely. Love—hell, no. Then the memory of her perfume came back with a vengeance.

"Exactly. Which is where yours should have been for the past ten years, Richard." Miss Georgina did a precise pivot to focus her criticism on her son. "If you hadn't left Tremé Corporation to traipse off—"

Richard puffed out his chest. "I'm one of the best amateur golfers in my group."

"Traveling all over the countryside to hit a little white ball isn't something to brag about." Miss Georgina glared at him. "You wouldn't be so smug if that fat trust fund dried up."

"What does that mean?" Richard glanced anxiously at Noel, then his mother.

"Most of it comes from company value, and that value is dropping like a rock," Miss Georgina said in a low yet sharp tone.

"Hold on," Noel broke in. "Grandmother, things aren't quite that bad. Profits have leveled off and I see evidence of a slide downward. But we haven't reached a critical point."

"Yet," Miss Georgina said. "I'm old, not stupid. We haven't kept pace with the competition. Willie stubbornly resisted changes to our marketing strategy for five years. He completely missed the mark on taking advantage of the Internet."

"What?" Richard looked at his mother as though she were from another planet. "How do you know all this?"

"I read the annual company reports, the *Times Picayune* business section, and the *Wall Street Journal*. So should you." Miss Georgina gazed at her son.

"Profits are rising," Noel said. "With hard work and the right strategy, Tremé Corporation will survive."

Miss Georgina looked out the window at the flowers blooming in an explosion of color. "Your grandfather literally worked to death for that place. He did it for his children."

"You would have made a dynamite CEO, Grandmother," Noel said. "Grandfather didn't mind telling everyone you helped make the company as much as he did."

Raymond and Georgina St. Denis were married for almost fifty years. For all his hard edges, Noel would give anything to find that kind of partnership with a woman.

Yet watching his parents had bred skepticism. Lyrissa's crystal clear laugh echoed in a corner of his mind. His grandmother's voice brought him back.

"But we're talking about the present. More important, I'm talking about the future."

"And as usual, blaming me," Richard said, a note of complaint in his voice. "Willie ran the company, for God's sake."

"Exactly. Where were you? You've never lived up to your potential," Miss Georgina said.

"I've been hearing that since I was ten years old."

"It's still true." Miss Georgina poked his forearm with a finger. "You and Willie would have balanced each other well. He's too rigid, and frankly, not a people person."

"She means most people detest him." Richard chuckled.

"While you spend too much time charming people and not enough working." Miss Georgina pressed on.

"I'm not interested in real estate or insurance." Richard waved a piece of toast in the air. "I was bored out of my mind at that office."

"There you have it," Miss Georgina said dryly. "A childish need to be amused every day."

"Just because I didn't find actuary stats and collecting rent exhilarating—"

Noel intervened to head off the same argument he'd been witnessing since childhood. "Let's not beat a dead horse," he quoted his grandfather.

Miss Georgina glared at Richard for a few seconds more, then nodded and looked out the window again. Richard tapped a teaspoon on the side of his coffee cup. Noel hated being a referee, but increasingly he found himself in that role.

"Dad was very unhappy at the company. It was bound to affect his performance as a manager." Noel did not flinch when his grandmother squinted at him.

"An understatement of monumental proportions," Richard cut in.

"Uncle Willie did a lot for the company. The employees respect him a great deal," Noel added, frowning at his father.

"Of course they do," Miss Georgina said.

"I have a 'but' to add, Grandmother." Noel sat back against the chair cushion. "He doesn't accept suggestions easily. Uncle Willie gets insulted easily and considers input a criticism of his leadership."

"Ha!" Richard mimicked Miss Georgina. "What did I say?"

"Will you two stop?" Noel glanced between them. He felt like a school principal between two angry children.

"You're right," Miss Georgina said. "The question is, what do we do now?"

"I'm considering several options. But we need to move fast, before we lose the confidence of our creditors," Noel said.

"What do you have in mind?" Richard leaned toward him.

"Raising capital would help. I'm looking at several properties we can sell. One of the warehouses in Chalmette, for instance."

"Good idea, Noel," Richard said. "It's in a prime area and almost half empty." He smiled at the surprised look his mother gave him. "Yes, Mother, I do keep up with some aspects of the company."

"There's one more thing. Our family art collection is probably worth quite a bit. Of course, with it spread out all over the place, who knows?"

Miss Georgina's mild expression of approval changed into a frown. "I thought you only wanted to use its value to raise the value of the company and attract venture capital. If we sell the collection, you'll have the entire city thinking we're in the poorhouse!"

"Mother is right, son. That kind of thing carries the stench of desperation. Talk about spooking our creditors." Richard shook his head with vigor. "Besides, it's the St. Denis and Rohas family legacy, for God's sake!"

"That art has been in the family for generations," Miss Georgina said.

"And in dusty attics for most of the last twenty-five years or more," Noel added.

"He has a point, Mother. I'm sure our relatives wouldn't mind raising extra cash." Richard rubbed his chin.

"It could mean a difference in the future of our company," Noel said quietly. "We can be selective in what we sell."

"Some of our dear relatives will scream bloody murder," Richard warned. He spread butter on another piece of toast.

"I'll ask Lyrissa to prepare a report in time for the next board meeting," Noel said. "I'm sure they'll see reason once I explain our situation."

"Strange, you have time to attend to such details, being such a busy executive." Richard's dark eyes twinkled.

Miss Georgina stared at him. "I'm sure your administrative assistant can deal with that, Noel."

"Attention to detail is what I'm paid for," Noel said mildly and stood. "Speaking of which, I'll take care of it right now."

"I can do it. You have a full day at the office," Miss Georgina said stiffly.

"Noel would prefer to handle Ms. Rideau, Mother." Richard smirked at him.

"Finish your breakfast." Noel ignored his dig and smiled at his grandmother. "I'm on my way out, so I might as well speak to her." He patted her arm. He could feel her stony gaze as he walked away.

6

Lyrissa darted down the hall. She just had time to step into the library before Noel appeared. His grandmother's voice stopped him, giving her more time. Miss Georgina's voice rang out as Lyrissa gently pushed the sliding doors together.

"You said you had a meeting in thirty minutes. You'll be late," Mrs. St. Denis said.

"No, I won't. Relax and have a nice day, sweetheart," Noel replied.

"Come on, Mother. I'll drive you to that United Way meeting," Richard said.

"Perfect," Lyrissa whispered, and closed the doors together with a thump.

She passed through the study hardly glancing at the bookcases. Her real goal was the room beyond. The walls were painted a rich earth green. Near the ceiling was a border of wallpaper with a thick pattern of vines with deep red flowers. The pattern was repeated in the draperies on three windows, one of which faced the street. Three display cases held eighteenth century documents. A will dated 1806 listed the bequests of one Don Jose Nicholas Rohas.

"I leave to Eufrosina Hisnard, my faithful servant, a certain parcel of land measuring sixty arpents." Lyrissa read the florid handwriting aloud. She easily translated it from French to English. Her grandmother had insisted she learn the language. Lyrissa had complained loud and often that it was useless. Time had proved Mama Grace right. French had been the official language in Louisiana for most of the eighteenth and nineteenth centuries. Business and legal documents were recorded in French.

Lyrissa moved on and read another document brown with age. She looked around the room until her gaze settled on a portrait of two small children. It was lovely, but her interest was in the wall safe the painting concealed. Lyrissa's fingers itched with the desire to get at its contents. Miss Georgina had told her there were more family papers locked inside. Excellent signposts along the trail Lyrissa would follow in her quest. She wrestled with the urge to try her hand at safe cracking.

"Don't be impatient and make a dumb move," Lyrissa mumbled.

"I hate to disturb you again."

Lyrissa started. The mellow male voice close to her ear wrapped around her like a sultry breeze, warm and steamy as only summer in New Orleans can be. She could feel his body heat through the fabric of her blouse. His breath brushed against her neck. "Disturb" was the right word. She felt disoriented and off-balance. What was he doing to her? A tickle of lust went through her pelvis and traveled up to circle both breasts. Lyrissa pictured herself pressed to him. Their bodies would meld together as he gripped her hips with strong hands.

"I don't understand," Lyrissa said calmly.

"I keep interrupting your work." Noel pointed to her notepad.

That voice combined with the smile sent a thrill through her. No wonder women for miles around came running when he appeared. Lyrissa went rigid. He could just fold up his little magic act. She wasn't going to be duped.

"I thought you'd left for the office," she blurted out. "Don't let me delay you." Lyrissa groaned silently. *You might as well wear an I'm-guilty sign on your chest.*

"I wanted to talk to you. Taking a look at the family jewels, I see."

"I couldn't resist. I hope you don't mind." Lyrissa recovered and flashed a charming smile.

"Not at all. Go anywhere you like. In fact, there are even more documents at our offices downtown."

"Actually, it might be a good idea to give them a quick look. If only to rule out that any of them has to do with the collection." Lyrissa's heart sped up at the plum that seemed to just drop in her lap.

"No problem. Let me know when you're ready. For the documents, I mean," he added with a smile that could melt the Arctic Circle.

"Right. I'll just finish up checking off the items on your list." Lyrissa started past him when he stopped her with a touch on her arm.

"Wait, I wanted to ask if you could give me a report

with a complete listing in, say, three weeks. We have a board meeting then."

Lyrissa worked to clear her head. The weight of his hand on her arm was a powerful distraction. "I, er, should be able to give you at least a list by then."

"Great. Then I'd better let you finish." Noel turned to leave, then faced her again. "In fact, let's make an appointment right now."

"What?" Lyrissa stared at him.

"You can come to my office. I'll help you get started with your research. I'll even bring the papers here to my office. Having them all together will make your job easier."

Lyrissa knew trouble when it was staring her in the face. "Just have your assistant set it up, and I'll—"

"No, I'll handle it personally. I know what you need." Noel smiled at her.

She suppressed a shiver at his words. She lifted her chin and assumed a reserved, all business posture. "I'll call your office to make the arrangements, then." She made a wide circle around him and went back to the study.

"I look forward to it." Noel offered his hand to her.

Lyrissa steeled herself not to react as she took it. Her body didn't obey. His velvety skin sent a finger of heat up her arm. She pulled free of his firm grasp.

"Goodbye," she said.

"Goodbye," he replied and left.

"Keep your eyes on the prize," she whispered. "And off his fine body."

Noel went to the conference room without stopping at his office. His cousin Carlton was on the second agenda item by the time he sat down. As usual, Carlton droned on about insurance rates. The five top managers appeared to pay avid attention to him. One of them was Julie Duval. Julie's mother and Noel's mother had been best friends since high school.

"Over here," Julie whispered and spun the swivel chair next to her out.

"Morning," Noel said and nodded to the others.

Julie leaned close until their shoulders touched. "You haven't missed much."

Carlton stopped talking and looked at his watch pointedly. "I decided it was best to start."

"Good, go on." Noel nodded to him.

He stared at Noel for several seconds. To avoid a scene, Noel pretended not to notice. Carlton took up where he'd left off. His monotone voice went on with dry details about the industry. After a few seconds Noel's thoughts wandered back to a vision of beauty in rose.

Lyrissa Rideau looked more tempting each time they met. Not even a business suit could disguise her lush figure. He imagined her slender fingers stroking him. All she had to do was glance his way and he ached to feel her touch. She must have noticed. How could she not? Noel was sure he'd worn the expression of a horny teenager. That wasn't him at all. He was used to being in the driver's seat. Aside from the usual fleeting crush, Noel had breezed along love's highway without even a fender bender. He'd slowed down occasionally for a liaison. But overall, Noel kept right on going . . . until Lyrissa. Now he found himself applying the brakes and circling the block. Not that she cared, from what he could tell.

Far from being annoyed, Noel was intrigued. She had a depth to her that he wanted to explore. *Hell, tell the truth. You want to dive in head first!* The lusty image raised his temperature by ten degrees at least. His cousin's voice was an unwelcome interruption. Noel swam out of a sensual fog.

"What did you say?"

"Maybe I should start over," Carlton said, an edge to his voice.

"Not at all. And I agree with Paul. We shouldn't go before the commission for a rate increase." Noel sat up straighter.

"I'm not sure about that, given our current state." Carlton drummed his fingers on the wood surface.

"We decided in the meeting last week," Noel said, careful to keep his voice level. "The figures don't add up."

"My breakdown clearly indicates a rate increase is essential. I sent a copy to you and the board." Carlton looked at him, resentment stamped on his wide face.

Noel counted to five before he spoke. "The Insurance Commission has turned down every other request this year." The commission served as the regulatory entity over insurance companies in the state.

"I've studied those requests. I think we can succeed where they failed."

"The commissioners are up for re-election. They're not going to raise rates," Noel explained in a measured, calm manner.

"The election is eleven months away. They won't play politics this early. Look this over. The commission meets again in August." Carlton passed blue folders around the table.

"Carlton—" Noel began.

"You've seen the information on pages one through

five. The updated figures begin on page six," Carlton cut him off.

Noel read the section Carlton had directed them to, then skimmed ahead to another section. "What's new in here?"

"Excuse me?" Carlton grimaced at him.

The other men exchanged glances. One by one they eased back in their chairs. Obviously they intended to get out of the line of fire. Julie kept her eyes on Noel as though waiting for her cue.

"From what I see, you're making the same arguments the other companies made. More house fires because of a cold winter. Legislation that made our costs bump up, etc., etc. I don't see anything different."

"The difference is, we're a minority company providing coverage to a vulnerable population," Carlton said.

"So what? Most of the commissioners are conservative. They oppose special contracts for minorities and affirmative action." Noel wanted to shake him for being so dense. "We talked about this before."

"That's your theory. Three of the commissioners are more attuned to the needs of the people," Carlton answered.

"Figure in the cost of our attorney to help plus the staff time, and it's not worth it." Noel's reservoir of patience was running low.

"I don't think so." Carlton's small eyes narrowed.

"We can't afford to waste resources. We need to increase income," Noel said curtly, hoping his tone would close the subject.

"Which is what a rate increase will do," Carlton replied sharply.

"Not if we don't get it." Noel glared back at him.

"Are you implying that I'm the reason our cash flow is down?" Carlton puffed like an overheated engine.

Noel refused to rise to the bait. "I'm saying we could make better use of our time. I have several strategies in mind." Noel slapped the folder before him closed.

"I thought we worked as a team, that you considered ideas other than your own." Carlton wore a stiff mask of suppressed anger.

"I did consider all the information and made a decision. Now, let's move on."

"My father and I think—" Carlton began.

"Julie, what about the warehouse on St. Peter?" Noel cut him off short.

Carlton gripped his Mont Blanc pen but said no more. The meeting went on for another hour. They were winding down on the last subject for discussion when Miss Georgina came in with Lyrissa. She introduced her to everyone. She glanced at Noel with no more recognition than she had for the other men. For their part, the managers became animated as they greeted her. Andre Wilkins, his youngest manager, jumped to his feet and held out a chair for Lyrissa.

"Here you go, ma'am. I'll get you both a cup of coffee," he said with a smarmy expression. He stood with his hand still on the back of her chair.

"I'll take herbal tea, if you have it." Lyrissa beamed at him.

"No problem. I brought my own. It's in the kitchen." Andre grinned back. "I'll have my secretary get us both a cup." He went to a phone on a side table.

The brazen kid was leering down the front of her blouse

the entire time he was talking. Noel felt an overpowering urge to slam him back into his seat. Instead, he ground his teeth as Lyrissa laughed at something else Andre said. Noel wondered what the hell was so damned amusing.

"Maybe you can finish *business* now," Noel cut in. The young man cleared his throat and took his seat.

Lyrissa sat in a chair lining the wall.

"What are we discussing?" Miss Georgina asked.

"Grandmother, you should be at home, resting," Carlton said with an indulgent expression.

"I've been resting for months." Miss Georgina placed her cane on the chair next to her. "I'm not so feeble I can't listen."

Noel stared at Andre. "Tell us about the micro-mall development on the West Bank."

"Right." The young man stuck out his chest and gave his report.

Finally the meeting ended and the staff filed out. Carlton did not move. He wore a sour expression. Julie started to leave, but paused when she glanced at Lyrissa.

"Have we met?" Julie asked her.

"Possibly. I graduated from St. Mary's," Lyrissa replied.

"Really? You had a scholarship?"

"No," Lyrissa said and smiled at her sweetly.

"Lyrissa works for Taylor Gallery. She's appraising the art collection and compiling an extensive history on it as well." Noel said.

"I see." Julie gave Lyrissa her own appraisal with one sweeping head-to-toe gaze.

"Lyrissa will get to work on the family papers today," Miss Georgina nodded to her. "I want to talk to you and Carlton, Noel."

"I'll show Lyrissa to the office I had Eddie set up." Noel stood.

"You stay here, Noel. I'll do that for you," Julie said.

"Thank you, dear." Miss Georgina smiled at her in appreciation.

Noel thought some message of understanding had passed between them. He started to assert his will, but decided against it. His irritation vanished when Lyrissa looked at him with her smoky topaz eyes. Julie led Lyrissa out of the room and shut the door with a firm thump. Miss Georgina's voice yanked him out of a budding sensuous reverie.

"We need to talk about the board meeting," she said.

Noel fought to concentrate as they went over the agenda.

Lyrissa pretended not to notice the way Julie glanced at her sideways from time to time. Julie examined her. They walked through a large office area with six desks arranged around it. Employees talked on phones and tapped computer keyboards.

"So how long have you known Noel?" Julie asked.

"I met him and Mrs. St. Denis only a couple of weeks ago at Taylor Gallery."

"I see." Julie looked straight ahead.

So do I. Lyrissa smiled. Julie saw her as competition for Noel's attention. They rounded a corner and approached a foyer. A pretty young woman sat at a desk outside a large door leading to another office. *Edwina Norcross* was etched in black letters on a brass nameplate that sat on her desk.

"Eddie, this is Lyrissa Rideau." Julie turned to Lyrissa. "Eddie is Noel's secretary."

"Administrative assistant," Eddie corrected. She smiled at Lyrissa and extended her hand as she stood. "Glad to meet you."

"Hello." Lyrissa decided she liked Eddie.

"She's here to do research and—"

"I know," Eddie broke in. "Mr. St. Denis told me."

Julie's expression tightened. "Fine, then get her a few supplies and take her to Roger's old office."

"That office is tiny and way on the other side, near the janitor's closet," Eddie said.

"The quiet will be just the thing for Ms. Rideau. I'm sure your work requires great concentration. Our office can get pretty noisy." Julie's smile lacked sincerity.

Lyrissa didn't mind. Distance from Noel would really help her to concentrate. "Thank you for being so considerate."

"Mr. St. Denis told me to let Ms. Rideau use the office right down the hall," Eddie said with a lift of one eyebrow.

"She's satisfied. Get the supplies." Julie stared at Eddie hard.

Eddie's nostrils flared, but she didn't argue. She turned to Lyrissa. "I'll be right back, Ms. Rideau."

"Call me Lyrissa, Eddie." Lyrissa smiled at her. "And the smaller office really is fine." She didn't want the young woman to suffer Julie's wrath because of her.

"Okay." Eddie smiled back at her. The smile winked off when she glanced at Julie again. She went down the hall and through a door.

"I appreciate your help. Don't let me keep you from your work," Lyrissa said.

"No problem. Noel will be tied up most of the day. Call me if you need anything," Julie replied.

"You're familiar with the St. Denis family papers?"

"Very. Noel and I practically grew up together." Julie wore a possessive expression when she said his name.

Lyrissa put on an innocent smile. "Like brother and sister. How nice."

Julie's eyes narrowed. "I wouldn't say that."

Eddie came back with supplies in her arms. "Here we go, Lyrissa. I've got a tape dispenser, stapler, paper clips, and three legal pads. This should get you started."

Noel walked up. "Good job, Eddie."

"Yeah. I'm just going to take her to *Roger's old office*." Eddie gave him a look heavy with meaning.

"I thought it would suit her needs better. It gets so busy at this end," Julie put in quickly, when he frowned.

"I think we can keep it quiet enough for a few days. The office right over here is better. Let me show it to you, Lyrissa." Noel started toward her.

"Noel, I need to talk to you," Julie said.

"I'll call you in a few minutes, when I'm through," he said, and put a hand under Lyrissa's elbow. "We put a file cabinet in it for you."

Lyrissa looked back at Julie. The thin woman's eyes blazed with hostility. "You really don't have to disrupt your day. Eddie will show me around."

"I can spare five minutes. Here we are." Noel led her down the hall and opened a door.

Lyrissa stared around in appreciation at the large room. A wide window let in bright light and gave her a view of Poydras Boulevard. An oak desk sat in one corner. She went to it and ran her hand along its smooth surface.

"I'm going to get you a desk set. Let's make sure the

phone is working." Noel picked up the receiver. "Yes. Eddie is going to get you a digital clock radio, too. What kind of music do you like, by the way?" He sat on the edge of the desk.

"Jazz while I work. Blues or R & B would make me dance instead of work." She laughed.

"Nice sound," Noel murmured.

"You like jazz?"

"I meant your laugh."

Lyrissa swallowed hard and looked away from those dangerously gorgeous eyes. "Thanks. I'll just get set up."

He stood straight. "Right. Let me know if you need anything at all."

"I'm sure Eddie will take good care of me." Lyrissa had no intention of calling him. She needed distance from him or she'd never get anything done.

Eddie came in with a wide, flat storage box. "Knock, knock. Got this from the vault."

"Thanks, Eddie." Noel took the box from her and placed it on the desk.

"Sure. See you later, Lyrissa." Eddie left again.

"There are about twenty of these, I'm afraid. My ancestors were obsessive record keepers," Noel said.

Lyrissa smiled with pleasure at the prospect of seeing the most intimate details of the St. Denis family history. "Lord bless them for it!"

"Only a historian would be happy about digging through all this."

"You have no idea." Lyrissa touched the box lovingly. Her hopes soared. Somewhere in these papers she'd find the information she needed.

"I'm glad you're pleased. Now I'll get out of the way."

Noel started to leave, then stopped. "Let's have lunch. You can tell me all about what you've found."

"I have plans. Thanks anyway." Lyrissa lifted the lid from the box. She removed a large folder with a brown ribbon tied around it.

"Okay. Maybe another time?" Noel said.

"Maybe," she answered in a soft voice. She put the folder down and took a pair of cotton gloves from her briefcase.

"What are those for?" Noel asked.

"Oil and perspiration from human hands damage old papers. I want to be extra careful." Lyrissa slipped them on.

"Right. Well, like I said, just call me."

"I'll be fine. Thanks." She gave him a distant smile.

"Right," he repeated. He seemed reluctant to leave.

"Is there something else?" Lyrissa asked.

"In other words, 'get out.' I'm gone." Noel grinned at her, then left.

Lyrissa shook her head slowly. She would have to avoid him whenever possible. She turned her attention to the stack of yellowing documents.

For two hours she panned for gold.

Lyrissa rubbed her eyes and rolled her shoulders. Her neck ached from bending over the documents. Enthusiasm had changed to teeth grinding exasperation as she waded through each stack.

The St. Denis ancestors had included every tedious detail of their lives. Lyrissa might have been interested under different circumstances. But time was running out. Mama Grace and Aunt Claire reminded her daily of that fact. The only other valuable property left from the Joubert legacy was Beau Rive, a crumbling Creole cottage near Meraux, not far from New Orleans. Preservationists had warned that it would be lost if action wasn't taken soon. Jules Joubert's grandfather, one of the few Creoles of color with a small plantation, had owned it. Jules had used it as a country home before moving to New Orleans in 1794. The Louisiana Historical Foundation would finance renovations, but only if they had at least one major artifact important to the state's history.

Lyrissa stared out the window, trying to think of ways to speed things along. A firm knock at the door sent a prickle of anticipation up her spine. She turned, knowing who it was, somehow. Or was it wishful thinking?

"Come in," she said.

Noel opened the door and stuck his head in. "Taking a break yet?"

"More like gathering my thoughts before I go back to work." Lyrissa nodded at the folder on the desk. "I'm trying to narrow my search."

"Told you my ancestors were obsessive about keeping records." Noel wore an apologetic grin.

"I know so much more than I ever wanted to about nineteenth century chamber pots." Lyrissa laughed.

Noel strolled over to the desk. He picked up a page encased in a Mylar envelope. "And the art?"

"I've found receipts for ten pieces of pottery, two sculptures, and a painting." Lyrissa gestured to a separate folder. "I put those aside. You need to keep them labeled. You'll need it for any art sale."

"For the provenance. I've been paying attention." Noel's full lips curved up at one corner, giving his smile a sensuous quality.

"Good." Lyrissa glanced down, as though interested in the papers.

"So you've made progress."

"Yes, but there's so much more I want to find." Lyrissa's thoughts went to one particular item.

"Maybe I can help." Noel hefted a second box onto a side table he'd had Eddie set up for her. He took off the lid.

"Please do!" Lyrissa joined him at the table.

"Here we have personal letters and journals by decade. Reference to the art would most likely be in here somewhere." He ran his fingertips across the sections divided by blue and yellow tabs.

"You think so?" Lyrissa leaned a hip against the table.

"They sometimes attached receipts to letters about items purchased. So you may not find what you're looking for in household lists." Noel moved closer to show her an example. "See?"

The scent of his cologne fogged her mind. "Yes, indeed," she murmured, and gazed at his strong jaw line instead of the document.

The creamy tan skin on his neck invited her to nuzzle it. Thick curls of bronze hair reached to his shirt collar. A tiny ember flamed into full-fledged sexual attraction. Lyrissa backed away and stumbled over a stack of boxes. Noel dropped the files he held and grabbed her.

"Careful! Are you okay?" He wore a concerned frown.

Lyrissa savored the feel of his strong hands holding both her arms. She stared into his eyes. Noel's frown relaxed into a smoldering temptation.

"I-I should look where I'm going." Lyrissa gave a shaky laugh. She drew her arms back, but Noel didn't let go.

"Maybe you should stop for today. You're probably

tired," he said softly. "I should have arranged these boxes for you."

"I'm fine." Lyrissa firmly tugged free of his grasp. "I won't be here much longer."

"With all this? I'd say you'll be here three weeks, at least." Noel swept a large hand around the room. "But I'm not complaining. Take all the time you need, Lyrissa."

Lyrissa tried not to return his gaze, but she couldn't resist. His golden eyes were a seductive lethal weapon. She was losing ground fast. As she'd had to do often when he was around, Lyrissa reminded herself of who he was and why she was really there.

"I'd better get back to the gallery." She stiffened her spine as she walked past him to the desk.

"Will you come tomorrow?" Noel asked quietly.

"No," she said quickly. "I mean, I've got classes." Lyrissa packed her briefcase.

"That's right. You're working on your doctorate. I'd like to hear more about your dissertation."

"Believe me, you'd be bored out of your mind."

"I doubt that very much," he replied.

Lyrissa did not risk glancing at him. He had a nasty habit of putting too much into a single sentence. "Besides, I know how busy you are. I wouldn't want to take up your valuable time."

"True, my days are pretty full." Noel handed her a notepad that she then put in her briefcase. "So let's have dinner," he said.

Her heart thumped at the prospect of gazing at him in a cozy, dimly lit restaurant. *Real smooth.* She fought her own reaction. "I don't think so," Lyrissa said in a cool voice.

"Why not?" Noel put a hand in one pocket of his slacks.

"I'm here on business."

"We'll talk about art, history, and appraisals. You are doing research on the St. Denis collection. I'm a St. Denis." Noel reached in front of her and picked up an art book. His shoulder brushed against her body in the process.

Lyrissa shut the briefcase with a loud crack. "You were born a bit late."

"I grew up listening to all the old stories. I can tell you which of my elderly relatives might help." Noel grinned at her with sultry charm.

"So could your grandmother. Maybe I should have dinner with *her*."

Noel threw back his handsome head and laughed. His baritone voice poured over her like creamy milk chocolate. Lyrissa stared at his mouth. She could almost taste the sinful sweetness of it on hers. God in heaven! Why did he have to be so beautiful?

"You could, but she wouldn't be as much fun. I'll treat you to dinner at Commander's Palace. What do you say?"

A hearty "Yes!" almost spilled from her lips. The man had his finger on all the buttons. Still, she hadn't lost her senses completely. Lyrissa stepped back from the ledge of lust.

"No, sorry," she rasped, then cleared her throat. "I think we should keep our business confined to this office."

Noel's face fell at her refusal. He recovered and smiled gamely. "Okay. I tried."

Lyrissa coughed to cover a laugh that almost escaped. Mr. Charisma obviously wasn't used to hearing "no" from women.

"I'll arrange my work before I leave." She looked at him.

"Until the next time, then." Noel rubbed his hands together.

"Right," Lyrissa echoed. Once he'd gone, she let out a long sigh. "Safe," she mumbled. A little voice replied, *For now!*

7

The next week, Noel showed her around the office. Lyrissa followed him as he described the divisions of Tremé Corporation and introduced her to employees. Lyrissa nodded as he talked, but her mind wasn't on business at all. She needed to set boundaries between them. The man was a hungry hound and in his mind she was the main course. Still, she couldn't afford to be too cold toward him, either. At least, not before she found the painting. Once more she reminded herself to practice being demure and tactful.

"Finally, this is the manager in charge of our residential properties. I'll take you back to your office." Noel wheeled around and started off.

"Goodness, I didn't realize y'all took up this entire floor." Lyrissa had to walk fast to keep up with his long-legged stride. "But you seem to have it all synthesized. I mean the insurance bonds go with the real estate side. You do property appraisals. Very impressive."

"Thank you," Noel said over his shoulder.

"You're poised to do very well with your construction arm—when it's up and running, that is."

Noel stopped suddenly and Lyrissa bumped into his back. She caught hold of him around the waist to keep from stumbling. When he turned around, she jumped back.

"Put on brake lights next time," she teased. The rock hard expression on his face said he wasn't amused.

"How did you know about the plans to expand into construction?"

Lyrissa felt as though she'd stumbled in more ways than one. She cast around for a logical explanation. "I read an article in the newspaper, the *New Orleans Chronicle*. I think your uncle said something about it."

She was grasping at a very flimsy straw. The *New Orleans Chronicle* was an African-American newspaper. Each year an entire issue was devoted to Black businesses. Surely at least once in the past five years or so his uncle had bragged. Lyrissa was sure the pompous guy would hardly resist such a chance. She gazed back at him steadily, determined not to blink once. Noel St. Denis had many faults. Being easily fooled was not one of them. Lyrissa held her breath as she watched his expression, praying he wouldn't realize she'd skillfully pumped information from his secretary.

"Right," Noel said after a long ten seconds of staring at her. "This way." He started off ahead of her again.

Lyrissa exhaled in relief. Time to smooth ointment on his bruised ego. "Listen, about your dinner invitation—"

"No problem." He waved a large hand in the air.

"No, wait." She tugged at his arm to stop him. "It's just that I don't want to compromise my work here or get distracted."

"I understand, sort of."

"I have my reputation to consider."

"And being seen with me would damage it?" Noel's dark brows drew down.

"I meant my professional reputation," Lyrissa said. "But you do have your own reputation when it comes to women."

Noel folded his arms across his broad chest. "Tell me what you've heard."

"Well . . ." Lyrissa saw the impish glint in his eyes. "I hear a long list of ladies have fallen victim to your fatal charm."

"Not *that* long a list. I do eat, sleep, and work."

"Okay, so half," Lyrissa quipped.

"Not as many as you think. But thanks for the confidence in my stamina," he added before she could retort.

Noel's smile broke through and lit up his face. He put one hand in his pants pocket. The movement was fluid, as though he were a jazz dancer. The thick eyebrows lifted slightly. That smile could melt stone. A flush of warmth seeped from the light in his eyes and into her body. Her pelvis tingled right down into the deepest, most tender regions. Despite her best efforts, her own libido seemed honed in on this guy's deadly wavelength. In a panic she blotted out a full-color fantasy that involved his stamina.

She focused on a distant point past his shoulder. "At any rate, I do apologize. Maybe I've met too many chumps in the dating scene." She turned away and wiped tiny beads of perspiration from her top lip. To cover her reaction to him, she started walking.

"Ah, so you've been busy yourself." Noel walked beside her down the hall.

"A few. Guess I'm picky," Lyrissa said.

"Me, too." He was silent for a moment. "So what does Mr. Right have for you?"

The question startled Lyrissa. "What?"

"Your ideal man, what's he like? I already know I don't qualify. Just curious."

She wasn't at all comfortable with this talk. "I'll know him when I meet him."

"Cop out. Straight up truth, now," Noel persisted.

"Well, for a start, he should be sensitive and caring. I don't like men with huge egos or who take themselves too seriously. And Lord! Deliver me from a dude with mood swings."

"Hmm, sounds like an easy order to fill. I take it you've met him? Of course you have. Fine looking women like you don't run around free for long."

Lyrissa stole a sideways glance at him. He seemed sincere, but she wasn't going down that easy again. "Slipped that one in. Real smart."

"No line, no lie. Or am I making you uncomfortable again?" He faced her when they reached the double doors leading to his office.

"If I seemed uncomfortable, it's only because I'm allergic to bull." Lyrissa smiled at him sweetly and batted her eyelashes.

"*Now* who's playing games? I've met few beautiful women who didn't know their power." Noel gazed at her from head to toe.

"I'm not vain, Mr. St. Denis."

"No, but you're poised in a natural way. You move with confidence." He studied her intently. "And call me Noel, please."

Lyrissa shook her head. "Everyone has insecurities, and I'm no exception. I went to St. Mary's. I didn't pass the Creole acid test—light skin color and 'good' hair."

Noel's amused expression turned sour. "I hope you took care of them! I had to myself. My best friend didn't pass that test, either."

Lyrissa was skeptical. "Really? So how many fights did you have?"

"One too many," Miss Georgina cut in. She stood in the open door to Noel's office. "Ronnie was too willing to swing his fists and you shouldn't have jumped in."

"Ronnie wasn't the problem." Noel was obviously ready to launch a tirade.

Miss Georgina waved a hand. "Yes, yes. Ronnie turned into a fine young man. Excuse us, Ms. Rideau. I need to talk to my grandson."

Lyrissa accepted the dismissal. She was not one of them. Miss Georgina's tone reminded her of that once again . . . as if she needed it.

"Of course." Lyrissa spun around and left them without looking back.

Noel watched her walk away. Some force, like a hook inside his gut, pulled at him to follow her. Lyrissa's curvaceous hips moved inside the taupe shirtdress in a delightful way. He admired the shapely legs just beneath the knee-length hem as well.

"Noel," Miss Georgina said sharply.

He turned to find two sets of eyes boring into him. Julie stood in the hallway, her facial muscles rigid with displeasure. After a few moments, she continued on her way.

"I have a lot of calls to make and two meetings," Noel said shortly. He nodded for his grandmother to precede him into his office.

"Don't patronize me, son. I helped build this company." Miss Georgina marched past him.

"Yes, ma'am, you did. And now I have to rebuild it." Noel kept his tone respectful, yet firm.

Her eyes narrowed as she regarded him in stony silence for several seconds. Then she nodded. "This won't take long."

Noel closed the door. He waited until she was comfortably seated before he sat next to her. "What did you want to talk to me about?"

"Your grandfather would be proud of you, Noel. You've done a fine job."

"Thank you. Somehow I sense that a 'but' is coming," Noel said with a slight smile.

"Not when it comes to running the business." Miss Georgina looked at him steadily. "Be careful with Lyrissa Rideau."

"How did we go from my performance as CEO to Lyrissa?" Noel's amusement started to fade.

"You have the entire family on your shoulders." She held up one hand to stop him from speaking. "I know it's not fair, but there it is."

"I know what the company means to us all," Noel said.

"You're not just the head of this company. You must realize that. There are our family and business relationships to consider." Miss Georgina brushed a wrinkle from her royal blue dress.

"And?" Noel had a nasty suspicion where she was headed.

"Julie deserves some consideration. She's a fine woman from a good family. At least have the decency not to flirt right in front of her."

"I'm not going there again, Grandmother," Noel warned.

Miss Georgina pressed anyway. "I know your father's weakness in that department. I'd hoped you had more restraint. But at least be discreet. Julie won't wait forever. And her father won't appreciate having his daughter humiliated."

"I will choose my female companions and one day I'll choose my own bride. Frankly, Julie didn't make the short list," Noel said curtly.

"Don't be crude." Miss Georgina pursed her lips.

"I have my priorities on straight, but thanks for your concern." Noel put a note of finality in his voice.

"In other words, butt out of your personal life?" Miss Georgina frowned at him. "Fine, the subject is closed."

Noel started to retort that he doubted it, but didn't. "Don't worry. This family taught me to be a realist when it comes to marriage."

"Marriage is more than some romantic trip down Lover's Lane. It's a partnership," Miss Georgina said, shaking a finger at him.

"Fine, fine." Noel did not want to hear that lecture again.

"Carlton is the other reason I wanted to talk to you. He's criticizing you to the board. He's doing it on the sly, of course."

"What else is new?"

"They might listen if you show poor judgment." She pressed her lips together.

Noel's anger spiked again. They were back to Lyrissa. "Not as long as the profits increase. With the money they've made, I'm sure they like my judgments just fine. Or you can let Uncle Willie and Carlton run this damn place."

"Don't fight with me. I don't want anything or anyone to stand in the way of your future." Miss Georgina gazed at him.

He got the message and smiled. "Don't worry about me. I've got my eye on the future *and* Carlton."

She gave a satisfied nod. "Good. I'll let you get back to work, then."

"Goodbye, Grandmother." He accepted her maternal peck on the cheek.

Much as he loved her, Georgina St. Denis could drive him up the wall. He sighed with relief once the door closed behind her. Noel thought about Lyrissa being only a few feet down the hall. His grandmother considered her a dangerous temptation, and she might be right. The last thing he needed was to lose his head over a woman. His father had taught him the perils of choosing the wrong woman. Noel did indeed have priorities. Being distracted by a lovely set of . . . everything was not on the agenda.

Three days of searching, and Lyrissa found it. She strained to read the faded ink of a letter dated 1888. Phillip Jean St. Denis had written to his lawyer about a large painting by "a passable local artist called J. Joubert."

"Yes!" Lyrissa made notes with a big smile on her face.

Noel walked in. "You look excited. Found the lost treasure of Jean Lafitte?"

"Ah, no. I've finally made some headway through most of the papers. I should be through soon." She shuffled the letter in with a stack of other sheets.

"Then we can celebrate over lunch. To discuss the appraisal, of course," he added quickly.

In a good mood, Lyrissa could see no harm in one quick lunch. "I suppose so." She carefully put the documents back in their protective folders.

"What?" He blinked in surprise. "So easy?"

"No, but I can tell you a bit more. Might as well be today." Lyrissa picked up her purse. "I'm ready."

"Great! I'll just let Eddie know." Noel held the door for her and they went toward his office.

Julie appeared around a corner. "Noel, I need to talk to you." She glanced at Lyrissa but didn't greet her.

"I'm on my way out to lunch. Unless it's an emergency, I'll call you when I get back," Noel said.

"I'm starving myself. Where do you want to go?" Julie fell in step with them.

"We were going to grab something and discuss the collection." Noel pointedly did not extend an invitation.

"We?" Julie said.

Noel stopped with a hand under Lyrissa's right elbow. "Yes, Lyrissa and I are going out to lunch."

Lyrissa glanced from him back to Julie. It was her turn. Julie plastered on a smile. Had to admire the woman for self-control, Lyrissa mused.

"I'd be interested in hearing about the collection. Besides, it would save time if I talked to you over lunch about the warehouse lease agreement. I need to take care of it today."

"Fine," Noel said with a curt nod.

Julie's smile took on a feline quality when she looked at Lyrissa. "I hate to bore you with dry business."

"Not at all." Lyrissa had no intention of being gracious and backing out now.

Julie switched tactics. "You must have a pretty busy schedule with school and a job."

"Not so busy I can't have lunch," Lyrissa smiled back.

"How nice." Julie looked as though she'd swallowed a bug.

Noel's eyes flickered irritation when he looked at Julie. "Okay, let's get going."

Noel drove. His Infiniti was parked in a public lot adjacent to the office building. Lyrissa graciously stepped back and allowed Julie to join him in front. Julie clenched her jaw at the gesture, but said nothing. Noel looked at Lyrissa before they both got in the car. The trip along the narrow streets in downtown New Orleans was tense.

"So Julie, where did you finish school?" Lyrissa asked in a chatty tone as though there was no undercurrent.

"Spelman," was the short reply.

"Wow, great school. I stayed right here at home. Saved money you know." Lyrissa sighed. "Dillard U. grad here."

"I see." Julie's voice was flat. She sat straight in the leather seat without looking left or right.

"And Noel is a Harvard man." Lyrissa looked up at the rearview mirror.

Noel's brown eyes danced with silent messages. "Yes, but only for my MBA."

"That's right, Howard for undergrad, wasn't it? I'd love to visit that campus one of these days."

Lyrissa gabbed on about nothing in particular. Her empty small talk flowed almost non-stop. Noel put in a few single sentence contributions. Julie spoke when forced to by a direct question. When they got to the restaurant fifteen minutes later, Noel looked drained.

As they'd expected, the place was already filling up. Still they managed to get a table next to the window. A slender young woman dressed in a crisp white shirt and black pants appeared with menus.

"Here y'all go. Lemme get you somethin' ta drink." She smiled at them warmly.

"Iced tea," Julie barked in a raspy voice.

"Same for me." Noel eyed Julie worriedly, as though looking at a boiling volcano.

"Diet cola. Gots to have my fizz." Lyrissa smiled at the waitress who smiled back.

"Got ya, bay. I'll be right back." The woman darted gracefully around tables.

"We're going to be seeing each other at the office," Julie said to Lyrissa, forcing the words out like sour seeds. She arranged her round face into a smile. "Do you mind if I call you Lyrissa?"

"Of course not," Lyrissa answered in a "Let's-be-pals" manner.

Lyrissa had to appreciate Julie's effort. It was obvious the woman wanted to strangle her and claim Noel over Lyrissa's dead body. She took time to study her. Julie was attractive, no doubt about it. Her skin was the color of dark cream with a hint of tan. Her long hair was a honey brown, darker in some places than others. She had a habit of tucking it back in place behind her ears. Perfect mating material for a St. Denis.

"Good. So tell me about the inventory." Julie glanced at Noel and Lyrissa expectantly.

"The family art is all over the place," Noel explained. "To get a real picture of the total worth, we've got to track it all down." He broke off when the waitress appeared.

Lyrissa spoke up once the woman left. "Mrs. St. Denis can point us in the right direction."

"Directions," Noel corrected and scowled. "Like I said, there are things spread all over."

"Sounds like a huge job, Lyrissa. More work than you can do in a few weeks of your summer break." Julie took a small sip of iced tea.

Lyrissa smiled. "Art historians are used to playing detective. Besides, Mrs. St. Denis will probably make it easy. She remembers a lot about who has what."

"I wouldn't count on her memory. It's not what it used to be. Don't tell her I said so." Noel grunted.

"No promises. I might need the leverage later on," Lyrissa teased. "So behave yourself."

Julie tapped the table with her knife a few times before she spoke. "Anyway, where will you start?"

"I drafted a revised list of the scattered pieces after checking my grandfather's will and talking to my grandmother." Noel took a long brown envelope from a pocket in his jacket. "Here's a photocopy."

Lyrissa took it from him and extracted a single legal-sized sheet. Her hands shook as she scanned the yellow lined page. There were forty-five items. Most of the descriptions were vague. A few were labeled simply "painting." Some were described by dimension but none had the artist listed next to it. Still Lyrissa's pulse raced at the thought that she was so close to her prize.

"You're excited about this—it's in your eyes," Noel said, breaking into her thoughts.

"I love old houses and dusty rooms with hidden treasures. Of course, most people call it junk." Lyrissa laughed.

"Art can bring in big bucks these days," Julie said in a thoughtful voice. "And if we could sell the collection . . ." She leaned toward Noel.

"I didn't suggest we sell the entire collection, just certain pieces. That's where Lyrissa comes in. She can set a value and help us make the decision." Noel nodded at Lyrissa.

"One valuable item could be a nice shot in the arm." Julie spoke to Noel as though Lyrissa had vanished. "We could go ahead with the renovations on the Basin Street property."

"No, any money from the art would be for long-term projects. I want us to take our time. Some of the works might be too important to our family historically." Noel shook his head.

"Y'all ready to order?" The waitress stood with her pen poised.

They made quick work of selecting their entrees. The talk turned to everyday things like local politics and news. Lyrissa watched Noel and Julie, two shining examples of the Talented Tenth's descendants carrying on the torch— except that they were the unique New Orleans Creole version. Suddenly Lyrissa had a familiar feeling. She was on the outside looking in. Her plain off-the-rack-clearance-sale dress was in sharp contrast to the Nicole Tracy suit Julie wore. Lyrissa resisted the urge to stare at herself. There was nothing wrong with the way she looked.

". . . Don't you think, Lyrissa?" Julie's finely arched eyebrows lifted.

"What was that?" Lyrissa blinked back to the conversation.

"Instead of Noel, maybe I could help you." Julie wore a calculating expression. "His hands are full working with Carlton right now."

"You're not exactly free, either. You've got two major projects going, plus training a new employee. You can't spare the time," Noel said, a true manager assessing resources.

"I'm almost through with the Richardson sale. That's the most time consuming. I'll be free in a matter of a few days." Julie waved a manicured hand.

"Thanks, but it's really not necessary." Noel did not budge from his position.

Lyrissa decided to rub it in. "Besides, no need to tie up two valuable top-level executives."

Noel nodded. "Good point. Anyway, this is a special family project that Grandmother expects me to handle."

"Fine," Julie said curtly. "I don't see why our food isn't here yet. Did they go out on Lake Ponchartrain to catch the damn fish? Waitress!"

The rest of lunch was strained, to say the least. Noel looked like a worm trying to get off the hook. He made every effort to be solicitous toward Julie. To his credit, he didn't give up. He was the perfect Creole gentleman.

Still, Lyrissa heard him let out a soft hiss of relief when they arrived back at the office and Julie finally left them.

"That was fun," Lyrissa said in a low voice. She watched Julie stride off, back rigid.

"Very funny. Now I'll spend weeks ducking razor sharp icicles aimed at my head." He headed for his office.

Lyrissa bit back a belly laugh as she followed him. "But Julie seems like such a sweetheart."

He guided her into his office and shut the door. Noel stood within tantalizing reach. Lyrissa could feel him even though they did not touch. Just a whisper of fragrant air was between them. He smelled of hardwood, mint, and spice. She searched her memory to name the cologne. That bothersome tickle between her thighs surged again. Resistance to the moment was like swimming against a strong current. She was getting in too deep with each second.

"You don't like Julie, do you?" His deep voice washed over her.

Lyrissa fought hard to control her breathing. She imagined his skin was the same even light brown all over. Muscles would ripple each time he reached for her or moved against her body. Her voice sounded scratchy when she did speak.

"The feeling is mutual." She tried to step back. Her buttocks bumped against the solid wood door.

"You went out of your way to set Julie off. Why?"

She turned her head, hoping to deflect some of his animal power. "I've had to take crap from girls like her all my life."

"It's more than that, but I'll let it go for now."

"How big of you," Lyrissa replied, gaze still averted.

She felt rather than saw the smile. Despite a tiny voice warning her not to, she looked at him. The tip of his nose brushed hers when she turned her head.

"Why are you trying so hard not to like *me?*" he said.

His voice was barely above a whisper. He looked at her as though searching for a clue in her eyes or in the shape of her face. His gaze traveled from her forehead down her neck. Lyrissa gasped as she watched him stop at the neckline of her blouse. He looked for all the world as though he was contemplating unbuttoning it. For a crazy moment time seemed suspended. If he reached out, she'd let him. Then the phone on his assistant's desk outside rang. The magic bubble popped and she came back to her senses. Lyrissa slid sideways away from him. Her escape wasn't graceful, but it worked. Added distance cleared her head a bit more.

"It's not as hard as you think," she wisecracked. Still she stumbled over to the carafe and poured herself a glass of water. She drank deeply to soothe her tight, dry throat.

Eddie knocked, then came in. Lyrissa kept her back to them as a bid for time to rally. She was sure the X-rated fantasies he inspired were written all over her face.

"Sorry to interrupt, but Ellis Singleton is on line three," she announced. "Hi, Lyrissa. You sure had your work cut out for you. So did y'all get a good start?"

Lyrissa turned around. "We—"

Noel's gaze trapped her as though she were a butterfly caught in a silken net. The glass in her hand shook. Lyrissa wanted to shout that he was wrong, that she didn't feel anything when he was near. Yet she could read the truth in his smoky eyes. She'd wanted him to touch her and he knew it.

"Yes, we sure have," Noel finished for her. "And it will get better as we go along."

8

Noel flipped through the pad of notes. "Anything else? I'll look over the lease purchase agreement on the Stinson Street warehouse later. I'm sure Val did a thorough job."

Andre pulled papers from a folder. "Yes, but I thought you wanted to talk about the construction plans."

"No need for that. I've been over them twice." Noel tapped his pen on the table. He glanced at his watch.

"Noel, I think we should at least discuss the alternative floor plans today," Julie pressed. "There are advantages and disadvantages to both. Now, I think—"

"I say we go with floor plan two," Noel broke in. "We don't want the building to be cramped with cubicles."

"I was thinking the same thing," Andre added. "One of the larger businesses could move in. We'd actually get more, in terms of income."

"Right. The Dauphine Street building can be used for

small struggling businesses." Noel nodded. "Well, that's settled."

"We could at least discuss our report for the board meeting," Julie said, with an edge to her voice.

Noel stood. "It's almost twelve. I say we pick this up in the morning, when we're all fresh."

"I feel like we just ran the fifty-yard dash through this agenda." Julie's shapely brows drew together.

"We covered everything, right?" Noel glanced at Andre, who lifted a shoulder without answering.

"We skimmed the surface on most of the items," Julie replied.

"You have questions? Andre?" Noel asked.

"No, I'm okay. See you later at the warehouse, Noel." Andre gathered up his folders and left.

Julie spoke as soon as the door clicked shut behind him. "I have color schemes we can review over lunch. That's not too taxing, is it?"

"We can do it later." Noel glanced at his Movado watch again. He looked up to find Julie staring at him hard.

"You've got an appointment for lunch, then," she said.

"Yes. Look, you've got such great taste. Pick out three of your top choices and we'll go from there." Noel came around the desk and walked her to the door.

"Thanks so much for the confidence," Julie said with acid in her tone. "No need to shove, I'm leaving."

"It's not like that, okay? When I get back, we'll take our time." Noel put his hand on the small of her back. He gently guided her toward the side door in his office that led down a rear hallway.

Julie brushed against him and smiled. "Okay, boss. I look forward to it." Her short skirt swayed as she walked away. She glanced back at him once before going around a corner. Noel turned and headed for the front door to find his secretary. He pushed it open and called out.

"Eddie, did you—"

"Two grilled chicken pita sandwiches with ranch dressing on the side, whole grain chips, and two diet cream sodas. All in an attractive insulated high tech lunch sack." Eddie handed him a compact dark blue bag.

"You're worth your weight in gold." Noel pinched her cheek, then took the bag.

"When should I expect the armored truck?" she shot back.

Noel only grinned in reply. "I'll be back no later than two-thirty. Keep Julie happy until then."

"Oh, Lord!" Eddie rolled her eyes.

He laughed. "Okay, I'll try to be back sooner."

City traffic was heavier than usual but it didn't irritate him today. Noel turned up the radio and sang along. He smiled at the bright blue sky and fluffy white clouds overhead. It was a perfect day to meet at the park. A light breeze shook dark green leaves of hundred-year-old oaks along St. Charles Avenue. As he'd expected, there were no close parking spaces. Still humming, Noel parked along a side street. Nothing seemed to touch his good mood, he realized. "Hmm, wonder why?"

Noel smiled as he walked down the sidewalk. The answer to his question was only minutes away. It was the thrill of the chase, he said to himself. Never before had a woman resisted him with such determination. Lyrissa was not playing hard to get. She really *didn't* want him to get close. He should be content. Still, he kept thinking of reasons for them to get together.

The entrance to City Park was marked by a huge stone arch with ornate carvings. Lyrissa had agreed to meet him here. A set of figurines from the family collection was on display in the art gallery in the park.

Lyrissa was sitting on a stone bench in the shade of a large magnolia tree. She stared across the park deep in thought. Her thick hair was pulled back into a ponytail. The black frames of her dark sunglasses gave her a look of casual elegance. Light glinted from her silver hoop earrings. Noel stopped to admire her from afar. She wore a crisp white cotton shirt tucked into a dark red skirt. The short sleeves left her bare arms exposed. A short red jacket was neatly folded across her lap. Sunlight gave her brown skin a golden glow.

"Wow," he mumbled to himself. He'd been with beautiful women before, but none as delectable as Lyrissa Rideau.

A tall man seemed to come from nowhere. He held a basset hound on a leash. He started to walk by, but doubled back. Lyrissa seemed to notice him about the same time. She shielded her eyes from the sun as she smiled up at him. Their laughter drifted on the breeze as they talked. Noel strode forward to drive out the intruder.

"Hi, Lyrissa," he said with forced cheer. "Sorry I'm a little late."

Lyrissa looked at him through the opaque dark lenses. "Only about ten minutes. No problem."

"I'm Noel St. Denis." He stuck out his hand.

"Tony Tate," the man said, as he shook hands with him.

"So . . ." Noel looked at Lyrissa with a questioning expression.

"Tony's an old pal from college." She smiled at Tony fondly.

"Nice to meet you. We should go," Noel said.

Tony stood. "Yeah, same here. Root Beer is ready to move on anyway." He held on to the leash that strained as the dog tried to wander off.

"Bye, Root Beer. You're still a cutie," Lyrissa called out.

"I'll give you a call," Tony said in a low tone and kissed her cheek. "Nice meeting you."

"Same here," Noel lied. He watched the man stroll away, then turned his attention to Lyrissa. "I brought a delicious lunch."

She watched the man walk away. "Thanks."

Noel sat next to her with an unpleasant, and unfamiliar, knot of jealousy in his gut. "Seems like a nice guy."

"He is. You want to eat first and then go into the museum gallery?" Lyrissa nodded toward the gray stone building nearby.

"Yes. Uh, you take classes with him?" Noel said in a casual tone.

"Tony is a high-powered businessman. He's in the MBA program at Tulane. He's not into the 'artsy stuff,' as he calls it." Lyrissa laughed and shook her head. She gazed in the direction the man had gone.

"Kind of short-sighted, I'd say." Noel didn't like the man. Tony had made Lyrissa laugh the way she'd never laughed with him.

"Takes all kinds, as they say. Tony is a real success story. You know, came out of the most notorious housing project and excelled in school. He's going places. I really admire him." Lyrissa accepted the sandwich wrapped in waxed paper he handed her.

"Impressive," Noel said, his throat tight. "Not like me,

you mean, born with a silver spoon in my mouth. Had everything handed to me?"

"I didn't mean that at all."

"Right," he replied shortly. "Here's a Barq's cream soda."

"Thanks. Tony gives back to the community. He could have just made his escape and not looked back."

"Unlike spoiled rich kids who spend their time and money with expensive toys?" Noel said.

Lyrissa glanced at him sideways. "You seem kinda irritable. Having a bad day, or something?"

"I'm fine. Just wonderful."

"Okay." Lyrissa shrugged.

Noel tore into the pita sandwich, even though his appetite was gone. What the hell did Tony Tate have that was so magical? Neither of them spoke for several minutes. Birds sang, people passing by talked, but the only sound between them was the rustle of paper as they unwrapped the food. Noel swallowed hard to move the lump in his throat. What had just happened? He didn't like this new set of feelings at all.

"Pretty good," Lyrissa said.

"What?" He blinked at her. It was not good at all, he thought.

"Aladdin's has the best Lebanese food around." She patted her mouth with a paper napkin.

"Oh yeah, the food." Noel put his half-eaten sandwich in the bag.

Lyrissa craned her neck to peek at his food. "You didn't eat much."

"I'm not really hungry," Noel mumbled.

"Well, if you don't want those chips, give 'em to me."

She took the yellow bag without waiting for an answer.

"Oh please, don't worry about me. I'll be fine." He frowned at her.

She munched on a crunchy chip for several seconds. "I know you will. You're Noel St. Denis."

"Which means?" He used aggressive swipes to wipe his hands with a napkin.

"You're rich, part of a powerful family—and, some would say, handsome." Lyrissa glanced at him and shrugged.

"Matter of opinion, huh?" Noel had never been insecure, but her attitude was disconcerting.

The game wasn't going according to plan. Her words stung him like dozens of tiny wasps. In the past he would have brushed them off and changed tactics. This time his emotions seemed to be involved. Bad sign.

"Sorry, but you do have a certain rep, you know."

"I accept that moving apology," he retorted.

"No, I really mean it. I'm sorry." Lyrissa put a hand out. "Truce?"

He took it and the warmth from her satin soft skin made his body hum. "Truce." They ate in silence for a while longer before Noel cleared his throat. "So you're dating this guy?"

"We dated for a while. Then he moved to Atlanta and the long distance thing didn't work. Not that it's any of your business."

Noel ignored the swipe. "So you're not dating now."

"Not for a while. But we might in the future," Lyrissa added quickly with a look at him.

Noel's sour mood began to lift. She wasn't telling the

truth, he could hear it in her tone. The sunshine that had dimmed was now bright again. They were back on familiar ground now. She was playing his game, pretending an old boyfriend meant more than he did. He tried to ignore just how happy that thought made him feel. His joy was deeper than he wanted to examine at the moment.

"I got ya." He beamed at her. "You ready to go inside?" He nodded toward the gallery.

Lyrissa eyed him with suspicion, but gave him an answering nod. "Sure."

They tossed their litter in a nearby trashcan, then entered the cool interior of the building. Large paintings were arranged along the wall in the main gallery. A few art lovers milled around. Some were seated on cushioned benches.

"The figurines are this way." Noel led her to another room with glass display cases arranged around the floor.

Lyrissa drew in her breath as they approached the first one. "It's fabulous."

"Yes, it is."

The first figurine was of a Black woman and child. They were dressed in Sunday finery. The little boy wore a blue suit with short pants. The woman wore a pale pink dress and a wide brimmed hat. The hand painted clay had been glazed to make it look like fine china.

"The artist seems to have breathed life into them." Lyrissa circled the case. "Look at the expression on the mother's face. So tender."

Noel had seen pictures of them before, but he'd never really looked at them. Her excitement was contagious. Lyrissa wandered from case to case.

"Jean-Claude Atier is the artist. He was the son of a

wealthy white planter and a placage, his mulatto mistress. Their father was said to have doted on them all, especially Jean-Claude." Lyrissa lectured as she walked.

"He was obviously very talented." Noel followed her, content to let her lead. He enjoyed seeing the gleam in her eyes.

"Look at the detail, the warmth in these figures."

Noel laughed. "You sound like he was an old friend of yours."

"I feel like I know him. He put so much of himself into his creations."

Noel's heart turned over. "I see what you mean," he mumbled in a thick voice. Cold air rushed in when she went to another display case. He followed, eager to recapture her warmth.

"This figure is actually as much a political statement." She admired a sculpture of a small Black boy dressed in ragged clothes.

"I don't see anything more than a kid playing in the dirt."

"This piece was done in 1839, during slavery. He's got a tiny book hidden under his shirt. Jean-Claude protested laws preventing Blacks from receiving a decent education."

He leaned closer to peer at the child. "Hey, you're right."

"In fact, a lot of Jean-Claude's figures make a statement about his values and beliefs. Take this figure of a blacksmith . . ."

Lyrissa went through each of the twenty-six figures. She examined them with an eye toward history as well as aesthetics. Noel was content to trail after her as a willing student. Illogical as it seemed, he was happy to be an indirect source of her enjoyment. It occurred to him that he could spend hours watching her eyes light up with discovery.

Lyrissa sighed with satisfaction after they'd finished their tour. They took a seat on a bench in the gallery. Their vantage point gave them a view of the entire room.

"Congratulations, Mr. St. Denis. Every one of these is a wonderful example of Jean-Claude's best work."

"I can't take credit. I just happen to be born into the right family." Noel grinned. "The truth is, I never appreciated it all, until you came along."

"Oh, the privileges of the rich and famous." Lyrissa lifted her nose in the air and imitated an upper-class snooty tone. "So many treasures, how can one take it seriously?"

"Cut it out. I don't walk around like that."

"I was thinking of Julie. 'Noel, pick me up in the Lexus 400 next time. The Mercedes is so out of style.' " Lyrissa pitched her voice in a whiny tone.

"Meow, your claws are showing!"

She batted her eyelashes in the same way Julie did. Noel laughed at her antics. Then his expression softened. The skin on her face looked like creamy caramel. He caressed her cheek with his forefinger. Surprise, then fascination, flitted across her face as she stared back at him. Lyrissa leaned forward in a clear invitation. At least, he took it as one. Noel met her halfway and brushed his lips against hers. It was a delicious appetizer that sharpened his hunger for more. Their surroundings faded into the background. Her mouth was like a warm marshmallow, sweet and pliant. Lyrissa rested both hands on his chest. Noel pulled her into his arms completely. The tender kiss became urgent as need pounded him like a hammer. He planted small kisses along her jaw line, then moved to her neck.

Noel wanted to get out of his clothes. Better yet, he wanted to get into hers. One kiss had sent him right over the edge. Hard as a rock, he shook like a hormone-crazed teenaged boy. Desire twirled him up into a whirlwind that took his breath away.

"Ah-ah-hem!"

"Young folks grope each other anywhere these days, Mabel!"

Noel and Lyrissa jumped apart and looked around. Two elderly women stood in the doorway. Lyrissa put a hand over her eyes. Noel forced a weak smile. The women shook their heads in unison and walked around the display cases. Yet they glanced over their shoulders at Lyrissa and Noel.

"I think we've made their day," Noel whispered, close to Lyrissa's ear.

Lyrissa sprang from the bench like a pretty bird taking flight. Noel almost had to run to catch her. He tried to pull her against him again.

"No, let me go." Lyrissa seemed frantic to escape.

"Those two ladies got a cheap thrill. So what?" Noel smiled softly. Still she struggled to get away.

"*Cheap* is exactly how I feel." Lyrissa yanked free and strode out of the museum.

Noel went after her. She stood underneath an oak with her back to him. He approached but did not try to touch her again, much as he wanted to.

"What are you talking about, Lyrissa?" he said quietly.

She closed her eyes. "I know about you and I still fell for it."

"What do you think you know about me?"

"This city is littered with women you've dumped."

"That's an exaggeration."

"Is it?" Lyrissa wore a hard expression as she stared at him.

Noel had never thought of his romantic life as a whole. It seemed to flash before his eyes in an instant. Women's faces whizzed by at high speed. He'd done his share of dating over the years. Yet he hadn't thought of himself as callous. He considered himself honest, straight up. There were no whispered declarations of love or promises made in the dark to haunt him.

"Yes, I've broken up with women before. Sometimes it was mutual." Noel shoved both hands in his pants pockets. "Stop looking at me like that."

"Pleading guilty, huh?" Lyrissa folded her arms.

"You didn't seem to mind that kiss," Noel said.

She visibly relaxed. "Well, I—you caught me off guard."

"Come on, Lyrissa. Tell the truth." Noel leaned closer to her.

"It shouldn't have happened." She moved away from him. "This is strictly business."

"Not anymore," he said promptly.

"Yes, it *is*." She put more space between them.

"Okay, okay. It was my fault for giving in to temptation. I apologize." Noel ignored a raging need to taste her again.

"We're not going there again. Got that?"

"Listen, Lyrissa—"

"No." Lyrissa shook her head.

"Why?"

"Because." She wore a stubborn expression.

"Can you be a bit more specific?" Noel tilted his head to one side.

"There are a lot of reasons."

"Name one." He smiled at her.

"We're too different. That kiss was a mistake, a silly impulse." Her lovely eyes narrowed. "You set the whole thing up when you asked me to meet you here. I should have known."

"No, I didn't—honestly," he added, when she gave a skeptical snort. "I was just as surprised as you."

"Planned or not, it won't happen again."

"We're not that different." Noel gazed at her.

"Tell your family that," she tossed back.

"My family doesn't have anything to do with it, okay?" Noel said quietly. "Have dinner with me." The words were the second time he'd surprised himself today.

Lyrissa returned his gaze. "That would be another mistake," she replied just as softly.

Noel sighed with pleasure at the enticing sound of her voice. She hadn't said no outright. He got up and walked to her until they were only inches apart. "I'll pick you up tonight around seven. I've got a late meeting. Please?"

"I don't think—"

"We'll talk about art, if that makes you feel better," he teased with a half-smile. He touched her hand lightly. "What's your address?"

She didn't look away from his eyes. For what seemed forever they stared at each other. Noel held his breath. All sounds around them seemed muffled as he waited for her answer.

"Six sixty-seven Erato Avenue," Lyrissa murmured.

Noel started to steal another kiss, but the anxiety in her eyes stopped him. "Okay," he said.

They parted and he walked back to his car. Noel wanted to believe his happiness came from the thrill of victory. He'd melted her resistance. Still, he had never experienced such intense anticipation of a first date. The shadow of her alluring smile followed him for the rest of the afternoon.

Julie sat across from Carlton with both elbows propped on the arms of her chair. She tapped the toe of her Ferragamo pump on the floor. "Noel is spending way too much time chasing this art thing."

"Humm, did you go over the report from Andre yet?" Carlton was engrossed in a memo on his desk.

"I've read it twice. You know the art sale should be handled correctly. We talked about that, remember?" Julie shifted in her seat.

"I've got the claims projections. I assume you talked to our accountant."

"Of course."

"Good." Carlton nodded.

"I don't like it." Julie pursed her lips.

"The claims report?"

"The way Noel is following that Rideau woman around like a puppy," Julie said.

"Let Noel waste his time on some flighty scheme. At least it will keep him out of my hair for a while."

"It's not a flighty scheme. A lot of large corporations buy art and sell it. It's totally legitimate to use art as an asset," she said defensively.

"You stick up for him no matter what." Carlton gazed at her over steepled fingers.

"Noel isn't plotting to cut you out of the company,

Carlton. He's only doing what he thinks is best." Julie lifted her chin.

"I suppose that's your totally objective assessment." Carlton grunted to emphasize his cynicism.

"Stop being paranoid. Noel hasn't made any kind of move against you. The three of us can take this place to the top again." Julie leaned forward with an intense expression.

"I feel so secure knowing you two are behind me," Carlton retorted.

"This childish rivalry is a waste of energy. The board made him CEO. Deal with it like a grown-up."

"He's CEO for now," Carlton said bitterly.

"Dream on. Noel has added the right color to this place, black ink on the balance sheets and lots of green in the bank. Compete with that!" Julie said with pride.

"He's not exactly the golden boy. He's made mistakes," Carlton complained.

"You're no shining example. I know about that stunt you pulled with the board."

"Julie, you don't know anything about me." Carlton's lip curled, making his wide face even less appealing.

"Don't I? You wanted to have Miss Georgina declared incompetent." Julie smiled at the effect of her words. "Oh yes, somebody squealed."

"That's impossible!"

"Anyone will talk if the right amount of pressure is applied. You didn't even wait a good twenty-four hours after she was admitted to the hospital last year." She crossed her shapely legs.

"That's an unsubstantiated accusation." Carlton stared at her hard.

"You're so predictable." Julie sighed. "It wasn't hard to guess you were up to something. Then there's the little matter of the financial audit. Wonder what it would show, hmmm?"

"Nothing," he barked at her. "Those expenditures were legitimate."

"Expenditures, huh? I didn't know about those. Tsk, tsk." Julie wagged a forefinger at him.

"They won't find anything I can't justify." Carlton balled his thick hands into fists.

"Okay, but don't be so defensive next time. It makes you look guilty."

"Don't forget, I'm your boss. I can—"

"Fire me? Go right ahead. I want to see you explain why. Have you forgotten my Aunt Barbara is a member of the board?"

"You've been a bitch since the cradle," he muttered.

"Now you're trying to get on my good side."

Carlton's eyes narrowed to slits. "Noel is waiting for the right time. I'm sure you've given him the dirt on me."

Julie shook her head slowly. "How little you understand me after all these years."

"Get to the point, Julie. What do you want?" he spat out.

"Noel."

Carlton let out a harsh sound that was supposed to be a laugh. "Number one, that's old news. Number two, I can't make him jump into your bed. You've been running after him for years. Take a hint!"

Julie struggled to maintain her cool exterior. She was betrayed by a slight tremor of her bottom lip. "We dated in high school."

"His mother forced him to take you to one prom."

"That's a lie. We went out more than once!" Julie breathed hard.

"Whatever gets you through those long lonely nights," he cackled.

"You help me, or I talk. Your grandmother isn't going to find my story amusing. And I'm sure you won't be laughing, either."

Carlton's mirth died quickly when he saw the wrath in her eyes. "This is nuts! I can't make Noel want you."

"Noel cares for me. He's just too much into work right now." Julie's expression dared him to disagree.

"I still don't see what I can do."

"Don't oppose his idea about using the art collection as a company asset. I want in on the whole thing." Julie stood up and paced.

"He and this Lyrissa Rideau should . . . *now* I get it. You're jealous of her." Carlton's eyebrows formed a single dark line.

"I don't want him sucked in by the slut. She's going to come out looking like some kind of savior. I want to get there first." She stood with her legs apart.

"I'm lost again." Carlton looked genuinely baffled.

"Just tell me which family members I can call about the art collection. I want to know about every knick-knack, every white elephant *before* she does."

Carton studied her in silence for a time. A cunning light went on in his coffee colored eyes. "I'm not going to be your puppet. Go on, talk. The worse I'll face is Grandmother's anger. My father will help me with her and the board."

Julie gazed back at him. "Okay, suffer through months of company politics."

"I can handle it." Carlton drew himself up.

"Her anger won't just be a temper tantrum. You know damn well it won't," Julie pressed. "But we can do a lot for each other."

"You're going to help me? Yeah, right!"

"I'll convince Noel to start his own company. He can get the money from the sale of even one valuable piece of the collection." Julie walked to the edge of his desk and leaned on it with both palms flat. "Tremé Corporation will be yours."

Carlton gazed at her for a time, then wrote on a notepad. "I suggest you start with my cousin, Vic. She just got back from St. Croix."

9

Blouses, pants, skirts and dresses in the closet mocked her. Lyrissa had been staring at them for twenty minutes now. A pile of rejects was on her bed. Once again she tried to convince herself to choose anything. Her outfit wasn't important. She didn't care what he thought of her looks.

"This will do," Lyrissa pulled out a pair of black Capri pants and a white sleeveless blouse. "No, I'll look like one of the waitresses. Oh, hell!"

"Lyrissa, what in the world are you doing in there?" Aunt Claire called as she climbed the stairs.

"I'm almost ready." Lyrissa quickly snatched up the clothes and threw them into the closet. She shut it just as Aunt Claire walked in.

"You can't be wearing that!" Aunt Claire pointed a

ring-bedecked forefinger at her. "Blue jeans cut-offs and a Tweety Bird t-shirt? No indeed!"

"I'm about to change." Lyrissa spied the array of make-up spread out. Maybe she wouldn't notice.

"Hmmm." Aunt Claire looked around the room, then back at her.

"I got caught up in this television show and lost track of time." She pointed to the television on the other side of her bed.

"With the sound turned all the way down? Those must have been riveting pictures." Aunt Claire eyed her in an appraising manner. "You care what this young man thinks of you."

"Puh-leeze! He's about as shallow as they come. I'm going to take a quick shower now." Lyrissa went into her bathroom with a handful of cosmetics.

"Come here a moment," Aunt Claire called out.

"I really should get moving."

"I understand, but this is important." Aunt Claire's voice was muffled.

Lyrissa walked back into the bedroom to find her in the closet. "What are you doing?"

"This red silk blouse will be just the thing. It's not too dressy, and the quarter-length sleeves are so in right now." Aunt Claire held up the cropped black pants and shirt to make her point.

She had to admit Aunt Claire was right. The blouse had a delicate shimmer. Her black open-toed mules would round out the ensemble perfectly. Lyrissa immediately decided on the jewelry she would wear.

"Those bold silver hoop earrings, the sterling watch

you got for Christmas, and your silver link bracelet are perfect." Aunt Claire hung the clothes on the oak valet near her bed. Then she picked up the clothes that had been flung onto the closet floor.

"You're going to make me believe you are psychic." Lyrissa rubbed the chill bumps on her arm.

"Maternal instinct. You forget how well I know you. This mess isn't like you." Aunt Claire made a clicking noise with her tongue.

"I've been busy lately."

Aunt Claire placed the last blouse on the rack and turned around. "Really, did you think I'd be fooled?"

"I'm late and you're jumping to conclusions." Lyrissa forced a casual flippancy into her voice. She turned her back and opened a dresser drawer.

"We'll see," Aunt Claire said. A knowing smile tugged at the corners of her bow-shaped mouth.

"Don't give me that look." Lyrissa scowled at her aunt's reflection in the dresser mirror.

Aunt Claire's expression did not change. "Hurry along, cher. I'll entertain Mr. St. Denis when he arrives."

She sailed out before Lyrissa could think of a suitable rebuttal to her unspoken assessment. Lyrissa whirled around to stare at herself in the mirror. Was she that transparent? She'd gone to sleep last night and promptly dreamed of him. It was no fairytale-type Cinderella dream with chaste kisses, either. She could taste his mouth, sweet and wet. In the dream they had not stopped at kissing. They'd undressed each other right there in the gallery. His skin was smooth and his muscles taut. Things had moved quickly as they can only in dreams. Suddenly she was on her back with her legs clamped tight around his hips. She had awakened to find the top sheet kicked onto the floor and the fitted bottom sheet damp with perspiration. Just thinking about it made her hot.

"I should throw a sack of ice in this shower."

What she did was let cold water stream over her. She had to get herself together to face him. Lyrissa was still in only her panties applying make-up when the doorbell chimed. Her hand slipped at the sound. A line of plum brandy lipstick went across her cheek.

Aunt Claire stuck her head in the door "Are you . . . oh dear! Is that a new fad?"

"Very funny. I'm two seconds from being totally pulled together."

Lyrissa swabbed the lipstick off. She deftly applied more face powder, slipped on her lacy red bra, and put on her slacks. With one hand, she combed her hair back, then shook her head. The loose curls bounced around her face. Then she used a brush to feather side bangs and added a finishing touch. Last, she put on the blouse.

"Ta-da!" Lyrissa faced her and put on her best diva smile.

"You look stunning. He won't know what hit him." Aunt Claire giggled.

"All part of the plan, sweet Tante. All part of the plan."

Lyrissa sashayed out of the bedroom and down the stairs. She marshaled every ounce of attitude she could along the way. No doubt she would need it tonight.

"Papa must be spinning in his grave. A St. Denis in our living room." Aunt Claire's tone was more of titillation than dismay. "This is going to be interesting."

"You devil. I think you're enjoying this," Lyrissa whispered.

"This reminds me of those old 'Mission Impossible' episodes."

"Oh, Aunt Claire." Lyrissa could not help but laugh.

Aunt Claire hummed the theme song from the vintage television series. *"Your mission, should you decide to accept it . . ."*

They both halted before entering the living room to regain their composure. A deep voice spoke in a respectful tone in answer to Mama Grace's.

"I'll go ahead of you. Make a dramatic entrance," Aunt Claire said low, then spoke louder as she went through the door. "Here we are. So nice to meet you, Mr. St. Denis."

Lyrissa meant to stroll in behind her with a blasé expression. Instead, she ran smack into Aunt Claire. "What the—"

"My Lord!" Aunt Claire breathed barely above a whisper.

Her aunt stood just across the threshold. Aunt Claire's eyes were wide and her mouth formed a small circle in astonishment. Lyrissa stared at her, then followed her gaze. Noel stood next to Mama Grace. Rather, he towered over her. They were discussing a framed antique map of New Orleans, circa 1801. Yet the showpiece was not hanging on the wall. Noel was magnificent in mocha colored slacks that hugged his hips and muscular thighs. He wore a pullover cotton knit shirt that matched the pants perfectly. His upper arms bulged from the short sleeves in a brown glory of smooth skin. The shirt was open at the neck. A dark brown leather belt and shoes completed the picture. Lyrissa groaned to herself. She seriously considered heading back upstairs for another cold shower. At that moment he faced them. Mocha fabric stretched across his fantasy-inspiring chest. Aunt Claire sighed. Lyrissa's knees sagged.

Mama Grace glared at them. "I assume you both will come in eventually," she said. Her jovial tone held an edge to it.

"How rude of me to stare. I was just thinking how much you look like your grandfather," Aunt Claire trilled. She recovered enough to smile at him graciously and walk in.

"I'm glad to meet you, too. Did you know my grandfather?" Noel said.

"Only from a distance," Mama Grace cut in smoothly. "Naturally, he was well-known in the city."

"Yes, yes," Aunt Claire added as she bobbed her head.

Lyrissa took a deep breath and let it out. She was ridiculously grateful for even such a brief respite. Then she stepped from behind Aunt Claire to face him.

"Hi." She braced herself for the impact of his smile.

"Hi. You're amazing." Noel stared at her with what seemed to be genuine wonder. He didn't smile. Instead, fire filled his brown eyes.

Aunt Claire bustled forward to break the charged silence. "Ahem, would you two like a glass of wine, or maybe amaretto, before you go?"

"Don't be silly, Claire. I'm sure they're eager to get to work," Mama Grace said.

"Humph, work, indeed," Aunt Claire murmured. She eyed Noel while he gazed at Lyrissa.

Mama Grace shot her a cutting glance, then cleared her throat. "I'm glad your grandmother made a full recovery from her illness last year. I do so admire her. Such a talented and gifted woman."

"Thank you. She is that." Noel smiled.

Aunt Claire coughed loudly. "Excuse me, something in my throat."

Mama Grace ignored her sister. "I read about the St. Denis family art exhibit at the Amistad Center."

"Yes, we're looking forward to sharing our art with the community. My grandmother is especially thrilled," Noel replied.

"Lyrissa tells me you're in charge of it all. So wonderful to see a young person interested in his family's heritage." Aunt Claire beamed at him.

"Thank you. History wasn't my favorite subject. Until now." Noel cast a glance at Lyrissa, then back to Aunt Claire.

"How convenient." Mama Grace wore a reserved but polite smile.

Lyrissa held her breath. She expected her to blow like a kettle filled with boiling water. "Noel is working very hard to make sure the art is properly showcased."

"I'm sure, given its worth to his family," Mama Grace said in a controlled voice.

"I want it preserved, and not just for us, but for the future," Noel said.

"Admirable." Mama Grace put on a stiff smile.

"Such a nice young man. Lyrissa tells me you're a hard-working businessman as well." Aunt Claire took his arm and led him off.

"Yes, ma'am." Noel looked at Lyrissa, a question in his dark eyes.

Lyrissa shrugged in reply. "I'll be here," she called out with a slight smile.

"Let me show you some more of our prints in the den.

Of course, they don't compare to your family's art." Aunt Claire babbled on rapidly as they walked.

"He has the same arrogant bearing as his grandparents," Mama Grace burst out, the moment they were gone.

"Aunt Claire seems charmed. She's a pretty good judge of character." Lyrissa stared down the hall, though they were gone.

"Oh please! She'll believe almost anything a handsome man says." Mama Grace pursed her lips.

"He's not exactly what we expected, though." Lyrissa crossed to a chair and sat down hard.

"Don't be silly. He's a St. Denis. Scratch the golden surface and you'll see brass." Mama Grace shed the last vestige of cordiality, now that they were alone.

"I suppose," Lyrissa said uncertainly.

"Don't tell me you've inherited your great aunt's gullibility. Lord give me strength! They're high-class con men, have been for generations. How do you think—"

"Yes, yes, I know. His ancestor scammed our ancestor out of a masterpiece."

Lyrissa squirmed on the upholstered seat. Her grandmother must have detected something in Lyrissa's tone. Mama Grace marched over and sat down on the settee across from Lyrissa. She stared at Lyrissa's outfit.

"Interesting ensemble for a business dinner," she said.

"I'm not—"

"Remember his reputation." Mama Grace poked her knee with a forefinger.

Lyrissa sat straight. "I'm not naïve."

"Good." Mama Grace was about to say more when Aunt Claire's twittering laugh moved closer.

"You know, I hadn't thought of it that way." Aunt Claire patted his arm like they were old pals.

"I'm sure his intentions were purely to document the times." Noel winked at her, which brought more laughter.

"Uncle Herbert did photograph Storyville quite a bit." Aunt Claire's eyebrows arched. "Grace, I believe we're on the verge of uncovering a family scandal."

Mama Grace assumed a mask of affability again. "What is that, darlin'?"

"Noel pointed out something I don't think we'd considered. Uncle Herbert must have spent hours in Storyville. What would a respected church deacon be doing in that notorious hotbed of debauchery?" Aunt Claire's green eyes twinkled.

"Interesting question." Mama Grace looked at her stonily.

"Ahem, time for us to leave," Lyrissa said, as she sprang to her feet.

"Right. I enjoyed my tour, Aunt Claire." Noel gave her hand a squeeze.

When Mama Grace rolled her eyes, Lyrissa blocked their view of her by bending down. She kissed her cheek. "Cut that out," she whispered, then added louder, "Good night, Mama."

"Good night, darlin'," Mama Grace said with a brittle smile. "I hope you come again, Mr. St. Denis."

"Call me Noel." He grasped her hand and held it for a few moments. "I'm really glad we met."

"So am I. Claire is right, you're a fine young man. But of course, what would we expect from the St. Denis family?" Mama Grace clasped his hand with both of hers.

Now Lyrissa wanted to roll her eyes. They'd need hip

boots to wade through the bull in another second. "Like I said, let's get going. The band will start in less than fifteen minutes."

"Good night, ladies," Noel called out. He seemed cheerfully unaware of any undercurrent.

They went out and got into his car. Noel turned on the radio to an FM jazz station. "Your grandmother and great-aunt are wonderful ladies."

"Real family treasures."

"Aunt Claire is sweet as a praline."

"Uh-huh."

Lyrissa wondered if he liked her because she seemed so credulous. Mama Grace's suspicions rang in her ears. Had one kiss scrambled her common sense? His mention of candy made her think of the sweetness of his mouth on hers. She wrestled with the sensation in an effort to beat it back. The sultry alto sax on the radio didn't help any. They were wrapped in its clear tones. The soft leather seats encouraged her to relax. The expertly engineered luxury car muffled street sounds.

"You're into the music," he said quietly, and placed a hand over hers on the seat. "I'm like that, too. I love getting lost in a melody."

Lyrissa trembled at his touch. She moved her hand to her lap. The loss of contact felt painful.

"Sorry, nothing so romantic. I was thinking about work." She felt his gaze, but didn't look at him.

Noel's sigh was barely audible. "Okay. We're going to talk shop, so don't get all tense."

"I'm not tense," Lyrissa said too fast.

"You did agree to come." His voice forced the issue gently.

"To talk to you about the collection. I've got final projects for school. I won't see you much in the next few weeks," Lyrissa parried.

"You told Julie you had lots of free time to spend at my office." Noel's lips twitched with mirth.

Lyrissa cleared her throat. "I said that to irritate her."

Noel grinned widely. "Yeah, I kinda figured it out."

"It's got nothing to do with you. I just don't like her," Lyrissa added defensively

"Yeah," Noel said, still grinning.

"Don't flatter yourself." Lyrissa inched closer to the passenger side window and away from him.

Noel drove down Royal Street and into a parking lot. He cut the engine and placed an arm along the back of the seat. "Come on. Let's be friends."

"Sorry," she muttered. There it was again, that word coming from her lips! Mama Grace was right. Noel St. Denis was obviously a chip off the old block.

"Stop measuring me by stupid gossip. Let's just kick back and get into some fine music."

Lyrissa breathed deeply. "We can agree on that, at least." She forced a weak smile. Her insides melted when she looked into his eyes. There was a soft light in them.

"Besides, Julie's no competition for you," he whispered and leaned toward her.

She watched him move in slow action. Lyrissa could not have dodged him if she'd wanted to, and she had no will to do so. Instead, she stared at his lips as though hypnotized. He stopped so close to her face she could feel his breath on her cheek. The tip of his nose brushed hers lightly. His cologne floated around her like exotic spices from a far-off land.

"Are you thinking about the work now?" he whispered to her again.

Lyrissa somehow managed to talk despite the huge knot in her throat. "Not exactly," was all she could manage.

"Tell me what's on your mind."

"I can't." She closed her eyes.

"Why?"

She bit her bottom lip to stop another honest and more explicit answer. Danger bells clanged in her head. No way could she tell him that in her mind they were already naked and wrapped around each other on a king-sized bed. Lyrissa was sure she would shock even sophisticated Noel St. Denis. If she leaned over, she'd give him an earful. Another warning bell sounded. Lyrissa's eyes flew open. Bells from St. Charles Cathedral announced the hour.

"Uh, I don't think we drove here to sit in the parking lot," she stammered and unlocked the car door.

"It's sorta cozy in here, though. But I guess you have a point." Noel gave an exaggerated sigh and got out of the car.

Lyrissa gulped deep breaths of the moist night air to reclaim her equilibrium. She took advantage of every moment available while he locked the car and turned on the alarm. "I hope we haven't missed too much of the show," she said.

Noel held out his hand to her. "I doubt it."

She had no choice but to take it. Her heart raced as she walked beside him. He held onto her hand in a firm grip. Noel chatted casually about the history of jazz in New Orleans, and in Basin Street in particular. Lyrissa kept up her end of the conversation, but just barely. Either he was an excellent actor, or he truly didn't know the effect he was having. As though it mattered. The fact was, he was in the driver's seat once more.

"Whoa, we'll never get in." Noel shook his head at the line of people at the door. "I've got a better idea. Who needs a crowd, anyway?"

"I do," Lyrissa whispered. The last thing she needed was more one-on-one time with him.

"I couldn't hear you over the noise." Noel leaned his head down.

"Nothing, nothing at all."

"There's a smaller club just down the way. The Court of Two Sisters."

They went down one block and around a corner. A black wrought-iron gate was set in a brick wall that dated back a hundred years. The arched doorway led through a small garden that opened up into a courtyard. Wrought-iron tables with lit candles and chairs were arranged around a wide patio. Another door led inside the nightclub. There were people sitting outside. A buxom waitress came up to them.

"Good evenin'. Y'all wanna chair out here or inside?" She gestured with her head to the door.

Noel looked at Lyrissa. "It's up to you."

"Inside," she said promptly. She needed all the cool air she could handle.

"This way." The woman bounced ahead of them.

She showed them to a table, took their order for wine, and left. Lyrissa glanced around with sinking spirits. The lighting was minimal from candles and the few lamps set flush to the walls. The club was elegant in an understated way. The atmosphere was intimate.

"You know, this is really a revival of the old club. My

parents used to come here in the seventies when they were dating. It's been closed for almost twenty years," Noel said. He propped one muscular arm along the back of her chair.

"Interesting," Lyrissa replied, and tried to match his casual pose. Of course he had the advantage of really being calm. A storm of desire raged inside her.

"Are you feeling all right?" Noel's dark eyebrows came together in an expression of concern. "You look tense. Am I doing something to make you uncomfortable?"

"You wish," she blurted out.

"So I'm getting to you. I'm glad." Noel's full lips parted in a sexy half-smile.

"I'm sure you are." Lyrissa folded her arms across her breasts.

Noel stopped smiling and looked serious. "But not for the reason you think. I don't know how to put it."

"I have trouble believing you're speechless." Lyrissa tried to be saucy, but it fell flat. The anticipation thumping inside her entire body defeated the effort.

"Yeah," Noel said, wonder in his voice as he gazed at her. His handsome features seemed to reflect puzzlement. "Saying I like you doesn't go far enough. It . . . it feels right."

"What does?" Lyrissa lost the battle. She breathed hard when his arm touched her shoulders.

"Everything. Sitting with you in my car, walking beside you, holding hands, being here, and even arguing. It all fits." Noel traced a line along her ear lobe with a fingertip.

"Really?" Lyrissa rasped. *Don't lose it. He's pulling out the big guns!* Her body, especially her heart, wasn't listening.

"You were right, in a way. I had you in my sights," Noel said quietly. He twirled a lock of her hair around the same finger.

"That's refreshingly honest." She should be outraged. Instead she wanted him to caress her face.

"I've met lots of women. But none of them are like you."

"If you say so." Lyrissa said nothing more while the waitress set two glasses of Sauvignon Blanc on the table.

"I'll bring the appetizers in a minute. They're free." The woman grinned at them, then took off.

"I really care about you, Lyrissa." Noel ignored the wine and continued to stare at her.

"Let's not get intense. I find you attractive, too." Lyrissa flashed a sassy smile. "We can enjoy each other. Nothing heavy."

"That's what you want, a casual affair?"

"We're grown-ups. Have you been madly in love with every lover you ever had?"

"No, but . . ." His voice trailed off as though he were trying to find the words.

She jumped in while she still had the upper hand. For once he was off-balance. "Let's take it nice and easy. Don't pretend some mad passion. It's not necessary with me."

Lyrissa congratulated herself on the blinding inspiration. In one fell swoop she could further her real agenda and satisfy this craving for him. It was purely physical, she told herself. Those stories of forever romance she'd inhaled as a teen had messed with her head. All her shivering came from too many months of abstinence after her last break-up. Scratch the itch and it would go away.

He cupped her face in one large hand. "What if I want more?"

"We can have something special with no strings." She let her tone and expression say take it or leave it.

"I think—" He stopped when a band came out and started to play.

Lyrissa leaned forward with a superior smile. It was good to be the boss. "Ye-es."

"We should dance," Noel said.

Noel ran his fingers down her arm, then pulled her to her feet. He worked fast. Lyrissa found herself wrapped in his arms swaying to the beat before she could speak. Her mouth worked as words tried to come out. She realized the "No!" was only inside her head. Her inner Amazonian guard had failed once again. Here she was exposed, or rather, enclosed. Still, the other part of her, that wimpy romantic, thought, what a luscious captivity. His arms cradled her as they moved. The music teased the dancers with sensuous notes from an alto sax, soft and sweet. Lyrissa stiffened when he pulled her closer.

"Relax, just an easy thing. Isn't that what you said?" Noel whispered in her ear.

Lyrissa refused to look up into his eyes. "Yes," she tossed back.

"Good," he answered, a smile implied in his voice.

The sneaky, low-down dog! She would beat him at this game if it killed her. Then he really hit below the belt. Noel pressed his body against hers. She could feel herself getting wet. Her breasts ached to be free so he could touch them with his fingertips.

"You're good," Noel said in a voice like melted butter, all warm and rich.

"What?" Lyrissa closed her eyes.

"A good dancer."

"Oh, um-hum," she mumbled back.

"Let's discuss this casual affair. How should we begin?" He used one strong forefinger under her chin to lift her face to his.

Flecks of burnished gold in his eyes mesmerized her. "Th-this is a good start. You know, da-ating," Lyrissa stammered out at last.

"The second act. What about the finale?"

Lyrissa tried for humor to fend him off. "And what happened to act one?"

"We met and you learned not to hate me on sight."

"I wasn't orchestrating a play!" she protested. His moves fascinated her, and not the ones on the dance floor, either.

He went on with a soft smile. "Act three, you agreed to our first date."

"This isn't supposed to be a date. And by the way, we really need to talk about the collection." Lyrissa added the last statement in desperation. A pitiful attempt—but all she had at the moment.

Noel was merciless in his offensive. His smile never wavered. "The last act, Lyrissa. There's always a climactic ending."

Lyrissa could not afford to look into his eyes again. Her Amazon had fled to the hills and left her exposed. "Go play with one of your debutantes."

"You put up a good fight, but I'm not the enemy, Lyrissa."

"Your family will—"

"—Just have to get over it," he finished, before she could.

Guilt seized her. Maybe she was a gullible idiot, but his voice rang with real tenderness for her. "You don't know what you're doing."

"I think you've written the ending to our little play," Lyrissa said softly. Her heart told her it would be a tragedy.

"You're wrong, and I'm going to prove it . . . if you'll let me."

Noel lifted her head again and kissed her. His tongue swept across her lips, then parted them. Lyrissa opened herself to him and clutched his forearms with both hands. He groaned deep in his throat at her acceptance. Her last feeble vestige of cynicism went up in smoke. She forgot about secret legacies and family retribution. She was a woman who'd found the one man whose soul matched hers.

The music stopped and her head cleared. She pulled back from the cliff she was about to jump off. "No music, time to sit down." Lyrissa walked away on butter soft legs.

"You're a tough one, lady," Noel said with good humor.

Not very, she thought to herself. She fell onto the chair at their table and fanned her face with a cocktail napkin. The waitress walked over.

"Y'all ready to order?" She smiled at Lyrissa.

"Bring me a tall glass of very cold anything and a glass of ice," Lyrissa said as she dabbed at her throat.

"Iced tea?" the young woman asked. She scribbled the order when Lyrissa nodded. "And food?"

Noel wore an amused expression. "Give us a few more minutes to decide." He glanced at Lyrissa. "You okay?"

"I'm just fine, thank you," Lyrissa clipped. "Why shouldn't I be?"

"You look upset."

"Me? No way." Lyrissa stared at the damp napkin she was waving and put it down. She picked up the menu.

The waitress came back with three glasses on a tray. Noel ordered a carafe of white wine along with their food. By the time the waitress had left, Lyrissa had recovered somewhat. Lyrissa avoided Noel's attempts to draw her out again. Instead, she steered the conversation back to his family's art collection. After three tries to change the subject, he gave in.

"Basically my idea is to select certain art objects and use them as a corporate asset," he said.

"You'll sell the precious St. Denis heritage to the highest bidder. So much for sentimental value." Lyrissa sipped from her glass.

"We'll choose very carefully if, and that's a big if, we sell anything. Mostly I'll use it to boost the company's value on paper. That's where you come in."

"Yeah," Lyrissa said.

"You don't think we appreciate what we've got, do you?" Noel said.

"Maybe it all came too easily," Lyrissa replied. "I mean, to your family."

Noel wore a thoughtful expression. "You're right, in a way. I try not to take what we have for granted. But I didn't choose my family any more than Tony Tate chose to be born in the projects."

Lyrissa studied his handsome face. "I guess you're right."

"With my schedule, I can't volunteer as much as he does, but I do what I can."

"I know how much you contribute to charities. You're all over the society pages." Lyrissa smiled.

"So you despise me for being one of those check writing philanthropists." Noel smiled back at her.

"No indeed. Those checks come in handy," she quipped.

Noel laughed. "Refreshingly honest."

Their food came and they talked for another hour over dinner. Lyrissa tried hard to remember she was on a mission. Still she found herself lost in the pleasure of being with an intelligent, sexy man. Noel could be playful in a charming boy-child way. He was quite different from the driven CEO who ran Tremé Corporation.

"Now, where do we go?" Noel wore an eager expression.

"Go?" she repeated, dazed. "Home?"

"Tipitina's. The Alvin Batiste Trio is playing there."

Lyrissa shook her head. "School night. I have an early meeting with my dissertation advisor."

"Next time?" Noel gazed at her steadily.

She didn't trust herself to answer. Lyrissa looked at her wristwatch. "Wow, look at the time. It's later than I thought. I really have to go."

"Sure."

Noel paid for dinner and they left. They were quiet during the drive to her house. Once they arrived, Noel parked in the driveway and turned to her. Lyrissa swallowed hard and looked back at him. Fatal error. His mouth curved lusciously into a smile. She wanted to run her tongue over his candy-coated lips. Noel reached for her and Lyrissa found herself sliding right into his arms. He kissed her tenderly, a slow, searching exploration that seemed to ask if there could be more. They both sighed when it ended.

"Good night, Lyrissa," his baritone voice rumbled.

"Good night." She rested her forehead against his. "I have to go in."

"It's not really all that late," he whispered.

Lyrissa trembled at the implication, or rather invitation. She wanted to give in. Her body tingled with the desire to hold him, kiss him, and make love to him. But she still had a measure of control despite his assault on her senses. With one last self-indulgent sniff of his sweet, musky scent, she sat back.

Noel walked her to the front door. Lyrissa stopped him from kissing her again. She wasn't sure she'd be able to leave him if he did. He left, but Lyrissa knew she'd hear his voice for the rest of the night.

10

"**Y**es indeed, it's time to shake it out of that bed!" the male voice said with exuberance.

"Oh, Lord!"

Lyrissa slapped her hand around on the nightstand trying to find the snooze button. The disc jockey rattled on, oblivious to the pain he inflicted. A stack of magazines flew to the floor before she finally hit the elusive target. Then she opened her eyes slowly. Sunlight cast a thin line onto the mauve carpet beneath her window. Lyrissa got up and opened the blinds. She took a deep breath. Now that she was up, it was a glorious morning. A bird trilled a lively song from the oak tree branch nearby. When footsteps approached, Lyrissa hopped back into bed and pretended to be sound sleep.

"Morning," Mama Grace said from the bedroom door.

"Mornin'." She shrank deeper under the floral sheet.

"I'm not surprised you're having trouble getting up. You came in very late."

Lyrissa peered up at her. "Uh, not too late."

"It was almost midnight," Mama Grace said.

Her expression would have made any professional gambler proud. It gave nothing away. It was no use hiding under the covers like a kid. There would be no escape. She had to face them both eventually. Lyrissa sat up and combed her hair with her fingers.

"Really? Well, I just came in and fell into bed. Didn't look at the clock." Lyrissa yawned loudly and stretched. "Guess I better get these bones moving."

"I suppose you talked about the art." Mama Grace picked up Lyrissa's shoes and placed them in the closet. She turned back to stare at her, waiting for an answer.

"Sure. Like I told you, they've spread the collection around. Guess rich families are like that." Lyrissa got out of bed.

"Careless, with no sense of appreciation for the things they own." Mama Grace eased down onto the bed.

"They do care, in their own way," she added quickly.

"Proud as peacocks. They love to strut in front of everyone else." Mama Grace clasped her hands tightly together in her lap.

"I suppose." Lyrissa searched through her lingerie drawer.

"That young man is no different. I can see it in him— arrogance. It's their most plentiful family legacy." Mama Grace's voice was rough with bitterness.

Lyrissa gazed at her. Deep lines etched her face. "Mama, I'm going to try very hard to find the painting. But it won't be easy."

"It's there."

"They might have sold it years ago."

"They're unscrupulous, greedy, and a lot of other things. But not stupid." Mama Grace wore a tight, humorless smile. "Georgina knows she's holding onto stolen goods."

"Maybe so." Lyrissa shifted uneasily.

"They're lying low, hoping the Joubert descendants don't even know that painting exists. But we do." Mama Grace's eyes blazed with the fire of revenge.

"Noel hasn't mentioned it. I think he might if I asked."

"No!" Mama Grace stood up. "He might get suspicious."

"I doubt that," Lyrissa said with a laugh. "Noel hasn't paid much attention to his family's collection."

"Oh, really?"

"Noel St. Denis has been into a lot of things, but vintage art isn't one of them." Lyrissa bustled around in preparation for getting dressed.

"No doubt he's a womanizer like his father and all those St. Denis men before him." Mama Grace pursed her lips with distaste.

Lyrissa ignored her jab at his character "He's a hardheaded businessman type. You know, the one always closing deals."

"He seems to know its value well enough. I'd say he's paid attention to it more than you think," Mama Grace insisted.

"You couldn't look at that collection and not realize it's worth something." Lyrissa twisted a small hairbrush in her hands. "He does seem to really appreciate some of it, I mean beyond its worth in money."

"I see," Mama Grace said in a flat tone.

Lyrissa glanced at her, then away. "What? All I said was . . ." Her voice trailed off.

"Sit down for a moment, child." Mama Grace looked grave as she patted the bedspread.

"I feel like I'm about to get a spanking," Lyrissa said with a nervous smile.

"No, just a reminder of whom you're dealing with. They're a breed apart." Mama Grace delivered her verdict with a frown.

"Come on, that's so twentieth century," Lyrissa joked. Or at least she tried to. Mama Grace didn't smile.

"It doesn't matter what century this is."

"Yes, but—" Lyrissa stopped at the look her grandmother gave her.

"He's not for you, cher. Noel St. Denis will find the 'right' girl." Mama Grace clutched Lyrissa's hand as though to make the point.

Lyrissa stared at herself in the dresser mirror. She touched the fingertips of one hand to her skin. Could every moment of last night have been an act?

"You're beautiful, but he'll never see it. Not the way he should."

Lyrissa closed her eyes against the harsh words. Her body grew hot at the thought of Noel's arms and legs entwined with hers. Mama Grace could well be right. Noel had beguiled women before her. She thought of Julie Duval. Surely the woman must have some reason to be so jealous. Lyrissa opened her eyes to reality. She looked at her grandmother and smiled.

"Don't worry. I'm sticking to the plan," she said firmly. Both of them, she mused. She would reclaim the painting *and* keep a firm grip on her heart.

Mama Grace continued to look at her for a time before she nodded. "Be very careful."

"They won't catch me. Not before we can sue to get the painting back." Lyrissa started to stand, but Mama Grace stopped her.

"Your own heart can betray you, cher. It can convince you of the most foolish things," she said softly.

"I'll be okay."

Lyrissa tried to sound more sure than she felt. She hoped the clear light of day would help. But the words they'd whispered to each other rushed back inside her head as she prepared for work.

The drive to Miss Georgina's mansion gave her more time to think. Noel had everything he could want, including his pick of women. Much as it hurt, she had to admit that Mama Grace made sense. Men like Noel always went back to women like Julie. He would not seriously consider bucking his entire family. Lyrissa called up the weight of her experience. That alone helped her gain perspective.

By the time Rosalie let her in, Lyrissa had herself in hand again. She stubbornly refused to acknowledge the kernel of regret in her stomach.

"I'm going to enjoy the ride and get off when I'm ready," she mumbled.

"What did you say? Had my mind on the grocery list." Rosalie stared at the paper in her hand.

"Nothing. How are you?" Lyrissa put on a bright smile.

"Humph! I could be a whole lot better. Had to deal with her highness already." Rosalie jerked a thumb to the ceiling.

"She's extra cranky today?"

"Cranky ain't the half of it, sugar." Rosalie made a hissing sound through her teeth.

"Mrs. St. Denis has her ways, but I'll bet she can be nice sometimes. She *can*," Lyrissa asserted, when the woman stared at her wide-eyed.

"Uh-huh. You don't mind hanging round here, I guess."

"I've dealt with more difficult rich folks, trust me."

Rosalie lifted an eyebrow. "Yeah. Speaking of which, Mr. Noel is here. Stopped by on his way to the office."

Lyrissa kept her expression neutral even though her pulse raced. "I've got a date with a dusty attic. Hopefully I'll be out of your hair for good soon."

"Sure you don't want to see him?" Rosalie stared hard at Lyrissa.

Lyrissa glanced away. "No, don't need to. Don't you just love this cool spring weather?"

"Uh-huh." Rosalie wore a knowing smile, but said no more. "Go on into the study. I'll bring you a cup of coffee in a minute." She took out a pair of reading glasses and looked at the list again.

Lyrissa nodded and went through the double oak doors. She found a copy of the list of art along with another sheet of paper on the desk. Names and addresses were handwritten in neat print with cryptic notes behind each. Rosalie came back with a tray loaded with a matched server set.

"Here ya go, darlin'. Miss Georgina is still getting dressed. She can't move so fast these days—not that I'd let her hear me sayin' that." Rosalie chuckled to herself. She set the tray down and poured rich, dark coffee into a cup. Lyrissa accepted it gratefully, inhaling the wonderful aroma.

"Thanks. She seems to do well for her age," Lyrissa said and took a sip.

"Yeah, especially when she's got a bee up her you-know-what," Rosalie said in a stage whisper.

Lyrissa laughed out loud then caught herself. "She's a very determined lady."

Rosalie grinned. "That's a nice way of puttin' it. Well, let me go. I gotta get this dinner party organized. The family is comin' over here Saturday night."

"Really?" Lyrissa hurried to delay her exit. "Bet it's a job, planning for all those people."

"Won't be that many, it's just that they're so darn picky, picky, picky."

"They like getting together, I suppose." Lyrissa probed gently, searching for insight into what was going on.

"Not that much, darlin'. I got a feelin' this is more family business than pleasure. Somethin' about the company."

"Oh." Lyrissa wondered if the art were involved. Rosalie's good-natured voice interrupted her thoughts.

"Good luck with her highness this morning." She patted Lyrissa's shoulder, then bustled out. "Yell if you need something."

"I will," Lyrissa called back. "Now, what are the chances I can get an invitation?" she murmured as Rosalie disappeared through the doors.

Noel rubbed his hands together as he stood at the window. Then he walked to the round antique mirror on the wall and gazed at himself. He straightened his shirt collar. His coat and tie were draped over the back of the sofa in his grandmother's sitting room. Miss Georgina sat at a small antique writing desk. She studied the neatly typed inventory arranged as a table with notations on age, location, and description. Noel glanced at the door several times. Finally he walked to the window again.

"You and Ms. Rideau need to look at these." Miss Georgina tapped a finger on the paper.

"That's what I'm going to set up today. I'll call Cousin Augustin and two others," he replied.

"Fine." Miss Georgina shuffled through her files, glasses perched on her nose.

Noel swung his arms and walked in a circle around a small table. He fiddled with flowers in a vase. A noise made him look up sharply. Seeing no one at the door, he let out a long breath and paced.

"Noel, take a look at these journals. I'm thinking of contacting the Amistad Center to display them." Miss Georgina glanced where she thought he was standing.

"Did you say something?" Noel rubbed his jaw as he stared outside.

Miss Georgina squinted at him. "What have you done?"

Noel turned and grinned at her. "I'm not ten years old anymore."

"I don't care how old you are. I know you."

"That old bluff won't work, Grandmother." He assumed a casual pose to throw her off the scent.

She gazed at him with a bland expression. "I'll find out soon enough. Might as well save us both the trouble and confess."

Noel laughed easily. "Dealing with the family has you paranoid, cherie."

"Mon Dieu!" Miss Georgina burst out with a scowl. "I swear some of them can be so infuriating!"

His grandmother launched into a diatribe about her

relatives. He sighed with relief that his tactic worked. The last thing he needed was drama about his relationship with Lyrissa. They'd not had a chance to talk it out. His heart hammered at the sweet memory of holding her in his arms. She'd felt so good. His body was still in shock.

"Wow," he said to himself.

"Wow is right! Your Aunt Aline is impossible!" Miss Georgina seemed to vibrate with outrage.

Noel blinked back to his surroundings. "Huh?"

"Pay attention. We've got serious matters at hand here. I know what you've been doing, Noel Phillip."

Noel stiffened. "You do?"

"You've been letting this tug of war with Carlton distract you. I thought you two would act like adults and work together."

Noel scowled at the mention of his cousin. "Carlton is like a big kid still angry because I took his toy."

"Be patient."

"I have been and it's getting old," Noel retorted.

Miss Georgina sighed and put down the sheet of paper she held. "I know you have. I also know how much stress you've been under, running the company. Being the boss of a family owned business isn't easy."

"The business part is easy. It's the family part that's a pain." Noel wore a grim smile. "But I'll handle them."

"I have no doubt of that. You're like your grandfather," she said proudly.

"I may have to deal with Carlton soon, Grandmother. I won't tolerate his running to board members behind my back much longer."

She nodded. "Do what you have to, son. Just give me

fair warning. I'll have to deal with his parents, you know."

Satisfied with her support, Noel nodded back. "Fair enough."

The intercom on the desk phone buzzed. "Miz Rideau is here," Rosalie said.

"Thank you, Rosalie. Let's join her in the study." Miss Georgina stood. She gazed at him. "Noel?"

"Yes, sweet one?" Noel put an arm around her shoulder.

"What were you thinking about so hard a moment ago? It wasn't Carlton or the company." Miss Georgina studied him closely as though she had the answer already.

"I'm always thinking about business. You know that," he replied smoothly.

"Hmm." She continued to study him. "Who are you dating these days?"

Noel shook his head in wonder. Georgina St. Denis missed nothing. She could zero in on a target like a fine-tuned guided missile.

"I'm thirty-two years old. Don't be nosy." Noel pecked her on the cheek.

"I know how old you are, Noel Phillip. It's time to settle down," she tossed back at him.

"Lyrissa is waiting, dear. You can lecture me on that well-worn subject later." Noel opened the door for her.

"Don't think I won't." Miss Georgina wore a resolute smile as she walked past him. "I need to talk to Rosalie first. I'll be there shortly."

Noel straightened his tie. "Good."

His grandmother's dark brows came together. "What?"

"I'm sure you're getting the dinner all planned," Noel replied.

Miss Georgina looked at him hard. "I won't be long."

"Take your time, sweet Grandmother. I'll answer any questions Ms. Rideau might have," he said over his shoulder as he headed down the hall.

Noel walked in and a blush started at the base of Lyrissa's spine and spread up. Her face felt hot. He was magnificent in a navy pinstriped Brooks Brothers suit. His broad shoulders filled out the fabric. He had the sleek grace of a powerful athlete and the polish of an old-fashioned Creole gentleman. The memory of being close to him brought back that now familiar tingle.

"Good morning, Lyrissa," Noel said, his voice sounding low and intimate.

She took a deep breath and let it out. "Good morning."

"Are you okay?"

Lyrissa sat ramrod straight and assumed a cool expression. "Of course."

"Oh, guess I shouldn't assume." Noel tilted his head to one side.

"Assume what?"

"That you felt the same rush I did when I saw you just now." Noel walked across the room and stood in front of the desk where she sat.

"Sorry I didn't melt into a puddle. I'm sure women do every time you bat those thick eyelashes." Lyrissa picked up her pen and started writing.

"So you like my eyelashes, huh?" Noel grinned at her.

"You've got a lot of confidence in your charm, I see." Lyrissa didn't look at him.

"Not with you, lady. You have a delicate way of shooting me right down." He picked up a crystal paperweight on the desk.

"Let me guess. You've never met anyone like me before. I make you feel like you've never felt before with a woman. Blah-blah-blah." Lyrissa waved a hand in the air.

Noel laughed softly. He didn't seem the least bit insulted. "Something like that. Of course I wouldn't have made it sound so phony."

"I'm sure you've got it down just right. I told you it's not necessary to play the game."

"I'm not playing a game, Lyrissa," he said in a quiet, firm tone. "I think you know it, too."

Lyrissa couldn't resist looking up at him. His dark eyes drew her in. She cleared her throat and looked away sharply. "No, I don't. But it doesn't matter."

"Yes it does. I can show you better than I can tell you."

Lyrissa shivered when she looked at him again. She had to ask. "How?"

Mrs. St. Denis marched in before he could answer. "Good morning, Ms. Rideau. Sorry I kept you waiting."

"No problem," Lyrissa said. She shook off the hypnotic spell he'd put on her.

Noel leaned forward while his grandmother was still on the other side of the large room. "We'll talk later," he whispered. He faced Mrs. St. Denis. "I'll take Lyrissa around to the relatives. We'll start soon, as you suggested."

"Running a large company requires most of your attention," Mrs. St. Denis replied.

"The collection is part of the business equation now and needs my attention." Noel smiled at Lyrissa.

"I'll take Ms. Rideau myself." His grandmother's voice held an edge.

"Don't tire yourself. You've got all kinds of social obligations. The doctor told you not to overdo," Noel said.

Lyrissa felt tension in the air. Mrs. St. Denis wore a stiff expression. She glanced from Noel to Lyrissa. Noel seemed not to notice. He sat down in one of the heavy chairs facing the desk, totally at ease.

"He's so thoughtful. But I'm fine. We can start this week." Mrs. St. Denis put on a tight smile that didn't include her eyes.

"I need to know as much about the collection as possible," Noel replied firmly. "I'll take care of it."

They looked at each other for several moments. Lyrissa held her breath at the silent battle of strong wills. Finally Mrs. St. Denis gave a slight nod and cleared her throat.

"Of course you do," she said.

Noel stood. He walked over to his grandmother and kissed her cheek. "I'm on my way, sweet. Lyrissa, I'll call you at your office this afternoon. Okay?"

"Sure. I mean, that's fine," Lyrissa stammered when Mrs. St. Denis turned a stony gaze her way.

"In fact, I think we could start tonight. I'm sure Cousin Augustin won't mind. I talked to him a few days ago," Noel said without looking at his grandmother. "I hope you're available."

"I think so." Lyrissa fidgeted with her pen.

"Why don't you check your day planner right now?" Noel persisted.

Lyrissa wanted to strangle him for pushing the issue. She took her planner out of her briefcase. "I'm tied up until three o'clock. I could go alone if you're busy. Just call Mr. St. Denis."

"I'll make time. This collection is too important. I'll

pick you up around five. You should be through by then, right?"

"I could meet you there," Lyrissa said in a strained voice. She looked at him, trying to send a silent message.

"No sense in taking two cars. I'll pick you up at your house. I'll treat you to dinner, since I'm making you work late." Noel rubbed his hands together as though the matter were settled.

Lyrissa stood. She put her planner back into her briefcase, along with the list of art and addresses. "Then I'll see you later. I've finished up here." No way was she going to be left alone with Mrs. St. Denis.

"I thought you needed to examine the pieces in the attic." Mrs. St. Denis stared at her steadily.

"I did. It didn't take long since I'd examined them before. I just needed one more look after finding information on them in an art book." Lyrissa tossed more of her work tools into the briefcase. She snapped it shut and picked up her small purse.

"I see," Mrs. St. Denis said. "Goodbye, then."

"Goodbye." Lyrissa forced a thin smile.

Noel put a hand under her elbow and walked beside her. Lyrissa glared at him. He smiled back at her serenely. Rosalie came down the hall as they left the library. Her eyes sparkled with mischief as she noted Noel's hand on Lyrissa's arm.

"Bye, Rosie," Noel called out.

"Bye, you rascal," Rosalie called back with a grin.

"Rascal is right," Lyrissa muttered.

Noel only laughed at her comment. They went to the circular driveway where his Infiniti was parked behind her Honda.

"Goodbye, Lyrissa. I look forward to seeing you this evening. Two nights in a row." He stood close to her.

Lyrissa wanted to swipe the smug look of victory from his face. At the same time she wanted to kiss him. The conflicting emotions left her feeling dazed. "Goodbye" was all she could say.

He walked with her to the car. He opened the door once she unlocked it. "Don't look so worried. We're going to have fun." Noel winked at her, then strolled to his car and got in.

Lyrissa gripped the steering wheel as she drove to her morning class. There was no denying the pleasant tickle of anticipation in her body.

"Well?" Carlton frowned as he stared over Julie's shoulder.

"No wonder Noel is doing an inventory. This collection is one hell of an asset." Julie chewed on her bottom lip as she read.

"Some members of the family are very disturbed with his plans." Carlton wore a pleased smile.

"You could be wrong, you know," Julie muttered without taking her eyes off the list.

"I know I'm right." Carlton stuck his chest out.

Julie cast a glance up at him. "Sure you are."

"What does that mean? I've made a few mistakes, but—" Carlton snapped.

"I didn't say a thing." Julie cut him off. She sat back against the chair with a long sigh.

"This is a waste of time," Carlton said, his jaw muscles working.

"Noel is working hard to get everything listed. I think

he has good reason to do so." Julie crossed her legs and stared at Carlton.

"Sure he has—her name is Lyrissa Rideau." Carlton leered.

"That woman is a phony," Julie shot back.

"Oops, didn't mean to touch a nerve." Carlton's pleased expression contradicted his words. "Guess that's why Noel isn't at the office much these days. They're out 'looking at art.' "

Julie stood abruptly, the sheet clutched in her fist. "But I've got something she doesn't have. I'm going to see Mr. Augustin this evening."

Carlton's gleeful grin faltered. A baffled look came into his small eyes. "I don't know why. Cousin Augustin is nuts."

"He's got the best of the collection."

"I haven't agreed to anything yet." Carlton stared at her hard.

"What are you talking about?" Julie glared at him.

"This scheme of yours is all to your benefit. You want to show up Lyrissa and score points with Noel. What do I get? I've already told a few of the family they should fight his proposal." Carlton crossed to his desk and sat down in his chair.

"What if you need to sell the collection, after all? You've given them ammunition to fight you, too."

"I won't change my mind. It's a stupid idea."

"Don't be an idiot, Carlton!" Julie burst out. "You're just saying that because it was Noel's idea!"

"No, I'm not." Carlton looked like a stubborn child despite his size.

"Oh, grow up! You've been acting like this toward Noel since we were kids." Julie put both hands on her hips.

"He's always tried to make me look bad." Carlton's eyes glittered with anger.

"You didn't need help!"

His eyes narrowed. "You're on his side. Why should I listen to you?"

"I want this company to thrive for our children—Noel's and mine." Julie spoke with steely resolve.

"Got your china pattern all picked out," Carlton wise-cracked.

She ignored his attempt at humor. "My point is my interest lies with making sure we all win. Stop fighting Noel out of stupid, childish jealousy. I'll help you."

"Really?" Carlton still wore a guarded expression.

Julie sat deep in thought while Carlton seemed to mull over her arguments. The only sound for five minutes was the ticking of a fancy brass clock. Carlton fiddled with his Mont Blanc pen. Julie seemed to be far away. She finally spoke, a calculating expression on her face.

"I think there's more to this collection than even Noel or Miss Georgina realizes," she said.

"We'll need more than your intuition."

"Shut up and listen," she hissed. "I've done a bit of digging. I'm in the process of researching all the artists. That's why I'm going to Mr. Augustin's house."

"I don't get it," Carlton said.

Julie huffed with exasperation. "What if there's a missing masterpiece in it? What if one item is worth a fortune?"

"Don't be ridiculous. Grandmother would know. My father would know." Carlton shook his head.

"How? Everything has been scattered for years, even before your father was born. There's no *definitive list*, Carlton."

"You really think so?" Carlton stared at the list in her hands with a hungry expression.

Julie's pretty features hardened. "There's only one way to find out. I'm going to make sure Miss Lyrissa Rideau doesn't get there first."

11

Noel stole sideways glances at Lyrissa. The strained but polite conversation had finally petered out. Now they rode in awkward silence. She sat far from him on the other end of the front seat. It felt as though there were miles of leather between them. Lyrissa appeared to be far from him in more than physical distance. Mindless conversation was better than nothing, he decided after ten minutes.

"At least the traffic isn't such a nightmare," he said.

"Hmm."

"But then, it's almost seven. Too bad we couldn't meet for dinner," Noel ventured with caution.

"I was busy," Lyrissa said.

"I know. I was just saying it would have been nice." Noel looked at her. Lyrissa stared out the window. "Okay, I give up. Tell me what I did."

"Nothing," she said in a crisp voice.

"I kind of maneuvered you into this trip. Is that it?" Noel tried again.

"No."

Noel was shaken by her coldness. If she'd been any other woman, he would have shrugged it off and moved on, fast. He had done it more times than he could count. But this wasn't just any other woman.

"If I'm being too pushy, say so." His heart thumped when she sighed. "What I mean is—"

"I'll let you know," she said, still staring ahead.

"Okay."

They rode on in silence. Noel's fingers ached from holding the steering wheel so tight. He willed his hands to loosen. Words crowded his head, but he couldn't seem to put them together in the right combination. Once again he was stumped by her effect on him. He had no point of reference on how to proceed. He wasn't nervous, exactly.

"You've got me all confused," she said finally.

Noel gasped with relief. "I was thinking exactly the same thing. I don't—" He stopped when she started.

"I'm not usually this—sorry." Lyrissa looked at him.

"No, no. You go." He guided the car into the exit lane.

"I cut you off." Lyrissa waved a hand.

"Ladies first." Noel wore a slight smile.

"Chicken," she teased.

"I'm okay with that, now finish what you started," Noel said.

Lyrissa half turned in her seat. "I had you all figured out, and then you mess things up by being . . . nice."

"I'm so sorry. Should I be a real fool from now on?"

"I'm serious. Practically all my life I had this idea of people like you."

He could feel her gaze like a soft cloth settling over him. He pulled up to a red light. "You came to our house sure of what kind of people we'd be."

Lyrissa nodded slowly. "I guess I'm a snob."

"Everyone has biases. But we can choose not to hold onto them."

"I guess you're right," she said in a pensive voice.

"Maybe the answer is knowing your biases and not being bound by them." Noel reached out and touched one of her hands.

"Did you have any preconceived notions about me?"

"Yes indeed. I thought you'd be boring and plain." Noel laughed. The light turned green and he pressed the accelerator.

"Very funny," she quipped. "Seriously, there are real problems with you and me becoming a couple."

"A couple of what?" Noel glanced at her sideways.

"Cut it out. You know what I mean." Lyrissa squinted at him.

"So tell me what you think stops us from being a couple."

"Let's see, there's difference in social status, money, your family's attitudes about bloodlines and skin color. Need I go on?" Lyrissa looked at him.

"Don't be shy, say what you think!"

"Look, I went to school with Creole girls. I thought they were my friends. Then one day I saw two of my 'friends' away from school with their parents at the mall. They pretended not to know me." Lyrissa stared ahead.

"Then you didn't lose much," Noel said angrily.

"That was my first lesson in prejudice, from my own race. But Creoles don't consider themselves Black, do they?"

"The whole issue is complicated, Lyrissa." Noel shook his head. "Some feel that way, others don't."

"Well, I haven't met the ones who don't yet."

"Yes, you have. Me." Noel put a hand over hers. "I'm African-American. We know that Marie Auguste Conque was a slave bought by a French planter in seventeen sixteen. Her granddaughter had ten children, seven of them for her owner."

Lyrissa's tense frown gave way to an expression of interest. She took a pad and pen out of her purse. "Why haven't you told me this before? I can include this information on her in my dissertation."

He smiled, glad that the tense moment had passed. "See, there was a good reason for us to be together tonight. By the way, I hope you got that little bigot back."

Lyrissa wore an evil grin. "Oh yeah. I'll bet she still can't open a locker without getting scared."

"You've got to tell me that story."

"Let's just say my friend Herbie's pet rat learned how to fly that day."

"Remind me not to make you mad."

Her expression became serious. "That was one of the few bright spots at St. Mary's."

Noel wanted to stop the car and take her in his arms. "I'm so sorry, Lyrissa."

"Thanks. Anyway, back to the St. Denis family. They won't be happy with you dating me."

"You're assuming my entire family is close-minded. That's not fair."

She wore a cynical smile. "I've met them, remember?"

"I make my own decisions," Noel said with force.

"Life is complicated enough for me right now. I've got school, *my* family to consider . . ."

"If we trust each other, we can handle them all."

"Let me think about it," Lyrissa said after a few moments.

"Fair enough. In the meantime, we can date, nothing too heavy," he added quickly when she started to speak. "A nice chaste kiss or two every now and then." He wore a half-smile.

"Noel . . ." Lyrissa shook a finger at him.

"I like the way you say my name," he murmured.

Lyrissa blushed. Her lips looked moist and delicious. Noel shifted to relieve the tension of his intense arousal. Still he knew better than to push her. She needed time to think about them. But then, so did he.

Fifteen minutes later they pulled into a long, circular driveway on Pontalba Avenue. The house was three stories tall with the first floor on street level. A staircase went up to a wide veranda on the second floor. It was a classic New Orleans design.

"My God," she whispered.

"We just had this talk, Lyrissa. We're not from another galaxy, okay?" From her expression, Noel was afraid he'd lost what little ground he'd gained.

She stared at the house. "It's lovely. I'd say around 1870."

"You're an expert on old houses, too?" Noel led her around to a side door.

"No, but I recognize some of the carved woodwork. It dates from that period."

Noel pressed a lighted doorbell button. "Cousin Augustin lives down here. His youngest daughter has the upper floors, but she's gone most of the time."

"On family business, I suppose." Lyrissa gazed around as though taking in every detail.

"No, she likes to investigate ghost sightings," Noel said with a straight face.

"Say what?" She blinked at him.

"She dances to her own music, you could say," he grinned.

"I guess she can afford to," Lyrissa murmured.

She became thoughtful again as she took in her surroundings. A lush garden could be seen despite the darkness. Noel decided not to mention the landscaped yard with a pond filled with exotic koi in the back. Lyrissa stared up at the house, then around at the old-money neighborhood. Noel was about to speak up about stereotypes when the door jerked open. A round faced man dressed in a designer sports shirt and slacks beamed at them. He was short and stocky. His eyes were hazel with hints of green.

"Ah, the young prodigal. Oh, wait, that's your father, isn't it? My, but he makes life interesting. How is Richard these days?"

"Not too different," Noel said with a mock frown.

"Wonderful! I like consistency. Be yourself, is what I say." The older man hugged Noel with affection. Then he turned his attention to Lyrissa.

"Cousin Augustin, this is Lyrissa Rideau. I told you about her."

"Yes, but you didn't mention she was a flower of female perfection. So pleased to meet you." Augustin took her hand and bowed.

"Thank you." Lyrissa glanced at Noel with an amused expression.

"He likes to lay it on thick. But don't take him too seriously. He's fickle," Noel said.

Augustin straightened and led Lyrissa inside. "In the interests of full disclosure, I'm fifty-two—"

"Fifty-nine," Noel corrected.

He swept on as though Noel hadn't spoken. "I have my own teeth, mostly. My children are all grown, I'm financially secure and love to travel."

"He's all talk, Lyrissa." Noel smiled at him.

"Scared of a little competition, young man? Come in. I've got wine and beer, and I mix a mean hurricane."

Cousin Augustin led them down a short hallway. Lyrissa hadn't gone two steps when she stopped to admire a framed painting. The two men were talking and didn't notice. She opened her portfolio and scanned the list.

"How beautiful," she said as she flipped pages.

"Lyrissa, would you like Chardonnay or . . ." Noel realized she wasn't behind him. He went back to stand beside her.

"Your lady is all business, son. You like it, Miss Rideau?" Cousin Augustin called out.

"This is by Tomas Daigrepont." Lyrissa seemed awed by her discovery. "It's described here, but I never dreamed!"

"Oh yes. I remember my grandmother mentioning him. Quite well thought of, I think." Cousin Augustin bustled to the bar. Glass tinkled as he prepared drinks.

"He was a notorious man in his day. Very talented, but he died young." Lyrissa furiously made notes.

"Thrown head first from a horse at forty." Cousin Augustin stirred the contents of a clear glass pitcher. "Martini for me, kids."

"I'm driving, so I'd better not. Definitely not one of your martinis." Noel waved at him when he held up the pitcher.

"Coward," Augustin said with a grin. "Now, I'll bet this spirited young thing will join me."

"No, thank you. Are these part of the collection?"

Lyrissa no longer looked at the list. She walked around examining sculptures and paintings.

Augustin swallowed some of his drink. "Hmm, just right, as usual. No, those are from my mother's side of the family."

"You're fortunate to be surrounded by such beauty." Lyrissa continued her tour.

"Dust catchers, that's what the lady who cleans for me calls them." Augustin took another generous sip from the glass, then set it down. "Since you insist on business, come with me."

"I'm sorry. I got carried away." Lyrissa looked embarrassed.

"Don't worry, dear. I make it a point to indulge beautiful women." Augustin beamed at her.

"Oh, man!" Noel rolled his eyes.

Lyrissa smiled at the older man without looking at Noel. "Careful, you'll turn my head."

"I'm past the age of turning a young girl's head, sad to say. Now, pretend I'm the Wizard and this is the Land of Oz." Augustin went before them with a bounce to his step.

"You're going to show me amazing sights and sounds?" Lyrissa seemed happy to join the game.

"I told you he was a bit unusual," Noel whispered close to her ear.

"He's adorable," Lyrissa whispered back.

"Thank you, dear," Augustin said gaily. "You warm an old man's heart."

Lyrissa laughed. "And he's got the hearing of a twenty-year-old."

"This way, children."

Augustin climbed the stairs slowly but without faltering once. He led them into a grand room furnished with antiques. Lyrissa gasped when she reached the top of the stairs. Louis XIV chairs and settees upholstered in raw silk filled the sumptuous yet tasteful room. A Persian rug of rich jewel tones of green, ruby red, and sapphire blue covered the floor.

"I could spend weeks here," she said with a delighted expression.

"I just may steal her away, after all, handsome young cousin." Augustin slapped Noel on the shoulder.

"You wish." Noel pretended to frown at him. He watched Lyrissa take her time as she made a circle around the room.

"So you two are . . . together?" Augustin spoke in a soft, discreet tone.

"Never mind about that," Noel said. He wanted to shout out how he felt. But he exercised self-control.

"I see, the delicate stages of a new romance. I understand completely," Augustin whispered.

"Don't start any gossip. I'm serious, Cousin Augustin." Noel wore a sober expression to press his point home.

"You don't have to worry about me. I can keep a secret." Augustin nodded and made a gesture as though locking his lips with a key.

"Like I believe you," Noel said with a grunt.

"I found eight items on the list. But . . ." Lyrissa hesitated before going on, then pointed to an item written on her sheet. "I don't see this large painting."

"Let's see." Augustin took out a pair of reading glasses and put them on.

"It's probably on the third floor." Noel followed him and looked at the list as well.

"Must be 'Sunday Stroll.' The thing is massive. Simply overpowered this room." Augustin swept a hand around while still reading the list.

" 'Sunday Stroll,' sir?" Lyrissa's voice cracked.

"You do need something to soothe your throat. I have just the thing. Amaretto." Augustin started to dart off but was brought up short when Lyrissa yanked on his sleeve.

"What's the full name of the painting?" she said.

"We've always called it 'The Stroll.' I'm not sure. Remember that dance from the fifties?"

"What?" Noel and Lyrissa said at the same time. Both blinked at him in confusion.

"Of course you don't. Years before you were born." Augustin hummed a tune and shuffled his feet.

"Sir, the painting. Who's the artist?" Lyrissa cut him off by walking in front of him.

"You've broken my rhythm. I can't move the way I used to. I could really shake a leg."

"Focus, Cousin Augustin. We're talking about the collection, not how you used to party." Noel shrugged at Lyrissa in apology.

"The painting—oh, of course."

"It's the largest one listed. I was sure you'd have it," Lyrissa said.

Noel wondered at the intensity of her interest. "Is it important?"

Lyrissa took a deep breath and smiled. "I doubt it. But it would be good to have everything accounted for before the board meeting."

"Lord in heaven! I'm not looking forward to that, or your grandmother's party. People are choosing up sides, from what Julie tells me."

"Julie?" Noel frowned at him.

"I visited the offices the other day. It could use a lot more pizzazz. Scatter a few French colonial tables around, and—"

"I'm sure it would look nice. About 'The Stroll,' sir." Lyrissa gently nudged him back on the subject of interest to her.

Augustin sat down heavily in a chair nearby. "Whew! Get me something cold and refreshing, kid." He gestured to Noel.

"And non-alcoholic," Noel added. "You should know better."

"It's come to this, being lectured by an infant." Augustin fanned his face.

"Could you describe it?" Lyrissa's voice was firm.

"What are we talking about, dear?" Augustin took a large white handkerchief from his pants pocket and wiped his brow.

"This painting," Lyrissa said loudly. She jabbed a finger at the list.

Noel struggled not to laugh at her frustration. On his best day Cousin Augustin had the attention span of a three-year-old. "The one you call 'The Stroll,' " he added to help her out.

"My brother's youngest has it," Cousin Augustin said. "You remember Ersalind, Noel. She lives in that huge house near Covington. It amazes me why she'd want to live there."

"Good! We can visit her soon," Lyrissa said.

"I think she has it. Or maybe I gave it to my son Kyle for his law office."

Lyrissa let out a gust of air like a deflated balloon. "Maybe we can call them tonight."

"Kyle is in Atlanta on business. I'm pretty sure he is. And try catching Ersalind at home." Augustin finished what was left of his martini.

"But you're sure one of them has it." Noel tried to help again.

"I'm almost sure. You must see this stunning watercolor. It was done by an artist who had an affair with Marie Leveau." Augustin sprang from his chair and out the room.

"Good Lord!" Lyrissa rubbed her forehead with the tips of her fingers.

"Our family tree has a few lovable nuts in it." Noel smiled as he walked over to her. He massaged her shoulders.

"It's like trying to grip a handful of Jell-O." Lyrissa groaned. "Why couldn't it just be in the attic or something?"

"My relatives aren't known for taking the easy way in anything." Noel laughed.

"A news flash," she retorted.

"Don't be too irritated with us. I promise to call my cousins tomorrow."

"Fine, fine," Lyrissa said.

"First thing in the morning, I swear. Hey, I'll bet that print really is nice." Noel tried to soothe her.

Lyrissa shrugged free of his touch. "Owning a collection like this is a sacred responsibility. What do you people do? Toss it around like second hand junk!"

"So maybe we could have been a bit more careful," Noel admitted.

"That's an understatement. You realize a painting like that could be priceless?" Lyrissa glared at him as though he'd personally thrown it away.

"You think you know what it is?" Noel came around the chair to face her.

"No, it's just . . . your family has treated these beautiful objects so casually." Lyrissa grimaced.

Noel smiled slightly and sat on the sofa across from her. "At least he narrowed it down to one branch of the family."

"You take everything for granted because it's been handed to you on a silver platter." Lyrissa stood up and walked around the room.

"Not everything," Noel said defensively. "My ancestors worked very hard."

"Sure, at snatching up real estate owned by the poor descendants of slaves. Then you collect art as though it's nothing." Lyrissa swept her arm out in an arc. "Look at this place."

"So we're crass and a bunch of crooks." He gazed at her intently.

"I'm just stating the facts."

"We're not talking about art anymore." Noel sat forward. "It's the entire Creole sub-culture of racism and classism, isn't it?"

"Here we are," Cousin Augustin burst in wearing a wide smile. He held a framed painting of irises. "Just look at these colors!"

Noel sat with his hands clenched together. He stared ahead without seeing anything. Lyrissa stood near the window, her back to them both. Augustin glanced at Noel, then Lyrissa, then back to Noel.

"Nice," Noel said finally without looking at it.

"The air in here is thick with tension. And I missed it!" He looked disappointed.

Lyrissa whirled around and grabbed her portfolio from the chair where she'd sat. "I'll document what you have."

"Of course," Augustin said in a quiet, diplomatic tone. "This way, dear."

Noel remained behind. He listened as they moved from room to room. Their voices faded in and out, signaling their locations. When they came back, he sat with a glass of white wine in his hand.

"Changed your mind, eh?" Augustin clapped his shoulder.

"I needed it," Noel said and looked at Lyrissa. She avoided his gaze.

"Hmm." Augustin gazed at them, then yawned. "I don't mean to rush you, but it's getting close to my bedtime."

"Not unless it's near midnight." Noel glanced at his wristwatch. "It's nine-thirty."

"I'm trying something new." Augustin put a hand under Noel's elbow and guided him from his seat.

"Sure you are," Noel said. His eyes narrowed with suspicion.

"You kids should go to Celestin's. Perfect spot to spend quiet time and talk things out." He motioned to Lyrissa and took her arm when she approached.

"You must have a hot date," Noel teased.

"For me to know and you to find out. I'm so glad you came. It was wonderful meeting you, Lyrissa." Augustin talked fast as they walked.

"Thank you for letting us come over, Mr. Augustin." Lyrissa spoke in a stiff formal voice.

"I was happy to do it, dear. Drive safely. Bye, now." He ushered them to the door.

"Bye, Cousin Augustin. I'll call you later." Noel turned around to talk to him.

"Of course. Remember, soft music and dim lights." Cousin Augustin winked at him and jerked his head as though pointing the way.

Noel glared at him. "I heard you," he said tightly.

"Good night, and thanks again." Lyrissa gave Augustin a polite nod, then strode to the car. She was inside and wearing her seatbelt in seconds.

"I think you owe me an explanation," Noel said after getting in behind the wheel.

"No I don't. I'm hired help. As long as I do my job, I don't owe you anything."

"Take the chip off your shoulder, Lyrissa. Stop putting up barriers between us." Noel did not start the engine.

"The barriers were up generations ago." Lyrissa rubbed her forehead. "It's been a long day and I've said too much already."

Noel took her hand. "Let's find a quiet place to talk. Please."

They didn't speak during the short drive. Noel stole glances at her at each stoplight. He turned on the compact disc player. Luther Vandross sang standards, love ballads that Noel hoped would ease the tension. Lyrissa did not bend at all. She sat rigid as though determined not to acknowledge him. Noel sighed inwardly. They finally reached Celestin's. He parked in the paved lot, but neither of them moved.

Lyrissa peered at the building. They got out and went inside. Dark stained wood, soft music, and dim lighting made the atmosphere intimate. A tall waiter led them to a table. He took their drink orders and left. They looked at each other for several seconds.

"Well?" Lyrissa prompted.

"Well," Noel replied with a smile.

"You wanted to talk, so talk."

Noel tilted his head to one side and looked at her profile. "You had some kind of plan and I wrecked it. Good."

Lyrissa blinked rapidly as though trying to think of a comeback. "What?"

"You had me all figured out, right? You were going to put me in my place and stay away from me."

"Oh, right." Lyrissa glanced away from him.

"You're special to me. What can I do to prove it?"

Noel had never felt such a strong need to be believed. Everything else became insignificant. All his concentration was on her. Lyrissa must have felt the vibrations coming from his body. When she turned to look into his eyes, there was no anger or skepticism. What he saw was a raw need to believe. He kissed her hard. She froze, but only for a moment. Then she relaxed in his arms and returned his kiss hungrily. Noel pulled away only to kiss her forehead, her eyes, her nose and her chin.

"I want to make love to you right now," he whispered.

"Noel, we . . ."

He smothered her words by kissing her again. He drew away and smiled. "No pressure."

Lyrissa touched the tips of her fingers to his mouth. "Oh no, you're being very subtle. We really should—"

"Take time and get to know each other," Noel finished for her.

"Yes," she said softly.

"I like football, the Saints disappoint me every year, but I'm still loyal. Blue is my favorite color. I like fishing but don't get to do it very often. What else?" Noel rubbed his cheek against hers.

"You keep avoiding the real issue." Lyrissa pulled away. "I'm not going to play your game."

Noel swallowed hard at the chill left when she moved from him. Still he resisted the strong urge to reclaim her warmth. "Tell me what's on your mind."

"I don't care what your society friends think of me." She put more distance between them as she spoke.

"Sounds good," Noel answered cautiously. He knew there was more.

"Your family is no problem. I mean, we're only dating." Lyrissa spoke in a practical tone.

"Okay," Noel said slowly. He didn't like the temporary way she made it sound but let her go on.

"So like I said, we don't need to generate drama. Let's date, talk, and . . ." Lyrissa shrugged.

"And?" Noel rubbed his fingers along her left arm. He watched goosebumps appear on her skin and wanted to kiss each one.

"And," she murmured as she looked at his fingers.

"Can't wait to fill in the blank," Noel whispered close to her ear.

"Stop that." She took a deep breath.

"No," he said simply.

She seemed to teeter on the brink of surrender but pulled back at the last moment. "Why are you doing this?"

"For once I'm not being practical."

"Maybe we should be," Lyrissa said with a solemn expression.

"Do we want to be practical—or happy?"

Noel was stunned by how deep that question reached into all his assumptions. His plan to have the "right" wife to fit into a neat picture of the "right" life suddenly seemed empty. Neither of them spoke for a time.

"I don't know what to say." She wore a bewildered expression.

Noel touched his temple to hers. "Say yes, we'll be together."

"It's not going to be as easy as you make it seem."

"Maybe not. Right now what matters is that we're together. Let's go to my apartment," Noel whispered.

Lyrissa picked up his hand and moved it. "We're going to just talk tonight."

"I love the sound of your voice." Noel was not going to play fair.

"You've got a devious streak, you know that?" She gazed at him.

"Is it working?"

"Yes, but we're going to stay here." Lyrissa did not move.

"Okay. I'm happy just being with you right now." Noel put both arms around her.

They talked for hours.

12

Lyrissa stood at the door and gritted her teeth. This was the third house she'd been to today. The St. Denis and Rohas clan was getting on her last nerve big time. She'd visited two older women at opposite ends of the city. Each of them had been more eccentric than Cousin Augustin by a mile. Lyrissa was convinced that Noel's family held the monopoly on nutty behavior. She sighed deeply and steeled herself before she pressed the doorbell. The chimes that followed played the opening song from *Phantom of the Opera*. Her spirits fell to the ground.

"Perfect ending to my 'X-Files' day," she muttered.

Five minutes ticked by. Part of her was relieved, the other irritated. She'd called Victorine St. Denis Vivant and made an appointment. Ms. Vivant had sounded relatively sane on the phone two days earlier, but that didn't mean a thing with this bunch. Lyrissa's jaw ached from clenching her teeth all day. Maybe this was a sign. She'd managed not to assault anyone verbally until now. God might be telling her to quit while she was ahead.

She turned to leave when she heard locks click. The door creaked open two inches. A pair of pretty gray-green eyes peeked around the edge. The shapely brows arched and the door swung open.

"You must be Miss Rideau. Hmm, I know your family background. Genealogy is my passion. One of many." The tall woman spoke in a familiar way, as though they were picking up a conversation.

"Miss Vivant?" Lyrissa knew her day was going to end as it had started when the woman nodded eagerly.

"Call me Vic, everyone does. Let's not stand on formality. So you want to see the art—what am I thinking? Come in, darlin'."

Vic stood at least five feet nine in flat ballet shoes that were bright red. They matched the silk tank shirt she wore over white Capri pants. Lyrissa knew from Cousin Augustin and Noel that Vic was forty-seven. Yet she appeared to be at least ten years younger. Her skin looked like smooth condensed milk. A mass of dark curls were piled high on her head. Lyrissa noticed she held a wine glass in her left hand. Could this day get worse? Vic chattered on, oblivious to the fact that her visitor only nodded occasionally. Lyrissa tried to break her rhythm three times before succeeding.

"Excuse me, Vic. Vic, *excuse me!*" Lyrissa raised her voice until she had her attention.

Vic blinked rapidly at her and smiled. "Yes, darlin'?"

"I'll just check this list and then get out of your way."

"Don't rush yourself, sugar. My evening is free for once. We can start in the sun room." She hooked one long arm through Lyrissa's and tugged her along.

"Oh, good." Lyrissa spoke through a tight smile that stretched her face to the limit.

"Rideau, the name dates back to the late 1790s, I believe. Or is it earlier? Quite prominent, too." Vic halted suddenly, causing Lyrissa to stumble.

"What's wrong?" Lyrissa dreaded her answer. Was this woman going to take weird behavior to new heights?

"Actually, you might be distantly related to the Bonapartes. You know, Napoleon and Josephine," she said in an exaggerated French accent.

"I doubt that." Lyrissa's anxiety shot up for another reason. This woman was too close to knowing her family origins.

"Hmm." Vic gave her a head-to-toe appraisal. "Maybe not. There were two branches."

Lyrissa nodded with relief. "Right, we're not all related. I have here—"

"Yes. One branch is thought to be descended from the white planter Ribeau. Some stupid clerk at the Cabildo copied it wrong."

"Really? I didn't know that."

Lyrissa knew very well about the legend of Francois Ribeau. She could have set Vic straight with the real story. But that would put her back onto Lyrissa's family, and that wouldn't do at all.

Vic lifted a shoulder. "My passion, as I said."

"Yes, fascinating. I understand you have three sculptures and two, possibly three, paintings. I'll just look at the paintings first." Lyrissa attempted to take control of the visit.

"Of course. Straight ahead." Vic marched on, dragging Lyrissa in her wake.

They did not follow a straight line at all. The house was designed to curve around a central courtyard. They walked down a hallway with glass on one side. Late afternoon sun slanted across a green lawn with flowerbeds arranged around stone benches. They entered an enchanting room filled with rattan furniture upholstered in green, yellow, and white. Two large ceiling fans whirred overhead.

"This is a beautiful room. In fact, it's my dream sun room." Lyrissa gazed at the gauze draperies pulled back from the windows. The room was cozy without being too cute.

"Thank you, sugar. Glad you like it. Ah! Here's one of the figures you wanted to see."

Lyrissa smiled at her genuinely. She liked Vic despite her ditzy manner. At least she could finish the day in lovely surroundings. She put her notebook down and picked up the ceramic figure of a nude female dancer. It was at least three feet tall.

"It looks as though she might move at any moment," Lyrissa murmured.

"Yes, if we played the right music." Vic touched the dancer's head with the tips of her fingers.

"I see you finally made it." A voice came from beyond the door.

Lyrissa turned to find Julie standing with a glass in her hand as well. *What are you doing here?* She managed to keep the question to herself.

"Hello."

"Good afternoon." Julie drawled the words and managed to make Lyrissa feel clumsy. She came into the room.

"Julie, darlin', I'm so sorry. Forgot you were in the study. Didn't I mention Julie was here? Julie Duval, this is—"

"We know each other," Julie broke in dryly. She looked past Lyrissa.

"Right! Aunt Georgina told me Lyrissa goes to the office. Excellent idea. Noel is totally brilliant." Vic hugged Lyrissa again.

"It was Miss Georgina's idea, not Noel's," Julie's said in a snippy tone.

"Was it? Now, why did I think that? Oh, Cousin Augustin said Noel really enjoys working with the lovely—ahem, never mind." Vic's eyes widened at the look Julie gave her.

"I understand you've been through most of the list," Julie snapped. Her dark eyes flashed with animosity as she stared at Lyrissa.

"Three-quarters of it so far. Your collection could be the last of it." Lyrissa turned to Vic in a deliberate dismissal of Julie.

"I suppose you'll give us all a report," Julie said.

"After I consult with Noel. And Mrs. St. Denis, of course." Lyrissa spoke over her shoulder. "May I see the rest?"

"Uh, of course, darlin'. Follow me." Vic's gray-green eyes sparkled with interest. She glanced between the two young women.

"Thanks."

Lyrissa smiled and lifted her head as she walked after Vic. Julie brought up the rear. It was as though she meant to keep an eye on Lyrissa.

"I've made a study of the collection myself," Julie said.

"So you know about art and art appraisal?" Lyrissa kept her tone polite and cool.

"My family has collected art for generations as an investment," Julie replied.

"I see. Not so much for your own pleasure." Lyrissa's voice was even.

"We are able to do both, invest and enjoy beauty. We're like other fine old families in that way," Julie said.

They walked into a long room with teakwood furniture, Audubon wildlife prints, and royal blue brocade draperies. Lyrissa turned to face Julie. Before she could hurl a suitable reply, Vic spoke.

"My late husband's study is filled with history. You'll be in heaven, Lyrissa." Vic made a full turn with her arms outstretched. "Dripping with old things."

Lyrissa gazed around the room and forgot about Julie's attempt to bait her. The prints were wonderful, but on a far wall hung the prize—her own Holy Grail. There in all its splendor was "Sunday Stroll on the Tremé Faubourg." She stood frozen, in awe. She walked slowly toward it.

"I . . . I think . . . that is, I'm sure this is on the list," Lyrissa stammered. She felt her chest tighten just looking at it.

"It's lovely," Julie said.

"Yes, quite nicely done. Here is my favorite!" She strode over to a tall modern sculpture. "It's called 'Man-Child's Promise.' "

"That's not part of the collection, Victorine. Honestly." Julie frowned at it and then Vic.

"I didn't say it was. But it's my favorite all the same." Vic did not lose her good humor.

Their voices faded as Lyrissa stared at "The Stroll." Pale blue faded into a deeper one to make the sky. Women in pink, white, and green walked along with heads held high. They were of different shades of brown. Trees in dark green made impressionistic silhouettes against the blue sky. In one corner of the painting was the signature of Jules Joubert. Jules had used his sister, his wife, and a cousin as models. Lyrissa felt a connection to the women.

"You seem mesmerized." Vic walked over and stood next to her. "It is lovely, though, in a quaint, old-world way."

"Yes, quaint," Lyrissa said.

"I looked at it earlier. 'The Stroll' is its title, I think." Julie joined them in front of the painting but studied Lyrissa instead.

"Yes, well—I'll make a note of it and the other pieces." Lyrissa forced herself to step back. She scribbled.

"It's not part of the collection, either," Vic announced in an off-hand manner.

Lyrissa's head jerked up. "Say what?"

"That painting is mine. Papa gave it to me years ago. I think he said his grandfather left it to him."

"But that can't be! I have a painting of its general description on the list." Lyrissa flipped pages.

"Let me see. I have my own copy right here. A twenty-four by thirty-six painting, nineteenth century, women walking in the park," Julie read aloud.

"Maybe I'm wrong. Besides, I think it's a reproduction," Vic said. "Anyone for iced tea?"

Lyrissa reeled from her words. "I'm sure this painting is authentic."

"No, dear heart. Papa told me all about it. Don't worry,

no caffeine. It's raspberry orange herbal tea." Vic brightly changed subjects.

"Ms. Vivant—"

"Ah, ah, you better call me Vic, or no treat for you." Vic wagged a finger with deep red lacquer on the nail.

"Vic, I know paintings, and this one can't be a reproduction." Lyrissa's throat tightened at the thought.

"I'm telling you what Papa said. He was furious when he found out it was a fake. You see, my great-grandfather was—well, not so honest." Vic's eyes twinkled. She didn't seem the least bit embarrassed.

"I really don't think you should go into family affairs." Julie's glance slid sideways briefly and she nodded at Lyrissa.

"Don't be silly, it's a well-known fact. Besides, the old rascal has been dead for a good sixty years." Vic laughed and walked through the door. "Come on, girls. Tea is waiting."

Lyrissa started after her, but Julie cut her off. Both women went down a long hall that entered a wide gourmet kitchen. A skylight let in sunshine. The kitchen opened onto a large family room with a big-screen television and furniture in cool blues and greens. At any other time Lyrissa would have taken time to admire it. She hardly noticed the elegance of it.

"Vic, I'm sure you're mistaken. Do you have any kind of documents? Mrs. St. Denis is certain she lent your father this painting." Lyrissa tried to keep her voice calm.

"I don't think we have any kind of papers. No reason we would." Vic went to the built-in refrigerator humming gaily.

"Tell me exactly what your father said." Lyrissa was

close behind her. She jumped when Vic whirled suddenly.

"Here we are! Sweet nectar from heaven, by way of southern California." Vic held up a clear glass pitcher of red liquid.

"Vic, try to remember." Lyrissa wanted to snatch it from her hands and shake her until she talked sense.

Vic went to the breakfast table and put the pitcher down. She got three tall pale green glasses from a side cupboard.

"Let's sit down and then we can talk," Vic said gaily.

Julie had been leaning against the center island with bar stools around it. She studied Lyrissa in silence for several moments before she joined them around the table. "You're really intense about that painting. Are you familiar with the artist?"

Lyrissa looked at her and could see wheels starting to turn. She cleared her throat. "Not really. He was considered a minor regional artist. Just being thorough."

"Really? Hmm." Julie's tone and expression said she was suspicious. She continued to examine Lyrissa closely.

"But it's no big deal, Vic. I'll check it out after we enjoy this delicious tea." Lyrissa willed herself to relax. She even managed to smile at Julie.

Vic chattered about the merits of herbal compounds. Lyrissa nodded while adding the occasional comment of her own. Julie continued to watch her surreptitiously. Lyrissa rolled out what she prayed was her strongest performance to date. Still Julie was not so easily distracted.

"The neighborhood in the painting looks lovely. It dates back at least two hundred years. Wealthy free Creoles lived there." Julie eyed Lyrissa.

"The Tremé Faubourg was a favorite setting for artists. So it could be a reproduction," Lyrissa said.

"*Fake*, cher. We shouldn't be so delicate." Vic laughed and drank a long sip of tea.

"Maybe we should have it examined by an expert," Julie said.

"Lyrissa *is* the expert, Julie. Such a sharp young thing." Vic winked at Lyrissa.

"I mean someone with more experience in authenticating art," Julie said firmly.

"That could come later. First, we should make sure it's part of the collection. Vic says it's not." Lyrissa shrugged again and made notes on a legal pad.

"Well you know, I'm not really sure now. Maybe I'm thinking of the landscape in the dining room." Vic screwed up her face.

"We'll sort it out eventually. No need to struggle with it now." Lyrissa smiled at Vic and drank some tea.

"The board meeting is in less than two weeks. I think you'd better *sort it out* before then. That's what we're expecting from you, as the *expert*." Julie stared hard at Lyrissa.

Lyrissa's smiled widened until it hurt. "You're right, of course. I'll be back in touch with you about the painting."

"Okey-dokey!" Vic replied with a wave of one hand.

The rest of the visit went by in a blur. Lyrissa's concentration was on being cool and nonchalant. She could feel Julie watching her every move. Vic seemed blissfully unaware of any tension. She gave a history of her family. Julie frowned several times at Vic's hearty candor.

"My great-grandfather was a fast-talking man. He almost got shot once. You know, it's been whispered that my ancestors were high-toned thieves." Vic dropped her voice in a mocking, confidential tone.

"Which might have included the art?" Lyrissa couldn't resist the opening.

"I wouldn't be a bit surprised, sugar!" Vic burst out.

"Vic!" Julie's mouth hung open for a second before she recovered.

"The older I get, the less I care what people think." Vic laughed. "Besides, it's all just entertaining historical tidbits."

Lyrissa sipped her tea and pretended only a mild interest in Vic's rambling stories. Julie squirmed, clearly bored but unwilling to leave them alone. She muttered a soft curse word when her cell phone rang.

"Another important business deal to close, I bet. I admire high-powered corporate women," Lyrissa said with a guileless expression.

Julie squinted at her but said nothing as she punched the buttons on the phone. "Yes, what is it?"

"Well, I don't envy them running around to meetings all day. So tedious. But then, someone has to keep the economy going, I guess." Vic beamed at Lyrissa. "Now *you've* got a dream career. You get paid for looking at beautiful things."

Lyrissa laughed. "I never thought about it that way. But I also study history."

"That can be exciting, too."

"Digging around dusty old books and buildings isn't exciting. Mostly I sneeze a lot."

"You're so funny! I can't wait for you to come back. I know, let's meet for lunch at Copeland's one day." Vic leaned forward with a look of anticipation.

Julie tried to follow their exchange but couldn't. "Say

that again. I'll be there in twenty minutes." She hit the off button on the phone.

"Duty calls?" Lyrissa said sweetly.

Julie's eyes flashed when she looked at her. "Nothing Noel and I won't be able to handle this evening. He wants me with him tonight at a meeting."

Lyrissa winced at her choice of words. "I'm sure you will."

"We work well together. We've been a team for six years now."

"Thank goodness. Carlton is a such a—" Vic blithely resumed telling tales out of school.

"Carlton has really grown in his position." Julie spoke in a measured manner.

Vic stopped. "Oops, loose lips, as they say."

Lyrissa pretended not to notice. Still she seethed at the vivid image of Julie hanging on Noel. She stood up. "I'd better go now."

"Don't tell me you're rushing off to a meeting. What about the leisurely academic life?" Vic stood, too.

"My schedule is anything but. I work and attend classes," Lyrissa said.

"She's on a scholarship or fellowship of some kind." Julie lifted one shapely eyebrow.

Lyrissa reminded herself of the invisible but no less substantial wall between them. She gazed at Vic and Julie. They wore their expensive clothes as easily as they wore their self-assurance. It was obvious neither had the experience of feeling out of place. At that moment the women represented generations of Creole smugness.

"How stupid of me to rattle on like some empty-headed dilettante. I wish I had half your brains and talent." Vic spoke in a sincere way, her eyes clouded with concern. "I didn't mean to imply—"

"It's okay." Lyrissa cut her off. She didn't need or want her pity. "Thanks for your time. I'll call again if I need to come back."

"Please do. I really mean that," Vic said. She glanced at Julie with a frown.

Julie did not accompany them as Vic walked Lyrissa to the front door. Vic talked in a nervous manner. Lyrissa nodded politely but remembered they were on opposite sides. Soon she would be at odds with Vic and the rest of the St. Denis family. Then Vic would not be so cordial.

"Thanks again," Lyrissa said in an attempt to leave.

"I'm glad you came. And don't pay attention to Julie. She's a bit possessive when it comes to . . ." Vic blinked hard. "I'm doing it again. I can't seem to stop making a fool of myself today."

"Don't worry about it. Bye-bye."

Lyrissa escaped after the third apology. She gazed around at the large homes, luxury cars, and neat lawns feeling like an alien from another planet. *Noel and Julie . . .*

The two names kept running through her mind for the rest of the afternoon.

"What's wrong?" Noel asked.

"Nothing," Lyrissa said, and knew it sounded false.

They sat on the sofa in the living room of his apartment. It was Friday evening. They'd had a quiet dinner at Semolina's, Noel's favorite Italian restaurant.

"Vic called me." Noel waited for her to answer.

"She's a nice person." Lyrissa did not look at him.

"Are we going to have that talk again?"

"What talk?"

"The one about how we come from different social classes and—" Noel put a hand on her knee.

"No," Lyrissa broke in. "We don't need to."

"Good. Then you can relax, right?" Noel bent forward to stare into her eyes directly.

"Sure," Lyrissa said and smiled.

"You're a strong woman. I can't believe you'd let anyone play you with stupid games."

Lyrissa knew he referred to Julie. So Vic wasn't such a ditzy heiress, after all. He was right. Yet little did he know that his statement applied to him, too. What if she was too distracted watching Julie to realize he was the real threat? Her chest tightened at the thought that his touch was false. She shivered when he stroked her cheekbone with a forefinger. Still she wanted to shift attention back to her real goal.

"I didn't think about that more than two seconds after I left." Lyrissa gazed back at him.

"Good. I'm going to tell my parents and grandmother about us."

"No!" Lyrissa blurted out.

"Why not?"

"I-I'd feel better if you waited. Just a little longer."

Noel nuzzled her neck. "You're too tense, baby."

"Promise you won't say anything until I'm ready."

"Relax," Noel whispered.

"Please," Lyrissa cajoled. "Just until I'm not so jumpy."

"If that's what you want. Now, let's not talk about it anymore."

"We should talk about this dinner party, not to mention the board meeting." Lyrissa tilted her head back to allow his kisses to progress.

"We talked about the collection too long already," Noel said, his voice muffled against her flesh.

She pulled away. "Time is getting tight." The dinner party was in one week and the board meeting would be the following Monday.

Noel sighed dramatically and let go of her arm with reluctance. "If you insist."

She left the sofa and retrieved her notes from the table near his front door. "You were right in thinking the collection has been undervalued all these years. You folks really should bring all the pieces together."

"What fun. Some of my loving relatives are grumbling about possession being nine-tenths of the law." Noel wore a sour expression.

"Nothing like warm family unity, huh?"

"Most didn't even know they had part of the collection," Noel said.

"It happens in the best of families. The thing is, we're talking a substantial asset for your company." Lyrissa showed him her preliminary appraisal.

"Why is there a question mark next to this painting?" Noel pointed to the listing of "Sunday Stroll on the Tremé Faubourg."

"Vic thinks it's a reproduction. I'll have to authenticate it first." Lyrissa's hand shook only a little as she uttered the lie. Noel seemed not to notice.

He nodded and read on to the total figure. "Whoa!"

"Yes, you're reading that right. I estimate it's worth 1.8 million dollars."

"Are you sure?" His eyes were wide with amazement.

"Noel, I found a Degas and Tunica Indian pottery, more than even I expected. In fact, I'm going to consult one of my professors. This might be conservative."

"My God," he whispered. "Wait until they see this."

Lyrissa pressed her lips together. The total figure would jump if the true value of the painting were added. She estimated it could add as much as $95,000. For a crazy moment she considered telling him. With the priceless items they already had, maybe one painting wouldn't make such a huge difference. They could still work through their feelings for each other and she could get the painting. Her fledgling hope crashed when he spoke.

"Close to two million. What if that painting is real?" Noel's eyes glittered with delight. "We could really attract investors."

She looked at him as he contemplated all the big time deals he could make. "What were you saying about your relatives?" she asked in a cryptic tone.

His dark brows drew together, the delight gone from his eyes. "Damn!"

"They'll hold on even tighter now. But at least the most valuable pieces are with Mrs. St. Denis and Augustin."

"We need every one of those items," Noel said in a hard voice. He paced the floor in front of the fireplace.

"For purposes of commerce," Lyrissa added coldly. She dropped the list onto the table.

Noel stopped pacing and looked at her. "No, not just as a business asset. Some of the top corporations have art as part of their holdings."

"Oh yeah, you really want to be like them. Strip miners, polluters, and destroyers of rainforest." She folded her arms.

"You know I'd never operate like that, don't you?" he said softly.

Lyrissa couldn't help but look into his brown eyes. They conjured up the image of warm pralines, dark and sweet. He was asking her to believe in him, to think the best of his motivations. His face was tantalizingly close. She breathed in his cologne, a tangy, warm scent that tickled her nose. To seal her fate, he leaned forward and planted a kiss between her eyes.

"I didn't say you would. But . . ." Lyrissa lost her train of thought when his lips found hers. He wasn't playing fair! But then, she was holding back information, so who was the real culprit? His tongue in her mouth, hot and insistent, cut off the rise of conflicting emotions. Craving took over, the need to wrap herself around him once more. Noel drew away to stare into her eyes again.

"Enough about business." He buried his fingers in her hair.

"But the report—" Lyrissa said as she closed her eyes.

"Later," he whispered and kissed her harder.

"We're supposed to take it slow, remember?" Lyrissa didn't stop his hands from roaming over her body.

"Vaguely," he said hoarsely. Noel stroked her breasts through the pink fabric of her blouse.

"Listen to me, mister. Oh!" She gasped when his tongue flickered across the tender spot between her breasts.

"I'm going to be a bad, bad boy," he whispered as he slipped a hand beneath her bottom and squeezed.

Lyrissa went limp when he rubbed the inside of her

thigh. His fingers inched up until he stroked her mound through the fabric of her matte jersey slacks. She lay back and caressed his hands as they moved over her body.

"I want you." Noel buried his face against her breasts and gently rubbed his cheek against them.

Lyrissa said nothing but held him tight. She closed her eyes against the world outside and reality. He moaned when she put both her arms around him. "What do you want from me, Noel?"

"Everything. I want to make love to you until we're both wringing wet and exhausted. But I want us to be together, heart and soul." Noel raised his face to gaze at her.

Lyrissa was lost in his sensuous eyes that flashed golden with passion. She wanted everything, too. Most of all she wanted to believe him. "I don't know what to say," she admitted.

"Tell me what you want from me." Noel put his head back on her breasts with a soft sigh.

"More time," she murmured.

Several beats passed before he answered. "You've got it. I ask just one thing."

Her pulse sounded like rushing water in her ears at that sultry, deep voice. She wanted to tear at his clothes and tell him to forget what she'd said. The time was right. Instead, she held on. "What?" she whispered.

"Give us a chance. Don't use my family or yours as a reason not to be with me. Concentrate on us." Noel caressed her breast until the nipple peaked through the fabric.

"You're not playing fair." Lyrissa lost the fight. Arching her back, she almost cried out when he sat back.

"That's not what I promised." He looked at her with a lusty grin, his hand still caressing the aching flesh.

With a strangled groan she opened the buttons to reveal more skin. Noel obliged her silent request by running his tongue over the mounds above the lacy pink bra. He deftly opened the front hook. His large fingers pushed aside the cups and his mouth closed over her aching nipple. Lyrissa shuddered with pleasure as he sucked gently. She cried out when his tongue ran over the swollen peak. The rough surface against the tender flesh sent shock waves down to her toes. Without conscious thought, Lyrissa stroked his erection stretched tight against his pants. Noel gasped her name and slid his hand under the waistband of her slacks. An insistent jangle intruded.

"You'd better answer the phone."

"Voice mail," he mumbled without taking his mouth from her breast. The phone stopped ringing as if at his command.

"Noel, we really shouldn't." Lyrissa took a deep breath and tugged her bra back in place. "Not yet. Please," she pleaded, not sure she could stop if he insisted.

With one last nip of her flesh, Noel sat back. "I'm going to give you the time you asked for. I want us both to be sure."

"I-I'd better go."

He twisted a lock of her hair around one forefinger. "Okay," he relented.

They held hands during the ride to her house. Her mind swirled with "what-if" scenarios, ways to sort through the situation. There was a dizzying twist of complications and implications of what they'd shared tonight.

Noel seemed to read her mind. He squeezed her hand several times as though to reassure her. Jazz played softly. The muted light from the dashboard lit his beautiful profile. Lyrissa wished she could make the rest of the world go away for a little longer. As if to answer her, they turned onto Erato Avenue and her house came into view. There would be no fantasy solution. Noel pulled into her drive and walked her to the front door.

"Lyrissa," he said and brushed his lips across her face.

She cupped his face with both hands. "Noel St. Denis."

"Remember, think about us."

Lyrissa nodded. He kissed her one last time. Noel held onto her hand as he walked away until they both let go. With one last wave, he drove away. She watched the red taillights until they disappeared.

"Think about us," she whispered. Lyrissa knew she would think of little else.

13

"**W**ell, this should be a barrel of laughs," Augustin muttered.

"It might not be so bad." Vic looked around at the grim faces. "Then again . . ."

"Oh, sure, as much fun as that delightful dinner party last week." Cousin Augustin made a sour face.

"God! I'd rather have a root canal than suffer through that ordeal again." Noel's third cousin, Harold St. Denis, winced.

Noel watched them all, ears attuned to each whispered comment. The boardroom was packed for this meeting. Family members that usually wore weary expressions seemed alert today. They sat or stood around the long mahogany oval table. Groups of two and three formed, broke up, and reformed. Carlton cast stony glances at Noel from time to time. The seventeen people present were dressed impeccably, as usual. Some held fine china cups filled with dark Louisiana coffee. A platter of beignets sat on a credenza with the large silver coffee pot, napkins, and a pile of fresh fruit. It was eight-thirty in the morning. The earlier-than-normal meeting had been his grandmother's idea. She'd suggested with graveyard humor that they might as well get the execution over with early. The dinner party had been a big bust in terms of creating family unity. Noel had not even been able to spend much time with Lyrissa as consolation. He'd been too busy trying to butter up quarrelsome kinfolk. At least they'd learned just how much lobbying Carlton had done. They would not be blind-sided in this meeting. It was something, though not much.

"We'll get started in a moment," Noel said. "Miss Rideau will be here with her report. I'll present it, but she'll answer any questions you might have."

"I hope we're going to talk about more than art," his gruff Uncle Laurence burst out. "This company needs more than doo-dads to support it!"

"I'd say the St. Denis Collection is a lot more than that, Mr. Rohas," Julie said in a respectful tone. "I've seen each piece, and—"

"Let's wait until everyone has settled down," Noel put in.

"Fine. I suppose you want her to take center stage here, too?" Julie whispered the last sentence.

"What does that mean?" Noel frowned.

"You know damn well what it means," she hissed.

"Not here, not now," he said sharply. Noel tried to feel sorry for her. Yet he felt stifled by her possessiveness.

"When?" Julie pressed closer to him.

Noel glanced around in time to see his father and aunt

watching them intently. He maneuvered her away from Vic and Augustin. Fortunately, the others were too distracted to notice Julie's dramatic performance.

"Later," he said.

"After the meeting? Today?" She searched his face with a desperate expression.

"Yes. Now please, Julie. We've got enough to deal with right now." Noel put a sense of urgency in his tone.

Julie looked over his shoulder and then into his eyes again. She smiled. "I'll be right by your side, Noel."

"Good. I know I can count on you."

He turned in time to see Lyrissa standing in the door. Her expression went hard as she looked at his hand still on Julie's arm. There was no time to explain or say anything.

Carlton chose that moment to clear his throat loudly. "Maybe we should get started," he said.

"Let's get down to it, for God's sake," Uncle Laurence rumbled. He walked to his chair with a rolling gait caused by arthritis in both hips. The other board members took seats around the table.

Miss Georgina stood in the open door leading to the executive offices, which were down a short private hall. She was dressed in an emerald green Carole Little business suit. There was a black-and-white silk kerchief in one breast pocket. Gold button earrings gleamed in the fluorescent lighting. Her silver gray hair was swept up in a French roll.

"Good morning, everyone. Laurence, I'm glad you're here." She fixed a baleful stare on the seventy-year-old curmudgeon.

"Morning, Georgina. You're looking hale and hearty for somebody supposed to be down for the count," Laurence said with a grunt. He tossed a glare at Carlton, who blinked hard.

She gave a composed laugh. "The reports of my death were greatly exaggerated."

"Ahem, Grandmother's trademark sense of humor," Carlton said with a watery smile. "As I was saying, we're here to discuss proposals to address the viability of this company."

Carlton's father marched over to stand beside him. "My son has a solid grasp on the road we need to take."

"Careful we don't end up going off a cliff, Willie," Richard said with a lopsided grin. He sat down next to Noel.

"Dad, please." Noel eyed his father. "We're here to work together."

"Not if we're on the wrong track," William said. He glared at Richard for a moment before going on. "My son has a proposal that makes sense."

"Sounds reasonable," a distant cousin said.

"Then get to it," Uncle Laurence added. "Don't waste time shillyshallying around."

Augustin raised a hand. "Ah, excuse me."

"Yes, Augustin," Miss Georgina said with a nod.

"Shouldn't we at least hear details of what we're supporting?"

"I thought that's what we came here for. I don't like being rushed at this hour of the morning," Vic said.

"I was simply making a general opening statement," William said tightly.

"We got the message." Augustin had a twinkle of mischief in his eyes.

Noel moved to shift the group into a more positive direction. "We can get started now. I believe we both have solid ideas to put on the table—right, Carlton?"

"For the most part," Carlton said with a cool smile.

As chairman, Uncle Laurence officially opened the meeting. For the next half-hour they reviewed a report of operating expenses and net profits. Eddie passed out manila folders as he spoke. Noel made it a point to keep his expression blank. He could feel glances from other members of the board. Lyrissa sat across from him. She stared down at a folder before her. The gray skirt, matching jacket, and crisp white blouse she wore fit her curves very well. Other women would have looked straitlaced in such an outfit. Not Lyrissa. Her business suit gave a hint of the sensual woman beneath the functional clothes. When she used one hand to brush her hair in place, heat shot through Noel's midsection. He smiled at the memory of the way she tasted.

Richard leaned close to him. "Keep your mind on business, son. William and Carlton are up to something."

Noel adjusted his tie and looked around the room. Several pairs of dark St. Denis eyes stared at him. Julie watched Lyrissa closely. His father was right; he needed to keep his mind on the present. Still, there was no place Lyrissa could sit that wouldn't light a fire inside him. He'd just have to focus, even with her so close.

Carlton leaned forward, both elbows on the table. "As I said, my proposal makes good business sense. Jack Castle, a top consultant in this area, endorses it. We could see a six percent rise in profit within the first quarter after my plan is implemented." Carlton wore a confident expression.

"I like it," Aunt Aline said promptly. "Well, this was relatively painless, as dry board meetings go. Very impressive, Carlton."

"Not bad," Uncle Laurence grumbled.

"Are we following Robert's Rules of Order?" Augustin asked, an innocent expression on his face.

William's eyes narrowed. "You know we are."

Augustin raised his hand like a schoolboy. "I ask to be recognized, then."

"Of course," Uncle Laurence said.

"Let's hear from the expert on art," Cousin Augustin said, his gaze on Noel.

"Let me conclude first," Carlton said quickly.

"You're not through yet?" Vic blurted out.

"I just wanted to point out that I did include the St. Denis art collection as an asset in my proposal." Carlton tapped his copy of the report.

"May I give information to the board?" Julie spoke up.

"Of course," Carlton said before anyone could object.

"I can name quite a few Fortune 500 corporations that list art in their asset reports. That's not really an issue." Julie's voice was neutral.

"Miss Rideau's appraisal confirms what I suspected." Noel nodded to Lyrissa. "The—"

"And I think we can leverage the value of the collection even more," Julie cut in with force.

Aunt Aline cast a cool glance at Lyrissa. Her expression softened when she looked at Julie. "You have something in mind, dear?"

Julie smiled tightly. "Yes, as a matter of fact. I even mentioned it to Noel a couple of weeks ago. I think you could display the art and sell limited edition prints, and even reproductions of some of the sculptures. Also, I've made some contacts with Sotheby's in New York. A few of the pieces could be auctioned for a considerable amount." Julie looked at Lyrissa as she talked.

Cousin Harold nodded his approval. "Which could increase income while we hold onto the art. Clever girl."

"I even have an idea to sell the reproductions on a major national shopping channel." Julie smiled in triumphant as she gazed at Lyrissa.

"I think we should hear Miss Rideau's report. She's a sharp cookie." Vic winked at Lyrissa.

"We can read it later," Julie snapped impatiently. "The point is, the collection is valuable."

Uncle Laurence nodded. "Not exactly news. Just needed a reliable dollar figure."

"There's more to Miss Rideau's report," Noel said. He had to work hard to keep irritation from his voice. "Could you give us a summary of your recommendations?"

Lyrissa cleared her throat. She looked at the yellow legal pad in front of her. "As Mr. Rohas has pointed out, there's no question that the collection is valuable. However, an accurate appraisal is essential. Of course, prices can go up at an auction."

Noel watched as she gave a concise summary of her findings and recommendations. She spoke with confidence and authority. He noticed every move she made, remembering the taste of her skin. Her words faded to a pleasant buzz. Or was it his libido turned way up?

"Finally, I talked to Professor Pat Smith, and—"

"I didn't know we'd paid for two experts," Julie interrupted. She glanced around at the board members.

"You didn't. Dr. Smith is my dissertation advisor and mentor. She has a national reputation for her expertise in African-American art preservation."

Vic clapped her hands excitedly. "Of course! She was the driving force behind that slave ship exhibition. Lyrissa can use university resources since she's a student. Brilliant, darlin'."

"I considered that when I asked Lyrissa to complete her report." Noel smiled at Vic and Lyrissa in turn. "And it's made all the difference." Noel gazed at her. She looked beautiful beneath the starched, buttoned-down veneer. Yet she did not return his glance.

"Thank you. In conclusion, I suggest an auction. Certain pieces may bring much higher bids alone."

Aline sniffed. "I'm still concerned about how this will look for the family."

"Some of the finest families in the country, even the world, have sold art they owned. Their reputations were even enhanced." Lyrissa looked around the room. "The pieces you have clearly show that your family not only had the money to acquire the best, but the good taste to choose well."

"She's right about that," Uncle Laurence said, and stuck out his chest.

"I say we compare all proposals," Cousin Harold put in.

"Agreed," Miss Georgina said before Carlton could speak.

When the others followed her lead, Carlton sat back with a resigned frown. Julie began a presentation on rental properties. Noel studied Lyrissa's face, hoping to find some clue to what she was thinking. She still stared down at her notes. He could tell she didn't really see them, though. There was something in her large brown eyes but he couldn't read it. Suddenly the meeting seemed to have dragged on longer than necessary.

"Noel, I think you have an update on the Insurance Commission?" Julie said.

Her tone sliced through to him like a butcher knife. Noel adjusted his shirt collar as the others looked at him. His aunt wore a frown. Richard gazed at him with one heavy eyebrow raised.

"Let's take a break. We've been in here for over two hours now," Noel pointed out.

"Bless you, child," Vic said passionately.

"I agree. My rear end is numb," Uncle Laurence said. "Fifteen minutes, folks. Let's come back in by eleven. Order lunch from Semolina's, Eddie."

Eddie nodded. "Yes, sir."

The young woman wrote furiously as Uncle Laurence and the others gave her their orders while they walked. Then, the board members once more clumped together in groups to drink coffee. Noel knew he should stay to get a feel for their mood. Yet the sight of Lyrissa leaving drove him through the door after her. She walked quickly in the direction of the elevators.

"Lyrissa, wait a minute," Noel called out.

She stopped but did not turn around immediately. When she did, her expression was impassive. "Yes?"

"I want to be with you tonight," he said simply.

"I'm busy. I don't think it's a good idea," Lyrissa replied promptly.

"Which is it and why?" Noel stared at her hard. He could feel a distance between them that had nothing to do with space.

Lyrissa took a deep breath and let it out. "Different galaxies," she whispered.

"This is the age of space travel." Noel took her by the elbow and drew her closer.

"We'll talk about it later."

Noel held on. "Tonight is as good a time as any."

"Don't make a scene. People are watching us." Lyrissa looked in all directions.

He let go and spoke in a normal tone. "Fine, then come to my office. We can discuss it in detail."

"Of course, Mr. St. Denis," she said in a crisp, businesslike voice.

They both turned to find his Aunt Aline, Carlton, Julie, and Augustin looking at them. Carlton wore an expression of curiosity. Aunt Aline clearly disapproved. Julie's eyes flashed lightning bolts of rage.

"This is certainly an interesting day." Augustin's black coffee eyes twinkled at them both.

Noel gazed back at them coolly. "I'll be back in five minutes." He led Lyrissa away.

14

"**W**ell!" Aunt Aline scraped Lyrissa with a head-to-toe examination.

"The meeting will start again soon, Noel," Julie said in a controlled tone. "We need you back in here now."

Noel kept walking. "I've got time. Excuse us."

Noel guided Lyrissa ahead of him with a hand firmly planted against her lower back. At that moment he did not care what they thought. Approval or disapproval from his relatives meant nothing. What worried him was the sound of "goodbye" in Lyrissa's voice. Once the door closed, Lyrissa spun around to confront him. She tossed her purse and portfolio down onto a nearby chair.

"Now you've done it!" she burst out.

Noel found her pouting lips irresistible. He leaned closer. "Done what?"

"You know what." Lyrissa pushed him away.

He shrugged and folded his arms. "Blame yourself. All you had to do was say you'd see me tonight."

Lyrissa frowned at him. "You're such an arrogant, spoiled brat. Used to having your way, aren't you?"

"So you don't want to be with me?" Noel cocked his head to one side.

Lyrissa waved her arms in the air. "That's not the point."

"That's the only point I'm interested in right now, Ms. Rideau," he teased. His expression turned serious. "Forget them."

"Right. I'll have one huge knife in my back before I leave here." Lyrissa eyed him steadily. "Julie is—"

"There is nothing between Julie and me."

"Not that I care." Lyrissa straightened her blouse.

"I'd be crazy with jealousy if I saw you with another man." Noel said the words so easily it stunned him.

"Think you know it all, don't you?" Lyrissa said in a small voice. She looked into his eyes like a woman under a spell.

"Maybe I do." He planted three small kisses on her forehead.

"And how do you plan to break this news flash?" Lyrissa breathed in short gasps.

"Straight and to the point."

Noel did not want to think about anyone else at the moment. He lost himself in the scent on her skin. Lyrissa met him more than halfway. She closed her eyes as he kissed her face again and again. They swayed to an internal rhythm only they felt. Lyrissa planted both her palms on his chest.

"You don't need the hassle right now. Your family is close to fighting another civil war."

Much as Noel hated to admit it, he knew she was right. He sighed deeply. "Okay, I'll give you that one."

Lyrissa backed up from him. "So we shouldn't see each other for a while."

"No way!" Noel said with force.

Lyrissa waved at him. "Keep your voice down."

"No games. If you don't want to be with me, then say so." He clenched both fists to fight off the pain.

"I didn't say that." She didn't meet his gaze.

He found hope in her cautious admission. She was holding back. It only made him want her more. Before he could speak, a firm knock sounded at the door. His assistant opened it slowly and peeked in with wide eyes.

Eddie glanced from him to Lyrissa. "Mr. Laurence says the meeting is about to resume."

"I'll be there in a few seconds," Noel replied without looking around.

"O-kay," the woman replied with an impish grin and withdrew quickly.

"You'd better go," Lyrissa said.

"I'll call you at home tonight."

Lyrissa paused for a moment before answering. "All right."

"You'll be there around eight?" Noel wanted to hear her say she'd wait for him, that there was no one else.

"Yes, I'll be there."

He exhaled. Only then did he realize he'd been holding his breath as he waited for her response. "Eight o'clock, don't forget." He kissed her as insurance.

"Go, before Julie sends in a swat team to rescue you from my clutches." Her eyes sparkled with humor.

Noel groaned with frustration. "I have to see you no matter what."

"We'll talk about it when you call," she said.

"Lyrissa—"

She picked up her briefcase and made a wide circle around him to the door. "Take care of business first."

Noel watched her walk away and enjoyed the sexy sway of her hips. He couldn't help but stare.

"Son, I sympathize. Lord knows I do," Richard said over his shoulder. "But we've got work ahead of us. Carlton and Willie have been scheming."

Noel took out his handkerchief and patted his face. "On my way."

"Can you focus?"

"Of course."

Noel talked to his father as they went down the hall. The men spoke in low confidential voices. As they entered the conference room, Richard made one last comment, then patted Noel's shoulder. They took their seats. The board members sat around the table again. Noel allowed Carlton to review where they'd left off. He felt energized. Lyrissa would be waiting for him at the end of the day. Not even Carlton could dampen his mood now. For another two hours the others squirmed and sighed. The rest of the meeting seemed to slip by with not one complaint from him.

"Maybe we should throw another dinner party." Richard pursed his lips in an obvious attempt to keep from laughing.

Mrs. St. Denis scowled. "Your sense of humor could use improvement."

"Really, Dad," Noel said. He squinted at his father. "And you didn't help one bit at the meeting."

"Let's not forget Augustin's contributions. And my daughter should have gotten more spankings as a child." Miss Georgina's scowl deepened.

Lyrissa tried to remain invisible. She'd been invited to give details on a possible auction. They were in the study at Mrs. St. Denis's home the day after the meeting. Richard sat with easy grace in a wingback chair. Mrs. St. Denis was on a chintz settee, while Noel sat behind the massive desk that dominated the room.

She gazed at each of them in turn. Noel had his father's handsome profile. There were differences, though. Richard seemed always ready to toss out a joke. He wore a smile that was charming at first glance but seemed fake upon closer examination. Noel had a resolute set to his jaw that reminded Lyrissa of a portrait of his grandfather. It was strange to see two generations so much alike, yet so different. Noel's expression was grave. The board meeting had been inconclusive.

"I tried my best to explain why we need to act." Noel tapped a Cartier pen.

His grandmother rubbed her temples with the tips of her fingers. "Please don't do that. My nerves are on edge as it is."

Noel put down the pen. "We need to raise capital. I looked at the latest income statement."

"Things are not getting better, I guess," Richard said.

"How bad is it?" Mrs. St. Denis looked at Noel.

"We could be in trouble with the insurance commission. Our reserves are low." Noel shook his head and sighed.

"A quick infusion of cash would be just the ticket," Richard said softly and looked at Lyrissa.

"You mean, a quick art sale," she said. Her heart sank. Thank God they didn't know about "The Stroll." Not yet, at least.

"Yes, dear," Mrs. St. Denis said with a nod. "Noel?"

"Would it be enough though?" Noel glanced at Lyrissa.

"You have two small paintings by Degas and a Henry Osawa Tanner, three Elizabeth Catlett sculptures, and a Clementine Hunter. An auction could easily bring close to a million dollars. The Degas paintings aren't from the best period in his career but are still valuable." Lyrissa wore a blank expression to mask her disapproval.

"Tidy change," Richard quipped with a grin.

"Certainly. Now the only problem is to pry them out of our loving kinfolk's hands." Mrs. St. Denis rubbed her temples again.

"Who has them?" Richard asked.

Lyrissa spoke even before Noel could finish flipping through her report to find the list. "Helene Auguillard Rohas owns—"

"No, she does not! None of them *owns* any of the pieces!" Mrs. St. Denis broke in angrily. "The collection is in my control."

"Excuse me, she has *possession* of the Tanner," Lyrissa replied.

"Jordan and Roberta have the Degas paintings," Noel said. "We'll need dynamite to blast it free from Jordan's greedy grip."

"Roberta chose poorly in marriage, for the *third time*," Mrs. St. Denis said in an acid tone.

Richard turned to Lyrissa and spoke in a confidential

voice. "Roberta is my second cousin's youngest. She married a self-made man who bought his way into certain circles."

"Except for the right ones?" Lyrissa gazed at him.

"Money can't buy everything, darlin'. We're civilized, of course. Always polite, but . . ." Richard let a careless shrug finish his sentence.

His words rang in her ears. Where did that leave her? She didn't have money or the right last name. Noel met her gaze when she looked across at him.

"It has nothing to do with his family tree. He's rude and likes to step on people," Noel said, as though reading her mind.

"And those are his good points," Mrs. St. Denis put in. "They're not the only ones we have to worry about."

Richard's good-humored playboy expression vanished. "Let's stop playing around with them. It's common knowledge we own those paintings. Kick ass and take them."

"You sound like your father for once," his mother said.

"I have my moments." Richard grinned back. "But I'm serious. No sense pretending we can avoid bad feelings."

"You're right. Noel, I know you want to approach this differently, but I don't see how we can," Mrs. St. Denis said.

"Not after Carlton's little behind-the-scenes campaign," Richard added. "But Willie probably did most of the talking. Hell, nobody pays half attention to Carlton."

"The last thing we need is our own family feud," Noel said.

Richard shrugged again. "It's been festering for years. It was bound to burst sometime."

They went on to discuss the best strategy. Lyrissa tuned

out their voices and became wrapped up in her own planning. The family fight that loomed would be to her advantage. All their attention would be on the two paintings in question. Which meant she could bide her time for the moment.

Miss Georgina rose. "Thank you, Ms. Rideau. You've been such a help in all this. I'm going to have coffee. Anyone else?"

"Yes." Richard stood.

"None for me," Noel said.

"Me either. Thanks." Lyrissa smiled politely.

Mrs. St. Denis headed down the hall. "Rosalie, I hope you have some of that strong coffee freshly made. I'm going to need it."

Richard hung back. He stared at Lyrissa. "I have a feeling we'll get to know you and your family."

"What are you talking about?" Noel asked.

"I'm an old hand at reading people, especially when it comes to romance. I've made it something of a hobby."

"More like a full-time occupation," Noel said.

"The fact is—" Richard raised a forefinger.

"Don't form opinions out of thin air, Mr. St. Denis," Lyrissa cut him off sharply.

"I apologize, Miss Rideau. My mouth moved faster than my good sense again." He made a courtly bow and left with one last glance at Noel.

Lyrissa hid the fear that clutched at her heart. Her mind spun wildly as she thought of how to deal with this latest threat. She couldn't afford to have them digging into her life just yet. Then there was Noel. Lyrissa had become her own worst enemy. Mama Grace and Aunt Claire looked forward to a moment of triumph. Their idea of a happy ending would be her tragedy. She'd fallen in love with Mr. Wrong.

"He wasn't being mean, Lyrissa. You just have to get to know Dad." Noel reached out for her.

Lyrissa nimbly moved away as though she hadn't seen his hand. "Not here."

"Fine. Come to my apartment tonight," he said.

The enticing scent of Aramis cologne made her light-headed with desire. Her breast ached at the memory of how he'd teased her nipples with his tongue. She clenched her fists to fight off the fire it started. Noel seemed to sense her vulnerability. Lyrissa backed farther away to avoid the temptation of his full lips coming closer to hers.

"I'd better go. I have a meeting with my advisor. Goodbye."

"I'll call you," he said.

Lyrissa waved as she walked quickly through the double doors and to safety. If she looked into his eyes again her act would crumble.

The next day, Lyrissa sat in her office at the gallery. She tried to concentrate on work, but the memory of her phone conversation with Noel made it tough. The sound of his sultry voice kept coming back to her. Mr. Taylor walked toward her studying a glossy catalogue. He glanced at her briefly before looking down at the pictures again.

"Mrs. St. Denis called," Mr. Taylor said. "She's anxious for us to finish."

Lyrissa frowned. "Really?"

"I assured her that you were being very thorough and would take good care of the famous collection as though each piece were your own."

Lyrissa laughed nervously. "How right you are."

Mr. Taylor sat down and crossed one long leg over another. "You know, she seemed particularly uptight."

Lyrissa's heart thumped hard. "Did she say anything?"

"Well, we talked about how you were searching the family history. I explained the importance of establishing a provenance." Mr. Taylor's eyes lit up. "Maybe there are some nasty family secrets you're close to uncovering."

"Nothing that exciting, I'm afraid."

Lyrissa's mind whirled, wondering if the wily old lady was on to her. Surely Noel's behavior might make her want to investigate Lyrissa. Julie would certainly encourage such a move. Time was running out.

A flutter of guilt unsettled her stomach. Lyrissa could only imagine Noel's reaction when the truth came out. Once, she'd looked forward to that day. The anticipated thrill of victory was definitely gone. Still, she had to go through with it. "The Stroll" belonged to her family. She thought of the pain passed down through generations. Even more, she thought of two proud, resourceful Joubert descendants. Mama Grace and Aunt Claire had done so much for Lyrissa all her life.

"Too bad. A spicy scandal would add to the value of the collection and give us publicity. You can't pay for that kind of advertising." Mr. Taylor grinned at her as he stood. "Keep digging, dear."

"I will." She watched him leave. "Believe me, I will." She had to go on. Yet the mental image of Noel smiling at her with trust and affection haunted her for the rest of the day.

15

"I hope this is important, Julie," Carlton snapped. "I've got a desk piled high with work." He walked ahead of her into his office. Contrary to his claim, the expensive walnut desk appeared very neat.

She glanced at the modest stack of files but did not comment. "I hired a private investigator to look into Lyrissa Rideau's background."

"You're obsessed with this woman," Carlton said with a slight smile of amused contempt. "Overkill, if you ask me. All because Noel has the hots for her."

Julie ignored the dig. "Here's his report."

Carlton sat down without looking at the folder in her hand.

"Parents died when she was young, raised by grand-mother and great-aunt, did well in school, the usual." Julie sat down in the leather chair facing his desk.

"Why should I be interested?" Carlton threw her an impatient glance, then went back to the file.

"Because the board listened to her advice about the collection, and Lord knows what else."

His head snapped up. "What does that mean?"

"Miss Georgina doesn't like it, but she has to rely on Lyrissa's input. Noel is more interested in her below the neck. Men are so stupid," she added with force.

Carlton rocked back in his chair. "Big surprise. Noel and Lyrissa are lovers."

Julie cringed at his terse statement. "She's a novelty. He'll dump her like the rest."

"Maybe."

"What are you talking about?" Julie snapped.

Carlton smiled. "Office gossip says Noel spent a lot of time in that office with her when she was working here."

"Like I said, he'll get tired of her soon."

"And you'll be right there when he does."

"Noel will come back to his roots," Julie replied.

"Great. You and Noel will stroll hand in hand one day. Anything else?" Carlton went back to reading the contents of a file on his desk.

"This investigation of Lyrissa Rideau skims the surface." Julie tapped the bound report on her knee as she spoke.

"Maybe that's all there is. She's just another pretty face trying to catch a rich husband."

"A pretty face with a master's degree in art history, working on her Ph.D." Julie pursed her lips.

Carlton wore a half-smile. "Not that it bothers you."

"I have my MBA," Julie snapped.

"But Noel isn't gazing at you over a glass of wine."

"Don't be so smug, Carlton," Julie shot back.

"Face it, babe. Noel is not going to buy you that three-carat engagement ring you want so badly. He's screwing both of us the way I see it."

Julie threw the report down onto his desk. "What are we going to do about it, then?"

"*We?*" Carlton let out a short laugh. "*I* plan to run this company one day."

"From a jail cell?"

Carlton blinked as though she'd slapped him. "What the hell are you talking about?"

"Noel is arranging an audit," she replied.

"Yes, a management consulting team will look into the way we run the business."

"And a financial audit." Julie nodded as his eyes widened.

"B-But the audit isn't due for seven months. He can't do that."

"He's the boss. You should have been paying attention," Julie added with a nasty smile.

"Damn it." Carlton rubbed his face hard.

"Look, we both want payback. I can help save your butt. Let's help each other." Julie sat forward.

Carlton took his hand down and cleared his throat. "I don't know what you mean."

"Don't waste time. I have a pretty good idea what you've been up to, but I'll need details." Julie's hazel eyes narrowed to slits. "Trust me or you'll go down."

"Why should I? You might end up with everything and leave me out in the cold." Carlton stared back at her.

"The board would never let me run this company, you know that. I'll help you get control, and you'll make me VP of operations," Julie said with confidence.

"And you'll get back at Noel. It's a thin line between love and hate, huh?"

She stood and looked down at him. "You want my help or not?"

"I don't have much choice. But don't fool yourself that I trust you," he said.

Julie's thin lips curled. "The feeling is mutual."

Lyrissa watched Noel out of the corner of her eye. He'd handled himself well. Of course he'd been schooled in the social graces like any well-bred Creole heir. Still, his reaction to her artsy friends had been admirably restrained. Especially considering the outfit her friend Izzy was wearing that afternoon. Isabel Canton breezed around the Beaux Arts Gallery in a diaphanous outfit of lime green, purple, pink, and royal blue. She wore hot pink tights beneath the long, flowing tunic. Izzy was the owner of the gallery. Noel had been pleased when Lyrissa had invited him to the opening of her latest exhibit.

"Lyrissa, babe!" Izzy threw out her arms and came at them like a runaway Mardi Gras float. "I'm thrilled you could come. And even more thrilled at what you brought," she said, eyeing Noel.

"Save me," Noel mumbled.

Lyrissa stifled a giggle. "Noel St. Denis, this is our hostess and longtime patroness of the arts Isabel Canton."

"Not that long a time. She makes me sound so old," Izzy purred at him.

Noel put an arm around Lyrissa's waist. "Nice to meet you."

Izzy put a hand on his free arm and squeezed it. "You

run Tremé Corporation. Solid muscles, for a man who sits at a desk most of the day."

Noel wore a gracious smile. "Thank you. Your show seems to be going over well." He skillfully extricated his arm from her grasp by putting Lyrissa between them.

If she was put out, Izzy didn't show it. Instead she continued to leer at him. "Yes, everything looks so good."

"Behave, Izzy. He's talking about the art," Lyrissa said firmly. She leaned against Noel.

"How selfish, Lyrissa." Izzy pouted at her, then her face cleared into a smile. "But I can't really blame you."

"Izzy, you're too much." Lyrissa laughed.

"Well, sugar, I'd better circulate. Helps the sales if I give the minglers lots of attention. Goodbye, Noel." She made a kissing noise at him and left.

"Whew! That was close." Noel shook his head as he watched her leave.

"Oh, please. With those strong arms I'm sure you could have gotten away from her." Lyrissa looked at Izzy. "Of course, she does know Tae Kwon Do."

"Very funny. Just don't ever leave me alone with her." Noel put his arm through hers as they walked around looking at paintings. "But she did give me an idea."

"Leave me out of that scene, honey." Lyrissa giggled at the scowl that brought.

"I meant about our collection. We could have a show like this." Noel nodded around the room.

"A show?"

"Yes. We have an old house nearby that's just been renovated. I'd like to show it to you. My property manager, Keisha, could be here in ten minutes."

Lyrissa's throat went dry. "I thought you hadn't decided to sell any of the art in your collection."

"I didn't say we'd *sell* anything, but we could at least generate interest." Noel took out his cell phone and hit a button. "We can go have coffee while we wait for Keisha."

"I think you're trying to run away from Izzy," Lyrissa joked with a grin. Still she tried to think of a way to head off this new idea.

"I think you're right," he said. "Hello, Kee. Listen . . ."

They were walking down Magazine and turning a corner onto Antoine Street ten minutes later. They sat outside a small coffee shop sipping café au lait and waited for his property manager. The weather was beautiful as they watched the Thursday afternoon traffic. Noel told funny stories about his family until Lyrissa was nearly in tears.

Lyrissa shook her head. "You're making this stuff up."

"You've met a few of them, right?"

"Oh, Lord, yes!"

"Then you know I don't have to make up wild stories." He grinned at her. "You see we're not all that bad."

"Solve a mystery for me." Lyrissa grew serious.

"I'll try." Noel took a sip from the dark brown mug.

"How can your family still think skin color matters? I mean, we've gone through decades of civil rights and the whole Black is Beautiful movement." Lyrissa expected him to become defensive. Instead, he looked thoughtful for a time.

"It's not simple to explain. The whole attitude about skin color got mixed up with snobbery about heritage and class. Skin color became a symbol of being descended from wealthy French or Spanish ruling class families."

"Maybe so, but it's still destructive. Racism mixed with classism is just another way we're divided."

"I agree. But it's not as bad as it used to be," Noel replied.

"Bad enough," she retorted.

"But better," he insisted. "And don't think I'm naïve."

Lyrissa smiled at him. "I can't imagine you being naïve about anything."

"Now you solve a mystery for me," he said. "What do women want?"

Her smile widened. "Sorry, I'm sworn to secrecy on that one."

"Come on, I answered your question. I'm serious." Noel playfully nudged her arm.

She shook her head. "There are as many answers to your question as there are women on this earth."

"Okay, I'll make it easier. What do *you* want?"

"I want to be a curator at a small museum. Then one day I'll open my own gallery."

"What about your personal life? Marriage, kids, a Lexus SUV?" Noel's easy smile didn't conceal his keen interest in her answer.

"I'm concentrating on the professional part right now. I can't see past getting this dissertation finished. Grad school is a killer." She neatly sidestepped his question.

"But you want security and a good lifestyle, or else you wouldn't be so ambitious."

"Don't we all?" Lyrissa studied his expression.

"Some women will do anything to get it, though. Men are like prizes, objects to be used." Noel's brow furrowed.

"Sounds like you're testifying based on personal experience."

"I've had my close calls," he said quietly. "But I don't want a model wife who looks good in the family portrait. I want something real."

"I see." Lyrissa looked away from his intense gaze. "Not like your parents, I suppose. Sorry—I shouldn't have said that."

"No, it's okay. They're the poster couple for how not to run a marriage." Noel sighed.

"Bet that was no fun for you, either."

"I learned to duck when the dishes started flying," he quipped. "It took me a long time to figure out marriages could be happy."

"So you know loving marriage isn't an oxymoron." Lyrissa laughed.

"Yeah, I'm learning something new all the time."

He put an arm around her chair. His smile softened into a lovely invitation. Lyrissa accepted it and leaned close until their lips touched. She closed her eyes. His light kiss felt like honey flowing into her body. When they broke apart, both were breathing heavily.

"Now what?" she murmured.

A young woman the color of cinnamon approached before he could answer. "Sorry, it took me a while to get here. Busy day, and it's not over yet! Hi." She smiled at Lyrissa.

Lyrissa smiled back. "Hi."

"Keisha Collins, this is Lyrissa Rideau. Sit down and take a deep breath. I'll get you a latte." Noel patted her arm.

"I wish, boss. I've got an appointment to meet a client in twenty minutes. He's interested in the Basin Street building. Here you go, the keys and the code card. I wrote down the number." Keisha handed him an envelope.

"Thanks, Kee." He took it from her.

"No prob. Gotta get moving. Nice meeting you, Lyrissa." She waved and strode to a black Acura Legend parked across the street.

"Let's go take a look," Noel said.

They walked back to Magazine Street. The day was still bright, even though it was early evening. Several joggers sped past them. Lyrissa admired several restored homes as they strolled the three blocks. Noel stopped in front of a three-story house painted pale yellow with white trim. A white wooden fence surrounded it and stone steps led up to a wide porch.

"Here we are. Built in 1843, it was the home of Thomas Chaisson. Tommy, as he was affectionately known by his friends, made his fortune in real estate."

"Very interesting. A relative?" Lyrissa added.

"His sister married into the family. Tommy never married." Noel led her up the steps and unlocked the door. A soft beeping sounded until he slid the code card in and punched in the number.

Lyrissa walked ahead of him as he locked the door behind them. She headed into what must have been the formal parlor. It faced the street. Floor-to-ceiling windows gave an excellent view of the neighborhood.

Noel joined her. "It still needs some work."

She turned in a circle. The fireplace had a mantel made of ivory Italian marble. "The atmosphere is a perfect backdrop for the collection, even the more modern pieces."

"Let's take a look upstairs." He took her hand and led the way.

"This is beautiful wood. What is it?" Lyrissa ran her fingers along the smooth surface.

"Rosewood. We had to strip several layers of varnish from it. This wallpaper is original, too." He pointed to the textured creamy walls.

They reached the second floor. A large center room had a lovely medallion set in the ceiling. Lyrissa studied the detailed carving with great interest. A few pieces of period furniture were scattered around. "This must have been a drawing room."

"This was the master bedroom," Noel said close to her ear.

She could feel his breath on her cheek. He pulled her into his arms. His hands trailed down her sides to her hips, and then he kissed her neck.

Lyrissa sighed when he pressed against her. He cupped a breast with one hand and ran the other up her skirt. She should have protested, but instead she sighed again. He guided her to an antique lounge chair.

"You feel so good, Lyrissa," he whispered.

She sank onto the chair with him. In seconds she'd kicked off her leather pumps and pantyhose. Noel unzipped his pants. He moaned when she reached inside the fly. Lyrissa kissed his face as her fingers gently massaged him until he was rock hard. His fingers rubbed her mound until she was senseless.

"We can't. We don't have a condom."

Noel opened her blouse and the front hook of her bra. "I have one," he whispered and sucked her nipple hard.

"You came prepared?"

"Since the first kiss I've been prepared."

Lyrissa tried to feel incensed. Instead, she only felt white hot with hunger. She arched against him as his tongue circled her tender peak. He moaned deep in his throat. Music played in the distance, soft chiming notes that soothed her. The notes chimed again insistently and she froze.

"The doorbell!" she said. "Someone's at the front door."

"They'll go away," he mumbled without taking his mouth from her breast.

She let go of him and tried to sit up. "It might be Keisha."

Noel ignored the racket. "Somebody at the wrong house."

"Then why do they keep knocking? We'd better see who it is." Lyrissa pulled her skirt down.

"Damn it. I'll get rid of the idiot." Noel quickly re-arranged his clothes with angry, jerky movements. "Don't move."

Lyrissa scrambled into her pantyhose and shoes. After checking her hair in a mirror, she went to the landing. Noel looked back at her and licked his lips. A series of hard knocks rattled the wooden door. He growled and went down the stairs. Moments later she heard the door open.

"What are you doing here?" Noel said.

16

Julie stared at him through her designer sunglasses. "Keisha mentioned you wanted the keys to this house. I thought maybe you were showing it to a prospective tenant. You might need my help, since I know a lot about the property." She peered around him into the house.

"I don't need help," Noel said in a short tone. "Thanks anyway."

"I see." Julie took off the sunglasses and stared over his shoulder. "Hello, Ms. Rideau."

Lyrissa cleared her throat. "Hi."

"What's going on?" Julie stared at Noel.

"We're planning a show of the collection," Lyrissa said. She tugged at her skirt, then stopped when Julie looked at her.

"I stored the old furniture and worked with Keisha on instructions to the man who restored the house."

Julie tried to walk past Noel into the foyer.

He shifted to block her entrance. "We really haven't gotten very far yet, Julie. I'll let you know when we do."

"Can I speak to you privately?" Julie asked in a taut voice.

"I'll just have a look around the rest of the house," Lyrissa said. She went down the hall and gently pulled a door closed. She could hear their muffled voices.

Minutes later she heard the staccato sound of high heels across the wooden floor of the porch. Noel opened the door.

"She's gone," he said, his expression grim.

"We should leave, too."

"We didn't finish our . . . talk. Let's see more of the house." Noel crossed the space between them in two long strides.

"Maybe her arrival was a sign we shouldn't finish." Lyrissa blushed at the way he gazed at her body.

"Bull." He nuzzled her neck.

Lyrissa moved away fast, afraid she'd give in. "We'd better go, or we'll set off the fire alarm," she teased.

"Then come to my apartment tonight." Noel held her hand. "I'll cook us dinner."

"We'll see. I—"

"*No excuses.*" Noel jerked her into his arms. "Please, baby." He sealed her fate by licking her bottom lip with the tip of his tongue.

"Okay," she whispered.

"There has to be something else!" Julie burst out in exasperation. The report landed on her desk with a thump when she threw it down.

The mild-mannered private investigator shrugged.

"Sorry, it's the usual stuff. Her parents had problems with too much partying and drinking. You can't blame her for that. The mother died when she was three, the father when she turned seven."

Julie glared at him but said nothing. They were in her office. Everyone except Carlton had gone home. The usually busy offices of Tremé Corporation were quiet for a change. Silence stretched between them, broken only by an occasional phone ringing in the background. The man gazed back at her with an impassive expression.

"Mr. Hausey, I was told Crescent City Investigations was the best."

He nodded. "You were told right."

"Then why is this damn report—" Julie took a deep breath and let it out. She seemed to call up her charm school lessons. "Sorry. There doesn't seem to be a lot here, Mr. Hausey."

"You paid for a background check. Then you asked us to expand our research to her family tree. We don't guarantee we'll find compromising information you can use."

"But—"

"Ms. Duval, you weren't specific about what we should look for," Mr. Hausey broke in.

"Yes, yes. I know." Julie rapped a fist on the arm of her chair.

"We did the usual criminal background check, credit history, and work history, and even poked into her old school records. You have the names of her great-great-grandparents and a little information on them," he went on in a cold, logical voice.

Julie didn't want logic. This was emotional and personal for her. She rocked forward in her chair. "Great. Maybe her nana was a kleptomaniac. How does that help me?"

Mr. Hausey stood and buttoned the jacket of his suit. "I suggest you read the report thoroughly, Miss Duval. You just might find something useful."

Her upper-class good manners slipped again. "Like you care. You've been paid," she muttered low.

"My report is very comprehensive. But if you get a lead on a particular avenue, call me." Mr. Hausey spoke like a man used to dealing with unreasonable clients.

"Goodbye," Julie said with a sour expression.

"Have a nice evening," Mr. Hausey replied without a trace of sarcasm and left.

"Here's your nice evening." Julie made a rude gesture as the door clicked shut.

Almost immediately Carlton stuck his head in. "Sorry I got tied up on the phone. What did he say?"

"He said to read his useless report," Julie barked out. She flipped the pages with a muttered profanity.

Carlton strolled over to stand at her shoulder. He read a few lines, then sat down on the edge of her desk. "Told you so. Money wasted."

"You wait until I see Giselle! Best in the business, my ass!" Julie slapped another page flat.

"GiGi Babin, huh? She gutted her ex-husband like he was a fish."

"Which is why I trusted her recommendation," Julie exclaimed.

"GiGi doesn't have the brains of a cucumber. Her father got the goods on poor Brandon." Carlton shook his head in sympathy.

"Crescent City Investigations did the digging. But I got nothing, *nothing*." She yanked another page open.

"Too bad. Now I'll have to keep pretending to respect Noel's opinions. At least for a while longer." Carlton made a face at the prospect.

"You mean until Miss Georgina is . . . out of the way."

"Of course not," he said quickly. "I meant until everyone sees I'm right. I'll be in control once he falls on his face."

"He won't. Noel is an astute businessman." Julie grimaced.

"Why does everyone heap praise on him?" Carlton complained with a morose frown.

"Noel could build his own company from the ground up the same way his grandparents made Tremé so profitable." Julie clenched her hands. "That Rideau woman has interfered with his work."

"He's not complaining, and I can see why," Carlton added quietly with a wistful sigh.

Julie didn't hear his comment. She was too intent on the puzzle of Noel's attraction to Lyrissa. Her eyes narrowed to slits. "She's so obvious. I can't believe he doesn't see through her."

Carlton pointed to the open report. "Well, if you didn't get ammunition from that, I guess you're out of options."

"Damn it! Totally useless piece of sh—" Julie froze in the act of tossing it aside. "Wait a minute."

"What? Did she get a parking ticket?" Carlton chuckled.

"There's something here that rings a bell." Julie waved him to silence with one hand. She continued to read as he ignored her signal.

"You've lost perspective on this thing, Julie. Too much emotion wrapped up in the outcome," Carlton said. "Typically female."

Julie looked up at him. Her eyes glittered with triumph. "Is that right? Well, this typical female just might be on to something that you typical males missed!"

"I hope you know what you're doing, girlfriend." Ebony crossed her arms and stared hard at Lyrissa. They were in her apartment for a night of watching old movies.

"Listen, I couldn't stop the art show. Besides, Julie is prowling around like an alleycat. At least this way I can keep an eye on things."

"What if an art expert sees your painting and blurts out how much it's worth?" Ebony plopped down on her sofa.

"Most experts have to be familiar with an artist's work to fix a value. None would toss out a figure at first glance. Besides, not many specialize in eighteenth century New Orleans Creole paintings."

Ebony munched on a cheese curl while she mulled over Lyrissa's argument. "Okay, so now you have your family's old letters, journals from Noel's archives, and letters you found at the Louisiana State Museum."

Lyrissa pointed a forefinger in the air. "Exactly. They even went to court. Now if I can find the trial minutes from 1822 when Gustave's son was sued by Jules's widow, we'll have it made."

"Leave well enough alone, girl. Make your getaway." Ebony wore a worried expression.

"I was nervous about it, too. But the show gives me an excuse to hang around, Ebony. I'm almost through with the appraisal. I need more time."

"I was talking about this thing with you and Noel, Lyrissa. Have you gone out with him again?" Ebony squinted at her.

"We had to talk about the show." Lyrissa avoided looking at her.

Ebony shook her head. "Girl, you're in deep trouble."

"Don't jump to conclusions." Lyrissa chewed hard on a corn chip.

"I know you." Ebony pointed a cheese curl at her. "Are you going to tell him about the painting?"

"No way! I know what would happen."

"So you're falling for him, but you don't trust him. Trouble, girl, *big* trouble. You're in the fast lane on the highway to heartbreak." Ebony shook her head again.

"I didn't say Noel would do something sneaky," Lyrissa said defensively. "His family might, though."

"Right. He's a genetic anomaly, nothing like his long line of cutthroat relatives." Ebony wore a skeptical frown. "And I haven't mentioned his rep with women."

"He's not like that." Lyrissa pounded a throw pillow. "Noel is very active in raising funds for charity. He puts in long hours at the company and still finds time to help the community."

"I'll give him a good citizen certificate *after* we get the painting back," Ebony said dryly.

"Cynical lawyer," Lyrissa retorted.

"So you're going to see him?" Ebony stared at her.

"Like I said—"

"You have to finish the appraisal and work on the exhibit," Ebony finished for her. "Yeah, right. And y'all have to work at his apartment."

"Oh, hell!" Lyrissa gave up trying to fool her best friend. "Why does he have to be so . . ."

"Fine, sexy, and a boy scout, too?" Ebony finished.

"I tried to stay out of his way, I really did."

"He's hot for you, too. If he's a good guy, then he'll do the right thing."

Lyrissa punched the pillow harder. "It's not just up to him. Besides, I'm not so sure he's that good. You know how they are."

"Right, close ranks and protect what's theirs. But you said he's different."

"I can't afford to risk everything on what I feel. I'm not thinking too clearly about him these days," Lyrissa confessed.

"Yeah, I can see that." Ebony shrugged when Lyrissa glared at her. "Hey, you said it first."

" 'The Stroll' means more to our family than money. I have to deal with him." Lyrissa moaned at the thought of giving up his kisses.

"Yeah, but can you deal with *you?*" Ebony said.

"I'll be okay. Let's watch a movie." Lyrissa jumped up and went to the VCR. "Something with lots of action. I'm definitely not in the mood for a love story. That stuff is too far from real life."

Lyrissa shifted in the chair behind her desk. The day had dragged on and on. Mr. Taylor scurried around between projects, but managed to drive her crazy in between. At least work kept her mind off Noel most of the time.

Mr. Taylor dashed into her office. "I'm going insane. I can't find the insurance file on the sculptures from Hobart's Fine Art." He raked his gray hair with one hand.

"Here, you gave it to me this morning. Everything is in order. The coverage is for $250,000." Lyrissa handed him the folder.

"Thank God!" Mr. Taylor clutched it to his chest. "I

don't know why I'm stressing myself out. Things are going well for us these days."

"Yeah, just dandy," Lyrissa muttered.

"What's with the gloomy face?" he asked.

"Nothing much. My stupid car is in the shop again, and look at this!" Lyrissa held up a wad of pink phone message slips.

"Uncle Shelton can help," he said in a sympathetic voice. "I'll return these calls. Hmm, all from Darlene Bracotta."

"The woman can't make up her mind," Lyrissa said with disgust.

"Don't worry about it, dear. I'll handle her." Mr. Taylor patted her arm paternally.

"Thanks." Lyrissa's expression didn't lighten.

"Are you sure there isn't something else?" Mr. Taylor sat on the edge of her desk.

Lyrissa sighed and shook her head. "I'm okay, just having one of those days."

"I'm only a few feet away if you need me." He beamed at her and left.

Lyrissa tried to concentrate on the invoices, but the numbers danced around like jumping beans. More than once she stared off into space. Her mind kept wandering back to Noel. Maybe she should tell him about the painting. He might understand. Then she thought about the St. Denis family.

"Yeah, right. And pigs might fly around the Garden District, too," she muttered to herself.

"Hi."

Lyrissa looked up to find Noel smiling at her. The familiar shiver went down her spine at the sight of him. He wore a charcoal gray suit with a light blue shirt.

"Hi. What are you doing here?"

He came in and closed the door. "You backed out on me last night and I want to know why."

"I thought it was best. I really was busy anyway." Lyrissa avoided his gaze.

"I was on my way to the office after a meeting when something bizarre happened." His expression was serious.

"Really?"

He nodded. "My car turned down this street and parked outside the gallery. I can't explain it."

"That *is* strange. You should get that car checked out."

"Nah, the car is just fine. It brought me where I needed to be." Noel sat down.

"I've decided to keep our relationship strictly business." Lyrissa lifted her chin when she looked at him.

"Because of your professional reputation," he said.

"Yes." Lyrissa turned away from his gorgeous brown eyes.

"Is this a game?" he snapped.

"We shouldn't have gotten carried away."

"More than once," he put in.

"Whatever. I realized what a mistake we were making. That's all."

Noel leaned forward. "I wouldn't call the way we touched a mistake."

Lyrissa gazed at him. The strong jaw and beautiful lines of his face hypnotized her. Noel St. Denis inspired lustful fantasies with just the lift of one dark eyebrow.

"The invitation is still open. I cook one mean pasta dinner," Noel said.

"I can't. Really." Lyrissa tried to ignore the way her body craved him. If he'd just leave, she might get through the day.

"We have to finish planning the show, Lyrissa." Noel frowned at her. "Your professional reputation is at stake, remember?"

"I'll iron out the details with Keisha." She stood her ground.

"No, you'll deal with the boss."

"Business only," Lyrissa said firmly. She was surprised when he smiled at her.

He held out a large hand. "Goodbye, Lyrissa."

She had no choice but to take it. Lyrissa braced herself for the reaction. Still she tingled when his warm flesh met hers. "Goodbye," she said.

Noel started to walk out, then turned to face her again. "I have a feeling we'll talk again."

"You don't give up."

"Like you said, I'm used to having my way." He left.

Lyrissa had to admit his confidence aroused her. "Lord have mercy," she said in a shaky voice.

17

Noel rocked in his chair and tapped the tip of his pen on the tabletop. Carlton, Julie, and two other employees sat around the table in the small conference room adjacent to his office. They gave their usual mid-week reports, a practice Noel had started when he became CEO. Andre's voice was only background buzz to Noel's thoughts.

Once again he wondered where Lyrissa was at this moment and what she was doing. For the past three days he'd thought about her at odd moments, suddenly daydreaming while stuck in traffic or sitting in his office. Lyrissa Rideau had accomplished a feat no other woman had before—she'd become a distraction. Noel's reaction swung between excitement, irritation at himself, and anxiety that he was not in control.

"So that's it. The micro-mall on Crowder Boulevard is

now at fifty-percent occupancy. We really need to renovate to attract new tenants," Andre said.

"Renovation might be an option. What do you think, Noel?" Julie asked. *"Noel,"* she repeated louder when he didn't answer.

He glanced around them with a slight frown. "What?"

Carlton lifted an eyebrow at him. "We've been talking about the mall on Crowder for the last fifteen minutes."

Noel smoothed down his silk tie. "I know that," he replied shortly and stopped rocking his chair. "Thanks for the report, Andre."

"And the renovations?" Carlton pursed his lips.

"Renovations?" Noel blinked at him.

"Yes, we were discussing the possibility of attracting new tenants. Obviously your mind is elsewhere," Julie said in a tense voice.

"Andre mentioned it to me two weeks ago. Excellent idea." Noel nodded at the young man. "In fact I've already talked to several contractors about bids."

"I say we sell. The whole area has gone down. Stats show that the upwardly mobile are moving to Chalmette and Mandeville. Let's follow the money," Carlton said.

"We should help revitalize these neighborhoods. The people who can't move need drugstores, grocery stores, and dress shops, too." Noel looked at his cousin.

"That property isn't profitable and won't be for years," Carlton replied. "What we need is to increase income, remember?"

"We will in other ways," Noel said evenly.

"A sale would bring a substantial infusion of money to help cash flow," Carlton persisted.

"We're working to create an enterprise zone," Noel

said. "In the short term we won't make as much money. In the long term the tax breaks combined with a vibrant community-based economy will be very profitable."

"Most enterprise zones don't. Besides, we're a business, not a charity. I'm talking about the bottom line."

Noel decided he'd been patient long enough. "So am I, Carlton. As for the mall, the board agrees with me." He stood to signal the meeting was over. "Andre, Eddie has a list of small business owners you can contact."

"Yes, sir," Andre said.

"Schedule appointments within the next two weeks. Mention the renovations, too." Noel glanced at Carlton's tight expression.

"Got it." Andre made notes then left.

Carlton didn't stand or follow him out. Instead he stared at Noel. "You couldn't at least pretend to respect my opinion in front of the employees?" he barked.

"I'm tired of listening to you say the same thing in every meeting. Same song, tenth verse," Noel said tersely.

"You mean I don't agree with everything the brilliant Noel says," Carlton shot back.

"This train is pulling out of the station. Ride or get off!" Noel wore a fierce expression.

"Oh, no. I'm not going anywhere. I'll be here right until the day they realize you can't deliver," Carlton said coldly. He shoved back his chair, stood, and strode out.

"If he spent as much energy doing his job, we'd all be richer," Noel retorted.

"Maybe you should be nicer to him," Julie said. "Carlton might cause you real trouble one day."

Noel waved a hand. "He'll try to hurt me, but not the business. I'm not worried about him."

"People will do anything if they're pushed into a corner." Julie gazed at him.

"Are we talking about Carlton, Julie?" Noel studied her until she looked away.

"Of course." She gathered up her copies of the reports and a legal pad. "I'm just saying you shouldn't forget that family and friends are important, too."

"Right. I'll try to remember that." Noel went into his office.

Julie followed him and closed the connecting door. "You seem out of it these days."

"I'm juggling ten different business issues on any given day. Guess I'm on edge. But I'm making progress, at least." He went to his desk and shuffled through a stack of phone messages.

"I'm talking personal now. You put in long days at the office." Julie came around his desk and put down the papers.

"Don't worry about me." Noel pinched the bridge of his nose. "I know when to stop."

"Do you?"

He glanced at her. "I've been taking care of myself for a long time now."

Julie smiled at him. "I know. Maybe you need to get away for a while. This is the perfect time for a trip to the beach. You know, I have a condo in Crystal Springs, Florida."

"That's nice of you to offer it to me, but I'm really too tied up at the moment." Noel pretended to misunderstand the invitation.

"Look, we could make a big push to prepare for a weekend away and—" She massaged his arm as though to soothe him.

"No," he said gently.

She jerked her hand away. "Don't make a fool of your-self with that Miss Social Climber!"

"We've had this discussion about us." Noel stared at her steadily. "Let's not have it again, Julie."

"No, let's not," Julie hissed. She snatched up her files. "I've heard the speech. So you're sleeping with her. You'll get what you deserve, then."

"Look, Julie, we've known each other too long. Let's not lose our friendship." Noel realized instantly that he'd poured gasoline on the flames.

Julie's eyes flashed. "Perfect, I get the 'Let's be friends' speech," she yelled.

"I'm not . . ." Noel walked toward her.

"I'll find a way to live without you, Noel St. Denis." Julie's bottom lip trembled. "In fact, I plan to live very well *without* you!" She spun and left, slamming his office door behind her.

Noel groaned in frustration. "I'll just fire everybody and run the damn place alone," he muttered.

Minutes later his grandmother came in after a per-functory knock. "Hello, son. What did you say to Julie? She seems upset."

"Why assume I'm the cause?" he said irritably.

"Because she came from your office and she's madly in love with you," Miss Georgina replied matter-of-factly.

"I don't think love enters into it with Julie, Grand-mother. I'm the perfect mating stock for her, that's all." Noel got up and poured them both a cup of coffee from the carafe on his credenza.

"I've told you what I think of that kind of attitude. I

don't want to have the same discussion again," Miss Georgina scolded.

"Good, because I have it memorized." Noel took a deep breath and let it out. "Now, sweet lady, I've got a lot of work today." Noel used the same blunt manner she used.

"Then I'll get right to the point. Stop this exhibition. I don't like it." Miss Georgina folded her hands in her lap.

"Lyrissa is doing a lot of hard work to make it a class act. She's got media interested and top art critics excited about seeing the collection."

"I don't care. Cancel it." Miss Georgina wore an inflexible expression.

"Impossible at this stage. We've invested too much and invitations have already gone out. We have a lot at stake."

"More than you know," she replied gravely.

Noel frowned at her. "Meaning?"

Miss Georgina did not answer him. Instead she rose and went to her late husband's portrait on the wall. She studied it in silence for a time, then turned to face Noel again.

"How much does the family name mean to you?" she asked.

"You know the answer to that, Grandmother. But what does that have to do with the show?"

"We can make Tremé Corporation great again without sacrificing family privacy. Lyrissa Rideau doesn't understand and never will. I don't like the way she's intruding on us." She lifted her nose in the air.

"Don't be ridiculous. We gave her access to the family archives. You knew she needed to search for information on the collection." Noel smiled indulgently. "Lyrissa has done a fine job and she's very discreet."

"I don't agree on either count. I want you to stop her," Miss Georgina commanded.

"People will definitely talk if we cancel at this point." Noel got up and crossed to her. "Look, cher, a few dusty old skeletons won't matter."

"Noel Phillip, you care more about an affair with that woman than you do about my feelings."

Noel wrestled with his temper for the third time that morning. He swallowed a tart reply. "Grandmother, tell me what this is really about."

"I don't know what you mean. And don't try to change the subject," she said stubbornly.

Noel's eyes narrowed. "This isn't about Lyrissa. You're hiding something. Don't withhold information from me, especially if it affects this company."

"I don't see why ancient slander should matter, but . . ." Her voice trailed off as she twisted the leather handle of her purse.

"Out with it," Noel prompted.

"Some disreputable nobodies accused our ancestors of being less than honest. I don't think digging up that kind of unfounded garbage is necessary," she said defensively.

He let out a short laugh that made her scowl at him in disapproval, then went back to his desk. "Is that all? Darlin', I'm afraid no one will be shocked to hear those stories again."

"I don't find anything funny about mud being slung on our family reputation!" Miss Georgina said sharply. "Besides, there are lurid details you haven't heard. Lies, of course—but all the same. . . ."

"Such as?"

"Nothing was ever proved," she blurted out. When Noel continued to stare at her hard, she went on. "There were stories that some of the art was not acquired properly."

"You mean stolen," he said dryly.

Miss Georgina pretended she hadn't heard him. "Then there was the matter of an affair your great-great-great-grandmother had with—well, never mind who with. Her husband died after a brief illness and there were filthy whispers. None of it true, of course. And then—"

"Wait a minute!" Noel cut in. "How many skeletons are we talking about here?"

"No one in our family has ever been to jail," she replied haughtily.

"Sounds like some of them *should* have been tossed in prison. Damn!" He rubbed his jaw.

His grandmother sat forward with a grim expression on her proud face. "All lies from jealous competitors. There are still people who resent our status. Lyrissa Rideau strikes me as one of those people. All this talk about art history could be just a cover."

"Lyrissa is only interested in doing research on the art. Remember, we asked her to. She's not planning to sell our story to the tabloids!"

"Stop thinking with your hormones. That woman has no loyalty to us. She's gone way beyond doing an appraisal."

"You're being silly about this whole thing. Lyrissa hasn't done anything without my knowledge."

"Julie can handle the collection from now on. She has the experience. She handled the estate sale when her grandmother died. She says—"

"Julie. I should have guessed she had something to do with this. She's out of line discussing this with you. I'm going to set her straight." Noel glared at her.

"You're being unreasonable in your defense of Lyrissa Rideau." Miss Georgina stood.

"Don't question my judgment based on your own prejudices."

"Noel Phillip, you've never spoken to me this way. I know who's the cause, too."

Noel's eyes narrowed. "The subject is closed, Grandmother."

She gazed at him for a time. "I'll keep the collection out of your hands if you can't be trusted with it."

"Do what you have to. I've earned the right to be boss around here, damn it! I won't roll over every time you decide you want to run things." Noel crossed his arms as he stared her down.

"You're as stubborn and impossible as your grandfather was—more. That man hated listening to me even when it was obvious I was right." Miss Georgina looked at the portrait with a deep frown. "Our parents were happier with our marriage than we ever were," she said.

Noel was stunned by her admission. "But I thought you were very happy."

"We had a partnership. We . . . suited each other in other ways that compensated." She drew herself up and turned back to Noel. "No romantic notions, Noel Phillip. Does that shock you?"

He shouldn't have been surprised. After all, most of his relatives had married under the same conditions. After thinking it over a few moments, he shook his head. Suddenly he felt sorry for her. They must have been two lonely people for much of their thirty-year marriage. They'd hidden it well.

"Stop worrying, Grandmère. I'm going to protect the family name and the collection. You really shouldn't listen to Julie's wild accusations." Noel patted her hand to reassure her.

"Speaking of Julie, that girl deserves to be treated better. She comes from a fine family." Miss Georgina deftly switched back to his marital prospects.

"Didn't we just cover marriages based on family preferences?" he said with a slight grin.

"You also have your father's smart mouth," she retorted. Still her frown melted into a soft affectionate smile. "I know you'll do what's best in the end. I trust your upbringing."

Noel decided to let that one pass. "Thank you, Grandmother. I'm going to live up to your trust in me with the company."

Her light brown eyes narrowed. "Noel Phillip St. Denis, I—"

He kissed her hand. "Now, sweetheart, let me take care of business," he said with a disarming smile.

"I can take a hint." Miss Georgina smiled back at him. She turned to leave, then stopped and looked at him. "We're not every family, son. Don't forget that."

Once the door finally closed behind her, Noel went back to his desk. "So much for getting anything done this morning," he muttered.

Dealing with Carlton, Julie and his grandmother left him feeling cranky and cynical. He needed to clear his head. One by one he rejected his usual methods of working off tension. A workout at the club didn't appeal to him. He could try to book an appointment with the club's masseuse instead. No, he wasn't in the mood. Noel drummed his fingers on the arm of his chair and stared at the telephone on his desk. What was she doing right now? Was she thinking of him?

"What the hell," he muttered, and dialed Lyrissa's office number.

18

Lyrissa darted sideways glances at Noel as he drove. So much for her declaration not to see him again. Well, she did need to stay close to her family's painting. *Yeah, right!*

Noel wore a slate blue Land's End t-shirt tucked into Tommy Hilfiger designer blue jeans. The cotton knit fabric stretched across his broad chest. More than once she caught herself staring at the muscles that rippled beneath it. His jeans fit snug enough to invite wicked fantasies. She tried to focus on the landscape, but it was no use. The Technicolor visions of their entwined bodies wouldn't go away. He was her worst nightmare and her deluxe erotic dream come true. God! What had she been thinking to accept this invitation?

His black Montero Sport whizzed down the highway toward Mandeville, a once sleepy town that had been transformed by an influx of wealthy escapees from the traffic and hustle of New Orleans. As the miles slipped by, leaving the city behind, he visibly relaxed.

"You're full of surprises." Lyrissa gazed ahead, too aware of the heat he generated.

He smiled. "Hmm, that sounds like a good thing."

"I mean, I didn't see you as a guy who owned an SUV and was into long drives in the country." She made the mistake of looking at him. He shifted his hips in the leather seat. A sharp ache shot through her pelvis.

"I'm a man of many layers. Not quite as shallow as you thought, huh?"

"I never thought of you as shallow, just a guy with a narrow focus," she quipped.

When his smile widened, the pleasant itch on the inside of her thighs intensified. Lyrissa swallowed hard and looked away from danger. She squirmed in her seat, hoping it would help. It didn't.

"Are you okay? You look a little jumpy. I hope you're not carsick." Noel put a hand on her knee.

Lyrissa gasped and moved away. She couldn't be held responsible if he touched her again. "No, no. I'm cool," she stammered.

"Sorry, I wasn't trying to start anything." The sexy curve of his full mouth told a different story.

"What a beautiful day!" Lyrissa blurted out. "I love this weather."

"Yes, we've had lovely weather lately. Though we could use some rain." Noel grinned at her. "Did that help?"

"Just drive, smart-ass," she retorted.

Noel laughed out loud at her frown of exasperation. "Let's both unwind, okay? No pressure of any kind."

"Agreed." Lyrissa willed herself to relax. "Don't mind

me. I'm stressed from juggling school and work. Too many deadlines."

Noel sighed in sympathy. "I know exactly what you mean. Some days I'm tempted to book a flight to a Caribbean island and not come back."

"Conquering the world can wear a brother down," Lyrissa teased.

He laughed again. "The world is easy. Dealing with my family is what wears a brother down."

"Well, at least you can see the humor in it." Lyrissa smiled at him.

"Being thirty miles out of town with you helps," he said. Noel blinked as though he'd surprised himself with the admission.

"Thanks," she said quietly.

They rode in silence for another ten minutes. The scenery had changed drastically. They drove on the Lake Ponchartrain Causeway. Sunlight reflected on the water causing it to sparkle like diamonds. Boats were scattered around the vast lake. Some drifted lazily while others raced along leaving white foaming wakes behind. Noel took the Mandeville exit.

"Boy, when you said you wanted to get away, you weren't kidding." Lyrissa looked around.

"Ever been out on the Tfecunte River in Tickfaw?" Noel changed lanes effortlessly.

"You're not serious?" She gaped at him.

"Sure. Enjoy the trip." Noel turned up the music. A driving hip-hop beat thumped through the speakers.

Lyrissa's mouth fell open even wider. "Who are you and where is the real Noel St. Denis?"

They laughed hard at her joke. An invisible force field

dropped. They exchanged an effortless banter about everything except the weather. Noel's sense of humor went from dry and sophisticated to silly one-liners. Lyrissa laughed so much she didn't notice the passage of time or miles. Noel parked the Montero at a boat landing.

"Here we are," he announced and swept a hand out.

"Okay, I'll play along. Where are we?"

"The river. Don't you ever get out of New Orleans?" He shook his head.

"Not often. I'm one of those folks who thinks nothing important happens outside the city." Lyrissa grinned back at him.

"Today you'll expand your view of the state." He got out and went around to open her door. "Come on, city girl."

Lyrissa threw up both hands. "Like I have a choice. You've got me."

His smile softened into an expression of mischievous seduction. He took her hand as she stepped to the ground. "I like the sound of *that*."

She blushed. "Behave."

"I'll try." He slammed the door shut.

"Don't try, do." Lyrissa didn't succeed in sounding severe. She couldn't seem to wipe the silly grin from her face. Her heart skipped when he took her hand as they walked into a store.

A sign that said "Thibeau's Boat Landing and Café" hung above the wide front porch. Small tables were arranged on the weathered cypress porch with a view of the river. Several couples sat nursing soft drinks and enjoying the balmy breeze from the water.

"What can I do for y'all today?" a female voice boomed as they walked through the door.

A tall woman the color of ebony stood behind the counter. Bags of corn chips and other goodies were stacked on either side of the wide surface. At the other end of the room a waitress took orders for food at another counter.

"We want to rent a party barge," Noel said.

"We do?" Lyrissa blurted out.

"Yes, we do." Noel put an arm around her waist.

"Okay," the woman grinned at them. "But where's the rest of the party?"

"This is it," Noel replied with a wink.

"Gotcha." The woman gave a lusty laugh. "I got just the thing, a six-seater. Enough room to spread out."

"Hey!" Lyrissa felt outnumbered.

"To picnic, boo! That's all I meant." The woman laughed again and winked at Noel.

"She your buddy or something?" Lyrissa squinted at him.

Noel held up both hands palms out. "Innocent."

"Oh, please!" Lyrissa rolled her eyes.

He bought a small cooler and packed it with soft drinks. While the woman readied the party barge, Noel ordered po-boys and fries for their lunch. Ten minutes later they pulled away from the landing with Noel at the wheel. He seemed to be expert at maneuvering the barge.

"We'll find a nice shady spot and eat before we take a walk," he said over the noise of the engine.

"Why not?" Lyrissa called back. She sat on a bench near him and savored the feel of the wind on her face.

Noel guided the barge down the river. He pointed out scenic spots of historical interest along the way. Fifteen minutes into the ride, he eased the nose of the barge to the bank. Weathered picnic tables were arranged around a clearing. Lyrissa gripped his hand and jumped to the mossy ground.

"Like I said, you're full of surprises." She gazed around.

"I was a Boy Scout. We used to camp out here and at Fountainebleau State Park. I have badges in boating, archery, and sewing."

"Did you say *sewing?*"

"Don't start with me, woman." Noel shook a finger at her.

"We've got a true case of alien abduction here." She shook her head in wonder.

"So how do you like me now?" Noel stared at her steadily.

He smiled, but she could hear the serious note in his voice. Did he need her approval? She studied the handsome face. A warm feeling touched her heart. Lyrissa had never thought of him as vulnerable before, yet out here he was so different. Of course he had feelings, she mused. Maybe her own bias about people in his social class had blinded her.

"He's all right," she said with a smile.

His brown eyes twinkled with delight at her modest answer. "Hey, I got it." He did an impromptu hip-hop dance step.

"Wait a minute. That Master P impression needs major work. Let me show you how it's done." Lyrissa bounced around and bobbed her head.

Soon they were laughing like kids. They twirled around, startling a family that emerged down a nature trail. Laughing at the sight they must have made, they sat down and ate their lunch. After they'd finished, they went for a leisurely hike along a winding path. They walked beneath huge oak and ash trees draped with Spanish moss. Lyrissa held his hand tightly, enjoying the firmness of his strong grip. After another hour they returned to the barge and headed back to the landing. It was six o'clock in the evening by the time they reached Thibeau's. Yet the sun was still bright in the late spring sky.

They were on the highway headed back to New Orleans twenty minutes later.

"Thanks for the great day trip," Lyrissa said.

"You're welcome. I had a lot of fun." Noel drove on for a time. "Tell you what, those sandwiches are gone. Let's have dinner. I've got all the ingredients for shrimp and pasta."

"At your apartment?" Lyrissa wore a slight frown.

"Sure. Is that a problem, Lyrissa?" he asked quietly. "No pressure."

"We've talked about us before and—" She broke off. Lyrissa was unsure how to go on, especially because she wanted to be with him.

"I know, I know. Look—I have this cynical view of happy-ever-after romance myself." Noel shrugged. "But why fight what we feel?"

"This little outing was nice, but we're on our way back to the real world."

Noel looked at her. "I really need to forget the real world for a while."

"Just you and me," she murmured, savoring the notion of them in their own cozy space.

"Yes. We'll deal with all the crap tomorrow." He placed a hand on her knee.

Lyrissa didn't move away this time. "Okay," she replied.

Noel grinned like a boy playing hooky from school.

"I'm going to shatter any doubts you have about my domestic skills."

She smiled back at him despite the flutter of fear in her stomach. Noel kept up a cheerful stream of chatter for the rest of the trip back to the city. Lyrissa answered in all the right places—at least, she thought she did. Noel parked in the reserved spot outside his luxury apartment.

"Lyrissa, come up only if you really want to. It's okay if you don't. I'll understand." Noel squeezed her hand.

Her pulse raced at the sensitive and caring tone in his voice. "I'm fine, really." Then raised an eyebrow. "Don't try to wiggle out of cooking me dinner, mister!"

"No way." Noel kissed her cheek and hopped from the car.

They went into his apartment, once again at ease with each other. Noel turned the radio to a jazz station and went into the kitchen. Lyrissa sat at the counter facing it while he worked. Good conversation and a great wine helped the time pass quickly. They sat down to dinner forty-five minutes later.

"Be honest, how does it taste?" Noel eyed her as she ate.

"Delicious. You get a gold star, Scout St. Denis." Lyrissa nodded. "This sauce is superb."

"I took a few cooking classes. Helps to be a well-rounded kinda guy, ya know." Noel looked genuinely pleased.

"Well, you told the truth. This is good." Lyrissa wound more pasta around her fork.

"I wouldn't lead you astray, baby," Noel said.

"So I can trust you, huh?" Lyrissa shot back.

Noel wore a serious expression. "Yes. I guess we should both learn to trust."

He put down his fork and brushed a finger along her jaw. Lyrissa watched as he leaned closer. He kissed her gently at first. Then he wrapped her in a strong embrace. His kiss became searching, urgent. It was as though he needed reassurance. Lyrissa sighed and gave in to him eagerly.

Noel tasted the inside of her mouth, his tongue caressing each soft spot. Lyrissa rubbed his chest with both hands as she pressed her mouth against his, wanting more of his sweetness. Without a thought about complications or difference, they rose as one. Noel lifted her until their hips touched. They held each other close for a few seconds before Noel led her to his bedroom. She hardly noticed the soft blue, green, and earth brown décor. Drapes reached down to the dark green carpet. He yanked the matching comforter from the bed and lay her down on soft sheets.

"You are so beautiful," he whispered.

He continued to murmur endearments as he slowly undressed her. Each took turns pausing to kiss the other's exposed flesh as their clothes came off. He cupped her breasts in his powerful hands, yet his touch was tender and loving. He massaged the nipples until Lyrissa moaned with pleasure. His tongue teased each one as he alternated between licking and nibbling them. She shivered at the delight of having pleasure delayed. Noel proved to be a master at foreplay. His hands roamed every inch of her body until she was mindless with need. Lyrissa moaned his name over and over.

"Now, baby?" he whispered.

Lyrissa nodded, unable to speak. She gazed into his eyes as she tightened her fingers around his erection. Noel closed his eyes while she massaged him. His groans became louder. He paused to put on a condom. When he finished, he stretched his long frame on top of her.

"I wanted you the first day we met," he confessed.

"Noel," she whispered.

They rocked together. Lyrissa sighed when he entered her. They moved in tandem with a steady pounding rhythm. Slowly they pushed each other to the brink only to pull back. Lyrissa clung to him, crying out at the joy of feeling him inside her. From far away she heard a female voice begging for more and a gruff male voice promising to give it. They rocked each other hard, lost in the frantic need to satisfy a raging hunger.

Lyrissa came first. She dug her fingernails into his back and cried out. Her contractions sent him into an orgasm. Noel thrust hard until Lyrissa came again.

"Please, please," Lyrissa whispered and wrapped her legs around him.

Noel sighed deeply and pressed his face against her neck. "Thank you, baby," he said in a shaky voice.

Lyrissa kissed the top of his head. "Why are you thanking me?"

"For giving me hope," he said simply.

"I don't understand."

"I grew up watching unhappy couples hurt each other," Noel said.

"Sounds pretty awful." Lyrissa stroked his dark thick curls.

"I assumed I'd have to settle for lukewarm at best when it came to a relationship." Noel kissed her skin. "Now I know for the first time that I don't have to."

"Noel, about the real world . . . I know what your fam-

ily expects. But have you really examined what you want?"
Lyrissa hated to say the words, but she couldn't run from
the truth.

"I'm that no-nonsense business geek, remember?"
Noel lifted his head to stare into her eyes. "No romantic
fantasies. I know what I want."

"It can't be this easy, just say what you want and your
family will knuckle under." Lyrissa pictured the formidable family matriarch. "Your grandmother will make a
hurricane seem tame when she finds out."

Noel shook his head like a stubborn little boy unwilling to give up his favorite toy. "Forget them. It's all about
us right now."

She didn't want to push the issue. He looked so happy,
as happy as she felt at that moment. Against her best
hardheaded, no-nonsense judgment, Lyrissa merely
sighed and held him close. They drifted into a dream state
holding onto each other.

Two hours later he drove her home. They sat in the
driveway holding hands and not talking. Noel kissed her
tenderly.

"Good night, baby. I'll call you tomorrow." He traced a
long finger around her mouth.

"Yes," she said and kissed it.

Lyrissa entered the house and headed upstairs to her
bedroom. She hummed the rap tune that had played as
they drove out of town. She was jarred out of her blissful
state when Mama Grace appeared in the hallway.

"Good news! That reporter called. She asked questions
about the St. Denis family scandals, just like you said she
would." Mama Grace beamed. "I told her you'd call her
tomorrow."

Aunt Claire came from the living room. She glanced at her sister, then studied Lyrissa's expression shrewdly. "She could break the story soon after the art show at Chaisson House. Just the way you planned, right?"

The real world crashed back around her with a vengeance. Lyrissa felt the weight of it on her chest. "Right, just like I planned."

19

Four critics drifted around the room. They took turns standing in various poses as they studied each work of art. All of them scribbled notes on small pads. Lyrissa looked at the elegant crowd of A-list people. A generous helping of society folks filled the historic Chaisson House. Waiters circulated with platters of appetizers. The caterer had a bar set up in the foyer.

Ebony walked up to Lyrissa. She balanced a small plate of smoked oysters on one hand and held a goblet of champagne in the other. "I'm dizzy from the smell of old money," she mumbled.

Lyrissa stifled a laugh. "Stop that!" she whispered back.

Vic swept toward them in a swirl of peacock blue silk. The caftan over matching silk pants suited her figure very well. "Brilliant, darlin'. You've done us proud," she gushed as she fluttered her fingers at friends.

"Thank you, Vic. I'm glad you're pleased. This is my friend Ebony Armstrong. Ebony, this is Vic Vivant, Noel's cousin," Lyrissa said.

"Nice to meet you." Ebony gawked at the expensive outfit. "I love that ensemble."

"Thank you, dear. Little something I picked up when I went to St. Kitts. It was made by a native designer. She's all the rage. She has a boutique in New York and one in Houston. I'll give you the address." Vic's rapid-fire chatter ended when she sipped wine. She spotted someone else she knew. "Oh, hello, Jessamine!"

"Uh, thanks." Ebony leaned close to Lyrissa. "I'd have to sell my car to afford it," she whispered.

"Stop!" Lyrissa hissed. Then smiled when Vic's attention turned back to them.

"As I was saying, lovely reception," Vic said.

"I didn't do it alone," Lyrissa replied.

"Nonsense, Noel has been singing your praises to us all." Vic pointed to him by waving a ring-bedecked hand toward where he stood.

Noel must have sensed he was the topic of conversation. He glanced at them and flashed a dazzling smile at Lyrissa. Her heart raced. Magnificent in black tie, Noel had females of all ages hovering around him. His charm was in full force as he entertained a group of society matrons. Lyrissa ground her teeth. Younger versions circled like greedy felines waiting to devour the catch of the day.

"He's a tasty dish," Vic commented archly. She took another delicate sip of wine. "Those aging debutantes would crawl through broken glass to get to him."

Lyrissa wanted to look away but couldn't. "He doesn't seem to notice."

"He hardly ever does, especially now." Vic wore a sly smile and winked at Lyrissa.

"I wouldn't know." Lyrissa struggled not to grin with glee.

"Noel has told everyone here what a genius you are and how you worked together *so closely* for weeks."

"Miss Georgina helped out quite a bit, also." Lyrissa assumed a neutral expression.

"Hmmm," was Vic's only reply. She continued to smile at Lyrissa.

Ebony cleared her throat. "I've enjoyed learning about the history of each piece. Especially those you own, Ms. Vivant."

"Vic, please! No formality between us tea girls. Which one of my lovelies do you like best?"

"The sculpture over here." Ebony led her away with a backward glance at Lyrissa.

Lyrissa mouthed "thank you" as they left. She couldn't help but smile at the endearingly eccentric woman. Her heart rate picked up speed again when Noel walked toward her. Julie stepped into his path. They spoke briefly, an exchange apparently not to Julie's satisfaction. Noel went around her and walked toward Lyrissa again. Julie wore a mask of controlled hostility.

"Everyone is impressed. Congratulations." Noel smiled and lifted his wine glass to her.

"Thanks. Not everyone is happy." Lyrissa gazed at Julie, who stared back at her.

Noel only glanced briefly at Julie. "Never mind. This is your night."

"Mr. Taylor helped a lot. He has years of experience with this sort of high-profile event." She nodded to her boss. Mr. Taylor mingled with the guests, laughing and having a wonderful time.

"Yes, but you worked with the decorators, arranged the art and set up all the media coverage. Take the applause, baby. You've earned it." Noel stood close to her with one hand under her arm.

"Uh, thanks." Lyrissa worked to tame a jolt of desire at his nearness. She put a few inches between them. "Nice turnout."

"Relax. I'm not going to make a pass at you here. I'll wait until we're alone." His baritone voice rumbled provocatively.

"People are already talking." Lyrissa smiled and nodded to an art reviewer for a suburban weekly newspaper.

"Like who?" he asked mildly.

"Vic, for one. She says you're telling people great things about me. Cut it out," she muttered, but kept smiling.

Noel's resonant laugh turned heads. Lyrissa was just as captivated as the other salivating females who watched him hungrily.

"I'll try to be less enthusiastic, but it won't be easy. You're so wonderful." Noel gazed at her as though there was no else in the room but her.

Mrs. St. Denis joined them with Julie right behind her. "Noel, Mr. Helaire wants a word with you," she said.

"Sure, Grandmother. I'll be back," he said to Lyrissa and walked away.

"Well," Mrs. St. Denis said with a stiff smile. "You've done an excellent job, Ms. Rideau."

"Thank you, Mrs. St. Denis." Lyrissa glanced around for an opening to escape.

Julie stared at her with barely concealed ire. "Interesting, how you chose to show certain pieces."

"I wanted a mix of different periods and media to showcase the best of the collection." Lyrissa repeated the well-worn answer she'd given all night.

"I see." Julie looked around the room. Her gaze stopped at the "Sunday Stroll on the Faubourg Tremé." "That painting, for instance. It's a real show stopper."

"Yes, it's quite attractive," Lyrissa replied calmly.

"Magnificent is the word," Mrs. St. Denis replied. She put on her eyeglasses to see it better as she walked toward it.

Lyrissa had no choice but to follow them. "Actually, the entire collection is outstanding. The pottery and sculpture have really impressed everyone."

Julie studied the painting for a few seconds, then turned to Lyrissa. "What do we know about the artist?"

"Not much, except that he wasn't particularly prolific," Lyrissa responded smoothly.

"Strange," Julie remarked, not looking at Lyrissa. "I would think such a talented nineteenth century artist would be well known to an expert."

"Some artists are harder to research than others." Lyrissa clenched her back teeth.

Mrs. St. Denis peered closer at it. "Such lovely lines. Was he from this area?"

"I believe he came here from one of the river parishes," Lyrissa said. That much was quite true.

Julie looked at Lyrissa. "Then his descendants should be able to help."

"That is one way we gather information," Lyrissa said.

"I love the vibrant colors." Miss Georgina turned from the painting and looked around the room. "But as you said, the entire collection is a treasure. Julie, there's the mayor and his new wife. I must thank him for helping us out last month with the charity drive." She left them alone.

"So you were saying about this artist?" Julie asked.

Ebony walked up at that moment. "Lyrissa, this show is marvelous." She turned to Julie. "Oh, hello. I'm Ebony Armstrong." She stuck out her hand.

"Julie Duval." Julie gave it a quick shake and let go.

"Lyrissa, the head of our firm would love to meet you. Would you excuse us?" Ebony whisked Lyrissa away before Julie could answer.

"Thanks. I owe you big time," Lyrissa said in an undertone.

"Honey, Julie D. wants to hurt you bad. Watch your back."

"I know, girl. She'd kill to have Noel," Lyrissa said in a low voice as she smiled at those around her.

"With her rep, I believe it! I have friends who have done business with her. She's ruthless."

"Yes, but I can handle her little bursts of jealousy." Still Lyrissa frowned as she thought of their exchange.

"Listen, I saw those two eyeing 'Sunday Stroll.' I say we get rolling. We can organize the documentation and meet next week. Then—"

"No," Lyrissa cut in sharply. She rubbed her forehead. A tension headache throbbed behind her eyes.

"I've been working my butt off for two weeks. Let's move," Ebony said with intensity.

"I know, but . . ." Lyrissa heaved a sigh. "I can't just hit him with it out of nowhere. Not now."

Ebony maneuvered them into an alcove away from the crowd. She jerked Lyrissa around by the arm until they were nose to nose. "You didn't!" She stared into her eyes and gasped. "Oh hell, you did!"

"I didn't plan it. We just sort of—"

"What, tripped and all your clothes flew off?" Ebony squinted at her. "Who do you think I am, Bozo the Fool?"

"You've seen him!" Lyrissa blurted out. She sighed again.

"Well . . ." Ebony took a deep breath and let it out. "I can't argue with you there. The brother has it all!"

"And then some." Lyrissa tingled all over just thinking about his hands on her body.

"So the plan is off completely? Please warn me to get out of town when you tell your grandmother!" Ebony gave a melodramatic shudder.

"I'm going to change the plan, not give it up."

"Since I'm your attorney, you might want to fill me in. I think we both need a fresh drink." Ebony darted off to catch a passing waiter. She gave him their empty glasses and came back with refills. "So tell me this new strategy."

"I haven't worked out the details yet," Lyrissa said with a slight frown.

"Just how far have you gotten?"

"Uh, that's it." Lyrissa wore a weak smile. "We'll think of something before we tell Mama Grace and Aunt Claire."

Ebony's eyes widened and she shook her head. "Forget it. I plan to have urgent business elsewhere that day, girlfriend."

Lyrissa gripped her forearm. "Oh, no you don't, *girlfriend*. You're going to help me."

"Lord, have mercy!" Ebony gulped a mouthful of wine and swallowed it. "You've forgotten something, Lyrissa. The story is going to run in the *Picayune* real soon."

"We've got to stop that reporter." Lyrissa chewed her bottom lip until her raisin lipstick came off.

"Right, stop Dionne Jackson from printing a juicy scandal about a prominent Black family. We've got all the makings of a movie of the week here. The woman loves that kinda stuff."

"You're a hot shot young lawyer. Talk to her." Lyrissa gripped her arm tighter.

"Let go before you amputate my arm." Ebony pried Lyrissa's fingers from her flesh.

"Sorry. I'm in deep, Eb. We've got to head this whole thing off." Lyrissa looked up to find Noel staring at her. He smiled. She managed to smile back.

Ebony followed her gaze. "Damn, this love thang has gotta be good. Okay, I'll talk to Dionne. I'll tell her we're not sure of the facts yet and mention the word 'libel.' Maybe that will get her attention."

"You're wonderful, Ebony." Lyrissa gave her a quick hug of gratitude. "No wonder you're considered one of the most intelligent and impressive young attorneys in the city. Hell, in the state. I—"

"Don't lay it on too thick, please. I didn't bring my hip boots," Ebony quipped. She looked at Noel again. "I have to say I don't blame you one bit, sugar."

Lyrissa gazed at him. He was six feet three inches of caramel delight on two legs. Yet he was more than a pretty package. She loved the way he approached life. Noel St. Denis seemed to take the best of his world and toss the crap that came with it. Noel nodded to her before a well-

dressed couple claimed his attention. When she turned,
Lyrissa met Mrs. St. Denis's stony gaze. Julie stood beside
her, whispering low in her ear.

"I've got to figure this out soon, Eb," Lyrissa murmured. "*Real* soon."

20

Two days later Lyrissa sat across from her grandmother at the breakfast table. Aunt Claire shot sideways glances at them as she ate her scrambled eggs and grits. She cleared her throat finally after ten more minutes of tense silence.

"We're supposed to get rain this afternoon. That cute new weatherman on Channel Six said so." Aunt Claire's tentative smile soon faded when no one answered. She tried again. "Take your umbrella now that you've been warned, Lyrissa," she said cheerily.

"She doesn't listen to good advice, Claire." Mama Grace dabbed her lips with a paper napkin. "Lyrissa thinks we're just a couple of old fools."

"I didn't say we should just forget the painting," Lyrissa blurted out.

"Warning them is the same thing, Lyrissa Michelle." Mama Grace threw down her napkin.

"Noel isn't the kind of man you think he is."

"I gave you more credit, child. He'll be on the phone to his lawyers the minute you walk out. Don't doubt it!" Mama Grace stabbed a forefinger at her nose.

Lyrissa crossed her arms. "I don't want him to read about it in the newspapers."

"He will put his family first. So should *you*." Mama Grace glared at her.

"I won't walk over him to get the painting. Isn't that why you despise them so? They didn't care who got hurt as long as they profited."

"Let me remind you that we're at a disadvantage in this situation, young lady."

"I don't believe Noel will want to keep 'Sunday Stroll' when I tell him the truth and what it means to us." Lyrissa wore a stubborn expression. "I'm sure he won't."

"A few moments of pleasure will not override years of upbringing." Her voice sliced through the air like a razor.

"That's enough, Grace," Aunt Claire said loudly.

"No, she has to hear the truth. The St. Denis family wasn't satisfied with holding onto stolen goods. They discredited your great-grandfather and ruined his business because he dared to tell everyone what they'd done. Now our family can't even preserve our ancestor's historic home because we're poor." Mama Grace stood and looked down at Lyrissa.

"You're judging Noel by people he never even knew— people who died decades before we were born. It's not fair." Lyrissa stared back at her.

"If life were fair, young lady, we wouldn't need to have this discussion! He's a St. Denis," Mama Grace shouted.

"Decide right now if you're going to turn your back on this family."

Lyrissa shoved her chair back and stood. "Don't be absurd. I'm going to get the painting back."

"Your father needed treatment, but we couldn't afford it. Our family's inheritance was stolen, our reputation destroyed by the St. Denis family. The consequences have haunted us for generations."

Lyrissa flinched with pain at the mention of her father. "I know how much Daddy suffered. But we can't blame everything on one act committed over a hundred years ago, Mama Grace."

"Can't you see that this is about more than one painting?" Mama Grace replied, her voice strained with frustration.

"You have to trust me on this," Lyrissa said forcefully. "We'll do it my way."

"You're only thinking of him. Well, I won't let you throw our legacy away." Mama Grace marched out of the kitchen.

"God!" Lyrissa sat down hard and put her head in her hands.

Aunt Claire put an arm around her shoulders. "I'm starting to think we've lost our way."

"No, Aunt Claire. Mama Grace has freaked out. She's more interested in revenge."

"Guilt," Aunt Claire murmured.

"What did you say?" Lyrissa looked at her.

Aunt Claire shook her head. "Ah, cherie, it's a sad story. She's right about one thing, though. The St. Denis family has dogged us for generations. This feud started with the painting and grew."

"Tell me the sad story." Lyrissa turned to her.

"You see us as little old ladies, a bit strange, but sweet." Aunt Claire smiled.

"No, babe. I think of you as lovable eccentrics." Lyrissa patted her cheek.

"Same thing. You're not far wrong, either." Aunt Claire waved a hand. "But we were young once, of course. You should have seen us back then, the Joubert sisters."

"I've seen the old photos." Lyrissa grinned. The faded black-and-white pictures showed two lovely young women.

"We went to parties every week. Mardi Gras season was the best, of course. And we had lots of gentlemen admirers, naturally."

"Naturally. But what's that got to do with 'Sunday Stroll on the Faubourg Tremé'?" Lyrissa blinked at her.

"That painting has a way of reaching into the future." Aunt Claire stared ahead as though looking back in time. When she spoke, her voice was so soft, Lyrissa had to lean close to hear her.

"We moved in the same social circles as all the best families. Of course, we were Jouberts. Our grandmothers insisted that we go to all the right parties. We even rubbed shoulders with Georgina Rohas. That was before she married into the St. Denis family."

"I thought—" Lyrissa broke off.

"That we weren't acceptable? Well, we weren't on the same level as the Rohases, St. Denises, and some others. But our grandfather had rebuilt the family business and we had money. Plus the Joubert name did mean something. So we got our share of invitations to the best functions."

"Mrs. St. Denis snubbed you every chance she got. I've

heard the stories." Lyrissa frowned. "And I know the feeling. Even some of the nuns treated the darker skinned kids in school differently."

Aunt Claire gazed at her in dismay. "Was it still so bad at St. Mary's? Lord, I never realized. You always seemed to enjoy school. You were in so many clubs and such."

"I didn't want you to worry about me. Anyway, I'm tough, like you two." Lyrissa smiled in spite of the dull ache from the memories. She still felt sad for the little girl who had felt so ugly.

"I'm sorry, baby. We only wanted you to have all the advantages." Aunt Claire wore a regretful expression.

"It was years ago. Besides, it wasn't all bad. I had two teachers who really encouraged me."

"God has a plan for good even from evil." Aunt Claire made the sign of the cross. "Thank you, Lord."

"Now back to the painting," Lyrissa prompted her.

"You never wondered how we knew Georgina had the painting?" Aunt Claire tilted her head to one side.

"You had old letters and journals from Jules. Right?"

"True, but they only referred to Gustave and his grandson as being in possession. Any of the descendants could have had it."

"Come on, tell me the whole story, then." Lyrissa sat back, eager to hear.

"Grace had more gentleman callers than most of us girls. Including a certain St. Denis boy. Phillip St. Denis," Aunt Claire said dramatically, and spread her arms wide.

"Get outta here! Mama Grace was tippin' with Georgina's man?" Lyrissa's mouth hung open with shock.

"Grace had him first, dear. Oh yes," Aunt Claire nodded with a grin. "They were quite the talk of New Orleans

Creole society. Mother was fit to be tied, let me tell you. Grandpapa demanded that Daddy put his foot down. Grace defied them all, but it just wasn't meant to be."

"He dumped her and married Georgina Rohas because she was from the right family," Lyrissa said with certainty.

"Tossed her aside like that." Aunt Claire snapped her fingers.

"I can see why she's so upset about Noel and me. But I still don't see the connection to the painting."

"While they were still courting, one of Phillip's elderly aunts died. Grace had always loved old houses. He took her to see all the antiques and fine furniture."

"Right, they were alone in a huge mansion to look at antiques." Lyrissa raised her eyebrows.

"Don't be impertinent." Aunt Claire's eyes danced with merriment. "The point is, Grace saw 'Sunday Stroll on the Faubourg Tremé' and naturally recognized it. She told Phillip. The poor dear trusted him."

"Oh." Lyrissa felt a chill as she remembered her defense of Noel to Mama Grace. How her words must have brought back painful memories.

Aunt Claire nodded slowly. "So you see, Phillip let Grace believe they would become engaged soon. He didn't outright promise, just said things like 'We'll be together, love.' Instead, he sent her a short note saying they couldn't see each other again. Then the painting vanished. By the time Grace told our parents and grandparents about it, well . . ."

"They'd assembled lawyers and stonewalled," Lyrissa added.

"That's about it. They put out all kinds of nasty innuendos about us. Grandpapa's business suffered." Aunt

Claire sighed deeply. "Grace has blamed herself for that and more since then."

"Did they really ruin his business on purpose?"

"Oh yes! Poor Grace. She read about Phillip's engagement to Georgina in the paper."

"Mama Grace really believes all our financial problems are her fault?" Lyrissa felt sorry now that she'd been so harsh with her grandmother.

"After years of struggling, Grandpapa was the first in years to rebuild the family fortunes. They made sure he lost business."

"I don't blame her for being angry. But it's not all her fault. Sounds to me like Great-grandpapa was overbearing and inflexible."

"True. Grandpapa was hot headed. He didn't follow his lawyer's advice. He even accused Phillip's grandfather of embezzling from the bank. Old Henry St. Denis was on the board of Citizens Trust." Aunt Claire shook her head. "Our father didn't help by trying to punch Phillip's father in the nose at the country club."

"Have mercy!" Lyrissa sighed. "Mama Grace needs to let it go, Aunt Claire. We can't let the past rule us anymore."

"Grace sees a lot of herself in you. You're both determined, stubborn and—"

"I get your point." Lyrissa cut her off with a grin. Her expression grew serious again. "She thinks I'm repeating her mistake. It *is* kinda spooky."

"Seems we've come full circle." Aunt Claire studied her for a time. "You're between a rock and a hard place, cher," she said quietly.

Lyrissa gazed out the window. Doubts crowded out her confidence in telling Noel everything. She'd felt so sure when she was in his arms. What if she were repeating the past in some cruel twist of fate?

"Any ideas on how I can straighten out this fix I'm in?" Lyrissa searched her face, hoping for an answer.

"It's going to be messy no matter what you do. The question is, what are you willing to give up?"

Lyrissa leaned both elbows on the table and wore a bleak expression. "That's not what I wanted to hear. But it's the truth. The light at the end of this tunnel is a speeding train."

21

Lyrissa flipped through the full-color glossy brochure with a grim expression. So far she'd found ten typos. "I just may have to kill somebody," she muttered.

The day was heading south big time. Blue Monday had started with a frustrating drive to work through city traffic. Mr. Taylor walked around in a crabby mood all morning. Now she had to give him the bad news about the brochure they needed in less than two weeks. The phone rang.

"Damn it! I can't get anything done." She snatched the receiver from the base and strained to be polite. "Hello, Taylor Gallery. How may I help you?"

"Hi, sweet thing. And how is your day going?" Noel said.

"Don't ask." Lyrissa balanced the receiver on her shoulder and continued to look at the photos of brass sculptures.

"Things will get better today, babe," he replied.

"Yeah, yeah. I'm hangin' on by a thread and it's not even noon. How are you?"

"Fine and mellow, now that I've heard your voice. Meet me for lunch and I'll make sure the rest of the day is better. I've got a nice surprise for you."

"Okay. I sure could use something good to make me forget this hellish morning." Her irritable mood eased at the thought of seeing him. Yet Noel's deep laughter through the phone sent chills through her.

"The real good stuff will come later."

"Can't wait. Meet you at twelve-thirty?"

"Yes, at the Gumbo Shop. Bye, baby." Noel made a kissing sound before the phone clicked off.

"Bye, darlin'."

Lyrissa smiled as she hung up the phone. Her smile faded as she remembered her dilemma. A small voice reminded her that time was running out.

"Okay, okay," she snapped at herself. "I'll tell him."

Mr. Taylor strode into her office. "What is going on with you and Georgina St. Denis?"

"Nothing that I know of. Why?" Her heart thumped.

"She just got through slicing and dicing my butt. Something about a reporter, slanderous lies, and we'll be hearing from her attorney. She says you have no integrity." He leaned on her desk, both palms flat. "Lyrissa, what in the world is the woman ranting about?"

Lyrissa dropped the brochure. "A reporter? She mentioned a reporter?"

"Aside from having Georgina St. Denis angry with me, this could be a very good thing, Lyrissa. Nothing like a touch of notoriety to make a collection valuable. Not to mention people will flock to my gallery." Mr. Taylor wore a calculating smile.

"What exactly did she say? Mr. Taylor!" Lyrissa raised her voice to get his attention.

"Hmm, oh just that this reporter called from the *New Orleans Chronicle* to get her comments on this story." Mr. Taylor stood straight and crossed his arms. "This is too good to be true." He beamed at Lyrissa.

"Dionne," Lyrissa groaned. "Damn!"

"Dionne Jackson? That's one tough investigative reporter. She loves to burn folks." Mr. Taylor waved his hands excitedly. "Could it get any better?"

"I'm going to run out and get a copy of that damn paper." Lyrissa sprang from her chair.

"Excellent idea." Mr. Taylor pulled out his wallet. He removed several bills and shoved them at her. "Here, get as many copies as you can. I'll keep them here in the gallery for customers to see!"

Lyrissa grabbed the money without looking at it. She headed for the door. "I've got to see what's in the article," she said, more to herself than to Mr. Taylor.

"By the way, what about this brochure?" He picked it up.

"Typos. It has to be done over. Call the printer. Chew him out," Lyrissa called over her shoulder as she raced across the lobby.

"No problem." Mr. Taylor did not lose his smile. "I'll deal with him. I'm sure he'll put his staff to work and get it done in time."

She barely heard him as she pushed out the door and onto the sidewalk. She strode quickly to the corner convenience store. A blue metal newspaper dispenser sat outside. The *Chronicle* took pride in "printing hard-hitting

stories" as they called them. They specialized in going after prominent people. She got change from the cashier
and fed the machine. As she reached in for a stack, the
bold headline made her stomach lurch.

"Famous Collection Stained By Scandal," she read
aloud. "Damn! I've got to call Noel fast."

Lyrissa whirled around and headed for the gallery. On
the way back she'd stop, read a few sentences, curse, and
start walking again. People gave her a wide berth, no
doubt convinced she'd gone insane. She didn't notice. The
only thing she could think of was Noel's reaction to the
story.

Lyrissa got back to the gallery.

"Give me, give me!" Mr. Taylor bubbled. "Louis from
Chartres Art Emporium just called. He's s-o-o-o jealous.
Says they mentioned us three times."

Lyrissa literally tossed him all of the copies except one.
She went into her office and paced in a circle as she read
the rest of the article. Kevin stuck his head in.

"Lyrissa, Tameka has a call for you. But I'll have her
take a message if you're busy."

Lyrissa heard his voice, but couldn't stop reading. "The
St. Denis family collection was seemingly acquired with
the same single-minded ruthlessness as they've shown in
business for decades."

"Tameka is going on her break again. She's part-time
and takes more breaks than I do," Kevin complained.
"Anyway, you're busy. I'll just take the message from Mr.
St. Denis."

"No, don't do that!" she yelled, causing him to jump
back. "Sorry, I'll take the call."

"Okay."

Kevin gazed at her with a curious expression as he backed out of her office. Moments later her phone rang. Lyrissa took a deep breath and let it out to steady her nerves. No good. She picked up the receiver with dread.

"Noel, I can explain," she began.

"Good. Come to my office."

"Now?" Lyrissa's voice wavered.

"I'll expect to see you in fifteen minutes, Lyrissa." He hung up the phone.

Lyrissa groaned and hung up. She grabbed her purse as she headed back out. Mr. Taylor emerged from his office waving the newspaper.

"Listen, about the show next month—"

"Later. I've got to go." Lyrissa didn't break her stride.

"Lyrissa, you can't leave now. We've got to talk about—"

"I can't right now, Mr. Taylor," Lyrissa shouted.

Traffic was still heavy. Lyrissa's mind raced as she tried to think of what she would say. Unlike her morning commute, the trip seemed too short. She needed more time. Yet there could never be enough hours in the day to help her prepare to face Noel. Eddie was at her desk when Lyrissa arrived outside Noel's office.

"Hi. He said you should go right in." Eddie's expression was grave. "Uh, Julie's already in there, and so is Carlton," she added.

"How bad is it?" Lyrissa fingered her copy of the *Chronicle*.

"I've never seen him this upset, and Carlton has a talent for getting on his nerves."

"Notify my next of kin," Lyrissa mumbled. She squared her shoulders and opened the door.

Julie, Carlton, and Noel stood holding copies of the

newspaper. Conversation stopped when they saw her. Julie wore a smirk. Noel gazed at her with a severe expression like chiseled stone.

"Let's sit down," Noel said and waved a hand at the seating area. The others followed him. They'd barely settled when he spoke again. "My grandmother is upset, and rightly so, Lyrissa."

"Upset is an understatement," Carlton put in. "She's in a rage. You know how she feels about the family name. She certainly doesn't like family business talked about publicly."

Three sets of eyes stared at her. "The stories all came from historical record," Lyrissa said carefully.

"The reporter seems to have been reading family documents from our archives," Carlton shot back.

"Or talking to someone who had," Julie added. "The documents you had access to for weeks."

"The Louisiana State Museum has documents, too. The reporter could have gotten information from there," Noel said quietly.

"How would she know what to look for, or even where to look? No, Noel, obviously this information was fed to her." Julie looked at Lyrissa again.

"Lyrissa has done publicity for the art show. She talked to reporters and art reviewers about the family history." Noel rubbed his jaw.

"Then she's done her job too damn well," Carlton snapped.

Julie's eyes narrowed. "This was part of your scheme, wasn't it, Ms. Rideau?" She looked like a large cat about to pounce on a bird.

"That's enough, Julie," Noel said.

"She saw you coming. All she did was wiggle her butt and your common sense flew out the window. She used you."

"You're going too far, Julie." Noel's eyes flashed a warning at her.

"Am I?" Julie stared at Lyrissa.

Noel glanced at the two women. His dark brows came together. "Lyrissa, what is she talking about?"

"No, I want the pleasure of telling you," Julie cut in before Lyrissa could speak. "She had a secret agenda. 'Sunday Stroll on the Faubourg Tremé' is an extremely valuable painting that was done by her ancestor. Her family had claimed for years that a St. Denis stole it. They've been plotting to get it back. Seducing you was part of the plan." She smiled with satisfaction.

"I'm afraid she played you, Noel," Carlton said in a dry tone.

Noel sat silent for several minutes. "I want to talk to Lyrissa alone," he said in a low voice.

"The board will want answers. We need to address this vicious attack on our reputation." Carlton held up the newspaper to emphasize his point.

"Later, Carlton," Noel replied without looking at him.

Lyrissa tried to gaze back at Noel, but the hurt in his eyes was too much to bear. She glanced away. No one spoke for several seconds more. Carlton huffed at being dismissed. Yet he merely glared at Noel.

"I'll check back with you later, Noel," Julie said smugly. "Come on, Carlton." He followed her out after frowning at Lyrissa once more.

Noel continued to stare at her. "Are they right? Did you use me?"

"Of course not. I didn't use sex to pry information out of you." Lyrissa went to the window and stared down at the street. "I already knew enough by the time we . . ."

"Why didn't you tell me?"

"I couldn't be sure how you'd react at first. I needed to check family records."

"I see. So you *did* use me." Noel's jaw muscles stretched tight.

"Noel, I—"

"You came here and searched for evidence. You stalled for more time until you found what you needed," he said in a cold, harsh voice.

"No, I didn't."

"Come on! You strung me along so you could stay longer." Noel stood and walked to her.

"The painting really does belong to my family. You even admitted that your ancestors were unscrupulous."

"Now I get it. We had long talks about my family history. No wonder you were so interested. I was stupid enough to think you enjoyed being with me." Noel looked into her eyes.

"That's not true and you know it."

"Do I?" Noel gave a short, bitter laugh. "I don't know much at all. I sure didn't have sense enough to see through you."

"It's just one painting. Your family has an entire collection of valuable art and a major business." Lyrissa shook her head. "You didn't even know what you had."

"Which makes what you did okay, I guess. We're rich, so anything goes."

"To you that painting is just another asset, a dollar figure to add to your balance sheet. My grandmother sees hat painting as the last hope she has to save our family's egacy. 'Sunday Stroll' is just about all we have left." Lyrissa ·ut a hand on his arm. "She's seen too much slip from her ·ands."

"In other words, the painting represents a chance to re-tore your family status. And you accuse us of being nobs." Noel shook her hand from his arm and walked to ·is desk.

Lyrissa sighed. "Mama Grace feels it's her responsibil-·ty to hold onto our heritage. She's a proud woman. I'm ·ure you understand."

Noel shook the newspaper. "According to this story, my ;randfather, his father, and *his* father were thieves. I feel a ·esponsibility to them."

"But they knew the truth, Noel. They knew the cir-·umstances of how that painting was acquired," Lyrissa ·aid forcefully.

"*Your* truth, Lyrissa. There are two sides to every ·tory, or history, in this case." He threw the newspaper ·nto his desk.

"I was going to tell you, Noel. This article caught me by ·urprise, too. I know how it looks, but I'm not lying to ·ou." Lyrissa tried to get close to him. His rigid stance ·topped her.

Noel's eyes narrowed. "You realized you didn't have to ·ettle for one painting. You would romance me and win ·he whole prize. Hell, why stop there? Go for stock op-·ions, a house, and my trust fund. Louisiana is a commu-·ity property state."

Lyrissa flinched at the way he looked at her. "You don't ·elieve what you're saying."

"I've been in this game before, baby. At least those

debutantes were honest. I knew what they wanted. But
you . . ." Noel clenched a fist.

"I didn't plan what happened between us. You wanted
to be with me, too, Noel." Lyrissa wanted to remind him
of the tenderness they'd shared. Instead, her words only
hardened his expression.

"So it was my fault. Okay, I'll give you that one. I let
your charm blind me." Noel wore a brutal smile. "But I'm
seeing you pretty clearly today."

"The painting is ours. But—"

"Our attorneys will deal with your claim," he broke in.

"Fine. Let's talk about us," Lyrissa said softly.

"For some reason I'm not feeling particularly romantic." Noel punched a button on his phone. "Eddie, get my
lawyer on the phone. Have the archives brought to my office. I'll need to review that stack of contracts we talked
about. I can't let our business grind to a halt."

Noel issued a string of instructions as he sorted
through papers on his desk. He seemed determined to
block out Lyrissa's existence. He succeeded. She felt invisible. A cold hollowness gripped her. She fully realized in
one awful moment the precious thing she'd lost. Despite
his heated words there had been no mistaking the anguish
reflected in his eyes. Lyrissa ached to explain but couldn't.
No words could go far enough to help him understand
her betrayal of his trust. His anger masked the pain and
he would use work to numb it. All she had left was the
pain.

Lyrissa picked up her purse from the table where she'd
left it and walked out his door.

22

After a week with no word from Noel, Lyrissa couldn't
stand it anymore. The two families fought each other with
dueling press releases and news articles. Mrs. St. Denis
had enlisted the aid of another prominent local magazine
edited by a longtime friend. The result was a series of articles in praise of the St. Denis family and a companion
piece on the life of Jules Joubert. The stories revealed that
Jules had a less than sterling reputation himself. Mama
Grace was livid. She demanded that Ebony issue ultima-
tums that barely stopped short of threatening physical vi-
olence. Lyrissa spent fifty percent of her emotional energy
trying to reason with the fiery matron. The other half was
tied up with thinking of Noel. He finally called, but she
took no comfort from the tone of his voice. She called Mr.
Taylor to let him know she'd be in after meeting with Noel
and headed for Tremé Corporation.

"Hi, Eddie. Let Noel know I'm here." Lyrissa nodded
toward the closed door.

"Hi. You okay?" Eddie wore a sympathetic expression.

Lyrissa teared up at the genuine concern in Eddie'
voice. She hadn't realized her emotions were so close to
the surface. Lyrissa took a deep breath before answering
"Sure. I'm doing okay."

"Good. He's on a long distance conference call, but he
should be through soon. I'll bring you a cup of coffee."
Eddie started toward the kitchen.

"Don't stop working because of me." Lyrissa twisted
the strap of her purse. She considered bolting while she
still had the chance.

"Any excuse will do." Eddie grinned at her. "I'll be right
back."

Lyrissa sat down on the sofa. She tapped a foot nervously and became lost in thought. Noel was angry, and
she could understand why. Yet they needed to clear the air
Or maybe Lyrissa just needed her conscience soothed. His
office door swung open and she steeled herself to face
him. Instead Julie walked out.

"I'm surprised you have the nerve to come here." Julie
stared down at her. When Lyrissa didn't reply, her mouth
lifted in a scornful smile. "Your 'assets' won't get you out
of trouble this time, honey."

Eddie came back carrying a tray that held a carafe and
cups. "I poured a fresh pot. I'm sure the one in Noel's office is empty by now, and—"

"You shouldn't have bothered. They won't be meeting
long enough for Miss Thang to even sit down." Julie
crossed her arms.

"Ahem, I'll tell him you're here." Eddie ignored Julie and went into Noel's office.

"Great," Lyrissa muttered, convinced she'd made a huge mistake in coming.

She braced herself for more condemnation. Noel came out of the office. Tall, and gorgeous as ever, he was dressed in tan slacks and a white shirt. She stared at the full lips that had left their mark on her body, the strong arms that had held her close. There was no denying how much she missed his touch.

He stood gazing at her for a few moments. Lyrissa felt exposed and guilty. Maybe he wanted to throw her out personally. His anger would be better than nothing at all. She'd use it as a starting point, at least. Silence was a more deadly weapon.

"Hello, Lyrissa. Come on in." His tone was mild, almost without inflection.

"I'm glad we can talk." Lyrissa stood.

Julie snorted. "You've got to be kidding. After what you pulled? Don't worry, Noel. I'll show her the exit."

"No more scenes, Julie," Noel said tersely. "I asked her to come here."

"You shouldn't talk to her without your attorney, Noel! Don't be her fool again," Julie snapped.

"Goodbye, Julie." He stared at her until she stomped off.

Lyrissa barely noticed her departure. She gazed at Noel. How she wanted to caress the smooth vanilla caramel skin. Even now she could not stop thinking about their night together. His cold gaze sent a shock through her. He nodded for her to walk ahead of him. Lyrissa lifted her chin and went into his office. Eddie was at his desk gathering papers. The young woman sent Lyrissa a silent message of support with her dark eyes then left. Once the door closed gently, Noel nodded to her again to take a seat.

"I haven't heard from your attorney." He sat across from her.

"She'll send a letter soon." Lyrissa fought hard not to shrink from his relentless gaze.

"Here, for services rendered." Noel handed her an envelope.

Lyrissa opened it and found a check. "Let's talk."

"About what?"

"You know the answer to that question, Noel."

He studied her for a while longer. "And you must know there's nothing left to talk about. You got what you came for, Lyrissa."

Lyrissa lost the staring battle and looked away. "Being with you wasn't part of the plan."

"Being with me," he echoed. "Nice way of saying it."

"I care about you so much. I really do," she protested when his jaw tightened into a cynical expression. The scornful glint in his eyes stung her already bleeding heart. "God, I wanted our relationship to work. Inside I still do, but I'm realistic. There is such a gulf between us, Noel."

"Right. So you don't feel so bad lying to me, is that what you're saying?" Noel's voice sounded strained with controlled anger.

"No, I feel terrible about everything that has happened. Why else would I come?" Lyrissa felt tears pushing at her eyelids again. "I'm sorry about this whole crazy mess."

"So am I, Lyrissa. But I'm not going to roll over." Noel glanced away from her for the first time. His jaw muscles worked as he clenched his teeth. "You can look as sexy and vulnerable as you want to, it won't work."

"What?" Lyrissa's heart sank at his words.

"Tell your lawyer to send the letter. Your act doesn't play anymore. My grandmother is determined to fight you. Frankly, I don't blame her." Noel stood.

"You think I'm lying about what I feel?" She looked up at him.

"Yes!"

Lyrissa stood and walked close to him until they were an inch apart. His anger radiated out in heat waves, yet there was more. Noel's expression wavered between resistance and desire. She found hope in the way he gazed at her face.

"Please talk to me. I know you feel betrayed. You really haven't let me explain it all to you." She touched his solid upper arm and instantly longed to feel his embrace.

He didn't move away. Instead he seemed to watch her in fascination as she leaned closer. With great care, Lyrissa brushed her lips across his. She put her arms around his narrow waist and sighed. Noel stood rigid for only a moment before he pulled her hard against his broad chest. He moaned as his mouth covered hers. His kiss was rough, needy. Then he let go abruptly and stood back.

"I can't believe I'm letting you play me all over again." He rubbed a hand across his face.

"I'm not and you know it." Lyrissa touched her fingertips to his chest. He placed a hand over them. "Let's be together tonight."

Noel seemed to fight a mental battle for a time. "I must be crazy, but . . ."

He fingered a tendril of her hair and kissed her again. This time it was a lingering exploration that was as much spiritual as physical. Lyrissa trembled at the jagged desire that tore at her. The aching lonely hours of being without him had taken a toll. She rubbed her hips against his hungrily. Noel responded by lifting her until she stood on tiptoes.

"God, I missed you," he murmured, his mouth still on hers.

"Tonight we'll work it all out," she whispered. "I'd better go, or we'll end up on your desk."

Noel cupped her face with one large hand. "Tonight," he said softly.

"Tonight." Lyrissa pried herself from him with great effort. She walked out of his office on a cloud.

Eddie looked at her hard as she walked out. "You might want to fix your lipstick." She gave her the thumbs-up signal and a big grin.

The rest of her day went smoothly. Nothing bothered her. Mr. Taylor's excitement about the publicity had been warranted. A steady stream of people curious to get the inside scoop on the scandal came to the gallery. He was even more delighted with the increase in serious buyers. Lyrissa was more than happy to let Mr. Taylor take center stage and deflect all the attention from her. At the end of the day, she sighed with contentment. Her good spirits vanished when Mama Grace met her at the door when she got home. Today seemed to be the day to face the music.

"Lyrissa." Mama Grace stared at her hard. "Ebony tells me you went to see *him*."

"I did." Lyrissa walked past her and put her briefcase down on the hall table.

"You went behind my back and risked our claim." Mama Grace glared at her.

"*You* went behind *my* back and released that damn story," she tossed back.

"I couldn't count on you to take action." Mama Grace lifted her nose in the air.

"So you didn't trust me," Lyrissa said through clenched teeth. "After I busted my butt researching, following leads, and setting up the whole thing? I planned for months."

"Yes, you did," Mama Grace agreed.

"I took a job with Taylor Gallery instead of that position clerking at the Presbytere. Do you know how hard it is to get in there?" Lyrissa put her hands on her hips.

"Yes, I know what you gave up. But you fell in love with Noel St. Denis."

Lyrissa shivered. Was she hopelessly in love with a man she could never have? She shoved away the frightening thought quickly and threw up her hands in exasperation. "I have no intention of giving up our painting!"

"Really?" Mama Grace gazed down her nose at her.

"We're going to meet tonight and work things out."

"While he's holding your hand and staring into your eyes, his lawyers will be hard at work," Mama Grace retorted.

"Well, you didn't help by tipping them off before I had a chance to test the waters. He might have been able to deal with his grandmother," Lyrissa said with a frown.

Mama Grace gave a sharp, humorless laugh. "You're definitely living in a fantasy world."

"Have you fed Dionne more dirt? I'm hoping the article today will be the last one."

"It won't. I could keep an army of reporters busy for

months with the scandals from that family." Mama Grace wore a victorious smile.

"Lord, have mercy! Mama Grace—" Lyrissa broke off when the phone rang. She marched to the phone. "Hello," she barked into it.

"Okay, I don't need to ask how you're doing," Ebony said. "I leave town for a few days and all hell breaks loose. Folks are buzzing about the war between the Joubert descendants and Mrs. St. Denis."

"I didn't release the stories. Mama Grace did it without consulting me!" Lyrissa raised her voice and frowned at her grandmother.

"Humph!" Mama Grace turned and walked off.

"Damn, girl. The legal sharks are circling as we speak. I'd better put on my armor and get my ammo ready."

"I'm trying to avoid a bloodbath." Lyrissa sighed.

"Too late. We have a subscription to *New Orleans Life*. Have you seen the stuff they printed about your illustrious ancestor?"

Lyrissa could hear pages rustling. She sighed again. "Yes. Some of it I knew. Anyway, I'm meeting with Noel tonight."

"You still sleeping with the enemy?" Ebony quipped. "Brave woman. Listen, he's no lightweight when it comes to taking out opponents. Remember, he's a St. Denis. They got their reputation the old fashioned way, they earned it!"

"I wish everyone would stop telling me that." Lyrissa rubbed her throbbing temples. Her good mood was definitely gone now.

"Oh right, you've got a secret weapon." The grin in Ebony's voice came through the phone lines clearly.

"Funny. I'll talk to you later." Lyrissa hung up and

glanced at her wristwatch. She had just enough time to run an errand before she met Noel.

He scanned his apartment again. "Relax," he told himself once more.

Soft New Orleans jazz flowed from the compact disc player. Noel paced in front of the double windows leading to the balcony. He alternately watched car headlights pass in the night and stared at nothing in particular. He drank from his wine glass, rolling the smooth Merlot on his tongue.

Crazy. He had to be out of his mind. Lyrissa had insinuated herself into his life, hell, into his soul, with an ulterior motive. Yet here he was, sweating for her. Maybe he should believe in voodoo love potions, he mused.

Noel opened the window and stepped out onto the balcony. The scent of gardenias mixed with Creole spice floated in the air. Huge oak trees rose in the dark like hulking giants. He loved every inch of this city even as others cursed its faults. History oozed up from the sidewalks. Noel imagined an army of St. Denis ghosts marching down Rampart Street. *Sins of the fathers,* he thought. Generations of proud, greedy Creoles reached into the future. Yet he'd come to understand his family history in a more complete way. Not a view his grandmother found appealing, for sure. Never mind how she railed when he dared to say Lyrissa's name. The doorbell chimed as if on cue. Lyrissa smiled nervously when he opened the door. She wore white Capri pants, white sandals, and an emerald green tank-style tunic. Her brown skin glowed as though she'd been brushed with warm butter.

"Hi," she said.

He swallowed hard. She'd pulled out the big guns. His pulse pounded when she walked by him, leaving a delicate trail of perfume behind. Noel closed the door. All he could think of was peeling the clingy slacks from her sexy body.

"Hello," he finally managed to say.

"How bad has your day been? Lyrissa turned to face him with a slight frown. "You look tired."

" 'Harassed' is a better word. But the world didn't come to an end." He smiled at her.

"Noel, I didn't know about some of those things in the paper. I—"

"Let's not talk about it just yet. I ordered dinner from La Madeleine's. Wine?" He wanted to hold the ugliness at bay for at least a few more magical moments.

"Yes indeed!" Lyrissa tossed her small handbag onto a chair.

He handed her a glass and they went out to the balcony. Neither spoke, content to watch the city around them. A gentle spring breeze stirred the sheer ivory draperies that framed the window.

"So, what will we talk about?" Noel said finally.

"Talking about us seems the best place to start. We'll get to the weather later." Lyrissa wore a gentle smile.

He drew her to him and looked into her eyes. "Lyrissa, you should have trusted me."

"I didn't know you. I had to think about my family," she said softly.

"So do I."

Lyrissa looked away. "We're back to problem number one. Your grandmother must have her way."

"Wait a minute. Why is this all about my family? You've got your own biases, too." Noel turned her face back to him.

"Which your relatives immediately confirmed," she countered.

"Not all of them. Admit it."

"True, but that doesn't include your parents and grandparents. Lord, I haven't even met your mother's parents." Lyrissa shook her head. "I've heard about them."

Noel heaved a sigh. "Okay, I can't argue with you. My grandmother is tolerant compared to them."

"See?" She moved away.

"I wouldn't let them keep us apart. Period," Noel said firmly.

"But they'd make life miserable for us. They might even disinherit you because of me." Lyrissa shook her head.

He laughed. "Baby, this isn't the eighteenth century."

"And what about Tremé Corporation? They'd fire you and make Carlton CEO," she persisted.

"Not a chance," Noel retorted. "There is one very important reason they won't fire me—money. I've turned the company around. They may be snobbish, but they're not stupid."

"Don't tell me Mrs. St. Denis wouldn't cut you out of her will." Lyrissa pointed a finger at him.

"Stop reading those romance novels. My grandmother couldn't if she wanted to. My grandfather set up an irrevocable trust, which means the money is mine." Noel put his arms around her.

"Oh." Her frown relaxed a little. "You'll lose all your fancy friends. I'll never be accepted in your social set."

"I don't care, it's fewer pretentious parties to attend. I'll live."

"You've never been on the outside looking in. I don't think you realize what you're giving up." Lyrissa traced a finger over the stitches of his olive cotton shirt.

"Yes I do. People I've known all my life, some of them relatives, will avoid us. I'm not naïve, baby." Noel touched his forehead to hers.

He kissed her sweet mouth until the image of ghosts and disapproving family faded. Desire for her spread through him like warm oil poured on his body. The warmth turned into raw heat when her tongue touched his. Her hands gripped his forearms as they kissed hard. He cupped a breast. Lyrissa wiggled closer as his thumb teased her nipple. She pulled back.

"We haven't finished talking, Noel. Nothing is settled." She panted when he gently squeezed her breast again.

"Keep talking." He bent his head and rubbed his lips against her neck.

"You know what I mean," she said softly. Lyrissa tilted her head back to let him go farther.

"I need to feel you," he whispered. "You know what I want."

He led her inside and did just what he'd fantasized about for days. He removed her clothes slowly and with relish.

Lyrissa opened his shirt and planted moist, hot kisses all over his chest. She took her own time removing his pants, her fingers caressing him until he cried out. They paused briefly while he put on a condom. Lyrissa pulled him on top of her as they went down to the floor. There would be no long foreplay tonight. Instead, Lyrissa guided him inside her and wrapped her legs around him. Noel moaned again at the sensation of entering her. He was enclosed by a deliciously hot, wet satin.

"Please, baby," she whispered.

"Not yet. I'm going to make you wait," he whispered back and lay still. In truth, he wanted to savor the first few moments of being engulfed, sucked under into a wonderful world.

Impatient, she rocked her hips and whispered his name. Noel couldn't resist longer than five minutes as need pounded him. He matched her rhythm with his own. Their lovemaking became frantic. Noel tumbled dizzily into senselessness, thrusting hard into her to satisfy his hunger for her. Lyrissa screamed once and shuddered as she came. Noel held on long enough to feel her muscles contract around his erection. The sensation pushed him into a powerful orgasm. Every one of his muscles seemed to quiver as sweat poured down his sides. After a time they lay still in each other's arms.

"Are you trying to drive me crazy, lady?" Noel mumbled, his face buried in her thick hair.

"No, I'm trying to be worth all the trouble I caused." Lyrissa stroked her fingers along his spine.

Noel shivered in her arms. "God knows you've succeeded."

"We'll have to face them all, Noel. We can't live in our own world away from everyone else," Lyrissa said softly.

"We can tonight. We can do it every night. Just shut the door and leave them all behind when we need to, baby." Noel breathed in the lush scent of her perfume mixed with perspiration.

"Can it be that simple?"

"Not simple, but damn sure worth it."

23

Lyrissa shifted enough to see the digital clock on the nightstand. The numbers glowed a muted orange showing it was six A.M.

"Oh, boy," she said softly so as not to wake him. "Mama Grace is probably mad as hell with me now."

"Hmm." Noel's large arm tightened around her waist.

She studied the contours of his face. Beautiful. Noel's long dark eyelashes stood out against his light brown skin. Lyrissa pressed her cheek against his chest. His heartbeat seemed in tune with hers.

"Baby," he whispered. "Time to get up."

"Hey, I thought you were asleep." She kissed his nipples.

"I am, almost." Noel stretched his long frame. "But I've got a busy day. Let's go to the French Market for breakfast."

"Deal. If we get up now, you'll have plenty of time before you go back to ruling the world." Lyrissa tapped his face playfully.

They showered and dressed together, teasing each other about which one would be in more trouble with their families. Lyrissa tried to make it a joke, yet her fears for him lingered.

Gloomy thoughts fled when they finally stepped into the sunshine. Noel drove them to the French Market, where they bought two tangelos and bananas. Next they walked to Café du Monde, where they enjoyed café au lait with their fruit. Lyrissa could almost believe that they could be like any other couple in love. Almost. Their conversation had lapsed into thoughtful silence.

"The party's over." Lyrissa toyed with a sliver of rind from the tangelo.

"I guess you're right. Let's see what new hell I'll have to tackle today." Noel went to buy a newspaper from a stand nearby. He glanced at a copy of the *Chronicle* and grimaced.

"I'm really sorry, baby," she said, when he came back to the table.

"You pointed them in the right direction. The secrets were waiting to be found. I just—" His cell phone trilled a series of musical notes. "Damn, now what?" he muttered as he looked at the caller ID.

"Who is it?"

He flipped open the phone. "My property manager. Yeah, Keisha. I hope this is urgent. What?" His frown deepened as he listened. "I'm on my way. No, I'll talk to the police when I get there."

"What's happened? Why are the police—" She stopped when he waved a hand at her.

"Right. I'm not far." Noel punched the end button and jumped up. "The Chaisson House is on fire. I've got to go. I'll drop you at your car on the way."

"I'm coming with you. What about the art? Did Keisha have a chance to move it yet?" Lyrissa almost had to jog to match his long strides back to his car.

"We were supposed to move them tomorrow." Noel unlocked the car with his remote. The horn blew as he turned off the alarm.

"Damn!" Lyrissa ran around and got in the passenger side.

Noel made good time weaving in and out of the early morning traffic. They reached Magazine Street in fifteen minutes. Lyrissa's stomach lurched at the column of black smoke in the sky. They had to park three blocks away and go around a barricade. Noel explained who he was to a policeman who allowed them to approach a fireman. Keisha rushed toward them. She was dressed in an over-sized t-shirt and jeans.

"What happened, Kee?" Noel asked.

Keisha gulped in air and wiped a large tear from her cheek. "Mrs. Barrett got to her antique shop about seven. She saw smoke and called 911."

A tall blond policeman walked up. "Sir, your employee says you can verify the contents of this building."

"I don't have a list of all the art, and I . . ." Keisha started to cry.

Lyrissa put an arm around her. "Come over here and sit down, honey. Noel will take care of everything. We have a list."

"Yeah, Kee," Noel said gently. "Go with Lyrissa." He looked at her in gratitude.

"We'll go down to the coffee shop. A good mocha latte will help steady your nerves." Lyrissa led her through a crowd of onlookers, which included one of the waitresses.

"Hey, I'll get y'all two cups right away." She patted Keisha on the shoulder and went ahead of them to the coffee shop.

They sat at a table near the large window. Keisha sniffled as she patted her nose with a tissue. "I don't understand how this happened. I know that house is in good condition. It can't have been electrical. I swear I got all the permits and hired the best people to work on it."

"It's an old house with old wiring. Anything could have happened. Don't start blaming yourself."

"The alarm didn't go off. But I swear I set it the last time I was there. And Earl, he's our security coordinator, would check the house at least once a day to be sure. Just until we finally moved the art, I mean." Keisha twisted the sodden paper between her fingers.

"Keisha, no one is going to say this is your fault," Lyrissa said calmly.

"Here you go, bay." The young white woman smiled at them. "I added a dash of vanilla. It's soothing."

"Thanks," Lyrissa said, and paid her.

"You don't know how Julie can be. She's never liked me." Keisha dabbed beneath her eyes. "I have to report to her."

"Julie isn't the boss. Noel will keep her in line."

"Yeah, you're right." Her anxious expression eased into a half-smile. "She tries to boss him around, but he sets him straight."

"Exactly. Nobody controls Noel St. Denis." Lyrissa grinned at her.

Noel walked up at that moment. He sat down hard and

ordered a cup of black coffee. "Andre is coming with the inventory of the art. Our insurance agent is coming with the adjuster in two hours."

"We need to get every piece of art some place secure . . . what's left of it." Lyrissa held her breath and waited.

"The fire wasn't that big. They contained it pretty fast. Seems it started in the kitchen pantry. Most of the damage is from smoke and water." Noel accepted his coffee from the waitress and drank deeply.

"How bad?" Lyrissa held her breath.

"The firefighters think it was arson to cover a burglary. They found a pile of oily rags stuffed in a corner of the pantry."

"What about the alarm?" Lyrissa said.

"The lines had been cut. Several neighbors reported their phones went dead late last night." Noel rubbed his eyes. "Keisha, they found Earl in one of the rooms upstairs. He'd been knocked out."

Keisha's eyes widened with horror. "Oh no! Is he—"

"He's alive, but barely. Smoke inhalation. The fire must have smoldered for a long time before smoke spread through the house. They just found him and took him to the hospital." Noel rose slowly, as though he carried a heavy weight.

"We have to call his mother," Keisha said through tears. She glanced at Lyrissa. "Earl is a single parent. Kamal is four and Jasmine is ten. His wife was killed two years ago in a car accident."

"Earl's sister is going to keep the kids. Can you go to the hospital and stay with his mother? I'll wait here for Andre and the insurance people."

Keisha stood up. She collected herself. "Of course. I'll make sure she's okay, then come back."

"Let me help," Lyrissa said to Noel.

"No, baby. I'll get you a cab back to the apartment. It was good having you here, though. I love you," he murmured and kissed her lightly.

Lyrissa watched him walk away. Keisha hurried off in the opposite direction with a distracted goodbye. She sat alone, gazing at the hustle of activity from firemen. The coffee shop filled with customers who talked about the fire and rumors they'd heard. Their voices were muffled. Lyrissa only heard echoes of Noel's deep voice saying, "I love you."

"What the hell happened?" Carlton paced the floor of his office and wrung his hands. "How did Earl get hurt?"

Julie sat in a leather chair. She seemed tense but in control. "Lower your voice or the whole office will hear you," she said in a clipped tone.

Carlton halted and darted a frightened glance at the closed door. He sat next to her. "The house was supposed to be empty. You didn't mention anything about a fire. The collection was supposed to be intact after all this settled down," he whispered harshly.

"I'd moved most of the good pieces to the front room after that wine and cheese party I hosted. Remember, they 'stole' most of it, anyway. Nothing valuable was seriously damaged." Julie waved a hand.

"And Earl?"

Julie wore an irritated frown. "That fool wasn't supposed to be there. He must have changed his schedule. Anyway, Keisha says he'll live."

"Was he burned?" Carlton flinched as though feeling the flames.

"No, just a bit of smoke inhalation. He might be in the hospital for a while, maybe have lung problems," Julie said in a distracted tone. Earl's health did not seem to be her real concern.

"Good God, Julie! Noel says the police will charge the arsonist with attempted murder if they catch them." Carlton rubbed his face with a shaky hand.

"That's a big *if*. Arson is a very difficult crime to solve." Julie tilted her head to one side. "Actually, the fire wasn't a dumb move. Anyway, those guys will make sure they don't get caught now."

"If they'd been smart, they would have made the fire look like an accident."

"I told Keisha that those rags had been left after the cleaning crew finished up. The fire actually started in a wall. So the fire department isn't sure it wasn't accidental now." Julie smiled at him.

"Yeah, and Keisha also told them all about the electrical contract work," Carlton shot back. "They've ruled that out as a cause."

"I never would have guessed she had that much intelligence." Julie's thin mouth turned down into a sour expression.

"Seems your plan wasn't so well thought out after all," Carlton snarled.

"A minor detail. They're calling it a suspicious fire. As I said, most arson cases are never solved. Except this one will be, with a little help from us."

"Well, I'm glad you're so cocky!" Carlton stood and went to his desk. He sat down hard.

"Stay calm and everything will fall into place. Lyrissa will get a nasty surprise very soon. Imagine thinking she could get away with such a scheme." Julie wore a nasty smile.

"Why should anyone believe she'd steal art?" He shook his head. "You must have been crazy to hire street criminals to commit burglary. Now Earl is hurt, and—"

"Shut up, Carlton!" Julie leaned forward and pointed a manicured finger at him. "It was *your* idea to frame her, or have you forgotten?"

He shrunk back against the chair. "Okay, okay. What's done is done," Carlton muttered. "Just make sure those men can be trusted to keep their mouths shut."

Julie snorted. "Hell no, they can't be trusted. They're scum! But they're well-paid scum who don't know who we are."

"How do you know those kind of people?" Carlton wore a curious expression.

"Never mind. Except for this little blip with Earl getting hurt, we can still win."

He studied her in silence for several seconds. "You're cold-blooded, Julie."

A slow smile spread across her face. "Worried?"

Carlton continued to look at her a few moments more before he shook his head. "No, your fingerprints are all over the dirty work. You made the contacts and set things in motion."

"Yes, I did. I can prove you gave me the money, though." Her eyes glittered with malice.

Tiny beads of sweat popped out on his forehead. "How?"

Julie stood and smoothed the front of her green Donna

Karan dress. "We're in this together. Don't make the mistake of thinking otherwise." She strolled out of his office without a backward glance.

Carlton rocked his chair back and forth in a jerky, nervous motion. "Bitch!" he mumbled low.

Lyrissa, Mama Grace, and Aunt Claire were in Ebony's law office on Camp Street. They were on the tenth floor of a twenty-story building. The window behind Ebony gave them a view of the New Orleans business district skyline. The brilliant blue sky was dotted with fluffy clouds. Yet the idyllic scene contrasted with the anger in the office.

"This is a plot to steal our painting again!" Mama Grace pounded on Ebony's desk as she spoke.

Ebony moved a crystal pen stand away from her. "Take it easy," she said.

"Noel wouldn't do such a thing," Lyrissa said for the tenth time in five minutes. "You're being paranoid."

"Grace has a point, Lyrissa. The St. Denis family can be very crafty," Aunt Claire said with nod.

"Look at the lies they've spread about Jules Joubert!" Mama Grace slapped a palm on a recent copy of the magazine with the stories.

"All those women and illegitimate children!" Aunt Claire's eyes twinkled. "He drank like a fish. We knew that. But, my goodness. When did he find the time, not to mention the energy, to paint?" She started to giggle, then stopped at a venomous look from Mama Grace.

"And he made copies of his own work, then sold them as the originals." Ebony shook her head. "I won't lie to you, this is bad."

"I want to sue them for defamation of character and

get our painting back." Mama Grace shook a finger at Ebony.

"You can't defame a dead person, Miss Grace," Ebony said patiently.

"You should have told us about Jules, Mama Grace," Lyrissa added. "We'd look like idiots, pressing a lawsuit now."

Mama Grace huffed for a few moments. "So he wasn't perfect," she admitted grudgingly.

Aunt Claire put a hand to her mouth as she smothered another giggle. Ebony cleared her throat loudly and glanced at Lyrissa.

"In other words, most of it's true."

"Which doesn't change one basic fact—they stole his painting and we've got the documents to prove it." Mama Grace wore an intractable scowl.

"We'd better wait. No need in pressing your claim now. I'm sure Mrs. St. Denis will dredge up more dirt on the old rascal. I mean Mr. Joubert," Ebony added quickly, when Mama Grace glared at her.

"Then there's the police investigation of the burglary." Lyrissa got up and walked around to the window. "Very smart thieves. They took five of the most valuable pieces."

"One of which just happened to be *our* painting. What a coincidence!" Mama Grace said, sarcasm dripping from her voice.

"She's got a point, Lyrissa. My suspicious legal mind tells me something is up," Ebony said.

Lyrissa spun around and looked at Ebony. Her friend's skeptical expression said it all. Mama Grace gave a curt nod. Aunt Claire lifted a shoulder. She wanted to refute the argument, but couldn't. She'd thought the same thing more than once.

"Noel isn't involved, even if what you're thinking is true," she insisted.

"Your totally objective assessment, of course," Ebony said quietly.

"I know him. Noel would fight us face to face. This kind of sneaky stunt isn't his style," Lyrissa said.

"He's a St. Denis! All charm, but deadly as a snake." Mama Grace spoke with conviction. "You've got to face the truth, Lyrissa Michelle."

"I know his family's reputation is deserved." Lyrissa stared out the window again. "But Noel wouldn't . . . either way, Ebony is right. We should wait."

"We don't even know where the painting is, anyway." Aunt Claire blinked rapidly as she glanced at them all in turn.

"That was going to be my next point, Miss Claire," Ebony said. "Let's use the time to make our documentation damn near irrefutable." Her eyes narrowed. "I don't intend to lose."

"I'll go over every piece of paper myself." Mama Grace stood. "Come on, Claire." Sure of her younger sister's obedience, she marched out without looking at her.

Aunt Claire rose from the chair slowly. She walked over to Ebony and pecked her on the cheek. "I know you'll kick legal butt."

Ebony laughed out loud. "Thanks for the vote of confidence, Auntie Claire."

"You're welcome. As for you, sugar," she went to Lyrissa and hugged her, "I know how you feel. I hope you're right about him. Bye-bye, girls."

Lyrissa sat on the edge of Ebony's desk with her arms folded. Ebony swiveled her captain's chair slowly back and forth. Neither woman spoke for a time. They listened to the distant sound of phones ringing outside Ebony's door.

"What a mess," Lyrissa said finally.

"Girl, I don't like this crap one bit. I'm getting a bad feeling about the whole thing." Ebony tapped a black Cross pen on her yellow legal pad.

"Me, too, Eb." Lyrissa watched a cloud shaped like a cotton ball drift across the blue sky. "I'm not going to sit and wait, though."

Ebony glanced at her. "What are you going to do?"

Lyrissa looked back at her with a determined smile. "I'm not sure, but I'm working on it."

24

Lyrissa walked beside Noel down one of the many paved paths in Audubon Park. The sunny morning had turned cloudy. Neither spoke more than a few words for thirty minutes. Noel held her hand loosely, a thoughtful frown on his handsome face. She'd allowed him time to think. Yet her anxiety grew as his expression became more distracted.

"It might rain. We should have come prepared, like good scouts." She tugged at his hand playfully.

"No, we didn't expect bad weather so soon."

"Let's sit down over here." Lyrissa pointed to a bench sheltered under a wide oak.

They strolled over and Noel brushed a few leaves from the seat. They sat down and Noel gazed out over the park. Lyrissa knew his mind wasn't on the view.

"We might as well say it out loud." Lyrissa looped her arm around his.

"This whole fight over a painting is way past crazy," Noel said.

"I'd suggest we negotiate, but I'm scared to put our grandmothers in the same room. I can see the headline, 'Septuagenarians Choke Each Other to Death,' " Lyrissa deadpanned.

"God, yes! All the family secrets are out there on both sides of this feud." Noel grew quiet again.

Lyrissa glanced at him. "What?"

Noel turned to her. "I'm proud of my family. Sure, my relatives, past and present, have done a few things close to the line. But those stories pretty much label us as gangsters."

"You've got to admit a lot of it is true. Most of the stories about Jules are hundred-year-old gossip," Lyrissa said defensively.

"At least three women declared him as the father of their children in court, and what about the copies of his paintings?" Noel let go of her hand.

"Accusations, not proof," she replied.

"Gustave St. Denis founded schools for poor blacks in New Orleans. His grandson helped freed slaves who poured into this city after the civil war," he replied in a stiff tone.

Lyrissa heard his grandmother's brand of pride in his voice. She looked at him hard, remembering Mama Grace's warnings. "Gustave St. Denis 'acquired' a lot of real estate in a shady fashion. He also supported the Confederate government in Louisiana. Then, once the

Union Army captured the city, he became a carpetbagger."

"He never truly supported the Confederacy or slavery. His journals prove that," Noel said heatedly.

"So he lied when it suited his needs. Oh, I almost forgot—he was a founding member of the Astoria Club. They didn't admit dark-skinned Blacks. Your parents are members, too." Lyrissa arched her eyebrows.

"Those days are gone and you know it," Noel snapped.

"On the surface, maybe," Lyrissa shot back.

"Don't generalize about my friends and family, damn it." Noel sat forward with his elbows propped on his knees. "Talk about being biased!"

They sat next to each other in tense silence. Lyrissa wondered why one of them didn't just get up and leave. Something held her to the bench, an invisible cord that connected her to him. Yet each angry word sawed away at it. Soon they'd be hanging on by a slender thread.

"Maybe we should stick to talking about the weather, after all," she said finally.

Noel sighed and sat back against the bench. "We haven't even gotten to the fire and the burglary."

"You know what my grandmother thinks." Lyrissa looked across the wide green lawn.

"That we set it up. My folks feel the same way about your family."

"I defended you," Lyrissa said with a faint smile.

"Thanks. I defended you until we were all shouting at each other." Noel leaned toward her and put an arm across the back of the bench.

She nodded. "Did you ever once think—"

"No," he broke in sharply. "Did you think I might have been responsible?"

"No, but . . ." Lyrissa plucked at the hem of her cotton blouse.

"Yeah, my family. They didn't do it, Lyrissa." Noel rubbed his jaw with one large hand. "The police said they're going to call you."

"They haven't yet. Of course, I'll tell them everything I know."

Noel wound a tendril of her hair around his forefinger. "I don't want to lose you," he said softly.

"I don't want to lose you, either, but we're up against a lot here."

"Then we have to be stronger than the scandals, the rumors, the prejudices, *and* our relatives." He pulled her against his chest.

"Right," Lyrissa murmured. A tall order indeed, she mused.

Miss Georgina scowled at Noel over the top of her reading glasses. "She's got you fooled, Noel Phillip!"

Noel sat on the large sofa in his grandmother's sun room. He folded his arms in a defensive posture and braced himself for another tirade. His parents sat on either side of his grandmother like soldiers supporting the general. Julie had joined them at his grandmother's request. She stood to one side with a cup of coffee in one hand.

"I understand why you're so angry, but Lyrissa isn't a thief," he replied in a calm tone. "I'm not going to listen to your accusations again."

His mother put down her coffee cup. "Be reasonable, son. You can't believe this sequence of events is a coincidence."

"It does seem a bit odd, Noel," his father put in. Richard lifted a shoulder. "The timing is suspicious."

"To say the least," his mother, Madeline St. Denis, added sharply.

Julie strolled over and sat next to Noel. "Her claim is pretty shaky. Maybe she realized her scam wouldn't work."

"Your objective conclusion?" Noel said coldly. They stared at each other until Julie looked away. He turned to his father. "Lyrissa isn't stupid. Besides, their evidence isn't shaky at all."

"You're the one who isn't objective," Miss Georgina said.

Madeline looked at Miss Georgina. "Just how close have they become?"

"Obviously much *too* close." Miss Georgina pursed her lips.

"Don't even go there, people," Noel growled. "This is about our family and the business. I've always stood by both."

"And now? Lyrissa Rideau is the test, Noel. You'll have to choose." Miss Georgina lifted her proud chin.

"No, I won't."

His grandmother shook her head. "This woman is determined to destroy us. You can't or won't see through her. For the first time, I don't trust your judgment."

"Carlton is talking to board members, Noel. You've got to take some kind of decisive action to head him off," Richard put in.

"I think we can prove the painting belongs to this family." Julie spoke in a smooth tone. "We can use Jules Joubert's reputation to cast doubt on their claim. He probably sold the painting for liquor, then lied to get it back."

"Exactly the kind of strategy we need. Thank you, dear.

At least *you're* thinking clearly. Noel, you should rely on Julie more," Miss Georgina said pointedly.

"Her loyalty is unquestionable," Madeline added as she stared at her son.

"This game of dueling accusations in the media hasn't helped, Grandmother. Julie, you shouldn't have gotten involved without consulting me." Noel glared at her.

Julie's expression remained composed. "Your grandmother asked for my advice and help. We can't allow people like Lyrissa Rideau to run over us."

"I think you should be grateful, young man," Madeline said. "Julie is looking out for your best interests."

Noel stood and buttoned his navy blue suit jacket. "I still run Tremé Corporation. No more interviews until I consult with our lawyers."

"The board won't be happy, Noel. Don't forget, we choose who runs the company." Miss Georgina's eyes flashed with anger.

"You want the company back? Fine with me. I don't need the headaches from a bunch of hardheaded, narrowminded dinosaurs who allowed it to get into a mess in the first damn place!" Noel shouted. He spun around and strode from the room.

Richard caught up with him in the hallway. "Son, I hope you know what you're doing." He walked beside Noel and put a hand on his arm.

"I do," Noel shot back.

"Uh, your grandmother is worried that you just dropped your resignation in her lap," Richard said. He yanked on Noel's arm. "Will you stop for a minute?"

Noel faced him. "I sure as hell don't intend to resign. They'll have to fire me."

"Good, but watch your back. Carlton we know about, but there are others you should keep an eye on." Richard spoke in a low voice.

"Julie just made the short list. The stunt she pulled with Grandmother proves she can't be trusted." Noel wore a fierce expression. He would deal with her today.

"I was thinking of Lyrissa Rideau, Noel," Richard said somberly. "Your grandmother could be right about her."

Noel walked away from him. "I'll call you later, Dad." He slammed the door hard behind him as he left his grandmother's house.

Lyrissa gripped the receiver and fought hard to control her temper. "Mr. Polk, the brochure has to be perfect. I don't care about your other jobs. We're paying you to get it right."

The part-time receptionist appeared at her office door. "Your grandmother is on line three," she whispered. "She says it's urgent."

Before she could answer, the printer whined in her ear about his schedules. "Mr. Polk, we can't hope no one notices twenty typos, one of them misspelling the name of our gallery!" she barked at him. "Your staff screwed up. Now, fix it! Mr. Taylor is talking lawsuit."

She'd said the magic word. Mr. Polk babbled on about how much he valued their business. Lyrissa softened her tone now that he was cowed. They agreed on a delivery date for the brochure. Lyrissa glanced up again to find that Tameka had gone back to her desk. She heard her raised voice.

"Yes, ma'am, but she's on an important call and—yes,

ma'am." She turned to Lyrissa with a silent plea in her wide eyes.

Lyrissa waved to her. She couldn't stop now that she'd finally made the mule-headed printer see reason. Besides, she didn't need another dose of Mama Grace's daily drama. Lyrissa endured her tirades each time a new article about Jules Joubert appeared.

Two men in suits walked through the front door while Tameka tried to soothe her grandmother. They scanned the gallery for a few seconds, then separated. One studied paintings that hung on the north wall of the lobby. The taller one walked past the reception desk to Mr. Taylor's office. His companion followed him seconds later.

"Yes, Mr. Polk. I understand how hard it is to find good workers," Lyrissa replied.

She propped the receiver against her shoulder as he continued to complain. Tameka hung up the phone and hustled across the floor to her door. Mr. Taylor walked ahead of the two men toward her office, but Tameka arrived first.

"Lyrissa, your grandmother is freaking out about something. You'd better call her, girl." The young woman waved her arms

"Not now, Tameka. Excuse us." Mr. Taylor nodded his head toward the reception desk.

Tameka backed up. "Yes, sir."

The two men walked into her office and Mr. Taylor closed the door. "These detectives are here to see you, Lyrissa."

The short man spoke first. "I'm Detective Campo, and this is Detective Murphy. We're with the New Orleans PD."

"Ma'am, a stolen painting was found at your place of

residence on"—he broke off to consult a notepad in his hand—"Erato Street."

"What?" Lyrissa sprang from her chair, still holding the receiver.

"You're under arrest on suspicion of arson, felony theft, and aggravated assault in the commission of a felony," Detective Murphy rattled off the charges.

"My God!" Mr. Taylor's mouth hung open.

"No way!" Lyrissa shot back. "I'm not guilty of anything."

"Ma'am, we don't determine guilt. That's for the courts to decide." Detective Campo spoke in an even, calm voice. "Let's just get this straightened out."

Detective Murphy closed in on her from the left. "Yes, ma'am. Just handle your business and we can leave quietly.

She hung up on Mr. Polk cutting him off in mid-sentence. "This is a big mistake."

"Of course it is, dear. I can't believe anyone would seriously think you're an art thief." Mr. Taylor twisted his hands together. "Uh, did any reporters follow you here, Officer?"

"We don't control the press, sir," Detective Campo said in a dry voice. "Ma'am, the owners have identified the painting as being part of the St. Denis collection."

Detective Murphy read from his notepad again. "It's called 'Sunday Stroll on the Faubourg Tremé.' "

"According to Mr. Carlton St. Denis you claimed the painting really belonged to your family. There is some legal dispute, I believe."

"Oh-oh." Mr. Taylor put a hand over his mouth.

"That doesn't mean I stole it. We had a good case. My attorney is confident we'll get it back." Lyrissa's voice strained with the effort to convince them. Mr. Taylor lifted his hands in a helpless gesture when she looked at him for support.

"Yes, ma'am. Speaking of attorneys," Detective Murphy said. He read her rights in a rapid-fire delivery. "You understand?"

"Yes," she answered in a numb voice. A weight settled on her chest.

"I don't think we need handcuffs, do we, ma'am?" Detective Campo raised an eyebrow at her. His expression implied he'd use whatever means necessary to subdue her.

"Of course not! Think how that would look!" Mr. Taylor blurted out.

He dashed to the front lobby and looked outside with a frightened expression. Tameka's eyes stretched wide as she watched them escort Lyrissa to the door. Kevin emerged from the back of the gallery.

"What the hell is goin' on?" he asked.

"Lyrissa has been arrested," Tameka said in a stage whisper.

"Call my lawyer, Ebony Armstrong," Lyrissa yelled over her shoulder. "Now!"

25

Lyrissa heard her name through a thick fog. The ominous voice grew louder and louder, coming closer with each passing second. Her heart hammered until her chest hurt. She felt trapped. Fear pressed her down until she couldn't breathe.

"Lyrissa. Lyrissa, wake up, baby."

She twisted around then sat up with a cry. Slowly her bedroom came into focus. "No bars," Lyrissa rasped from her bone-dry throat.

"You're home safe and sound, cherie. Nothing is going to hurt you here." Aunt Claire put her plump arms around Lyrissa and rocked her.

Lyrissa hugged her aunt as the pounding in her chest subsided. "What time is it?"

"Ten o'clock in the morning. I've got breakfast waiting

for you." Aunt Claire brushed a strand of damp hair from her forehead.

"I'd better call Mr. Taylor."

"Shelton already called. He says you can take off all the time you need."

"He means I'm fired," Lyrissa muttered.

"Now, baby, he didn't say you were fired. He meant you needed time off."

"The last thing he needs is a suspected art thief working for him. I can't blame him, either." Lyrissa let go of her aunt. She pressed the heels of her hands against her eyes.

"He'll stand by you, dear. We had a little talk." Aunt Claire's sweet tone gave way to one of steel. "I reminded him how we helped him years ago when he first opened that gallery."

"Thanks, sweetie, but I don't want him to lose his business because of me." Lyrissa threw the twisted sheets back and swung her legs over the side of the bed.

Aunt Claire rubbed the small of her back. "We're going to fight. You can't hide in your bedroom forever. You've been in here for two days already." She got up and put away piles of clothes.

Ebony came to the bedroom door. "Hey, girl. How are you doing?" She put her briefcase on the vanity.

"I was just telling her to get up," Aunt Claire said as she tossed clothes in the hamper.

"Sorry. Being booked as a felon and tossed in a cage is a little unsettling." Lyrissa waved her arms.

"Of course it was awful. But we got you out double quick, babe." Ebony unbuttoned her blazer and sat down.

Aunt Claire paused in the act of folding a t-shirt. "All

the evidence is circumstantial. Someone is trying to frame you, no pun intended. They can't place you at the scene of the crime."

"You've been reading those legal thrillers too much." Lyrissa gave her a weary smile that faded.

"She's right. I mean, the painting is stolen and then pops up in your garage? Puh-leeze!" Ebony placed a hand on one hip. "I'll rip that kind of evidence apart. That's the good news."

"Eb, there *is* no *good news*." Lyrissa cradled her head in both hands. "God! What a nightmare."

"Honey, get dressed. I baked your favorite apple cinnamon muffins, scrambled two eggs, and Ebony brought Jamaican Blue Mountain coffee." Aunt Claire pulled her hands down.

"Yeah, girl. Get out of this room." Ebony glanced around at the piles of clothes and magazines. "Looks like a bunch of gerbils are nesting in here."

"Uh-huh, I'll have to come out for my trial anyway," Lyrissa retorted.

"Don't frown like that. You'll leave lines on your face. Now, take a nice warm shower and put these on." Aunt Claire neatly draped a pair of blue jeans and a blue t-shirt with tiny white flowers over the stuffed chair next to her bed.

"Yeah, yeah." Lyrissa didn't move.

"Okay, the St. Denis gang set you up, but the good news is—"

"Wonderful, more good news," Lyrissa muttered.

"Listen, our case must be damn strong. Why else would someone go to all this trouble?" Ebony leaned forward as she spoke.

"Sure."

Lyrissa had lost interest in the painting. She'd thought of little else except that Noel hadn't called. His silence meant he either believed she was guilty, or he knew his family had indeed set her up. Noel St. Denis, cut from the same cloth as his family. Mama Grace had warned her. Was she right?

"This whiny crybaby isn't the Lyrissa I know." Ebony slapped the bed hard. "Hey, I'm talking to you."

"I'll go fix you both a cup of coffee. Make her come out of this room, Ebony." Aunt Claire patted Ebony's shoulder, then left.

"We'll be there in fifteen minutes." Ebony stood. "You heard her. Move!" She pointed to Lyrissa's bathroom.

"Geez, who appointed you queen of the world?" she muttered irritably. She went in and turned on the shower.

"So you haven't heard from him, I guess. That explains that pitiful 'I-got-the-low-down-blues' look on your face."

"I can't hear you," Lyrissa lied. She took off her gown and stepped into the shower.

Warm pellets from the shower massage beat against her neck, shoulders, and back. Lyrissa covered herself in bath foam, then stood under the shower and rinsed off. She stepped out and dried off with a fluffy pink bath towel. She found clean panties and a bra on the bathroom counter.

"Thanks," she called out as she put them on. Ebony had made up her bed by the time she padded back into her room.

"You're welcome. Listen, word on the street is, Noel's got his hands full. I hear there's a real family fight going on. That could be why he hasn't called."

"Must be Carlton. His cousin thinks he should be CEO. Still no excuse." Lyrissa pulled the shirt over her head. She went to the mirror and brushed her hair.

"According to reliable sources, things are pretty nasty. By the way, that witch Julie Duval is having a field day." Ebony raised an eyebrow at her.

Lyrissa whirled around. "What do you mean?"

"She's suddenly become the company spokeswoman. She all but said you're guilty in one news interview."

"Humph! I'm sure she's climbing all over Noel." Lyrissa tossed her hairbrush across the room.

"Whoa!" Ebony's eyes stretched wide.

"What else did that skeezer say?" Lyrissa crossed her arms.

"It's more what she *doesn't* say. She implies a lot without coming out and saying what she means." Ebony pursed her lips for a moment. "Kinda like a lawyer."

"I'll bet." Lyrissa's eyes narrowed to slits. "So that's how it is, huh? Well, I'm not going down easy, you witch!"

Ebony grinned. "All right, girl. Let's rock 'em until they can't see straight."

"We'll talk about it over breakfast. I'm suddenly very hungry." She marched out ahead of her.

"You might want to put on your pants and some shoes." Ebony laughed. "Just a suggestion. I'll see you in the kitchen."

They exchanged a glance, then burst into laughter. Lyrissa got dressed and went to the kitchen. Mama Grace sat at the table alone. She didn't look up when Lyrissa walked in.

"Where is everybody?" Lyrissa went to the coffee pot and poured herself a cup.

"Ebony is on the phone. Claire's in the laundry room," Mama Grace replied.

"Oh." She considered leaving. She stood at the kitchen counter.

"Sit down. We have to talk."

Lyrissa heaved a sigh and obeyed. "Go on and say it. I wouldn't be in this fix if I'd listened to you. Noel hasn't called. The whole thing is a setup. I—"

"I can speak for myself," Mama Grace broke in.

"Yes, ma'am, you sure can."

"I did tell you that those people are ruthless. And yes, you let your heart rule when your brains should have taken over."

"I know." Lyrissa drank a gulp of the smooth dark liquid to bolster herself.

"*But* . . . I pushed you into getting involved. I called that reporter. All those stories forced them to do something desperate. You were right. I should have let you handle things your way." Mama Grace sniffed. "I'm the reason they're after you."

Mama Grace pressed her lips together. Deep lines crisscrossed her face. Her shoulders slumped, making her look shrunken. Lyrissa put down her coffee mug and placed an arm around her shoulders.

"It's not your fault," she said gently.

"Yes, it is. I should have known they'd try to destroy you the way they destroyed your great-great-grandfather." A tear slid down her cheek.

"You've been beating yourself up for way too long. None of what happened now or fifty years ago is your fault." Lyrissa pressed her cheek against Mama Grace's face.

"We lost our house, the business, everything. All be-

cause I wouldn't listen to anyone. I had to have my way."
Mama Grace covered her face with her hands.

Lyrissa tugged her grandmother's hand down. "Let it
go. You were young and in love. The St. Denis family did
what they do best, steamroll over people."

Aunt Claire joined them. "She's right, Grace. You've
been carrying around guilt and bitterness for too long.
Let it go."

Mama Grace smiled sadly. "I'm too old and stubborn
to change. Bitterness is the only thing that kept me going
for the past twenty years. That, and caring for you." She
touched Lyrissa's face.

"Papa, Mama and the rest would want us to be happy
no matter what. We put too much value on one object.
That painting isn't worth all this suffering," Aunt Claire
said fiercely.

"I'm so scared for you, baby." Mama Grace wiped her
eyes. "The important thing now is to clear your name."

"And keep her out of the slammer!" Aunt Claire
slapped a fist into her palm.

"You should stop reading those hard-boiled detective
novels, too," Lyrissa said with a laugh.

Ebony came in at that moment. "I put some well-oiled
legal wheels in motion."

"Good." Mama Grace nodded with approval. She rose
slowly. "I know you girls will do the right thing."

Mama Grace moved stiffly, as though each step was an
effort. Aunt Claire held her arm as they left together.
Lyrissa watched them leave with a worried frown.

"I've never seen Mama Grace look so worn out, Ebony.
She tried to be strong, but this ordeal has taken a toll on
her. If they find out about my father's drug problem and

that he overdosed..." Lyrissa shook her head. She couldn't bear to think of what such a public airing would do to the proud old woman.

"Yeah." Ebony dropped into a chair.

"I'm going to see Noel."

Ebony's long braids bounced as she shook her head hard. "No way. Bad idea. Don't do it."

"Mama Grace can't take much more." Lyrissa looked at her friend.

"You're going to settle? Mrs. St. Denis won't accept anything less than complete surrender," Ebony warned.

"Which is why I should talk to Noel first. He still has some influence with her."

"I don't know. Things are shaky with him these days. He could even be tossed out of the family business." Ebony cleared her throat. "Uh, remember I told you about my reliable source?"

"Yes."

"Well, I didn't tell you the whole story. Seems the family is pissed about you and Noel. They blame him for the bad publicity. Investors are backing off. All because he got involved with the wrong sort of woman." Ebony sucked in a deep breath.

"I'm not surprised." Lyrissa clenched her teeth.

"Noel might be willing to do anything to save his position with the company and his family." Ebony put a hand on her arm. "I hate to say it, but he's got a lot to lose. Social position, a major company..." Ebony's voice faded.

Lyrissa's throat tightened. Ebony had put Lyrissa's thoughts into words. *He hasn't called.* Noel could have decided to cut his losses.

"Okay, so maybe you're right. I'm still going. The bottom line is, 'Sunday Stroll on the Faubourg Tremé' belongs to us. Old Jules was a bum. But Gustave St. Denis exploited his weaknesses to snatch that painting."

"At least let me coach you on what to say. Don't agree to anything definite. Talk in 'maybes' and 'ifs' only. Let me deal with his attorneys to hammer out the details."

Lyrissa nodded as Ebony talked. She only half listened to her friend's instructions. An image of Noel, naked and brown lying next to her, filled her head.

Lyrissa strode into the offices of Tremé Corporation with her head up. Three of Noel's employees did a double take when they recognized her. A woman whispered, "Shouldn't we call someone?" Lyrissa kept walking. Eddie's mouth dropped open when she looked up and saw her.

"Hi, Eddie. I'm here to see your boss."

"Oh, boy." Eddie's mouth worked.

"I know he's here," Lyrissa repeated with a nod to his door.

"I, he . . ." Eddie blinked rapidly, a look of confusion on her face.

Julie raced down the opposite hallway. "Security will be here shortly to throw her out!" Her eyes gleamed with anticipation. "I can't wait."

Lyrissa ignored her. "He'll see me. Just let him know I'm here," she said to Eddie.

Julie walked up to her. "Noel will watch them toss you out on your ass and enjoy it. I'd advise you to leave voluntarily."

"I'd advise you to get out of my face," Lyrissa said in a deadly calm tone.

Eddie stepped between them. "Everybody just cool down," she said loudly.

Noel opened the door to his office. "What the hell is going on out here?" He stopped short when he saw Lyrissa. "Come in," he said to her.

Julie glared at him. "You can't be serious! The board will find out about this, Noel."

"In that case make sure you don't leave anything out," Noel snapped. He glanced at Lyrissa. "If you came here to stir things up, you've succeeded. Was that your only goal?"

Lyrissa strode into his office without answering. Noel closed the door and leaned against it. They stared at each other in silence.

"How are you?" he said finally.

"Take a guess."

Noel nodded and crossed to her. "So far, they're only going to charge you with receiving stolen goods."

"Ironic, isn't it, since the painting really belongs to us?"

He studied her expression. "We can settle the question of who owns the painting through our lawyers."

"If that's the way it has to be," she replied.

"I think it's the best way. Present your documentation and we'll go from there. My grandmother won't be satisfied otherwise."

"Right. You can't make your grandmother unhappy. Let her call the shots. Or is this really your decision?" Lyrissa gazed at him steadily.

"Mine. Besides, neither of our families will settle. A judge's decision should finally put an end to the whole affair." Noel's gaze traveled down her body and back to her eyes.

Lyrissa tingled as though he'd put his hands on her. "Yes, it will."

Noel rubbed a hand over his face. She noticed how drained he looked. He rolled his shoulders to relieve tension.

"Not soon enough," he said in a weary voice.

"I hear you've had a rough time in the last few days. At least you weren't hauled off to jail." She folded her arms to restrain the urge to hold him.

"Sit down, have some coffee." Noel sighed when she didn't move. "Please?"

Lyrissa sat in a chair that faced his desk. Noel poured two cups of coffee from the carafe on his desk. He handed one to her. She stared into the steaming liquid.

"I've had too much of this stuff lately. I should be drinking fruit juice," Lyrissa said with a grimace.

Noel punched the speaker button on his phone. "Eddie, would you mind bringing us two bottles of apple juice from the machine?"

"No problem," Eddie said promptly.

He took the cups and set them on the credenza. "Good idea. We're both on edge as it is."

"I—" Lyrissa broke off when Eddie knocked.

She came in with two half-pint bottles and two glasses on a tray. "Here you go. Uh, boss, Julie is demanding to see you right now."

"You know what to tell her," he said evenly.

"Oh, yeah." Eddie grinned and left.

"I'm not sure why I came to tell you the truth. I could have let Ebony call your attorney." Lyrissa bit her lower lip. "We sure can't solve anything."

"I'm sorry you were treated like a criminal," Noel said.

"You couldn't have been too worried." Lyrissa stared down at the floor.

"I called, but your grandmother suggested I give you time. I waited to hear from you. Then I thought maybe . . ." Noel raked his fingers through his hair. "Maybe you decided to bail out on me."

"*Me*, bail out on *you*?"

Noel sat across from her. "You wouldn't have been stupid enough to hide the painting at your house. Any chance your grandmother—"

"Hell, no!" Lyrissa shouted.

"Okay, okay. I'm just saying. Emotions are running kind of high. I know how intense she is about that painting."

Lyrissa huffed for several moments. Then she shrugged. "To tell you the truth, the thought did cross my mind. *Briefly*," she added with force.

"I didn't say anything." Noel held up his hands palms out.

"Yeah, well. I dismissed the idea because my grandmother wouldn't be that stupid either. Besides, she wanted to humiliate your family publicly as much as she wanted the painting. She's been spoiling for this fight for years."

"I have to say, some of those stories about my ancestors are pretty embarrassing. My grandmother has been hiding out for weeks." Noel rubbed his jaw.

"What about my ancestor? I was told he died young, a broken man, because his art had been stolen and his family left destitute." Lyrissa snorted in disgust. "Between bouts of drinking and marathon sex orgies, I'm surprised he didn't drop dead sooner!"

Noel laughed. "He wasn't that bad. My skeletons beat yours by sheer numbers."

"I don't know. If we give your grandmother and Julie more time, I'm sure they'll dig up more." Lyrissa smiled at him. "Why are we laughing? There's nothing funny in all this."

"Sure there is. Both our families are trying to preserve their good names. The problem is, our dirty laundry keeps tumbling out in public." He smiled back at her.

Lyrissa's expression became serious again. "Noel, let's have the lawyers handle it quietly. We have to stop these nasty stories from being published."

"The press is like a pack of wild dogs. You can't stop them once they're let loose. They're selling papers and magazines like crazy."

"Yes, but the whole thing will eventually die down if our grandmothers stop feeding them." Lyrissa sat forward.

"You just said your grandmother has been waiting to let us have it for years. She's having too much fun to stop." Noel lifted a shoulder.

Lyrissa shook her head. "No, she's not. Mama Grace didn't count on just how ugly things would get."

He rubbed his face harder. "My problem is more complicated."

"Your cousin and the board," Lyrissa said.

He exhaled. "I've spent the last twenty-four hours doing damage control. Carlton wants my ass roasted and served on a silver platter. Julie is in on it I'm sure."

"Julie? It's a thin line, huh?"

"Obviously." Noel scowled.

"You've got more to worry about than me, mister. Julie wants your ass, too. Don't doubt it." Lyrissa pointed a finger at his chest.

"Carlton doesn't need much help being vindictive.

She's probably just giving him a shoulder to cry." Noel waved a hand.

"The woman has been planning your wedding since she was in kindergarten. She's obsessed. I'll bet she's helping him a lot."

"Julie has known for a long time we weren't going to be a couple." Noel shook his head.

"She's probably still hoping you'll change your mind."

"I won't. I don't really give a damn about that painting, Lyrissa." He pulled her from her seat and into his arms.

"Hey! You're in enough trouble, Mr. St. Denis. If they walk in and catch you smooching with the enemy—"

Noel kissed her before she could say more. Lyrissa didn't try to escape, despite her words. Surprise and desire made her skin sizzle. She moaned when his wide hands slid down her body to her hips. He pressed his pelvis against hers. They both sighed when the kiss ended.

"I was in trouble the first day I saw you," he whispered.

"We'll have to fight one battle after another. *You'll* have to fight most of them." Lyrissa clung to him.

"I don't mind at all. Are you sure you want all the hassle?" Noel kissed her nose, then her eyelids.

"I'm sure that being with you is worth anything anybody can throw at me," she said.

"That's all I need to hear."

Noel kissed her long and hard. He guided her to the leather sofa and eased her down onto it. His hand lifted her skirt. Lyrissa panted when he trailed his fingertips along the inside of her thigh.

"Cut it out," she murmured and squirmed to allow his hand to go higher.

"Uh-uh, feels too good," he replied softly.

Lyrissa planted her palms on his chest and pushed him away. "We've got work to do, hot pants."

Noel smiled at her. "You've got that right." He tried to kiss her again.

Lyrissa slid from his grasp. "You know what I mean."

"Okay, okay. Rain check."

"Agreed." Lyrissa gave him one last kiss on the cheek. "Now, where do we go from here?"

He straightened his tie as he sat back. "Someone is trying to play both of us. I say we find 'em and kick ass."

"Don't get mad, but my money is on your family. Staging the fire and the burglary would keep me busy. Our claim would be discredited and you—"

"Hey!" he protested.

"Your family would keep the painting. Sending me to jail would be icing on the cake." Lyrissa gazed at him with her head to one side. "Well?"

"My grandmother has her faults, but she doesn't do lunch with felons. I don't see anyone in my family planning such a thing. Not even Carlton. He's devious, but not smart enough." Noel shrugged.

"You *have* been reading the papers, right?" Lyrissa quipped.

He winced. "Ouch! But that was history—ancient history, at that. I'm talking about now. I know these people, baby."

"So 'Sunday Stroll on the Faubourg Tremé' walked to my house and into my garage? Please!" Lyrissa rolled her eyes.

"Good point. Someone is responsible. Guess we'd better get to work on the who and why." Noel put a hand on her knee.

" 'We,' I like the sound of that word," she murmured.

"Me and you, you and I, us," Noel leaned close and whispered in her ear. "I love you."

"I love you back," she whispered. Lyrissa lifted his hand and placed it on his knee. "But if you don't stop we'll never make it off this sofa."

"A brother has to try." He grinned at her.

"We'll make up for lost time later. Now, where do we start in this quest for truth and justice?"

He thought for a minute. "I say we keep our alliance a secret."

"What?"

"I want to stir the gumbo pot until it boils over. If whoever is behind this whole thing thinks they've succeeded . . ." He raised an eyebrow at her.

"You mean lie and set a trap?" Lyrissa smiled. "You sneaky devil. In the blood, huh?"

Noel laughed again. "Using my powers for good this time. Let's do it."

He nodded toward the door. Lyrissa nodded back. She retrieved her purse and followed him. Noel jerked the door open.

"I don't think there's anything left to say, Lyrissa. Our painting didn't just walk to your house!" he said loudly. "Did you really think that act would work?"

"How dare you call me a thief, after what your family has done? I should have known you'd stick up for them. You chump!" Lyrissa shouted.

"Goodbye and get out," Noel growled.

Lyrissa slammed the door in his face. "Cold-blooded snake."

Eddie gasped. "Lyrissa, I thought—"

"Forget it, Eddie. To hell with him—and *all* of 'em."
Lyrissa waved a hand and stormed off toward the elevators.

Julie appeared out of nowhere wearing a malicious
smile. "Guess the thrill is gone, Miss Thang!"

"Kiss my ass," Lyrissa hissed at her. She smiled when
the elevator doors whisked shut and she was alone. "Perfect timing, *Miss Thang*."

26

"Come in, Carlton." Noel beckoned him inside with a wave of his hand. He stood behind his desk with his back to the window.

Carlton strolled in, his expression mild. He glanced around the office. Noel would have sworn he was calculating how to redecorate the corner office to his satisfaction. Good. Let him be sure of himself, for a while, at least. Noel went to the table in his seating area. He poured two cups of coffee and handed one to his cousin.

"Let's talk." He nodded at a chair and waited until Carlton had sat down. Noel stood gazing down at him.

Carlton crossed his legs. His mouth shifted sideways in a smirk when he gazed up at Noel. "What's this about? You lonely in here, or something?"

"It's been a hell of a week," Noel admitted. "The board is really on my back. But then, you knew that."

"Too bad," Carlton said in a monotone that lacked sympathy.

" 'Bad' isn't the word. They're furious about this whole mess with the collection. They blame me for trusting an outsider—Lyrissa Rideau."

"We did warn you," Carlton replied.

"They say I allowed her to influence me and now the company is suffering. They're questioning all my decisions, including my plans for the warehouses, the micro-malls, everything!" Noel blew out a gust of breath in frustration.

"Really?" Carlton leaned forward with a predatory gleam in his eye.

"You know how I wanted to develop the Crowder Boulevard property, right?"

"We talked about it." Carlton pursed his lips.

"Argued, is what you mean. Anyway, all of a sudden, Uncle Laurence is against it. I don't get him or any of them." Noel dropped down onto a chair.

"Interesting. He was your biggest supporter. Too bad." Carlton sipped from his cup again.

"Our net profits have risen steadily since I became CEO. You have to admit that, even though we've had our disagreements." Noel gazed at him as though anxious for a sliver of support.

Carlton shrugged. "That's gratitude for you."

"But this financial report really puzzles me." Noel picked up a file folder from the table between them.

"What financial report? The audit was clean." Carlton's satisfied pose slipped a notch.

"I know. But one of the accountants became curious about certain contracts and payments."

"I didn't hear anything about problems in that area." Carlton sat at attention.

"You know about the recent scandals involving certain companies and the way they do business," Noel said.

"Yes."

"This young man researched the companies we do business with, just to see if any red flags popped up." Noel flipped through the pages of the report.

"What did he find?" Carlton blinked rapidly.

"Look at page seventeen."

Noel handed him the open report. He watched him read in silence for several moments. Then he stood over him and clamped a hand on Carlton's shoulder. His cousin jumped.

"Someone has been diverting money. Clever method, but this sharp young man was able to trace it all the same. I couldn't believe it."

Carlton grimaced. "These figures aren't conclusive. I'm sure there's a good explanation."

"God, I hope so. I can't afford more problems. The board will blame me for this, too." Noel frowned and raked a hand through his hair.

"I delegated a lot of work to Andre and Keisha. Maybe that was a mistake. I'll look into this for you, Noel. Don't worry, I'll handle it. I'm sure we can straighten this all out," Carlton said in a rush as he sprang from his chair.

Noel looked up at him. "You think Andre or Keisha could be responsible?"

"I don't want to accuse anyone yet, but they did handle some of these transactions." Carlton stared at the report in his hands. "I have confidence in my employees, but I'll get to the bottom of this and do what I have to."

"Yes, I'm sure you will." Noel stood. "Thanks, Carlton. I knew when it hit the fan I could count on you." He put an arm around his cousin's shoulder.

"Like you said, we have to stick together. I'll look into the questions raised by this report immediately. Can I keep it?" Carlton clutched the report as though Noel would have to rip it from his hands.

"Definitely. Read it cover to cover. I know you'll find it *interesting.*"

Noel watched his cousin scurry out. He balled his hands into large, menacing fists when his office door closed.

Lyrissa walked into the small café on the corner of St. Charles and Third Street. Only a few customers were scattered around at the tables. She checked her watch. Ten minutes before two in the afternoon. Most of the lunch crowd had cleared out. Lyrissa took a seat and waited for Julie. She'd arrived early to get the advantage, since Julie had suggested where they meet. Also, Lyrissa wanted to appear anxious.

Five minutes later Julie drove up in her late-model dark red two-seater BMW. She turned a corner and parked on a side street.

Julie strolled inside wearing dark sunglasses. A waitress approached, took her order for diet soda, then left. She scanned the dining room, then smiled briefly when she saw Lyrissa. Lyrissa folded her hands and rested them on the table as she approached.

"Are you sure this is a good idea, under the circumstances?" Julie tucked her navy leather clutch bag under one arm.

"Hi. Thanks for coming," Lyrissa said with a jittery

smile that faded quickly. "I know Noel and the others would be angry if they knew. I—"

"I meant for *you*. *I'm* not the one in deep trouble." Julie raised her eyebrows until they arched above the gold rims of her sunglasses.

"I'm an arson and theft suspect, my boss fired me, and Noel doesn't believe me. What have I got to lose?" Lyrissa swallowed hard.

Julie stared at her for a few seconds, then lifted a shoulder. She sat down. The waitress brought their drinks and left.

"Good point, but I don't see why you're talking to me. Make your case to Noel," Julie said.

"I tried. We had a terrible fight. I couldn't believe the way he talked to me!" Lyrissa's bottom lip trembled. Then she reminded herself not to lay it on too thick. She stopped short of squeezing out a tear.

"He's not stupid. You must have known he'd see right through you eventually. And he's very loyal to his family." Julie removed her sunglasses and gazed at her.

"I'm innocent. Okay, I didn't tell him about the painting," she added quickly, when Julie's expression turned skeptical. "But I didn't set that fire or steal anything!"

"Fine. Your lawyer will get you off. The fact that the police found the stolen painting at your house looks bad, though." Her lips twitched into a smirk.

"I don't understand how it got there, Julie. I swear!" Lyrissa frowned. "A lot of people have decided I'm guilty already. Noel is one of them. My career is probably ruined in this business."

"Too bad," Julie said in a flat tone. "I still don't know why you're talking to me."

"I—" Lyrissa broke off when the waitress led two men in suits to a nearby table. She leaned forward and lowered her voice. "I was nowhere *near* that house when it caught fire. I was with Noel. Uh, sorry," she put in, when Julie winced.

"The theory is you hired someone to do your dirty work," Julie retorted with a stiff expression. "A suspicious type would say being with Noel was the perfect set-up."

"That's crazy! I'd never do such a thing." Lyrissa wrung her hands. "Look, I know we've had our problems."

"Yes."

"But I think we can help each other," Lyrissa went on.

"This I've got to hear." Julie folded her arms and gazed at her. "I can't think of one reason why I should care what happens to you or why I need *your* help."

"Noel is being difficult." Lyrissa wore a miserable expression.

"He's a St. Denis, darlin'. They don't easily forgive, and they *never* forget."

Lyrissa lifted her chin. "But he wants to believe me real bad, Julie. He's agreed to see me again. I've still got a chance."

"He's not that big a fool for you!" Julie snarled.

"Don't count on it," Lyrissa tossed back. "No matter what you'd like to think, the man still wants me. I'm more than his latest distraction."

"You're so wrong. I've seen him toss aside better women than you," Julie huffed in anger.

"Are you sure?"

Lyrissa watched fury and uncertainty flash in her eyes. So her guess had been correct: Julie still held out hope that she could have Noel.

"Noel has too much to lose," Julie blurted out. "The board would fire him. His family would cut him off cold. You wouldn't get your hands on their money."

"Maybe not, but I'd have *him*. You wouldn't. Then there's the small matter of his substantial trust fund." Lyrissa wore a tight smile. "We wouldn't exactly starve, from what he's told me."

"What makes you think I care at this point? He's no prize if you're his taste these days!" Julie hissed.

"Don't try it, Julie. You want him so bad you can't see straight," Lyrissa retorted.

Julie blinked as if she'd been slapped hard across the face. She recovered after a few seconds. "Why should you give him up?"

"As you pointed out, his family will shun us both. I won't have the bigger prize, their money. I won't have status. Hell, I might not even have the painting they stole."

Julie's eyes narrowed. "I knew it! You were after his money and social position all along."

"Then there's the problem of these charges hanging over my head." Lyrissa scowled. "He's not worth that much to me. Besides, hiring the best criminal lawyer could wipe out his nice trust fund like that!" She snapped her fingers. Such callous words about the man she loved dearly made Lyrissa's stomach twist, but she had to be convincing.

"You're too devious," Julie murmured. She wore an expression close to admiration.

"But I'll take what I can get *if* . . ." Lyrissa let her voice trail off as she stared hard at Julie.

They studied each other in silence for several minutes, each looking for weakness in the other. Julie sipped from her glass from time to time as the seconds ticked by. Finally she shrugged.

"What do you think I can do?" Julie patted her lips with a cocktail napkin.

"Call off the dogs," Lyrissa said bluntly.

"I don't know what you're talking about." Julie's expression didn't change.

Lyrissa leaned forward and lowered her voice even more. "I know I didn't set the fire or steal the painting. I've been thinking about who else had a motive. I came up with you and Carlton. Noel told me about the audit."

"You are desperate," Julie said with a snort. "Nobody would believe that fairytale."

"If I'm out of the picture, you could play Noel the way you want. Otherwise, I'll encourage him to follow up on the audit. They'll find dirt on Carlton, maybe even you. Noel would still be CEO and I would get the whole package."

"His family would never accept *you*." Julie stabbed a forefinger in Lyrissa's face.

"Fine. Take the chance. I've got nothing to lose either way. How bad do you want him?" Lyrissa said fiercely.

Julie drummed her fingers on the white linen tablecloth. "I'll consider it. I might just decide he's not worth it to me."

"You might, but I don't think you will." Lyrissa let out a shaky breath. "Look, don't be stupid. All I want is to stay out of jail and at least salvage my career. I didn't plan on being arrested."

A slow, confident smile spread across Julie's face. "You *are* in a tough situation, aren't you?" She put on her sunglasses and stood. "I'll be in touch."

Lyrissa watched her stride out of the café, head held high. "Yeah, do that, bitch!" she muttered.

Noel slammed a fist down on the oval table. Lyrissa and Eddie both jumped and exchanged a glance. The three of them were in the small conference room next to Noel's office. He stared at the thick final audit report before him.

"Good thing Carlton isn't here right now," Eddie whispered aside to Lyrissa.

"Honey, I thought you'd calmed down," Lyrissa told Noel.

"Every time I think about what they pulled—" His jaw muscles worked as he controlled his rage. Noel held up his hands palm out. "Right, right. There'll be plenty of time to crush those two later. The report will fix Carlton."

"You really think Julie will talk? She's pretty tricky," Lyrissa said.

"And arrogant. So is Carlton. They think they've won," Noel replied with a scowl.

"Yeah, they're both walking around like they run the place already," Eddie said with disgust in her voice.

Noel looked at her. "Did you set up the speaker phone? I don't want them to notice it's on."

"No problem, boss. They won't, not the way I positioned it. I've got it set to the vacant office down the hall. We can listen in and they'll never suspect a thing." Eddie grinned.

"You're pretty tricky yourself, Mr. St. Denis." Lyrissa looked at him.

He grinned. "It's in the blood, remember?"

Eddie stood. "I'll make sure no one is in the hall so Lyrissa can sneak into the office."

"Right. Then get back to your desk fast. Julie will be looking for you soon," Noel said.

"Check, boss! This is s-o-o-o cool." Eddie giggled.

Lyrissa started to follow her out when Noel pulled her into his embrace. She wrapped her arms around his muscular body as he kissed her.

"What was that for?" she asked when they parted.

"I needed something sweet. This whole thing has put a nasty taste in my mouth." Noel brushed her hair with one hand. "You were right about my family, baby."

"Come on. I've said a few nasty things about them, but every family has its share of shady characters." Lyrissa snuggled closer to soothe him.

"I have to face facts. The St. Denis family has a monopoly on low people in high places," he said in a dry tone.

"We can't change the past or take the whole burden for what they did."

Noel let out a long breath. "I want to try and right some of those wrongs. I can't brag about the good and avoid responsibility for the bad."

Lyrissa caressed his face. "Another reason I love you, Noel St. Denis."

He kissed the tip of her nose. "I love you back."

Eddie peeked in the door. "They're circling like vultures, Noel." She came in with both hands on her hips. "Listen, people, we're in the middle of a critical operation here. Save the gooey stuff for later."

"Yes, ma'am." Lyrissa saluted her.

"Sorry, chief." Noel winked at Eddie.

"All right. Come on, Lyrissa. Andre has everyone distracted." Eddie herded her out the door.

Lyrissa waved to Noel and darted out the side door. She

strode quickly down the hall and into the vacant office. A phone sat on the desk. A green light glowed, indicating the speaker was on. Seconds went by and Lyrissa grew antsy. A loud thump from the speaker made her yelp in surprise. Lyrissa clamped a hand over her mouth and prayed.

"What was that?" Carlton's voice came through.

"Sorry, I dropped my pad and pen," Eddie said.

Lyrissa let out a silent sigh of relief and turned down the volume on the phone. There was more rustling and a second solid thump. The others entered the large conference room and closed the door.

"Let's get going. I've got one hell of a busy day," Noel said.

"Fine," Julie said. Her voice was crisp and composed. "I've already met with Carlton about the audit findings."

"He told me. Why isn't Andre here? I think we should nail his ass. Carlton says—"

"There's no need to bring Andre in at this point," Noel cut her off.

Carlton spoke up. "He's been stealing from us. I realize you hired him and don't want to believe it. We all know the board won't be happy to hear this latest news."

Lyrissa grimaced at his gloating tone. The guy had nerve. She itched to slap him across his moon-shaped face.

"I'm not convinced Andre has done anything wrong, Carlton," Noel said calmly.

"Don't be ridiculous. I gave you the results of my investigation. The evidence against him couldn't be clearer," Carlton replied.

"I had our accountant hire a specialist, a forensic accountant is what I think they're called. He hasn't quite untangled the mess. Someone has been very clever, but not quite clever enough."

Carlton spluttered. "I-I don't understand. Why didn't you consult me? I've spent hours working to find out what was going on. I could help this forensic accountant."

"That's great, but I decided to put it in the hands of an expert on this sort of thing. Damn it, I left his preliminary report in my office." Noel sounded harassed.

"I'll get it for you," Eddie said.

"No, I locked it in my file drawer. Besides, Tyson is faxing me more details. It should be coming in on my machine now. I'll be right back."

The door opened and closed again. Seconds later Noel joined Lyrissa in the empty office. He wore a fierce expression on his handsome face. Lyrissa gasped at the sight of him. He towered over her as he placed both hands on the desk and leaned forward over the speakerphone. Noel looked like a beautiful avenging angel about to deliver justice. She couldn't resist touching him. His eyes softened with affection when her hand covered one of his large ones.

"I'll get you guys something to drink, since we have to wait," Eddie said after a time. Once more the door opened and closed.

"He knows," Carlton burst out.

"Sit down and get ahold of yourself. Did you do what I told you to?" Julie snapped.

"Yes! I posted payments to contractors we actually used. The money passed through the active company bank accounts. Then I made it look like clerical errors whenever I could. I don't see how they could find out."

"They'll reach a dead end. We can still hang it on Andre and Keisha if we work fast. I said sit down!" she barked. "Noel could walk in here any second."

Carlton groaned. "God, I hope that guy didn't find those foreign bank accounts. I haven't had a chance to close them all yet."

"You idiot!" Julie's voice cracked like a whip.

"I need more time, Julie," Carlton whined. "I've been up to my neck in work, trying to juggle it all."

"All right, all right. Let's just calm down."

Julie was silent for a while. Lyrissa could almost hear the wheels turning in her head.

"Okay, look, we probably do have a little time. But you take care of those damn accounts today. Stay up all night, if you have to," she commanded.

"Today," Carlton repeated.

"In the meantime, we could use a diversion." Julie gave a vicious laugh. "I'll make sure the rest of those stolen items are traced to Lyrissa no later than tomorrow."

"She hasn't been charged yet. So far, your brilliant plan hasn't worked."

"My plan is going better than yours," she shot back. "The woman had the nerve to try and bargain with me. She should have known better than to threaten *me*!"

"I hope you burn her good. She's caused us too much trouble not to pay for it."

"Poor Lyrissa. Pretty soon she'll be wearing one of those lovely orange jumpsuits with 'Orleans Parish Prison' stenciled across the back." Julie laughed again.

"Great, but what about me? I'm not sure I can handle the accounts, deal with Andre—"

"Don't whine," Julie cut him short. "Give me a list of the accounts. In the meantime, I'll keep Noel busy."

"How? You know how single-minded he can be."

"Now that I've eliminated Lyrissa Rideau, I'll work my magic on him," Julie replied with confidence.

"The witch." Lyrissa glared at the phone.

Noel put a finger to his lips. "Shh," he said softly.

As Julie prompted him with sharp questions, Carlton explained how he had diverted money into his accounts. Noel scribbled notes until he'd filled two pages of a legal pad.

"I'm going back in now," he whispered close to Lyrissa's ear. "Come in. You'll know when." He pointed to the phone.

Lyrissa nodded and Noel left the office. A minute later he was back in the conference room with Julie and Carlton.

"Did you find out anything?" Julie asked.

"Everything I needed to know," Noel replied.

"But you couldn't have—" Carlton croaked. He cleared his throat. "I mean, did you get the fax?"

"I didn't need Tyson's addendum. In fact, I have a confession. I wasn't expecting a fax. I made that up," Noel said in a placid tone.

"We're in a crisis. I think you have enough problems with the board, don't you? Stop playing games," Julie said.

"You're right. I played a game, *yours*. Guess what? You lose."

Lyrissa left the office and met Eddie coming down the hallway. They strode into the conference room together. Julie and Carlton babbled at the same time. They threw accusations and insults at Noel. Noel slammed a fist on the table so hard it wobbled. They stopped talking, eyes wide with shock.

"You told me what I needed to know. Now all I have to

do is have Tyson track the foreign accounts, the changed ledger entries, and the phony contracts."

Julie was the first to recover. She turned on Lyrissa. "I should have known. You've been listening to that slut again."

Lyrissa smiled at Julie. "Eddie, you can turn off the speaker phone now."

Eddie went over to a side table and took the phone from behind a large plant. She picked it up and pressed a button. Julie and Carlton watched with horrified expressions.

"We also know you framed Lyrissa. We'll prove that, too." Noel put an arm around Lyrissa's waist.

Carlton looked around frantically. "I tried to talk to her, Noel. When I found out what she was up to—"

"What the hell—" Julie swung her hand at his head and Carlton ducked. He scrambled from his chair as she shouted a stream of profanity at him.

"Such language from a young woman of your breeding!" Lyrissa clapped a hand to her face.

"You! I ought to break your neck!" Julie took a step toward her.

Lyrissa squinted at her. "Do it and I'll plant my Liz Claiborne pumps up your blueblood behind!"

Two burly security officers strode into the room. "What's the problem, Mr. St. Denis?" one of them asked.

Noel grabbed Carlton and shoved him out into the hall. "Escort these two out of the building. Eddie will box up any personal belongings from your offices and send them by messenger."

"I'm going to call Grandmother," Carlton yelled.

"Good. She's expecting an explanation," Noel retorted.

"I'll pay you back for this, you bitch!" Julie pointed a

finger at Lyrissa. She stomped past the guards. "Get away from me, you overgrown monkeys!" One of the guards followed her.

Carlton's defiant posture crumbled. "Look, Noel, we're family. You can't seriously throw me out of here in front of everyone. I'll be humiliated. The employees will spread it all over town, and—"

"Get out while I can still control myself, Carlton." Noel glowered at him until Carlton backed away.

They watched him leave with the other security guard close on his heels. Eddie shook her head in wonder. Noel let out a long, slow breath.

"Wish I had all this on videotape!" Eddie said.

Lyrissa rubbed Noel's arms until he relaxed. "It's over, baby," she said softly.

"No, it's just starting. Talk about a family scandal . . ."

"We'll get through it. You and me, remember?" Lyrissa put her arms around his waist.

"Me and you," he replied with a tender smile.

"Now I'm going to get out of your way and let you handle business." Lyrissa kissed him on the cheek. Before she could move, he held her tight.

"Give me more of that, lady." Noel kissed her hard for a moment. "Much better. The day won't be quite so unpleasant. I'll see you later?"

Lyrissa smiled up at him. "You bet."

EPILOGUE

A month later they walked arm in arm on the beach on the island of St. Lucia. Noel wore a relaxed expression for the first time in weeks. He was dressed in ocean blue swim trunks with a white racing strip down the sides, a white t-shirt, and sandals, and his buttery brown skin glistened in the sunshine. Lyrissa wore a lime green swimsuit covered by a matching big shirt. She swung a straw tote in her free hand. A trio of women hungrily stared at Noel's body as though Lyrissa was invisible.

"Hi, ladies!" She waved at them gaily. The women giggled and hurried on. "You're attracting a crowd, mister," Lyrissa teased.

"I think they might be here for the beach, babe," he said with a grin.

"They weren't staring at the water. But I can't blame them. You're the catch of the day." Lyrissa sighed.

"So are you, pretty lady." Noel patted her fanny. "I haven't noticed anything else but you. Did I mention that running away to a tropical island was a great idea?"

"About a dozen times, but who's counting?" She laughed. "And it was *your* idea. You told me so once when we were talking about your family."

Noel winced. "Yeah. My family. Grandmother took it hard, you know."

"Carlton got off easy, though. All he's lost so far is his cushy job. You were generous to find him even a minor job in one of your other businesses," Lyrissa said.

"He's family. Why make his wife and kids suffer?" Noel kicked a bit of sand. "He can't do much damage managing those duplex apartments."

"What's the latest on Julie?" Lyrissa squinted despite the sunglasses she wore.

"Those guys she hired got greedy and tried to sell one of the small sculptures. Her lawyer is working on a plea agreement." Noel shook his head slowly. "She really went over the edge this time."

"I feel sorry for Julie. I do," Lyrissa protested when Noel looked at her skeptically. "She's been a pampered princess all her life. Prison could scar her for life."

"Julie is tough as nails. Don't let that weepy act she's been putting on for the television cameras fool you. She'll get probation. Her lawyer is expensive for a reason."

"I don't know. She looked pretty pitiful, and—"

Noel kissed her and cut off her words. "It's all about us for the next seven days," he murmured.

Lyrissa smiled at him lovingly. "Agreed."

They walked on for another few minutes. The bright blue sky stretched out above the water. Gentle waves rolled up. They took off their sandals and let the water wash over their feet as they strolled along.

"Mama Grace cried when I brought her the painting. Thanks, baby. I know what it cost you." Lyrissa didn't mean money. Some in his family might never forgive him. His grandmother had agreed only after their lawyer explained she had little choice given the evidence.

"Besides being the right thing to do, I would give you the world if it made you happy." Noel squeezed her hand.

"You know people are going to say I slept with you to get my hands on 'Sunday Stroll on the Faubourg Tremé,'" she said after a while.

"Hmm, you know, I think you're right." Noel looked down at her through his dark sunglasses. An impish smile tugged his full mouth up. "That's a valuable painting, too. You've got a huge debt with high interest, lady."

Lyrissa pulled him around until they were face to face. She kissed him for a long, sweet time. "Yeah, but the terms are very reasonable."

Check these sizzlers
from sisters who deliver!

Blackboard bestselling author
Beverly Jenkins

BEFORE THE DAWN
0-380-81375-0/$5.99 US/$7.99 Can

NIGHT SONG
0-380-77658-8/$5.99 US/$7.99 Can

TOPAZ
0-380-78660-5/$5.99 US/$7.99 Can

THROUGH THE STORM
0-380-79864-6/$5.99 US/$7.99 Can

THE TAMING OF JESSI ROSE
0-380-79865-4/$5.99 US/$7.99 Can

ALWAYS AND FOREVER
0-380-81374-2/$5.99 US/$7.99 Can